DAVID HEWSON

The Cemetery of Secrets

D0581347

PAN BOOKS

First published in the UK in 2001 as Lucifer's Shadow by Harper Collins
First Published in the US 2004 by Delacorte, an imprint of Bantam Dell,
a division of Ramdom House, Inc., New York

This edition published 2009 by Pan Books
an imprint of Pan Macmillan Ltd
Pan Macmillan, 20 New Wharf Road, London N1 9RR
Basingstoke and Oxford
Associated companies throughout the world
www.panmacmillan.com

ISBN 978-0-330-50876-6

A CIP catalogue record for this book is available from
the British Library.

Printed and bound in the UK by CPI Mackays, Chatham ME5 8TD

Visit **www.panmacmillan.com** to read more about all our books
and to buy them. You will also find features, author interviews and
news of any author events, and you can sign up for e-newsletters
so that you're always first to hear about our new releases.

For Helen, Catherine, and Thomas,
whose music led me here

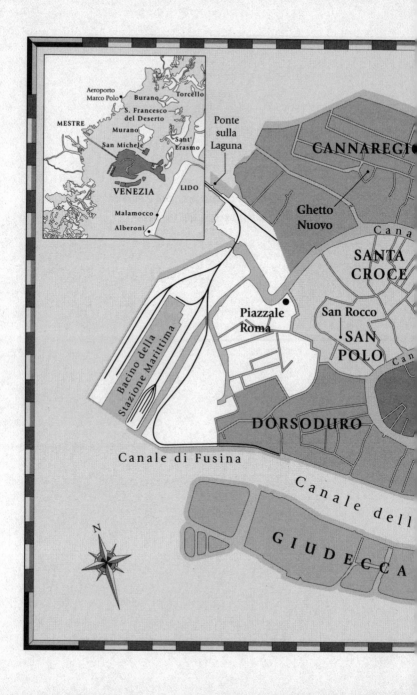

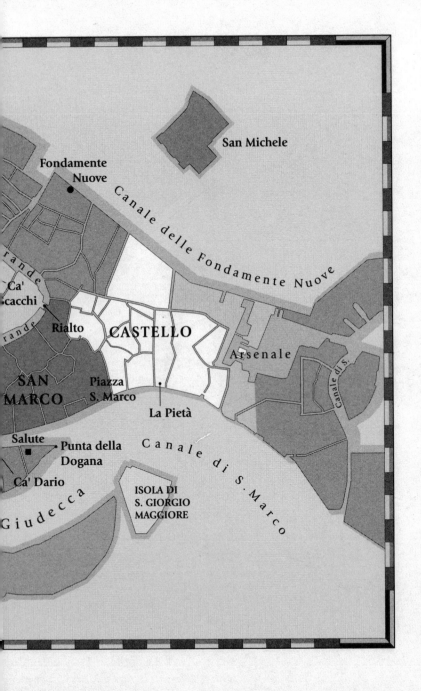

San Michele

Fondamente
Nuove

Canale delle Fondamente Nuove

Ca'
cacchi

Rialto

CASTELLO

Arsenale

SAN
MARCO

Piazza
S. Marco

La Pietà

Canale di S.

Salute

Punta della
Dogana

Canale di S. Marco

Ca' Dario

ISOLA DI
S. GIORGIO
MAGGIORE

Giudecca

San Michele

HE REMEMBERED TO WEAR BLACK. THE CHEAP, THIN suit from Standa. Shiny office shoes. A pair of fake Ray-Ban Predators stolen from some Japanese tourist straight off the coach at Piazzale Roma.

Rizzo lit a cigarette and waited by the gatehouse at San Michele. It was the first Sunday in July. The lagoon was entering summer, the change marked by the chittering of swallows above his head and a torpid heat rising from the water. A spirited breeze rippled the cypresses that dotted the cemetery like exclamation marks. In the shade of an alcove to his right, discreetly hidden, was an ordered stack of empty pine coffins. Rizzo watched something move in a beam of sunlight catching the corner of the nearest casket. A small lizard, dots running down its spine, dashed into the patch of gold, paused, then scurried back into the cracked brickwork.

Some job, Rizzo thought. Getting paid for checking up on a corpse.

The cemetery supervisor came out of his office and stared at the cigarette until Rizzo stamped it out. The man was short and fat, sweating in his bright white cotton shirt. He looked about forty, with a thick head of greasy hair and a weedy moustache like a comb snapped in half then stuck above a pair of fleshy lips.

"You got the papers?"

Rizzo nodded and tried to offer him half a smile. The supervisor wore a sour look, as if he suspected something was wrong. Rizzo was twenty-five but could pass for thirty dressed like this. Still, he guessed he looked a little young to be claiming possession of some stray cadaver, as if it were luggage left to be retrieved from a locker at the station.

He pulled out the documents the Englishman had given him that morning in the big, palatial apartment behind the Guggenheim Gallery. Massiter said they'd work. They'd cost enough.

"You're a relative?" the supervisor asked, staring at the lines of fine type on the page.

"Cousin," Rizzo replied.

"No other family?"

"All gone."

"Huh." The man folded up the papers and stuffed them in his pocket. "You could have waited another four weeks, you know. Ten years, they get. To the day. Seen plenty of people coming here late. Not seen many turn up early."

"Commitments."

The supervisor grimaced. "Sure. The dead got to fit themselves in to your calendar. Not the other way round. Still…" He favoured Rizzo with a professional glance that might have harboured a grain of sympathy in it. "Least you're here. You'd be amazed how many of those poor things just never get claimed at all. Run up their decade in the ground and then we just take 'em to the public ossuary. No choice, you see. No room."

Everyone in Venice knew the score, Rizzo thought. If you

wanted to be buried in San Michele, you had to follow the rules. The little island that sat between Murano and the northern shore of the city was full. The big names the tourists came to see could lie secure in their graves. Everyone else was on a temporary permit that lasted precisely ten years. Once the lease on that little plot of ground ran out, it was up to the relatives to take the bones elsewhere or leave the city to do the job for them.

The Englishman knew all about it too. For reasons Rizzo did not wish to know, he had fixed the disinterment papers early so he was the first to know what was in the box. Maybe there was someone else interested in this rotting corpse, someone who would stick to the ten-year deadline. Maybe not. Rizzo still didn't see the point. Was this to check there really was a body inside the casket? That had to be it. In truth, he didn't care. If the guy was willing to pay him a thousand euros just to flutter a couple of pages of forged paperwork around, he was more than happy. It made a change from lifting wallets in the crowds milling around San Marco.

"We have ways of doing this," the man said. "We like to do things nice and proper."

Rizzo followed him, past the tidy collection of shiny new coffins, out into the beating sun. They walked through the first section of the cemetery, where the dead had long-term residency, then on to an outlying area used for the relentless cycle of temporary burials. Green tarpaulins marked the areas where the current crop of bodies was being harvested. Each tiny headstone carried a photograph: young and old, frozen in a moment of time, looking at the camera as if they believed they would never die at all. They stopped by *Recinto 1, Campo B*, amid a fragrant ocean of flowers. The supervisor pointed to the headstone. On it was her name, reversed like all those in the cemetery: *Gianni*

Susanna. Just turned eighteen when she died. The grave was empty, the earth freshly dug.

Her portrait sat in an oval frame attached to the marble headstone. Rizzo couldn't take his eyes off it. Susanna Gianni was as beautiful a girl as any he'd ever seen. The photograph must have been taken outside, on a sunny day, perhaps close to the time of her death. She didn't appear sick. She wore a purple T-shirt. Her long, dark hair fell to her shoulders. Her face and neck were tanned, her mouth set in a natural, open smile. She looked like a kid about to graduate from university, innocent, but with an expression in her gaze that said she'd been places, she knew a few tricks too. Rizzo closed his eyes behind the dark glasses and tried to still his thoughts. It was crazy, he knew, but he could feel himself hardening at the sight of this unknown girl who had died, of what he couldn't begin to guess, almost a decade before.

"You want the headstone?" The supervisor's voice cut through this sudden, half-scary, half-delicious reverie. "If you want it, you can take it away with the casket. I guess you organised a boat, huh?"

Rizzo didn't answer the questions. He pushed his hands deep into the pockets of his cheap jacket and held them in front of him, wondering if the man had noticed.

"Where is she?" he asked.

"Send the boatmen round. They know where to come."

"Where is she?" Rizzo repeated. The Englishman had been specific about what he wanted.

"We got a place." The supervisor said this with a sigh, as if he knew what was coming next.

"Show me."

Without a word, the man turned and headed for a deserted corner in the northern part of the cemetery. One of the big ferries destined for Burano and Torcello passed on the right.

Gulls hung in the choppy air. A scattering of figures moved through the headstones, some with bouquets in their hands. Rizzo had been here only once before, with an old girlfriend, going to see her grandmama. The place spooked him. When he went, he wanted to go out in a puff of flame, a sudden fire inside the municipal crematorium on the mainland. Not lie around beneath the dry San Michele earth, waiting to be dug up a decade later.

They walked to a small, low building with a single tiny window. The supervisor fished a keychain out of his pocket and opened the door. Rizzo took off his sunglasses and followed him inside. Then he waited as the man threw the light switch, waited as his eyes adjusted to the abrupt transition from the piercing sunlight into the dark and then back into the thinner glare of the one fluorescent tube in the ceiling.

The coffin sat on a trestle in the middle of the room. The wood was a lifeless, flat grey colour. It was as if the thing, and what it contained, had been desiccated over the few years it had rested beneath the surface.

"Like I said," the man repeated, "send your men here. They'll know what to do. You don't want to watch. Believe me."

The Englishman had given his instructions.

"Open it."

The supervisor swore softly, folded his arms, and glowered into the dark corner beyond the casket. "No can do," he murmured. "What kind of game are you playing, kid?"

Rizzo reached into his pocket and pulled out two hundred euro notes. Massiter had known there might be incidentals along the way.

"Listen," he said. "The Giannis are a real close family. Just let me see my sweet little cousin one more time and then I'm on my way, OK?"

"Shit," the man said, then pocketed the notes and picked up a crowbar leaning against the wall. "You want me to take the lid off? Or do you feel so close to her you want to do that too?"

What Rizzo felt like was a cigarette. The tiny room was airless. A smell, musty and pervasive, was coming from the coffin. "Do it," he said, and nodded at the casket.

The man grunted, lifted the crowbar, and jammed it beneath the cover of the coffin. He barely looked at what he was doing. He'd popped these things a million times, Rizzo guessed. It was like working in a slaughterhouse or a morgue. After a while you never even thought about what was going on.

The iron worked its way around the wooden box slowly, lifting it just a few centimetres at a time, exposing the bent, rusty nails that held the thing together. The man completed a circle of the casket, then looked at Rizzo one final time.

"You sure about this, kid? A lot of you guys are real brave out there in the light of day, but it doesn't seem such a good idea when you're in here and it's time."

Rizzo didn't like being called "kid." Again he said, "Do it."

The supervisor carefully eased the bar beneath the cover, then pushed down, levering it open. The wood shattered into two pieces with a sudden, piercing crack. Rizzo jumped, in spite of himself. Dust and particles filled the air. Behind them came a persistent, noisome smell that was identifiably human in origin. Just one look, he thought. That was all the Englishman asked for.

He leaned over and peered into the casket. Her head was in the shadow cast by the corner of the box. The long hair was grey now, grey and fine and dry-looking. It hung down both sides of her skull, to which some flesh was still attached, like flaps of old brown leather. There was something in the eye sockets. He didn't want to look too closely. Around what remained of her shoulders were the straps of what must once have been a white shroud.

Rizzo thought he was going to stare at the skull and wonder where that lovely face had disappeared to. The nascent erection was all but gone now. He felt cold in the room. The air swam in front of him. He wouldn't be surprised if, pretty soon, he threw up. Not through horror and disgust, but from the insidious, choking atmosphere of the place. It was like standing in a cloud of human dust formed by every single being that had passed through the gates of San Michele over the centuries.

But he didn't look at the skull for long. Her arms were folded over her chest, long arms now reduced to a skeletal skinniness. To his surprise, they enclosed something, an object large enough to run from beneath her chin to the lower part of her body. He stared at it and knew the cemetery supervisor was doing the same. It was so out of place that it took a long time before he finally realised what this shape was. The corpse of Susanna Gianni, whoever she might have been, had been buried clutching an ancient violin case, her arms wrapped lovingly around the thing as if it were an infant.

The Englishman hadn't said anything about this. He just said to see the bones and then get going. It was a done deal, Rizzo thought, and no one could blame a man if he took a little incidental profit along the way.

He reached down, gently pried the grip of the dead arms from the case, then started to slide it out from underneath the cold, dry flesh.

The supervisor glowered at him. "You shouldn't be doing that."

Rizzo stopped and sighed. He was tired of this little man. He was tired of this place. Rizzo reached into his pocket and pulled out the small flick blade he took everywhere. Looking at the fat man, he pushed the button on the side, let the thin sliver of blade bite into the musty air, then grabbed him by the collar, watched the terror in his face grow. He thrust the tip into the fleshy underside of the man's left eyelid. The point lifted the flabby skin into a tiny pyramid, pricking through the surface just hard enough for Rizzo to see a tiny bubble of blood there.

"Do what?" he asked calmly. "I didn't do a thing."

The fat man froze and didn't speak. Rizzo reached into the man's jacket pocket, took out a cheap plastic wallet, and looked at the identity card. The caretaker lived in one of the public housing blocks north of him, in the Cannaregio. He could walk it in five minutes.

"Be smart," Rizzo hissed. "Or maybe I come back here and make you bury yourself. Huh?"

The supervisor's eyes had the flat, glazed look of terror. Rizzo pulled his arm away, let go of the man, then went back to the coffin, lifted the dead arms again, and removed the violin case. Using the sleeve of his cheap jacket, he brushed away the dust on the surface and saw her name there on a faded paper label. Then he slipped his fingers through the handle. The case swung solidly beneath his arm. There was something inside, for sure. Maybe it was just rocks. Even crazy people didn't bury their dead with treasure these days.

The fat man cowered in the darkness, peeing himself in all probability, wishing he were home with his equally fat wife, waiting to be fed. Rizzo grimaced, then pulled out another couple of 50 euro notes and stuffed them into the man's shirt pocket. "Your lucky day, friend. It's just a little family business. OK?"

The supervisor took out the notes and rustled them. The money gave him back some respect. They were now, in a sense, even. Rizzo could appreciate that. There wasn't enough respect in the world. He put his fake Predators back on his face, turned, and walked outside.

The voice rose up from behind him. "Hey! Where are the boatmen? They got to deal with this now."

Rizzo looked back from the door at the coffin and the squat little man standing next to it, still in the darkness. "What boatmen?"

"For the bones, for God's sake! I thought you brought her up early to take care of things yourself."

"I never said that," Rizzo answered.

"Jesus! So what do I do with them now?"

Rizzo shrugged. His jacket felt too tight. He hated having to buy these cheap things when what he really wanted were those clothes they sold in San Marco: Moschino, Valentino, and Armani.

"Do what you like," he replied, then looked at the man. Maybe he had pushed it too far. The guy looked ready to burst into tears or maybe pick a fight, even though he knew Rizzo would use the knife in his pocket. It was wrong, Rizzo thought, to let crazy people work in cemeteries. But maybe that was the only kind that took the job.

"Hey," he said. "Calm down. Keep your mouth shut. Stop looking like a crazy man. You could scare people like that."

Then he walked briskly out into the cemetery, retracing his steps through *Campo B*, past what had been Susanna Gianni's grave, not looking at the headstone, because something told him it would be a bad idea to see that picture of her again.

The *vaporetto* from Murano was half-full. He stood in the centre section, open to the air, and noticed how people moved away from him. The violin case stank, even on the deck with the lagoon breeze stiffening to the occasional gust. The boat slowed, then came to a halt. In front of the Fondamente Nuove, where the vessel would dock, some kind of regatta was taking place. A group of racing boats chased each other along the waterfront, cheered on by spectators from the bars behind the jetty. Rizzo cursed them. The violin felt heavy. The smell was getting worse. The *vaporetto* rolled drunkenly on the grey chop of the waves.

Rizzo closed his eyes. When he opened them, he was staring back at the island. Three police launches, sirens flashing, were heading for the jetty. He couldn't believe his eyes. He couldn't believe the fat little caretaker could be that stupid.

Still clutching the case, he lurched for the sliding metal bar that blocked the exit way and vomited over the edge, into the greasy, churning waters. The gulls that seemed fixed to the eggshell-blue sky watched him avidly. San Michele swam in the distance, a white-and-green blur between the city and the low, solid outline of Murano. Rizzo glared at the pure white church by the landing where the boats docked. He swore he would never pass through its gate again.

Ascension Day

Mark this moment: Ascension Day, Thursday, May the fourteenth, in the Year of Our Lord Seventeen Hundred and Thirty-three. Lorenzo Scacchi, a tall and handsome lad of nineteen years and seven months, stands on the broad stone apron of San Giorgio Maggiore gazing across St. Mark's Basin, watching the Doge renew his courtship with the ocean. The water is alive with humanity. Gondolas the colour of night scrap for places near the gold-and-scarlet *Bucintoro* as it makes its stately course past the Rio del Palazzo, on towards the twin columns of San Marco and San Teodoro and the towering pinnacle of the campanile.

There is a tremor in the air here. The Doge, they say, is sick, mulling over a successor to commend to the Grand Council. The Serene Republic stands balanced between splendour and decay. What man might save the day? What sublime genius might restore the city's fortunes and send the greasy Turks packing back to the East?

No one knows. But wait! The *Bucintoro* turns, away from the filigreed façade of the palace, away from the seething waterfront. Slowly, propelled by the forest of glinting, golden oars that prickle from its sides like the legs of some fanciful, jewelled insect, it glides across the Basin, towards the young man standing by the lapping edge of the waves, hands on slim hips, legs apart, face to the water, golden hair ablaze in the sun. The oarsmen heave into it with their backs and race across the channel at full tilt. Then the gorgeous vessel slows respectfully to reach the flat grey island on which the young man waits, and comes to a graceful halt, a vast, majestic token of power above him. Not for an instant does he waver.

"Lorenzo!" cries the Doge in a voice broken with age but still possessed of the majestic authority of his position. "I ask you again, sir. For the love of the Serenissima! For everything our Republic holds dear! Reconsider, I beg you! Lead us out of this darkness and into the light!"

A single cloud crosses the perfect azure sky, and for a moment, none may see the turmoil in the young man's face. Then it is gone, and his smile, kind yet firm, a wise and noble countenance in one so young, is revealed to all.

"Sure thing, boss," he responds in a raw, country brogue, and humbly shrugs his shoulders. The joyous cries of thousands rise up from the lagoon like thunder reversing its customary journey, soaring upwards to the heavens in a raucous clamour. A new Doge is found and soon . . .

There, dear sister. Do I have your attention *now*? If I have to write these letters like some tuppenny tale hawked around the streets by mendicants and cripples just to keep you reading, then be assured, I'll do it. It is now six weeks since we left Treviso, orphaned by a vicious fate. Do not make me feel alone in this world. You are my elder by two long, important years. I need your wisdom. I need your love. One letter, and that complaining largely of indigestion, does not provide the sustenance I crave.

Still, before I bore you, let me return to the narrative! Of the above, you may ignore everything save the beginning. It is indeed Ascension Day, and I did stand beneath the great stone monolith of San Giorgio; for how long I have no idea. It requires a better writer than this one to paint today's picture for you in mere words, so I shan't even try. Venice is a world of wonders, be assured. Even now I turn mundane corners and find myself in awe when confronted by everyday splendours that beggar the imagination. When the fathers have something to celebrate and decide to push out the boat—oops, sorry about that!—there's nothing else to do but stand and stare. You came here once with Papa, I believe. I never ventured much further than our little town until after that sad day of the funeral. For a straw-chewing farm lad, this is quite some place.

There are men here I wish you could meet. Picture our Uncle Leo up by the water's edge now, a skinny fellow, arms crossed, in plain dress, watching that big barge drift slowly in front of the palace. He looks as if he's seen this spectacle a million times, and nothing might move him again in all creation. But he is a Venetian, a man of the world, who would never have followed our dear father into such a quiet life as farming. Spectacle runs through his blood like an everyday humour. One should expect nothing less. He will, I believe, be a good guardian, and teach me the intricacies of the publisher's trade so that I may earn an honest living.

By his side is the English gentleman Oliver Delapole, a noble and aristocrat about our uncle's age, perhaps thirty-five, but of an altogether different background and with a little paunch at his elegantly attired belly. Mr. Delapole is a moneyed fellow in fine, perhaps overly extravagant clothing. He has a rosy, kindly face marred only by what I take to be a duelling scar, which runs beneath his right eye like a scimitar on its side. Yet I see no sign of a bellicose nature. In truth he possesses an engaging grin and a genial manner that makes every man—and woman (come, we are country folk and should not shy from such matters)—retire from his company smiling.

Of all those comments, remember that one concerning money; it is the most important word you will hear anywhere in this lagoon. Mr. Delapole is Capital personified, and for that reason half the city sticks to his coattails whenever he happens to pass, though he takes the attention in his stride. He came to our house last week and left his hat in the parlour. I raced after, clutching it, out into the *campo,* hoping to catch him before he reached the Grand Canal and found one of those ruffian gondoliers to take him home. When, out of breath and unable to speak, I reached him, he smiled pleasantly and asked, almost beside himself with laughter, "Why are you chasing me, lad? Am I the only man left in Venice with a little cash?"

Ducats open doors—most any door in the city, to be frank—and Mr. Delapole is a generous bestower of them. Word is he distributes the cash so quickly the money-lenders must make up the gap between his benevolence and the arrival of yet more funds from London. This is no complaint, you understand. With luck, the House of Scacchi will bring to the public several works from new writers and composers, and all at Mr. Delapole's expense. He has already shown some small kindness to Mr. Vivaldi, the famous musical priest at La Pietà, the ramshackle church a little along the waterfront from today's proceedings. Nor has the local artist Canale (known to all as "Canaletto" to distinguish him from his father, who follows a similar trade) been left out of the party. This is a chap who can apparently sniff the scent of silver from several miles. As I compose this, he sits in front of us all, on a great platform of wood poised above the rest of the party, toiling away on a canvas destined for some rich man's wall.

Canaletto is an odd fellow, most argumentative and, some wonder, perhaps a fraud too. He uses something called a *camera ottica*, a device he claims as his own invention. This is hidden from our eyes inside a black fabric tent in which the artist works, dashing outside from time to time to check that the real world is still there. Apparently the device throws an image of the scene through some kind of glass lens onto an interior screen, where it may be traced prior to painting. Out of curiosity I clambered up the scaffolding and examined the exterior of the contrivance, getting a sour look and a mouthful of Venetian cussing when he stuck his head out to investigate my clatter.

"If one more smart-ass tells me I'm cheating, I shall, I swear, punch his miserable lights out," Canaletto hissed at me by way of warning.

Undeterred, I peered at the mechanism through the gap in the fabric created by his hand. It seems most clever. "How can a little science in the aid of art be described as cheating, sir?" I asked honestly. "On that basis, you would surely be accused of trickery if you failed to use the selfsame paints the Romans favoured for their walls?"

That did the trick. At least I received what I took to be as close to a nod of approval as Mr. Canaletto might own.

"What you need next," I added, "is simply some alchemical canvas which recognises the image itself and moulds its atoms to the relevant pigment. Then you'd have no need of the brush at all!"

I heard a snigger from Mr. Delapole's manservant, Gobbo, and beat a sensible retreat back down the woodwork! I trust you have found a friend. I have, of sorts. Luigi Gobbo is an

ugly chap with, believe it or not, the makings of the hump
which his surname would suggest. He joined the Englishman
in France some time back, I believe. In all this company,
Gobbo is the most down-to-earth of fellows, always ready
with a roguish joke and the occasional impious suggestion.
The moment he discovered my fate, he took me under his
wing, promising to let no Venetian rogue relieve me of my
meagre purse. I like the chap, though we are not much
similar. Our parents may have spoiled us with our
homegrown education. Thinking that Gobbo might have
read a little literature, too, I asked him if he was any relation
of the famous Lancelot, and whether he had abandoned a
notorious Jew for the service of Mr. Delapole, a man
assuredly as amiable as Bassanio himself, if rather more
wealthy. Gobbo looked at me as if I were witless or, worse,
mocking him. English playwrights did not enter into his
education. Still, he has my best interests at heart, and I his.
There is amity in the city after all.

Now to more weighty matters (which are short, so do not
yawn and put down the page, please). It is a week since
Manzini last wrote about the estate (and yes, I agree with you,
it is wrong that he must deal with me, not you, but that is the
law). I hold out no great hopes. Our parents invested heavily
in the farm and that precious library we both adored. Had
they lived longer, we would all surely have benefited from their
generosity. Since the cholera decided otherwise, we must
make the best of what we have. So I shall strike a bargain with
you, Lucia. Let us be honest with each other in reporting our
failings. Let us write truly of those around us. And let us work
diligently to make ourselves worthy of the name Scacchi—until
some dashing Spanish blade steals yours away, of course!

I love you, Lucia, my darling sister, and I would trade an

eternity of this magnificence for one moment together with our dear parents in that ragged little farmhouse back in the wild meadows of our home. That cannot be, so we must look to the future.

Wait! I see the famed Canaletto scowling down from his perch once more. A little line of fat Dutchmen waddling together like a flock of ducks are attempting to possess his eyrie and steal a peek at his precious painting. More fools them . . .

"Bloody tourists," the artist barks, and emits a flurry of arcane curses which none beyond Cannaregio may understand. "Off with your ugly snouts and your herring-stink breath!"

"Be bold and wave a florin in his face, sirs," shouts Mr. Delapole, egging them on. "Any man smells sweet to Canaletto who has coin in his pocket!"

Muttering darkly, our intruders shuffle off. I suspect our painter friend is somewhat beyond their means.

While Canaletto was waving his fist at them, he left the door to his mysterious tented palace open. I leapt stealthily onto the woodwork myself and saw, with great amazement, how far this canvas had progressed in little more than an hour. This man is no fraud. It will, I think, be a fine painting. One day, when you have settled enough in Seville to earn the time and money to return to visit your native Veneto, I shall, I fancy, take you to see it. We shall measure the way our pains have diminished and our fortunes increased in the months that have passed since the *Bucintoro* found its way onto Canaletto's piece of rough canvas. Here is a wondrous talent, to trap a piece of glorious time in amber, for all the ensuing centuries to witness. All I have to offer are these words, but they come freely given and from an adoring heart.

3

A name from the past

GIULIA MORELLI SIFTED THE REPORT SHEETS ON HER desk. Giulia was duty captain on the evening shift. It was hot inside the modern police block by Piazzale Roma, and the work was beginning to bore her. Sometimes she thought of applying for a transfer. Rome, maybe, or Milan. Anywhere she might find some kind of challenge to keep her mind turning.

Then she stared at the pages in front of her and felt the years roll away in an instant. The dead girl's name seemed to yell at her. Giulia Morelli stabbed at the phone and managed to catch the reporting officer. He was changing before coming off shift, and none too keen to hang around the overheated police station. The tone of her voice ensured he would not leave without telling his story.

She listened keenly for five minutes, finding herself increasingly perplexed, then put the phone down, walked to the window, threw it open, and lit a cigarette. Outside, the last commuters were heading for their cars in the vast multi-storey close to the bridge to terra firma and Mestre, where most of them lived. She watched the straggle of figures and thought about what the officer had just told her. It made no sense.

Perhaps it did not say anything about the case of Susanna Gianni at all.

They had been called to San Michele by an irate undertaker whose party had arrived on time for the ceremony, only to find the superintendent missing. They finally found the man in a building used for disinterments, apparently in some kind of distress. When the undertaker remonstrated with him, the superintendent turned violent and attacked two of the party before being restrained.

The senior officer called to the incident attempted to interview the cemetery employee, but to little avail. According to the report, the unfortunate event was caused by a sudden loss of temper in the heat. The superintendent was cautioned for minor assault, then allowed to go home. The authorities were to be told, but there would be no formal action. Only one unusual detail was noted on the report, and the officer had again confirmed it, though with no further information, when she had spoken to him. In the disinterment room was the coffin of one Susanna Gianni. It had been opened to expose the corpse. And, so it seemed to the officer, something had been removed from the casket. The shape of a long object, perhaps a metre high, was superimposed against the remains of the cadaver.

With the care and foresight she had come to expect of the uniformed branch, the officer had thought this worthy of mention but not of action. Once he had arranged for the superintendent to be taken home by police launch, he had allowed the removal of the casket—and, with it, Susanna Gianni's bones—to continue. It appeared there was no private arrangement. The disposal of the body was carried out that afternoon by the city cemetery service. The box would be ashes by now. What remained of Susanna Gianni—even the girl's name still made the policewoman's blood race—would be strewn among the sea of skeletons which made up the public ossuary on one of the lagoon's smaller islands.

Giulia Morelli lacked the energy to curse the idiot. She picked up the phone, arranged for a launch, and within five minutes found herself heading up the Grand Canal for Cannaregio, wondering what might have made a cemetery superintendent, one surely used to dealing with corpses over the years, lose his mind so quickly and in such unusual company. Wondering, too, about who had taken that mysterious object from the murdered girl's coffin, and why.

She ordered the launch to dock at Sant' Alvise and walked briskly south into the tangle of fascist-era apartment blocks. She had told the launch to wait for her and, against standing orders, planned to conduct the interview alone. The details of the Gianni case were now, a decade later, somewhat hazy in her memory. Even so, she recalled the care with which it was discussed, particularly in the company of a lowly cadet as she was then. There was no reason to raise a fuss now, not until she saw something worth fighting for.

He lived in a block at the edge of the development. The building was clean but shabby. She walked into the dingy communal hallway and pressed the light switch. A perpendicular line of dim yellow bulbs came on overhead. His apartment was on the third floor. She looked for the light. It was out. Giulia Morelli, for no reason she could fully understand, found she was patting her purse to feel the shape of the small police pistol that lived there.

"Stupid," she hissed quietly, and began to climb the stairs.

The third floor was in virtual darkness. She cursed herself for having left the flashlight behind, wondered, too, why she had been so anxious to interview the man alone. The case was a decade old. The uniformed officer at the helm of her launch had not even been in the force when Susanna Gianni died.

The apartment was at the end of the corridor, somewhere in an inky pool of darkness. She called the man's name and immediately sensed she had made some kind of a mistake. There was a noise coming from ahead. A glimmer of dull yellow light leaked out from behind a door that stood no more than an inch ajar. She edged closer to it, hearing more clearly: it was a long, breathy moan, a sound that could betoken anything from ecstasy to death.

She reached into her bag and took out the police radio. The signal was dead. Mussolini had built these old apartment blocks well. Giulia Morelli kept the handset tight in her left hand, then reached into the bag for the gun, grasped the weapon, and walked briskly through the door, taking care to stand in the shadow cast by the wan light from a single bulb.

There were words in her throat, cold, officious words, ones which worked on most occasions, sending a little fear into the small-time crooks who were, almost exclusively, her customers. The words died before she was able to say them. Giulia Morelli took in what she could of the scene—the light was poor and the protagonist was deep in shadow, his face invisible to her. All that was apparent of him was a single, lean arm wielding a long, bloodied knife and a smell: cheap, strong cigarettes—African, maybe—and the rank odour of sweaty fear.

She could think of nothing but the painting, the damn painting that had haunted her ever since she'd seen it as a child. It stood in the chancel of San Stae, Tiepolo's *Martyrdom of Saint Bartholomew*, depicting a man apparently in rapture, arm raised to heaven, a half-hidden attacker carefully testing his skin, wondering where to begin with the blade. She had asked her mother about the painting, always seeking to know the story.

Her mother had evaded the question, mumbling something she failed to understand: that the saint was to be "flayed." It was only later, when she found the word in a dictionary, that she understood. This was the moment before the horror. The executioner was planning the act, that of skinning his victim alive. And the condemned man was looking to heaven in bliss, awaiting his deliverance with joy, something Giulia Morelli knew she would never understand.

The cemetery superintendent was not in rapture. He was, she thought, dead already, or at least she hoped as much. His throat was cut, carefully, from side to side, revealing a broad, bloody band of flesh and sinew. And his murderer, who remained out of sight—though he was, she knew, now moving—was slowly finishing the job, stabbing into the tendons, severing what he could find in the man's throat.

She gripped the gun. It wriggled in her sweaty grasp. Her fingers twisted on the grip, then slipped, and she heard the metal clatter on the tiled floor. Giulia Morelli could look at nothing but the dead man, wondering, wondering.

A shape rose to her left. A leg came out and kicked her hard. She fell to her knees, waiting for the blow, wondering if she had the courage to look upwards, to heaven, to nothingness, like the saint in the painting. But he was there and she did not wish to see his face.

She tried to speak, but there were no intelligible words in her head. Something silver flashed in front of her eyes. She felt a sudden slash of pain in her side, followed shortly afterwards by the rush of warm blood. Her breath came in sudden, jerky gasps. She waited.

And then the radio came to life in her palm. She had, she realised, been gripping tight on the panic button. Somehow her faint call for help had leaked out of Mussolini's brickwork and found a human ear. A voice barked at them. At the foot of the stairs outside in the communal hallway, which might have been on the far side of the world as far as she was concerned, there were footsteps. Too soon for the police, she knew, but the dark shape above her, dropping blood from the knife onto her face, could not know that.

"You are under arrest," Giulia Morelli said, and wondered why she felt like laughing. He was gone. There was no one else in the room. No one but the dead superintendent, who stared back at her with glassy, terrified eyes and a gory gash for what was once a throat.

She placed a hand on her side, felt the wound the knife had made. She'd live. She would find this man. She would discover why he had robbed Susanna Gianni's grave and what he had stolen from it. There was work to be done, much of it.

Giulia Morelli stumbled to her feet. There were men at the door. A caretaker, perhaps. Another resident. It was important, she knew, to take control.

"Touch nothing," she said, trying to think straight, trying to establish the kind of control which was required.

They gaped at her, half-amazed, half-terrified. She followed the direction of their gaze and saw the blood staining her jacket, running down her short skirt, coagulating hot and sticky on her knees.

"Touch…" she repeated, then felt her eyes turn upwards in her head, saw the murky yellow light of the apartment turn black and, finally, disappear altogether.

4

Spritz! Spritz! Spritz!

T HREE WEEKS AFTER THE OPENING OF SUSANNA Gianni's grave and the death of a certain cemetery superintendent in Cannaregio, Daniel Forster walked out of the arrivals area of Marco Polo airport carrying a violin case which was neither old nor malodorous. It was as modest as the instrument inside and the small, soft suitcase which hung from his other arm and contained almost his entire wardrobe: enough clothes, he hoped, to see him through the next five weeks. The flight from Stansted had taken two hours, crossing the snow-covered Alps before descending rapidly into the northeast corner of the Adriatic. Though he had just turned twenty, this was Daniel's first trip abroad. His new passport, still without a stamp inside, sat in the pocket of his green cotton windcheater along with the plastic envelope from Thomas Cook which contained 300 euros, almost the entire contents of his student current account.

He stood a little under six feet tall, with flowing fair hair and a pleasant, innocuous face still somewhat unformed by adult-hood. Hovering uncertainly in the airport hall, he looked like a trainee tour-guide waiting for his first assignment. Then a large man dressed in dark trousers and a baggy blue sweatshirt marched over, bent down to peer in his eyes, and inquired, "Mr. Daniel?"

Daniel blinked, surprised. "Signor Scacchi?"

The man laughed, a grand, booming noise that rose from somewhere deep within his vast stomach. He was in his late thirties, perhaps, and had the ruddy, weather-worn face of a farmer or fisherman. There was a bittersweet smell of alcohol on his breath. "Signor Scacchi! Do I look like a peacock? Do you think I can trill? Come! Come!"

Daniel followed this stranger out of the hall and found they were, within a few steps, by the side of the lagoon. A dozen or more sleek water taxis, each with finely polished wood decks, sat waiting for customers. They walked past them to the public jetty, where an old blue motorised fishing boat sat. In the prow, slumped against each other like lovers, were two slender men. In the mid part of the vessel, a woman wearing jeans and a purple T-shirt bustled over two plastic picnic hampers, her back turned. Next to her, a small, pure-black field spaniel with short ears and a compact nose peered curiously at the contents of the boxes and was shooed away, constantly and to little avail.

The large man looked at the passengers in the boat, waited for a moment to see if their attention would come his way, then, realising this was a lost cause, clapped his hands loudly and announced, "Please! Please! Our guest is arrived! We must welcome him."

The smaller of the two men stood up. He wore a fawn suit, well-cut, and was, Daniel judged, in his late sixties. This was, he assumed, his host, Signor Scacchi. His face was tanned and lined, almost to the point of emaciation. He appeared ill, as did the younger man by his side, who now lay back on the pillows in the stern of the boat and favoured the newcomer with an expressionless glance.

"Daniel!" the old man said, smiling to reveal a set of too-white dentures. He was short, with a slight hunch. "Daniel! He has come! See, Paul. See, Laura. I told you. Ten days' notice and us complete strangers. Still, he has come!"

The woman turned to face him. She had a fine, attractive face, with round, full cheeks tapering to a delicate chin. Her large eyes were an extraordinary shade of green. Her hair, long and straight, falling to her shoulders, was a subtle shade of auburn. She peered at Daniel as if he were a creature from outer space, but with a friendly curiosity, as if his presence somehow amused her.

"He did come," she said in a soft voice only lightly coloured by the Venetian accent, then almost automatically reached into her handbag, took out a pair of large plastic sunglasses, and placed them on her face.

"Well, who'd have thought it?" Paul murmured. He was, Daniel thought, American. He wore a faded denim shirt and jeans of a similar colour. Sprawled in the front of the boat, he had the awkward lack of grace of a teenager and, at first glance, young looks, too, though a moment's consideration showed them to be cracked and faded, like those of a fifty-year-old trying to appear thirty.

"Of course," the large man said, then passed the luggage to Laura and extended a huge hand to help Daniel into the lazily shifting boat. "Who wouldn't come to Venice when asked? I am Piero, since no one seems minded to conclude the introductions," the man announced. "The fool of the family, though a distant relative so that scarcely matters. And this is my boat, the lovely *Sophia*, a lady who is loyal, true, and always starts when you need her, which means, I guess, she's no lady at all.

Not that I would know about such matters—there, I said it before Laura said it for me."

The dog nudged at Daniel's trousers. Piero reached down and ruffled its head with affection. "And this is Xerxes. So called because he is the finest general of the marshes you will find. No duck escapes his beady little eyes, eh?"

The merest mention of the word "duck" had set the dog's stumpy tail wagging. Piero chucked him lovingly underneath the chin, then reached into one of the hampers and fed a small circle of salami into Xerxes' gaping mouth.

Scacchi leaned forward, rocking the little motorboat, pumped his empty hand up and down in a drinking gesture, and announced, "Spritz! Spritz! Spritz!"

"Naturally," Laura replied from behind the sunglasses, then reached into the second hamper, withdrawing a set of bottles.

"Seats, please," Piero bellowed, then, with a tug on the starter rope, brought the small diesel engine into life and clambered to the rear to steer it. One of the water-taxi drivers sitting on his gleaming vessel stared at the grubby little boat and said something in a dialect which Daniel could not begin to understand. Piero replied just as unfathomably and extended a single digit at the man. The boat lurched back to clear the jetty, and then they were moving, out from the airport, out into the flat expanse of the Venetian lagoon. What had for years been an idea, an entire imagined universe inside Daniel Forster's head, suddenly became real. In the far distance, rising from the sea like some bizarre forest, the outline of Venice, of campaniles and palaces, slowly became visible, growing tantalisingly larger as they travelled towards it.

"Spritz," Scacchi repeated.

Laura gave the old man three bottles: one of Campari, one of white Veneto wine, and a third of sparkling mineral water. Then she made up five glasses with ice, a segment of precut lemon, and, from a small jar, a single green olive in each, and passed them to the old man.

Scacchi looked at him, and for the first time Daniel saw something sly in his face. "You know what this is?"

"I read about it," he replied. "I wondered what it would taste like."

"You hear that?" Scacchi declared. "Such a fine Italian accent! This is spritz, my lad, and it tells you much you need to know about this city. Look. Campari, for our potent blood. Wine for our love of life. Water for our purity—no laughing there, Paul. An olive for our earthiness. And, finally, lemon, to remind you that if you bite us, we bite back. Here."

He passed him a glass, full to the brim with the dark-red drink. Daniel took a sip. It was mainly Campari, strong and with the same bittersweet aroma he had smelled on Piero's breath.

Laura smiled at him as if expecting some reaction. "And food too," she said, offering a plate full of flat breads filled with cheese and Parma ham. Daniel took one and realised he had no idea of her age. The plain, cheap clothes and obscuring glasses seemed designed to make her look older, and in this they failed. She was, perhaps, twenty-eight or even younger, not in the early to mid thirties which her dress seemed to indicate.

"To Daniel!" Scacchi announced. The four of them raised their glasses. Xerxes barked softly. The boat rocked a little. Scacchi wisely went back to his seat next to Paul. "May these next few weeks open his eyes to the world!"

"To Daniel!" they repeated.

"I'm honoured," he said in return. "And I hope I shall do the job well."

"Of course you will," Scacchi said with a wave of his skeletal hand. "I knew that when I asked you. For the rest, I have fixed some amusements. All other time is your own."

"I shall try to use it well."

"As you see fit," Scacchi said with a yawn.

Then the old man took a long swig from the glass, placed it on the wooden bench seat that ran around the interior of the boat, leaned his head against Paul's shoulder, and, with no more ado, fell fast asleep in the prow.

The *moto topo Sophia* edged its way out towards the wide expanse of the lagoon, following the channel from the airport at first, then picking a shorter route to the miniature city perched on the bow. They fell into silence while Scacchi slept. Paul touched the old man's hair occasionally. Piero drank. Laura offered Daniel a cigarette, seemed pleased when he refused, lit one anyway, and tapped the ash over the side. After a while Paul slept, too, curling his arms around Scacchi, placing his head against the old man's in a fond gesture which seemed touched with sadness. Piero and Laura exchanged glances. She refilled Piero's glass more than once. The July day was beginning to fade, casting the city ahead in a gorgeous pink-and-gold light.

Piero whistled softly to the dog and it came to the stern. He held out a small leather loop attached to the tiller and waited as Xerxes turned to face the prow, then took the strap in his mouth.

"*Avanti!*" Piero whispered, and the dog's eyes fixed immediately ahead of the boat, on the far horizon. "Go straight, my little beauty. Papa needs a break."

He came and sat with Laura and Daniel in the middle, balancing his weight on one side against their combined on the opposite.

"You see this, Daniel?" he asked, looking at the two sleeping men. "This pair love each other like a couple of little doves. Don't mind the American, now. He's Scacchi's choice, for better or worse, and jealousy's such a mean little thing. Men loving men...I don't get it. But what's it to me? Nothing."

Daniel was silent.

"And nothing to you, my new friend, I know," Piero added. "That's not why Scacchi invited you here. He told me. Not that a fool like me pretends to understand. He says these things you wrote..."

"My paper," Daniel offered.

"Yeah. He says they're the best. OK? But...just be patient. See that dog?"

Xerxes stood stiffly in the stern, eyes on the horizon, leather strap lodged firmly in his jaws.

"He's a marvel," Daniel observed, and truly believed as much.

"More than that. He is proof of the existence of God."

"Piero!" Laura scolded him. "That is sacrilegious."

The big man's eyes were a little glassy. Daniel did not want to consider how much Campari had been consumed on the long, slow voyage across the lagoon to the airport.

"Not at all. He is a proof of the existence of God, and I shall tell you why. You are aware, Daniel, that he is a G-dog. I may not say the G-word out loud, of course, since he'll be off that tiller in a moment, sending us around in circles, barking like a she-wolf in season, and waking those two slumbering lovers over there. You understand my meaning?"

Turning his body to ensure the dog did not see him, Daniel mimed the action of pulling a shotgun to the shoulder and releasing the trigger.

"Exactly. Yet he is the most ancient of breeds. Why, I shall take you to Torcello in the good ship *Sophia* one day and show you the great, great-to-greatest grandfather of this very dog sitting in a mosaic on the wall there. All that, long before the G-things even existed! Explain that, my girl."

Laura slapped him on the knee. "It is called evolution, you fool."

"It is called the work of God. For God, you see, does not know time as we do. When He invents the spaniel, He does so understanding that one day some other of His creatures shall invent the G-thing. So He places within the animal's blood the knowledge of it there already, saving Himself the trouble of inventing some new animal when the need arises. For God, Time is just another of His creations. Like trees. And men. And water. And..."

He extended the plastic beaker. "Spritz! Furthermore..."

Laura filled it to halfway, tut-tutting. "Furthermore, Piero, you are dead drunk."

He looked miserable all of a sudden. "I guess." Then he sniffed the air as if it had changed, and peered at the dog, with its dark, damp nose held high in the stern. The boat had shifted direction to the east, though no one had noticed. Piero walked to the back of the boat and straightened up the tiller to put them back on course.

"*Avanti*, Xerxes," he said gently. "We go home to Sant' Erasmo later. After we drop these good people off in the city. Home."

Laura threw him a couple of pillows from her side of the boat.

"Home," the big man repeated, then stared at Daniel. "Scacchi said you didn't have one. That right?"

"My mother died a year ago," Daniel answered. "My father left before I was born. But I have somewhere to live."

"No relations?"

"None close."

"And you a clever guy too?" Piero seemed surprised. "So much for what the books say."

Laura tut-tutted again, stumbled to the other side of the boat, made the pillows into a makeshift bed, then came back to sit beside Daniel.

"A man who has no home has nothing," Piero declared. "Like that Paul there. It's Scacchi's choice. OK. And God knows the old man pays for it, what with that disease the American gave him. But this isn't his home. He doesn't have one. Where are they going to put him when he dies? Probably in a casket on some plane back to America, where he came from."

"Piero," Laura said with only the hint of scolding in her voice. "You sleep, now. Please."

"Yes," the large man said, and lay down on the pillows, fitting his enormous frame onto the narrow wooden ledge with a precision that could only have come from much practice. In the stern the dog gave a low whine but never once let go of the leather strap. Daniel Forster looked at Laura. She raised her glass to him and said, "*Salute.*" San Michele, with its endless round of recycled graves, was beginning to make itself apparent to their left. Daniel touched his plastic beaker to hers and tried to think of the famous names buried there: Diaghilev and Stràvinsky and Ezra Pound... The city had lived inside his thoughts for so long, its districts memorised, its history picked over for months on end. He had wondered if the reality might turn out to be a disappointment, a living theme park preserved only for the tourists. Something told him already this would not be the case, but also that the real city, the real lagoon, would be different from the picture he had built in his imagination out of the constant stream of books he had borrowed from the college library.

His thoughts clouded over, became confused. Then he realised that Laura had extended a long, slim, tanned hand and that she was very pretty indeed.

"I am the servant here," she said. "I am cook, housekeeper, nursemaid, and anything else you can think of. You must know that Scacchi, while he has his foibles, is the kindest man on earth. You will remember this, please, in your dealings with him."

"Yes," he replied, shaking the hand awkwardly, wondering whether this was a warning about his own behaviour or that of the master of the house. Wondering, too, whether she really expected him to kiss that small patch of tanned flesh she held out to him.

"And as for Piero," she continued, "he is a holy fool. Paul and Scacchi are—you have a phrase in English—'like two peas from the same pod.' It is just that one bears his fate more bravely than the other, though perhaps a sense of guilt has something to say about the matter there also. I love them both, and will be grateful if, for the period of your stay here, you either learn to love them, too, or affect to do so."

"I shall, of course."

She tapped him lightly on the knee. "Silly boy. How can you say that? You don't even know us yet."

He smiled, feeling she had caught him out. "Then what would you have me say?"

"Nothing. Just listen. And wait. I know men find these things difficult. Oh, damn!"

The boat had shifted direction again. Xerxes was trembling in the stern.

"To think he can let a dog steer us home."

Laura made her way carefully to the back of the *Sophia* and took the tiller from Xerxes. The dog let out a grateful growl before perching on the rear platform of the vessel, where he lifted a leg and let loose a lively stream of liquid over the side. Then Xerxes stared balefully at Laura until he realised she had no intention of letting him regain the tiller. The animal shuffled amidships, placed its muzzle tenderly in Piero's groin, and closed its eyes.

Three sleeping drunks and a dog called Xerxes. And a strange, intriguing woman staring at him from the back of the boat, carefully directing them towards the city. In his head Daniel

Forster had played the scene of his entry to the city on many occasions. None of these imagined arrivals came close to matching the reality.

Nor could he have predicted what occurred next. As the ancient boat made a slow but steady passage along the Cannaregio waterfront, they were joined by a long, sleek police speedboat which came alongside, then slowed to match their speed. Laura sat in the helm, unmoved by the vessel's presence. In the rear of the speedboat stood a thin woman with short blonde hair. She wore a two-piece blue suit with a tightly cut jacket and a skirt that stopped just above the knee. In her hand was a megaphone. Daniel looked at the three sleeping men, as did the policewoman. Then the police officer stared at Laura, who merely smiled back at her and shrugged her shoulders.

It was too noisy and too distant to be certain, but Daniel felt sure that the policewoman had sworn at this point, then barked an order to the officer at the wheel of the launch. The boat lurched under a surge of power, then raced off, buoyed on its own seething platform of foam.

"See," Laura noted. "Even the police come out to greet you, Daniel."

But he scarcely heard her words. The *Sophia* had veered sharply and was now headed for the mouth of what he surmised was the Cannaregio canal. It was busy with small boats. A '52 *vaporetto* chugged towards them. They passed beneath the odd, geometrical outline of the Tre Archi bridge, Laura dodging the traffic expertly, and then the *Sophia* set off along the straight haul to the Grand Canal. To his left, Daniel knew, lay the older part of Cannaregio, with the original Jewish ghetto hidden somewhere in its midst. To the right was the busy commercial and tourist quarter around the station.

"You know why you are here?" Laura asked, unflustered by

the multitude of vessels of all shapes, sizes, and colours around her.

"To catalogue Signor Scacchi's library," he said, speaking loudly over the sound of the canal.

"Library!" She laughed out loud, and it made her seem much younger, he thought. "He called it that!"

The junction with the Grand Canal was ahead of them. The *Sophia* bobbed on the swell from the throng of boats milling in the busy waterway.

"Then why am I here?" he yelled, not knowing where to look.

She beamed at him and said something that was lost in the angry horn of a *vaporetto* shooing a gondola of Japanese tourists out of its way. Daniel was unsure, and did not want to ask, but wondered if she had answered: *To save us.* There was no time for introspection. They had turned, abruptly and with a sudden burst of speed, and were now midstream of the Grand Canal. Nothing—no photograph, no painting, no words on the page— had prepared him for this sight. The city's beating jugular lay before him. Great buildings rose on both sides, Gothic and Renaissance, Baroque and Neoclassical, a startling juxtaposition of styles in which the centuries tripped over each other's feet. *Vaporetti* and water taxis, haulage boats and gondolas bustled across the water like insects skating over a pond. It was a world which appeared to live in multiple dimensions: on every side, above in the towering palaces and churches, and below in the shifting black waters of the lagoon.

"And one thing we all forgot to say," Laura added.

"What was that?" he asked.

She removed the sunglasses, and a pair of warm green eyes appraised him. "Why," she said with a thoughtful smile that briefly made him forget the view, "welcome to Venice, Mr. Daniel Forster."

5

A boy's new home

Our uncle gives me a sideways look when I call this place the "Palazzo Scacchi." Strictly speaking, it is a house, in Venetian parlance Ca' Scacchi, but anywhere else in the world this would surely be regarded as a palace, albeit one in need of a little care and attention.

We live in the parish of San Cassian, on the border of the *sestieri* San Polo and Santa Croce. Our house is by the side of the little *rio* San Cassian (which any but a Venetian would call a canal) and small *campo* of the same name. We have the usual door which leads onto the street, and two entrances from the water. One runs under a grand, rounded arch into the ground floor of the house, which, as is customary in this city, is used as a cellar for storage. The second belongs to the warehouse and printing studio, which represents the Scacchis' contribution to the world of commerce. This is situated in an adjoining building, some three storeys high (our home is four!), attached to the north side, towards the Grand Canal.

Finally, there is yet another mode of exit: a wooden bridge with handrails runs from the first floor of the house between

the two river entrances straight over the canal and into
the square itself. Consequently I can wander over it in the
morning and find fresh water from the well in the centre of
the *campo* while still rubbing the sleep from my eyes. Or I may
hail a gondola from my bedroom window, find it waiting for
me by the time I get downstairs, and, but a single minute
later, be in the midst of the greatest waterway on earth,
almost slap opposite the magnificence of the Ca' d'Oro!
And this does not deserve the name "palace"?

The house is almost two hundred years old, I am told, with
weathered brickwork the colour of chestnuts that have lain
on the ground all winter and handsome arched windows,
most with their own miniature Doric columns which frame
green-painted shutters designed to keep out the cruel
summer heat. I live on the third floor in the third room to the
right (things always come in threes, they say). When I lie in
bed at night, I can hear the lapping of the water, the chatter
and songs of the passing gondoliers, and, in the square, the
occasional bawdy chatter of the local whores. The
neighbourhood has something of a reputation for the latter,
I'm afraid (but this is a city, remember—I am sure you have
the same in Seville). Nevertheless, I understand why Uncle
pursues his trade here. The prices are not so steep. The
location is central and easy for our clients to find.
Furthermore, the printing trade has many roots in this area.
Scotto and Gardano, Rampazetto and Novimagio all made
their homes hereabouts at some time. The quarter has the
spirit of a community of bookmen about it, even if some of
the old names are now nothing more than fading title pieces
on the shelves of the Rialto antiquaries.

Oh, sister! I pray for the day when I can show you these
things instead of struggling to describe them in a letter which

may take Heaven knows how long to reach you in Spain!
Venice is like a vast simulacrum of our old library at home,
one that stretches forever, unfathomed, full of dark corners
and random wonders, some on my very doorstep. Last night,
while rooting around in the jumbled corners of the
warehouse cellar, I found behind a pile of unsold (and,
frankly, inferior) cantatas a single copy of Aristotle's *Poetics*,
published in the city in 1502 by Aldus Manutius himself. The
imprint of the Aldine academy is on the title page—that
famous colophon of the anchor and dolphin which our
father told us about! I raced to Uncle Leo with my discovery
and—now, here's a victory—something very close to a smile
broke the thin, flat line of the Scacchi lips. "A find, boy! You'll
pay your way yet. This'll fetch good money when I hawk it
down the Rialto."

"May I read a little first, sir?" I asked, and felt a degree of
trepidation when I made the request. Uncle Leo has a
forbidding manner at times.

"Books are for selling, not reading," he replied firmly. But
at least I had it for the night, since the dealers were by that
hour closed. I have since searched diligently in other chaotic
corners for similar jewels but found little of importance.
Our uncle is a businessman first and a publisher second,
though he has an ear for music too. Sometimes he asks me
to play pieces that are sent for setting, and, by accident,
I discovered he once had ambitions in this field (the
Scacchis are born polymaths, girl, even if fate sometimes
thwarts us).

There is an ancient harpsichord in what passes for the
parlour, on the first floor, above the main bridge. The
tone . . . well, imagine holding a couple of our old Leghorn
hens, the ones past laying age, and trying to extract a sound

in unison by tickling their feathered breasts. "Cck-cluck, Cck-cluck, Cck-cluck...CCK-CLUCK!"

Still, as Leo says, an instrument is only one half of the bargain. Even such an amateur as I may extract something akin to a melody from the keyboard. Music or literature, most of the compositions we print are turned into ink and paper out of vanity, of course. The "author" pays, or, if he has found a patron, then some poor sap with a surfeit of unwanted cash foots the bill. Some show merit, though. Three nights ago Leo placed a single sheet in front of me and barked, "Play that!" then afterwards asked my opinion (not a common occurrence).

Something told me this was a time to be politic. "An interesting piece, Uncle, but I find it hard to judge on a single page. Is there no more?"

"None!" he said with a sardonic grin on his face. He held up his right hand in front of me and I saw what previously I had only glimpsed. The little finger and the index were horribly bent, as if the sinews of each had decided to withdraw on themselves and pull the flesh tightly into the palm. I had wondered why Leo was so slow at setting type. Now I knew. His musical days were surely past, at least as a player. "Nor will there be any more with a hand like this."

"This was your work?" I tried not to look too surprised. Just between you and me, Lucia, it was rather good.

"Something to impress the Red Priest and his little girls at La Pietà. Had I finished it before this *claw* appeared."

"I'm sorry, sir. If you like, you could dictate to me and see if I might turn your ideas into something on a page."

"And if I go blind, perhaps you will paint on my instructions so that I may rival Canaletto?"

It seemed best to say nothing. Uncle Leo has few friends,

and none female as far as I can judge, a shame since a wife
might mellow him. His trade is his life, and a hard trade it is,
too, with hours too long for much in the way of romance.
The two of us must do everything in this publishing process,
from setting the type to working the press, though Leo
assures me he will seek hired help should the contract
warrant it. If Aldus Manutius (or Aldo Manuzio, as the locals
knew him better) could not make a living as a publisher in
Venice, I wonder sometimes how a mere Scacchi might
manage.

I reread that last sentence, and how I hate it! To hell with
pessimism (excuse my language). We are Scacchis, all. There
is a profession here, a good one, that keeps me close to
words and music. We may not be artists ourselves, but we
are, at least, their mouthpiece, and that counts for
something. Nor is any of this a simple way to make a living.
Today, tired from the previous night's work, I misunderstood
Leo's instructions and arranged the imposition wrongly for
the printing of a small pamphlet on the nature of the
rhinoceros. Everything will have to be redone, at Uncle's
expense; there is no unmaking my mistake (printing is a
business which punishes errors very severely). Leo beat me,
but not hard, and I deserved it. An apprentice is there to
learn.

Across from our house, in the parish church, is a painting
of the martyrdom of San Cassian, the patron saint of
teachers, if you recall. I stared at it for ages this evening.
It is a dark, gloomy work with no joy inside the pigment
(martyrdoms, which litter the churches here, tend to fall into
that category, I suppose!). Cassian's bare, muscular form fills
the foreground; around him, madness in their faces, wielding
pens and knives and even an adze, the saint's tormentors

prepare to send him to eternity. The tale the priest tells is that Cassian was their master; the pupils turned on him when he sought to teach them Christian ways.

There is an important allegory there. The priest assures me so. Still, I cannot help but wonder. What would make not one but several pupils turn on their master with such deadly intent? Had he punished them more than they deserved? They are fallen; you can see it in their faces. But what made them fall? I see no sign of Satan anywhere in the picture.

I feel the tone of this letter is becoming cheerless, so you have perhaps put it to one side already and gone with your newfound friends to the dancing and the *fiesta*. I send you my fond love, my dearest sister, and am glad to hear your health is much improved.

An appointment with the Englishman

HUGO MASSITER WAS FIFTY-ONE. HE SEEMED, IN RIZZO'S eyes, like a character out of one of those sixties films that sometimes came up late at night on RAI. Movies where the women always wore short skirts and too much makeup and the men seemed possessed by some weird version of Mediterranean cool, like ageing playboys pretending to be teenagers. Massiter dressed straight out of that era. Today the Englishman wore a pair of fawn slacks with a knife-edge crease down the front, a white shirt ironed so much it had the appearance of a fancy restaurant tablecloth and—the finishing touch—a light-blue silk neck scarf tucked in at the open collar.

He was tall and must have been good-looking once. His face had a patrician cragginess. He was tanned in the cracked way the English male went when he spent too much time under the hot sun. He could break into a sudden smile that seemed permeated with some genuine warmth if he wanted. But his hairline was receding, and, against all obvious attempts to hide the fact, a shiny red patch of forehead was growing larger all the time. More memorably, there was the question of the eyes. Massiter had grey eyes, large, intelligent, and piercing. He looked at people as if he had some extra sense of focus, seeing more than their outward appearance. When Rizzo wanted to know what Hugo Massiter was really thinking, all he had to do was seek the answer in those eyes. In their cold frankness lay all the answers and, Rizzo felt, the true measure of Massiter's character. It was the eyes that made him fear the Englishman. Sometimes they looked only half-human.

It was three weeks since Susanna Gianni's early disinterment, and Massiter ought to be thinking of other things. He sipped from a glass of sparkling mineral water, then stared out of the window at the Grand Canal. The small apartment was in Dorsoduro, between the Accademia and Salute. It was on the second floor of a converted palace and must, Rizzo knew, have cost a fortune. Massiter could afford it. He had homes in London and New York too. The art trade paid better than thieving from tourists, though Rizzo suspected that if everything were out in the open, there might be precious little moral daylight between them.

Massiter turned and stared at him. Rizzo knew the expression. It said: *I know when you are lying.* Rizzo thought: *Yeah?*

"Tell me again what happened."

"Hey. The same as I told you a million times. What else is there to say?"

"Describe her."

Massiter scared him. Still, there were limits. "Listen. If you'd wanted a picture taken, you should have said. There was some dead woman there. End of story."

The words jogged something in Massiter's memory. He walked to the antique desk by the window and retrieved a folder. Then he took a photograph from it and came to sit next to Rizzo, very close. The pale leather sofa breathed expensively with the weight of his body. Rizzo stared at the painting on the opposite wall: a swirl of modernist colours. The feeling that he was trapped inside some old movie came to him again. Maybe Fellini's corpse was stuffed behind one of the floor-length mirrored wardrobes that lined the room. Maybe Massiter kept some ancient white open-topped Alfa Spyder in the car park at Piazzale Roma and drove it down the coast road on fine days, letting what hair he had left fly in the wind. Scalp apart, the man seemed impervious to time.

"Take a look at the picture."

This was a new photo. The girl was standing outside La Pietà, the big white church down from San Marco. She wore a black dress and held in her hands the old, fat fiddle that was now safely tucked away in a left-luggage locker at Mestre station. It was a sunny day. In the background there were other musicians, as if this were before or after a concert. It was impossible for Rizzo to take his eyes off the girl. She shone from the picture, full of happiness and life, eyes bright and...it came to him. *Focused*. She was smiling at the person behind the camera. Massiter, in all probability. With a touch more hair ten years ago, maybe, when that white Spyder had a little less rust. It came to Rizzo, too, that his first impression, gained from the image on the headstone, was no mistake. She was in the process of some change, turning from girl to woman, and it was impossible not to want to sit and stare as it happened. Some head-turning, magnetic beauty was emerging from inside her, being revealed like a work of art in the process of creation. Was this why Massiter was so obsessed with her? It didn't fit. Those cold grey eyes had no room in them for that kind of feeling.

"You're sure this is the girl in the coffin?"

"Am I sure? She'd been dead for ten years. What do you think?"

"It could have been her?"

"Sure."

"The hair?"

"Sure. The hair was just like that. To the tee." There was no explaining to Massiter that some change had happened, a change the girl had never expected when Massiter had snapped her image one sunny day a decade ago.

"And there was nothing else in the coffin? No note, for example?"

Rizzo looked straight into the Englishman's face, not flinching from his gaze. "There was a dead body in a shroud. Nothing else. Like I told you a million times. I'm sorry."

Massiter sighed and placed the photograph on the table. Rizzo tried hard not to stare at it.

"And then there is the matter of this dead superintendent."

Rizzo prayed he wouldn't pee himself. "What?"

Massiter's eyes turned on him. Rizzo felt cold.

"Oh, come! Poor chap murdered the very same day. You must have read about it?"

Rizzo nodded, surprised how calm he was. "Sure. I read about it. Never made the connection, that's all."

Massiter blinked, then sorted through a sheaf of newspaper cuttings on the table and pulled out a report of the killing. There was a bad picture of the dead superintendent accompanying the story. He looked a lot younger. "You didn't see him? In the cemetery?"

"Don't recall," Rizzo replied, making sure he looked intently at the photograph. "No. Not the guy I spoke to."

The Englishman made a noncommittal noise, then went to the table, picked up a white cardboard box full of tissue paper, and, as carefully as a surgeon, withdrew from it a small painted object. It was a tiny, primitive ikon of the Virgin, the kind of bauble the antique shops stole out east, then sold to the tourists.

Rizzo knew people who knocked up cheap copies in a backstreet studio on Giudecca. This looked like the genuine article. The halo round the Virgin's head shone like pure gold.

"See this," Massiter said, holding the ikon in front of him. "Next week I'll put it through an auction in New York. It'll fetch fifty, maybe sixty thousand dollars. That's where your money comes from."

Rizzo whistled. "Whoa. Am I in the wrong business."

"You're a thief," Massiter said bluntly. "That's how we know each other."

That much was true enough. He had tried to lift the Englishman's wallet one Sunday morning near Salute. Massiter was smart enough to spot the trick and then, to Rizzo's amazement, invite him for a coffee instead of an appointment with the cops. It was a neat way of finding someone to do the odd dirty job. Rizzo guessed he had his equivalents in New York and London, maybe found in pretty much the same way.

"You've got me there," he said.

Massiter placed the ikon in his hands. It felt tiny, delicate.

"It came out of Serbia," Massiter said. "Do you ever stop to think about the merchandise that's available from the Balkans these days?"

"Can't say I have." Rizzo felt slightly shocked to hear it called "merchandise." Art was art, even if it was stolen. He placed the object back in Massiter's hands. He didn't like having that kind of money perched between his fingers.

"No," Massiter said. "I imagine not. This is from a small monastery on the Kosovo border. Taken by some Christians I know, as it happens, but I'm strictly agnostic in these matters. I'll deal with anybody."

Rizzo could believe that. "Business, huh."

"You know what they're like? The kind of people who do this?"

Rizzo knew. There were Balkan crooks everywhere these days, Bosnian and Kosovan, Albanian and Serb. They would carve your eyes out with spoons just for saying "*Ciao*" in the wrong accent.

He nodded. Massiter shuffled closer to him on the pale leather sofa, then placed a hand on his knee. The Englishman had long, powerful hands, Rizzo saw, and wondered why he had never noticed that before.

"Last year, one of these...people stole from me. Really. It's true. I help them in their business. I pay them on time. I send them gifts. I pat their children on their filthy, lice-ridden heads."

Rizzo's chest felt tight. "I would never do that, Signor Massiter. You've got to know I would *never* do that to you, not in a million y—"

"Quiet."

Massiter had moved his hand and placed two fingers firmly on Rizzo's lips now. The big grey eyes filled Rizzo's gaze, like twin planets full of ice and hate.

"They stole from me, Rizzo," he said. "After all the trust I placed in them."

There was a smell on him, Rizzo realised. More perfume than aftershave, almost like incense.

He took his fingers away from Rizzo's face. Rizzo hoped he wouldn't piss himself.

"Stupid idea, huh?"

Massiter nodded. "I think so. Are you following me?"

"I'm following," he said.

"No. You're not." Massiter took a sip of his water. His hand was steady as a rock. "You're a thief. Which is useful up to a point. The lesson you must learn is this. Stealing what passes through my hands is bad. Stealing something that's mine is much, much worse."

"I wouldn't steal..."

Massiter broke into a smile, the warm, welcome-to-the-party smile that might have got him a bit part in the movies. "Oh, do be quiet, old chap. I am trying to explain. Some things I possess in order to sell them. Some things—objects of a greater beauty—I possess for myself alone. If you steal the former, I am angry. If you steal the latter, well...it would be impolite to spell it out, don't you think?"

Rizzo said nothing. Massiter laughed. "Do you know the difference between us, Rizzo?"

"You're smart. I'm dumb."

The Englishman laughed again and patted Rizzo lightly on the shoulder. "Oh, I wouldn't say that. You're quite the clever boy. No. The difference is that you steal things for themselves. While I...acquire them in order that I might, if they are of suitable quality, become their owner. What interests you is the object. What interests me is the act of possession."

"Got you," Rizzo said uncertainly.

"Let me put it more succinctly. You are a thief. I am a collector. We'll leave it at that, shall we?"

The Englishman got up, stretching his legs as if they hurt.

"That girl owned an object which belongs to me. I have missed it since her death. I hear things, Rizzo. I hear something very like it could be for sale right now, if a man were to go to the right place and offer the right kind of money. I wonder where it is. I wonder how it got there."

Rizzo made sure he didn't move a single muscle in his face. "What do you want me to do?"

"Why," Massiter replied, with the warm, beaming smile again, "watch. Listen. Be my eyes. Be my ears." He looked at the large and expensive watch on his wrist. It was close to one. "Then tell me everything you know. But for now, you'd best get the hell out of here. I have a reception to attend, with people who know me to be the very picture of modern rectitude. And since I'm paying for the thing, I'll be damned if I don't get a little entertainment while they drink my wine."

Beyond the law

Intrigue! Intrigue!

There. I have you instantly. None of this is fiction, either. Your hapless brother is in the thick of it, and I cannot help but wonder what dangers and mysteries lurk around the corner.

Yesterday Leo called me in to the parlour and said very gravely that I was to go about important and confidential business on behalf of the House of Scacchi. Vivaldi, that Red Priest of great fame, is teetering on his throne. His muse, it seems, has left him, and so have several of his players. The priest's reputation rests, of course, on the little band of female musicians he had gathered together at La Pietà. Well, sickness, arguments (plenty of them), and attrition over the years have left him short. Vivaldi must play his usual concert season, yet lacks the talent to perform his works.

I thought for one ghastly moment that Leo was expecting me to don a frock and enter the lists, and was about to plead terror, incontinence, or a sudden stiffness in the hands—anything I could think of. Uncle shook his head impatiently, reading my mind, and explained. "Not you, lad. He needs a fiddle-player, and I know just the one. I'm too busy. Be the girl's chaperone. Take a gondola there and back. Spare no expense. Vivaldi's a fading power in this city, no doubt, but even a ghost may have influence."

"You want me to accompany the lady to the church, sir? Is she ill?"

"No," he replied, and I thought I saw a touch of sly fear in his eyes. "She is a *Jew*!"

I had not the faintest idea what to make of this. "A Jew? But this is impossible. How can she play in a Christian church, Uncle? I don't believe Vivaldi may allow it."

"I don't believe Vivaldi need know! The lady in question is presentable and highly talented. She can play anything the priest may throw at her—and more. If she were Gentile, and a man, I daresay she'd be packing the concert hall by herself. But she's a Jew and a pretty little thing, so that's that. She has neither a hook nose nor a beard. Provided you can get her there safely and persuade her to remove her red scarf before you enter the church, Vivaldi won't think twice. And once he hears her play, he's caught!"

The dusty parlour felt cold as he said this. I may not know much about Jews, but I do know they are not allowed to walk the streets without some badge announcing their breeding and may not, under any circumstance, enter a church. Imprisonment, or worse, would surely follow. And prison, too, for any who encouraged them to break the Doge's law.

"I think the schedule is not so busy, sir, that you may not undertake this yourself. I am just a lad. I don't know the city so well as you."

Leo's eyes, dark at the best of times, narrowed and became unreadable. "I believe I am the one who enters the daily catalogue of this trade's calendar, Lorenzo. When I took

you in from penury and made you my apprentice, you agreed
to do my every bidding. Now, kindly meet that side of your
contract."

"But, sir! What if we are caught!"

"Then I shall be most disappointed and deny all
knowledge of your tricks. This is a dirty world. You cannot
prosper without dipping your hands into the muck from time
to time."

Yes, I thought. *My* hands.

"Besides, boy. You may find it more enjoyable than you
expect."

I said nothing, hoping he would relent. But Uncle Leo is
made of stiff board. He never bends. He never so much as
wavers.

"And if I refuse, sir?"

"Then you can pack your bag and find your own way
through this life. If I don't have a congratulatory letter from
Vivaldi on my desk by tomorrow morning, you might as well
do that anyway. Fat use you are to me in the press room,
spilling ink and printing pages upside down."

With that he thrust some small coinage into my hand—
enough for the gondola only if I walked all the way to meet
my Hebrew charge and back again—and a scribbled piece of
paper, then went back to reading the proofs of some piece
of medical quackery destined for the Arabs.

I am, sister, still alive, of course, and free enough to write
this letter, which you will, I trust, burn immediately. So you
may see that, so far anyway, this adventure has not yet
devoured the life of your little brother, though it gives me
small opportunity to sleep at night, for a variety of reasons.

A *mission*

DANIEL FORSTER'S FIRST FULL DAY IN THE CITY WAS, AT Scacchi's suggestion, spent in some solitary sightseeing. He arrived back at the large house by the square of San Cassian at five and was summoned, on the ringing of the church bells at six, for the evening ritual: spritz. Scacchi drank three large tumblers, each bloodred, Paul a little less. Laura, both servant and guest, had but a single glass.

Scacchi looked fitter today. His face had more colour to it, and his mood seemed much improved. Daniel understood the nature of the illness afflicting both men yet believed he could not begin to appreciate how deeply it might alter their moods. Laura's plea for his consideration towards both of them was not, in truth, necessary.

"You know how this young man found his way here, Laura?" Scacchi asked.

She exchanged a glance with Paul. "You may have mentioned it once or twice. But do, please, jog my memory."

"Why, through genius! There he is, writing some thesis on the Venetian printing industry in that famed college of his in Oxford. And what does he do? Finds that one of the humbler printing houses still exists! In bricks and mortar alone, of course. I salute your dedication, Daniel!" Scacchi's glass bobbed up and down. "It is more than two hundred and fifty years since a page was printed on these premises, and still you track us down!"

Daniel recalled the moment. Out of a whim he had looked up the records for the Venice phone directory while in the college library and cross-checked the entries there with the printing houses he was researching for his thesis. Every single name survived, scattered across the Veneto region. But there were only a handful of Scacchis, and one, to his amazement, lived at the very address which had, since the early sixteenth century, housed a once-famous city press. He was proud of his detective work. Since the death of his mother, he had immersed himself in research, partly as a form of escape but also because he found some private enjoyment in these old books and musical scores. Life in the college was pleasantly measured and ordered, if somewhat solitary. He had, in spite of himself, acquired the reputation of being bookish, a little remote, perhaps. There were acquaintances, if no close friends. He was aware that some distance existed between him and his fellow students. He had spent the last few years caring for a dying parent while those around him moved and grew in ways he could only guess at. In a sense, he felt he had only begun to develop on the day his mother died, though the thought filled him with guilt and pain.

A soft hand fell on his arm. Laura smiled at him, a little concerned, he thought.

"I'm sorry," he stuttered. "I was daydreaming. You were saying?"

Scacchi waved a forkful of meat in the air. "I was speechless when that letter arrived, wasn't I, Paul?"

"You are never speechless, Scacchi. Surprised, perhaps."

"What impertinence! I shall not rise to the bait. The city knows us, Daniel, if it knows us at all, as a couple of old queens who make a living buying and selling antiques from time to time. Yet you, with your computers and your talent for research, discover something that was little more than an old family rumour for me."

"But you knew," Daniel asked, "there was a famous publisher here, surely?"

Scacchi guffawed. "Flattery! All of this was so long ago and through different lines of the family. The name may be the same, but this house has been passed from relative to relative, branch to branch, for centuries. My own line goes back only three generations and inherited it from some bankrupt cousin. We ran a small warehousing business from the adjoining building for many years, until the demand for that collapsed. Now I am the last of the Scacchis. There will be none after me. And no Ca' Scacchi."

He stared at his plate and said without emotion, "As if that matters."

Laura bristled. "It matters to all of us, Scacchi. Remove that hangdog expression instantly, please. It does not suit you. And as to why Daniel is here . . . you invited him, if you recall. To help catalogue the . . ." she stared at Daniel, ". . . 'library.'"

"Ah." All were silent. Daniel found himself wondering once again about this complex trio and, most of all, the role Laura played within it. She was both servant and friend, confidante and guardian to these two much older men. It would be an onerous task at times—that much was obvious—but he did not doubt she adored it.

Scacchi looked at the table, an awkward grin on his lips. "A little exaggeration, perhaps. But nevertheless I think you will find this all most instructive. In any case, Laura, I paid the lad's ticket, didn't I? And a little pocket money for his stay. *And* a place at that nice little circus in La Pietà so that he may exercise that bow arm of his. Yes, I read your letters very carefully, Daniel, as you may see."

"La Pietà?"

"More of that later. For now..."

The old man stood up and, as he did so, retrieved from his pocket a set of keys dangling on a long chain attached to his belt. "Come one! Come all! We explore Ca' Scacchi and corners where none of you has ventured before!"

Laura saw the eagerness in his face and the direction he was headed, to the door which led to the ground-floor cellar. "We go to the warehouse? Are there rats?"

"My dear! There are rats everywhere in Venice."

"I think I'll clear up, thank you."

"Me too," Paul agreed. "The dust down there gets on my lungs, Scacchi."

The old man took it in his stride. "As you see fit. Come, Daniel. We venture into this netherworld on our own."

They went down a narrow set of stairs to the ground floor of the main house. It was dark and dusty, full of ancient furniture and crates. A single yellowing lightbulb lit the room. Scacchi picked up two large electric lanterns at the foot of the stairs and headed for a door to the left.

"Into the bowels we go," he declared. "It's dark as hell in there. No window. No electricity. You'll need these, and I'd be grateful if you tread as little dust into the house as possible. Laura can be a martinet over the merest hint of a dirty boot."

Daniel followed the old man through the ancient door. The lanterns cast twin yellow beams ahead of them. The adjoining room seemed even more disordered than the basement of the house itself. Dusty covers sat on shapeless forms, some only a few feet high, others towering to the height of a man. The space was the length and breadth of the house itself, seeming to stretch forever. At the front came a little light from two cracked wooden doors filling what must once have been the water-level trade entrance to the workshop.

"What is this, Scacchi?" he asked.

"Why, it's the remains of a print shop, I imagine. With some of the junk that must once have filled the three floors above us, dumped here when the business folded. When we were warehousing, we simply used the top floors and took everything in by hoist. Those stairs to the first floor are too narrow for carrying much, believe me. After you found me and got me thinking about this place's history, I decided to take a little look down here. Soon after, I thought to invite you to examine it yourself. Look…"

He lifted a corner of the fabric covering a towering rectangular object set to the side of the entrance arch, revealing the foot of some vast machine.

"A press?" Daniel asked.

"Some such junk. Worthless, from my enquiries. Not much call for this kind of thing. The world wants works of art, not ancient machinery. Paper, perhaps, but there I am lost. Show me a musical instrument, a painting, or a piece of ormolu and I can value it. Words on a page … they never meant much to me. A fine Scacchi I am, eh?"

Daniel heard something squeak, then scuttle off towards the light leaking through the doorway. Laura was absolutely right about the rats. She was, he thought, probably right about most things and generally ignored. He hoped that Scacchi understood how lucky he was in his choice of housekeeper.

"Some library, I suppose," Scacchi said, his face positioned out of the yellow lantern light, where it was impossible for

Daniel to discern his expression. "I'm a fraud. Say as much, please. I lure you here under false pretences and then show you a room full of dust and demand it be panned for gold."

"No! No! I would have come anyway. Even if you had only one scrap of yellow paper for me. I would fly here just to breathe the air."

Scacchi patted a low pile of papers near him. A miniature thunderstorm of dust rose from it and enveloped them. For some reason he seemed mildly upset. "Why do you say that, Daniel? We are strangers. I have lured you from your home on false pretences. Go on, admit it."

He was amazed the old man saw so little. "I've longed to come here. Always. My mother was English, but she lived in the city once, as a student. Where do you think I first learnt Italian? I grew up with her books and her stories. When I look around me..."

Daniel hesitated. Something, the dust perhaps, pricked at his eyes. "...I feel I see this place through her eyes and that here she's still close to me."

Scacchi coughed and gave him a sideways glance. Some scrap of intimacy had passed between them, though neither was ready to acknowledge as much.

"Credulity is the man's weakness but the child's strength, they say," Scacchi murmured. "Twenty years old, Daniel, and which are you?"

"A little between the two, I imagine," he answered honestly. "But set in the right direction."

Scacchi turned his head to stare into the darkness. "You remind me. Tomorrow there is something in San Rocco I must show you. Before your visit to La Pietà—which I think you shall enjoy immensely."

"You're too kind."

Scacchi tapped at the papers again, but more gently. Still, the dust came forth. "I am?"

"Perhaps not *too* kind."

The old man picked up the lanterns. It was time to go. "Daniel," he said. "Find something in here for me. Something I may sell. We laugh and joke and act as if there's no tomorrow. In a sense, for Paul and me there is no tomorrow, or not much, anyway. But not yet, and I need you to find me something in here I can sell, for good money too. I wish to die beneath this roof, not have to sell it to some American who has a fancy to remodel a Venetian *palazzo*. And I wish to leave our dear Laura enough to give her a fresh start in life. God knows she deserves it. For that we need some grubby cash."

Daniel was shocked. The change in Scacchi's tone was so unexpected. "I hadn't realised. You must stop this expense on me at once. I can work for nothing. You feed me. You bought my ticket. Please."

Scacchi patted him on the shoulder. "Oh, nonsense, Daniel. The pittance I am paying you is neither here nor there. I need money, not small change. There's providence working some-where here. It sent you to me. It sends you to this room. Search and you'll find, I know."

He fell silent. Daniel touched the old man gently on the sleeve. Some small amount of moisture glistened in the corner of his eyes. Had Laura been there at this moment, she would, he knew, possess the right words, the correct gestures to comfort him.

"This is Aladdin's cave," Daniel said, trying his best.

"Or Pandora's box."

"Either way. I'll find you something here to sell."

Scacchi turned to go. Daniel picked up the sheets of paper which had produced the dust cloud and peered at them in the dank yellow light. The ink ran across the page like smudged mascara. The warehouse was at ground level, next to the *rio*. At some stage, perhaps on many occasions, the flood of *acqua alta* must have penetrated into the room at least a good three feet deep, destroying everything it touched.

9

The route to the ghetto

The piece of paper Leo gave me read, "Dr. Levi, Ghetto Nuovo." Nothing else. No directions. No instructions on what to do when I got there. I left Ca' Scacchi just after midday in a state of mild anxiety, walked straight into the *campo* to the wellhead, and gulped down a cup of musty water. From across the square came a long, familiar whistle. Gobbo was there, ostensibly seeking out some rare kind of mushroom for his epicurean master from the markets round the corner, though I think the unmistakable smirk on his face as he watched a few of the painted ladies go by told of another intent.

"Tell me where the Ghetto Nuovo is, Gobbo," I pleaded.

"Why do you want that place?" he asked, instantly suspicious. "You're not a little Jew in disguise, are you?"

I would trust Gobbo greatly, but not with my life. One Venetian improvisation of which I was uncomfortably aware at that moment was the gilded and gaping lion's mouth one sees on street corners and in important buildings. These lions are there for the suspicious to rat anonymously on their fellow citizens for whatever civic misdeeds they suspect. I did not fancy finding myself in the Doge's Palace, explaining away my actions, just because Gobbo failed to keep his trap shut down some Dorsoduro drinking dive.

"Of course not, you fool! My master is a printer. Some Hebrew wants his memoirs put on the page. If they pay the money, we'll publish it, however dreary the old fart happens to be."

"Glad to hear it!" he said, relieved, and gave me a painful slap on the back. "It seems to me . . ."—he pulled himself up almost to my own height, to add weight to this coming observation—"that those slimy bastards got off altogether too lightly for murdering our Lord like that."

"Your grasp of learning never ceases to amaze me, Gobbo," I sighed. "I had no idea theology was among your talents."

A quick grin split his ugly face. "Really? Thanks. The Ghetto Nuovo's up in Cannaregio. Fifteen minutes on the water at the most."

I held out my hand with the paltry coins in it. He looked at them and grimaced. "Leo's a tight-fisted bastard, eh? In that case, you'll have to leg it over the Rialto and head past San Fosca. Won't take you more than half an hour, provided no one whacks you on the head along the way."

"Thanks . . ."

"I had a master like that in Turin. Stuck him with a penknife before I decamped out of the window with a bag full of silver. Pick a generous guvnor next, my friend. It saves so much grief."

"I'm an apprentice, Gobbo. Not a servant."

"Oh!" he said with a mock bow. "I *do* apologise, sir. I'd give you a lift on my way back, of course, but it's in the wrong direction, and one couldn't expect one to share a seat

with the hoi polloi. Besides . . ." A ragged-haired whore with
a painted face had just made eyes at him from the warren of
alleys beyond the church. "I may be a little time."

Without wasting another breath on the infuriating chap,
I strode off eastwards, following the tangle of "streets," little
more than dark corridors, which I knew would take me to the
Rialto. I have thus far not told you the truth about walking
around this fair city of mine, dear sister, and that is for one
reason alone: I do not wish to worry you. I am now
sufficiently familiar with its ways to know I can survive, but
many, I fear, never reach that happy stage. Even by day,
Venice is a nightmare to navigate on foot, a tangled warren
of passages and gangways, few of them running in a straight
line for even ten paces, and mostly built up on both sides so
that the weary and confused wanderer can scarcely see where
he is going. If an alley should turn into a cul-de-sac—and one
that may deposit you in the unsavoury waters of the canal—
you may be assured there will be no warning of the fact until
the point at which you almost tumble into the grey and
greasy lagoon. Should there be the luxury of a bridge, be
assured that it will have no handrails, so that a single false
step in the dark will tip you once again straight into the
drink. On Saturday nights, when the *osteria* around the corner
from our house fills to the seams with rowdy boozers, I lie in
bed listening to them trying—and failing—to cross the
plankwork that spans the *rio* into the Calle dei Morti (so
called, I imagine, because this is the quick way to walk coffins
into the church). For a good two hours after midnight, it is
always the same: *plop, curse, plop, curse, plop* . . . Ah, Venice.

The Rialto is no such bridge. It is the single way to cross
the Grand Canal on foot and, as such, must naturally reflect
the glory of the Republic. It does, too, in abundance, being a

veritable community above the water, with shops and houses and hawkers and quacks, the latter bellowing their wares into the hubbub as the water seethes with traffic beneath them.

I had no time to dawdle in this pleasant mêlée of humanity. The Jewess awaited me, and Vivaldi after that, so I broke into a loping jog and pushed my way through the throng, past churches, through oddly shaped squares and the low, vulgar architecture of Cannaregio, on to the area where Gobbo had directed me. Then, turning a corner, I found the Ghetto Nuovo, a sight so odd I stopped in my tracks, leaned against the nearest wall, and wondered whether to turn on my heels at that very moment, return to Ca' Scacchi, and pack my bags.

What stood before me seemed to be a single, small island in the city, like many others, but guarded by a wooden drawbridge—yes, the kind that goes up at night—with a bored soldier scratching his backside by the entrance. Behind, on the island, like some monstrous building that had grown of its own accord, towered a single line of housing six or seven floors tall, with washing hanging out of every window and such a cacophony of cries, young and old, singing, too, and a yowl of argument, that I wondered if an entire city might live behind these black, bleak walls. For a second, I thought that I had taken a wrong turning and stumbled upon the Republic's prison instead. But no. I walked entirely around this curious kingdom in miniature—no larger, sister, than that little field at the back of our farm where our father grew those waving heads of artichoke in the summer—and found two more such bridges, each with a solitary guard and each capable of being drawn up when required. This tiny piece of land, surrounded on each side by canal, was indeed the Ghetto Nuovo, and I cursed my uncle once again for failing to tell me what lay in store when he ejected me so ruthlessly into the street.

As boldly as I could, I walked up to the guard and said, "I wish to see Dr. Levi, sir. Is he at home?"

The soldier almost clouted me on the head with his fist. "What do you think I am, son? Personal secretary to these bloody monsters? You get your arse in there and find the little kike for yourself. Don't go asking the Republic's soldiers to do your dirty work for you."

I apologised profusely, touching my cap several times, and stumbled over the bridge beneath a dark arch and found myself, wide-eyed and more than a touch fearful, in the realm of the Jews.

10

An awkward interview

GIULIA MORELLI RANG THE BELL ON THE ANCIENT house in San Cassian. The housekeeper answered the door. She wore a plain nylon housecoat and smiled uncomfortably when she saw the police ID. The woman was blinking at the sunlight, as if she hated to be outside.

The policewoman remembered the last time she interviewed Scacchi. It was at the station, at his own request, in the company of a cheap lawyer. Nothing came of the discussion. Scacchi was as slippery as an eel, but charming too.

She peered at the servant, as if half recognising her. "Have we met before?"

"I don't believe so," the woman replied briskly. "What do you want, please?"

Yet they had exchanged glances at least once, when she had seen Scacchi on the boat, fast asleep, and realised that he might be able to offer some insight into the strange events which followed the disinterment of Susanna Gianni. The housekeeper had been at the helm of the craft, steering it with a professional air of disdain towards the mass of waterborne traffic on the Cannaregio canal.

"I would like an interview with Signor Scacchi. Is he at home?"

"Yes. For what reason?"

"I will discuss that with him myself. It is a private matter."

The housekeeper bristled. "He is tired. I will not allow him to be disturbed. Do the police not make appointments?"

Giulia Morelli found it impossible not to smile. The woman was implacable in her determination to protect the man and had moved her body to fill the doorway, as if she would block any intruder with her physical presence. "I am sorry. You are quite correct. I should have called beforehand. Most of my appointments are not with gentlemen like Scacchi, you understand. I forget myself."

The white housecoat did not move from the door. There was a noise from inside the hallway.

"I wanted to ask Scacchi's advice on a matter of which he has specialist knowledge. Nothing more."

The old man shuffled into view. From the expression on the housekeeper's face, she was unaware he had been eavesdropping.

"One must always help the police, Laura," Scacchi insisted, and beckoned Giulia Morelli into the house. "Some coffee, Captain? We haven't spoken since you sought that lost bauble from St. Petersburg, I believe."

She followed him up the stairs into an elegant living room, sitting on the sofa at his beckoning. He slumped into an armchair opposite. The young man from the boat was in the corner, peering at a set of ancient books.

"Daniel," Scacchi declared. "Cease your studies and meet a Venetian police officer. Captain Giulia Morelli. Daniel Forster. Daniel is English—at least it says as much on his passport—but we are fast developing a theory that he is a foundling who was spirited away to that cold climate as an infant."

Daniel Forster was handsome, though somewhat ingenuous, she thought. Was it possible he was blushing?

"You are on holiday?" she asked.

"He does a little research for me," Scacchi interrupted.

"Work which is as good as a holiday," Daniel said in near-perfect Italian. "I can't thank Signor Scacchi sufficiently for the kindness he has shown me."

She watched the old man's expression. It seemed troubled. Scacchi was not a man to dispense kindness without a purpose. The housekeeper returned with two small cups of coffee. Scacchi waved at the door. "The captain is on police business. I think you should take your books elsewhere, Daniel. You, too, Laura."

They left, a little reluctantly, it seemed to her. The old man folded his hands on his knees, smiled, and said, "Well, Captain. What have you come to arrest me for this time?"

"Scacchi." She beamed. "I have only arrested you once before and was unable, or unwilling, to press charges, in any case. You are most unfair."

"Huh! I have the single most ambitious woman in the Venice police in my parlour and she wishes me to think this is a social call?"

"Not at all. As I told your charming and most protective housekeeper, I merely seek your advice. And have some to offer in return too."

His face was grey and miserable when he allowed the pleasantries to drop. Scacchi was sick. It was obvious the rumours she had heard were correct. Giulia Morelli felt sorry for the old man.

"You know why I have come, surely?"

"I am an antiquarian, my dear. Not a psychic."

"The Gianni girl. You were familiar with the family."

He stared at her sourly. "Ten years ago. Who wants to drag up that terrible story again?"

"You read about the murdered cemetery superintendent. Surely? What the papers did not tell you is that earlier that day he had exhumed the poor girl's body, on forged papers too. And something was in that coffin, Scacchi."

"What?" he asked immediately.

"I don't know. A personal object of some value. Of some size too. I think it was too large to be jewellery."

He opened his hands as if bemused. "You are asking my advice about an object you cannot identify which may or may not have been taken from a casket which has lain underground for a decade. What do you expect me to say?"

Giulia Morelli hesitated. She had so little information.

"You knew the Giannis...."

"Only slightly."

"You met the girl. Perhaps you knew what she was buried with."

He shook his head. "Fantasies, my dear."

"Perhaps." There was another reason she had come. "But you must know something, Scacchi. Whatever was taken from that coffin has caused one man's death already. If someone should be unwise enough to accept it, perhaps there will be more. There is something strange here, and dangerous. Think of that, and call me."

Scacchi sighed. "You are young. You still have a romantic, a distant, notion about death."

She thought of the blade flashing through the air of the grubby apartment and the corpse opposite her. "I think not."

He studied her face with weary, perceptive eyes. "I read about your...ordeal in the paper. I am glad you were not seriously hurt. You have chosen a dangerous profession, Captain."

Was that a threat? she wondered. Scacchi's perfect manners surely made such a thing impossible.

"Sometimes we invite danger into our lives without even knowing," she replied. "I thought I was going to interview an irate cemetery superintendent. Not interrupt a murder."

Scacchi coughed, a dry, dead sound. "Surely not, my dear," he remarked. "You thought you saw the ghost of that poor dead girl. And you couldn't resist chasing it."

Giulia Morelli said nothing. From beyond the door she heard the sound of the housekeeper and the young man, Daniel. They were laughing, an easy, intimate laughter of a kind she rarely heard. She looked at Scacchi and wondered if she had been crazy to think he could help.

Outside, the bell of San Cassian tolled twelve.

11

From the past

RIZZO SAT IN THE SMALL, BARE APARTMENT BEHIND A locked door and closed curtains. He lived in a basic public-housing block in Cannaregio, not far from the old Jewish ghetto. His neighbours were, in the main, elderly, and wisely kept their noses out of his business. It was an ideal location from which to pursue his chosen trade.

The violin was safe inside its case in the luggage locker in Mestre. Even if it was discovered there, nothing linked him to the stolen instrument. All the risk came from any attempt to realise its value. He had to find a buyer, one who understood its worth and was willing to pay the price. And he had to achieve all this without making his disloyalty known to Massiter. In the gossipy world of stolen artefacts, this was no easy task. Rizzo had on occasion dealt in contraband tobacco, cocaine, and marijuana in addition to the run-of-the-mill objects he lifted from tourist pockets. These were all saleable items which could be moved through any number of third parties familiar to him. An ancient violin was a different matter. In order to establish the kind of price it might fetch, he needed the right advice and, to back up what that told him, some research of his own.

There was one possible solution. Three years before, he had, by a roundabout route, come into possession of a small, decorative antique carriage-clock, an item of little interest to the customary outlets he used for moving stolen goods. After some phone calls, he had established three individuals who might offer him a price for it: two dealers—one in Mestre, one in Treviso—and a third figure, a city man he knew as Arturo, who seemed ready to buy and sell on an occasional basis, though only through a third party so that the two of them never met. The Treviso dealer had taken the clock in the end, for a miserly price, but Rizzo had carefully filed away the dealers' numbers for future reference. The day after he acquired the violin, he had phoned all three anonymously, described the instrument as accurately as he could, with its markings and the curious inscription on the label. The first two dealers had laughed at him. The violin must be a fake, they said. Even if it were not, no one could possibly buy it. Any instrument of that calibre would be bought by an active, performing musician who would never take the risk of using a stolen violin in public.

Arturo had made the same point, yet there was, Rizzo felt, a note of measurable interest in his voice. He had asked detailed questions about the instrument: its colour, its size, and whether it had two parallel lines of stain on its belly—a sign, Rizzo judged, of a particular maker. When he confirmed the last point, Arturo fell silent for a moment, then asked, unwisely, what price Rizzo had in mind. The figure came straight out of Rizzo's head: $100,000. Arturo had whistled and said the game was too rich for him. No one would pay such a sum for an instrument that could never be played in a concert hall. But he asked for Rizzo's name and number and, when they were refused, suggested they speak again later, when his caller was willing to accept a more realistic price.

The conversation ended with both parties knowing it would one day, at Rizzo's choosing, resume. Yet it was hardly an ideal position. Rizzo preferred to have several potential buyers, each bidding against the others. With just three calls he had, in some way he failed to understand, managed to alert Massiter to the existence of the violin. To widen the net would be to invite Massiter's discovery of his theft, the consequences of which Rizzo cared not to contemplate. There were only two options: to take the thing out of its locker and throw it into the marshland out by the airport, where it could rot in the filthy salt waters of the lagoon, hidden forever. Or to squeeze the best price he could out of Arturo and get the thing off his hands as quickly as possible. To achieve the latter demanded information about the goods he had for sale. There seemed no better way to acquire that than to look into the background of its last owner.

Rizzo spent two hours in the city library, going through back issues of *Il Gazzettino*, and came away with ten photocopied pages of cuttings. Susanna Gianni's death had caused quite a stir in the city at the time, prompting a string of stories, each accompanied by the same photograph that he had seen on her headstone. It was perhaps this buried memory that had made her long-dead face so mesmeric when he had encountered it on San Michele. There had been a time when it was present on the front pages of the newspapers almost every day.

She was a local girl who grew up on the Lido. Her devoted single mother had, the reporters said, taken on extra cleaning work in the beachfront hotels in order to pay for her music lessons. By the time Susanna was twelve, the word "prodigy" was being used, an idea helped by the rumour, spread about by her mother, that the family was in some way distantly related to the legendary maestro Paganini. Only one mention was made of her instrument. In the year of her death, a preview of the concert which closed the summer school at La Pietà reported that she had been bought a fine and valuable fiddle by an anonymous admirer. No value had been placed upon the violin, which was described as a Giuseppe Guarneri from Cremona. Nor was there a photograph of her with anything which looked like the fiddle Rizzo had taken from her dead arms. Nevertheless, he knew this later instrument had to be the one which was now in his possession. Clearly visible on the label of the fiddle now in Mestre was the name Joseph Guarnerius and a date, 1733. It was also, without doubt, the one in the photograph Massiter had shown him in the apartment.

The newspaper accounts told of her music, not of Susanna Gianni. There was no hint of affairs or a darker side to her character, though knowing *Il Gazzettino*, he doubted such tittle-tattle would be carried even if it existed. At the start of the last summer of her life, there was every expectation that she would be the star of the summer school paid for by the great benefactor Massiter and, in all probability, move on to the international circuit afterwards. The girl had gone missing after the closing concert, where she had performed triumph-antly. Two days later her naked body was found in a *rio* near Piazzale Roma. She had been badly beaten, but the cause of death was drowning. Susanna Gianni was last seen at the farewell party hosted by Hugo Massiter in the Hotel Danieli. The police had no witnesses who saw her leave or any idea of how or why she had travelled from the waterfront by San Marco across the canal to the dank quarter on the far side of the city where she met her death. Nor was there any mention of the violin, a detail which, it seemed to Rizzo, would surely have been noted had the fiddle been found next to the body, lending the scene a melodramatic touch the papers would surely not have missed. He knew nothing of music. Perhaps the violin had remained at the school and was reunited with its late owner only when she was interred.

Murder is a rarity in Venice. The savage attack on Susanna Gianni and the lack of any progress by the police in finding her killer provided the papers with their best story in years. A week later it was over as sensationally as it had begun. Anatole Singer, the leader of the school, a lean, balding Russian in his late forties, was found hanged in his suite in the Gritti Palace. In a suicide note Singer confessed to attacking the girl when she refused his advances. He had lured her to a remote meeting place near Piazzale Roma after the farewell party on the pretext of meeting an American agent who would find her work in New York. Susanna rebuffed him, and so he raped her in a drunken rage, then threw her, unconscious, into the water.

All this, it seemed to Rizzo, was described in a very pat, logical way for a man who was about to hang himself. As a criminal by trade, Rizzo believed that confession, under any circumstances, was a most unnatural act. Even if one did feel the need to make a clean breast of matters, why do so just before committing suicide? What was the point? Every crime needed a purpose. He had not murdered the cemetery superintendent lightly. The man's death was required in order to save his own skin, since Massiter would surely kill him if he knew about the fiddle. And where was the gain in Singer's confession? These doubts did not trouble the heads of the city detectives, however. They had declared the case closed. Within a fortnight, the Gianni story was dead, as dead as its apparent protagonists.

The last cutting in the file was a tribute to Susanna from Hugo Massiter himself. Rizzo stared at the decade-old picture of Massiter. He had only a little more hair and the same dress sense, with a neck scarf folded neatly over his throat. The article described Massiter as the "well-known international art expert and philanthropist." Rizzo stifled a laugh. It was difficult to decide who was more stupid: the press or the police.

He picked up the phone and dialled the local number. A woman answered, then called Arturo to the phone. The familiar thin, reedy voice came on the line. Rizzo explained his proposition: $80,000, not a penny less.

"Give me time," the thin voice said.

"Two weeks. There's some guy in Rome who's creaming himself for this thing."

"Two weeks," the voice repeated glumly. "*Ciao*."

In the small, dark apartment, Rizzo smiled. There was triumph in the air. He even knew Arturo's full name. The servant had said it when she called to him.

"*Ciao*, Scacchi," Rizzo said, then hung up.

12

♣

The mysterious Levis

What should I have expected? The smell of incense in the air?
Strange people in strange clothes eyeing this suspicious
Gentile invader from the world outside? I had no idea. The
very oddness of this task had banished imagination from my
head. When I walked over that wooden bridge, I might have
been ready to enter the Tower of Babel. Instead, I discovered
ordinariness in abundance. The ghetto is much like any other
corner of the city, only plainer. The towering buildings which
line the circular perimeter of the island are just a few rooms
deep. Beyond them is a small cobbled square with a well in
its centre, a scattering of modest-sized trees, and—the only
curiosity—men and women dressed uniformly in dark clothes,
sitting on benches, toying with beads, and reading books.

I asked a young chap with a wispy black beard where I
might find Dr. Levi (speaking very slowly and clearly so he
might understand). He pointed with a long, pale finger at a
house in the corner of the square, next to a curious jumble of
buildings surmounted by what looked like the wooden cabin
of Noah's Ark. I crossed and entered by the downstairs door.
There was the smell of cooking—potato and cabbage—and

the noise of young families. I read the list of names on the wall, then climbed—and climbed—all six floors, past doors half-open, past arguments and banter, the bawl of infants, and, once, the unmistakable sound of sobbing, and was relieved when I reached the top to find myself in something that might pass for silence.

I knocked on the single door. It opened and a young man's affable face, clean-shaven, intelligent, with glittering brown eyes and a high forehead, met mine, smiling, with an amused expression upon it.

"Scacchi sends his lad," he said to someone behind him. "Obviously not man enough for the job himself. Come in. We won't bite. Like some tea?"

I entered the place and found myself in a tiny, ill-lit room requiring candles even in the middle of the day. There was a pleasant smell not unlike attar of roses. The floor was carpeted, and every seat was covered in some kind of soft drape. On the lone table stood a globe and several books. In the corner, obscured by the shadow cast from the window shutter, a lady sat most upright, as if observing me.

"I think we should be going, sir," I answered. "Vivaldi abhors lateness."

"Decisive, eh! I think they found you a man in the city at last, Rebecca. You will take good care of her . . . um?"

"Lorenzo, sir. Lorenzo Scacchi. My uncle sent me."

"Quite. I am sorry I cannot cure his claw, by the way. Even Hebrew medics have their limitations."

Some kind of debt was being repaid here, I gathered. I was risking my neck not just to ingratiate ourselves with the Red Priest but to save Leo a doctor's bill.

"I am Doctor Jacopo Levi. You shall call me Jacopo," he told me, extending a hand. "And your ward shall be my

much-loved sister, Rebecca, Lorenzo. I'd do this myself,
but that would only double the risk and I fear this city is too
unruly for her to venture out alone. So be wary. I don't want
to rescue either of you from the Doge's dungeons."

"I will do my best, sir," I replied earnestly, watching the
lady rise from the corner and move towards us, into the
narrow shaft of light that entered the room from the single,
small window facing onto the square. "I will do everything in
my power . . ."

And do you know? I haven't a clue what I said after that.
These next few moments are burned upon my memory, but
they contain only images, nothing as mundane as words. I
am back where I started when I tried to describe the wonder
of St. Mark's Basin on Ascension Day. Some things defy
those clumsy old foot soldiers of the alphabet. Ovid could
dedicate an entire work to this lady, and perhaps in another
incarnation did, but all my humble pen can give you are
facts.

Rebecca Levi is, she tells me, just turned twenty-five,
though she seems to me closer to my own age. She is a touch
beneath my height, very slim, but with an upright bearing,
straight-backed, and a strong pair of shoulders (there's the
fiddle player for you). On our first meeting she wore a fine
black velvet dress that ran from her neck to ankles, sleeves cut
to the elbow, as plain as you might ask for. Around her slim
white throat was a narrow band of roped gold, and from her
ears fell two gems, each scarlet red, of what breed I haven't
a clue, nor could I care. Rebecca has no need of jewels. Her
face shone out of the gloom like that of a Madonna painted
by a master in order to enlighten some dank church corner
(there goes my soul—perhaps this letter is not for posting
after all).

Let me start with the chin, which is delicately rounded and always facing up to you, as if to speak. Her mouth is inquisitive. She has the whitest teeth I have ever seen, each like some small, exquisite pearl. Her nose is modestly snubbed. Her skin has the pale, luminescent quality of a full winter moon, with only a faint trace of colour to her cheeks. She has brown eyes the shape of some precious opal from an emperor's crown, eyes that twinkle, as if laughing, and never leave the person she is facing, not until their business is done. And above all this loveliness, like a frame to some gorgeous piece of classical portraiture, is as wild a head of hair as you might find on one of those gypsy lasses who used to tease us at the fair: loose and cascading, a sea of feral, shining curls and waves the colour of chestnuts fresh from the tree in October. It falls around that superlative face all the way to her shoulders, and I have no idea how much of this is artifice and how much simple wilful abandonment, though I can say that from time to time she runs her fingers through her locks as if to free or shape them, and this provides a moment which will leave an entire monastery of monks praying for instant release back into the wicked world.

My auditory senses appeared to fail me until I heard two quick, deliberate coughs from behind: Jacopo trying to bring me to my senses. I felt hot and somewhat giddy and hoped the room's darkness was enough to cover the blood that had undoubtedly risen in my cheeks.

"He does speak, doesn't he?" she asked in a voice, slightly accented, that is as light and musical as a flute.

Jacopo's face came round to meet mine, his expression mock quizzical. "He *did*. You haven't bewitched another, old girl? I'm clean out of broken-heart ointment."

She giggled. No, be truthful now. She snorted! Quite unladylike, and I couldn't help bursting into laughter too.

"There," she said, and, with a sudden purpose, picked up a battered fiddle case from the floor, then pulled a scarlet silk scarf from her skirt pockets and tucked the best part of those lovely tresses beneath it. "Lorenzo has found his voice again. May we go now?"

Jacopo bent down to kiss his sister, an act which made my heart perform a rapid somersault inside my chest. Then he took me by the arm. "Take care of her, my boy. She'll impress the hell out of this priest of yours, and then the fun really begins. But if anyone should challenge you, profess all ignorance and say I sent you both on this escapade, on pain of death. You'll be amazed the things they'll believe of a Jew in this town."

"I will do no such thing, sir!"

Jacopo's eyes blazed at me with a sudden anger. "You will follow my instructions to the letter, lad, or drop this escapade at once. There's danger behind this laughter, and none of us should forget it!"

There. Two threats in the space of a single afternoon. One from my good Christian uncle, promising to incriminate me in something of which I am quite innocent. The second from some Hebrew stranger who pledged to exculpate me of a crime I was about to commit in full knowledge of my guilt.

"Very well," I agreed, making it clear from my tone that this last part was not to my taste at all. "If you insist, then I seem to have little choice in this matter."

"Splendid." Jacopo was his old, amiable self again.

Outside, in the ghetto square, none looked at us twice. We strode quickly out beneath a nearby arch, over the bridge, past the guard, and into the city. Close to the church of San

Marcuola and a jetty where we might find an inexpensive boat to San Marco, Rebecca suddenly grasped my arm and pulled me into a dark alley by a fish vendor's stall. There she snatched the scarf off her head, shook her hair as if to free it from some prison, and ran her strong, slim fingers through the curls.

"If anyone asks, Lorenzo, we are cousins and visitors to the city, and any offence we may have caused comes from our ignorance alone."

"Yes, my lady."

"Lorenzo!"

"Yes, Rebecca."

She seemed pleased with that. "Aren't you even the tiniest bit afraid? I am."

In all honesty, the thought had not occurred to me. I was too engrossed in other matters to consider much the cost of failure. I worded my reply carefully. "My father often said that fear is mainly a reason men cite for doing things they'd rather not. And that what we should fear most doesn't lie in the external world but in our own hearts."

"Clever man," she said.

"I believe he was. I miss him, and my mother also. It is because they are dead that I must live with my uncle."

She regarded me with an expression I could not decipher. "I am sorry to hear that, Lorenzo. Tell me. Do you think any will look at me now and see a Jew?"

"No," I answered honestly. *But they will look at you anyway*, I thought. *Who could blame them?*

13

At large in the city

ON THE WAY TO LA PIETÀ, FIDDLE CASE AT THE END OF his arm, Daniel enjoyed the promised detour. Scacchi had led him, at a slow but steady pace, south from San Cassian into San Polo, past the great Gothic hulk of the Frari, with its tall campanile, to the Scuola di San Rocco. Daniel recalled the place from the books in the college library. The *scuole* were charity brotherhoods, like Masonic lodges, each with its own funds and premises and each competing to display the finest art. San Rocco was the home of Tintoretto, whose cycle of paintings seemed to cover almost every inch of the interior.

Scacchi insisted that he pay the entry fee, then led Daniel upstairs to the Sala dell' Albergo, where they marvelled at the centrepiece depiction of Saint Roch towering over them, and the great panoramic crucifixion. Scacchi quoted Henry James on the latter and added, "Not that I have read anything else of his, of course. Much too tedious."

Then they went back into the main hall and he pointed out to Daniel the work which was, he claimed, the reason for their visit.

"There," he said. They both strained their necks upwards. In the corner, close to the door which led to the *sala*, was a large dark canvas depicting two figures. The first, a handsome young man with blond curls and a pleasant smile, looked upwards to the second, holding two rocks in his hand. The object of his plea, clearly Christ, from the halo that shone out of the darkness around his head, was half turned to him, as if in consideration.

"Subject, please?" Scacchi demanded.

"Painting is not my field," Daniel objected.

"Then use your head. That's why it's there."

It was, in a sense, obvious, although there was something highly unusual about the work. "It's the Temptation of Christ in the desert," Daniel suggested. "The lower figure is Satan holding out the rocks, which are shaped like loaves, with the idea that the starving Christ should turn them into bread."

"Spot on!" said Scacchi, beaming. "The date?"

"About 1570?"

"Ten years too early, but a good try. Now, please, tell me why this canvas is so very curious."

Daniel stared at the painting on the ceiling. "Because the focus is almost entirely upon the Devil, not Christ."

"Yes?" Scacchi required more.

"And because he is so...ordinary."

"Ordinary? Surely not. Look again."

The old man was right. "Because he is so fetching. So attractive," Daniel said.

"Precisely! Compare this to Bosch's *Temptation of St. Anthony*, painted probably no more than eighty years before. There you have devils with tails and snouts, demons ready to devour your entrails. This chap has nothing but a few feathers as his cloak and a smile as fetching as any sweet soul on earth. There you have it, Daniel. Everything you need to know about the Venetian Lucifer. That he wears such an engaging grin it is hard not to sup with him. Such a modern concept, don't you think? Except if you look at the canvas there..."

Scacchi pointed to an oval work on the ceiling at the centre of the room.

"You will see the selfsame pose used for Eve offering Adam the fated apple. There was always a touch of misogyny in Tintoretto, if you ask me. On the way out we'll take a look at the *Annunciation* downstairs. Poor girl looks as if she should never have stepped outside the kitchen, let alone mothered the Son of God."

Daniel found it difficult to take his eyes off the figure of Satan, with its perplexing smile and pleading expression. "Why did you bring me here, Scacchi?"

"For your betterment. A man must recognise Satan when he sees him, Daniel. Particularly in a city such as this. I am no moralist, so personally I care little whether you run with one side or the other. What matters, I think, is that it is you who decides. When the Devil comes to you, there are only three options. Do you do what he wants? What 'goodness' demands? Or what your own nature tells you, and that may be either or none of the aforementioned? The answer, naturally, should be the last. But unless you see him—or her—for what he truly is, you can't even begin to decide. Are you with me?"

It seemed, to Daniel, a distant argument. "I am not sure I have met the Devil. Or care to."

Scacchi gazed at him, seeming disappointed. "That is the child inside you talking. You should be wary of him. This Venetian Lucifer will come, in his or her own time. Now..." He looked at his wristwatch. "We must be going. Musicians hate a latecomer."

After leaving the *scuola*, they caught the *vaporetto*, disembarking at San Zaccaria accompanied by hordes of tourists headed for the

Doge's Palace and the famous piazza. On the way Scacchi announced that he had enrolled Daniel into the summer music school at the church as a speculative gift, a small pleasure to relieve the tedium of sifting the papers in the cellar. If the course was not to Daniel's taste, he could leave at any time, though the old man hoped he would persevere. The event had some fame. It took place every two years under the sponsorship of Massiters, the international art agency whose eponymous English founder, an occasional Venetian resident, appeared at irregular intervals to applaud and inspect the beneficiaries of his generosity.

The programme attracted young musicians from around the world, partly through reputation and partly because of its location in the church of La Pietà, "Vivaldi's church," as the sign outside had it, though Scacchi quickly denounced this as a fraud. The original was rebuilt shortly after the composer's death, he explained. The white classical façade photographed by thousands of tourists each week had been tacked on at the beginning of the twentieth century. The Red Priest would recognise precious little of the modern church, Scacchi said, and certainly not the lush oval interior which had replaced the customary bare, dark medieval space still seen elsewhere in the city.

The large double doors were open, giving the tourists a direct view into the nave. A middle-aged woman in a flowery dress was perched behind a desk at the foot of the steps, checking the credentials of those arriving for the event. She smiled brightly at Scacchi and greeted him with affection. Too rapidly for Daniel, and in a smattering of Italian and dialect, Scacchi spoke to her and pushed a piece of paper into her hand. Her eyebrows rose. She shrugged. Then she scribbled Daniel's name on a plastic name badge and passed it over the table. Scacchi took it up gratefully and with profuse thanks.

"We locals get a discount on the boats and buses," the old man explained with a victorious grin. "So why not for a little music course too? These foreigners..." He waved his hand at the crowd of young people milling inside the church. "They have money to burn."

"Speaking of money, Signor Scacchi," said the woman behind the table, "would you like me to present the *fattura* to your house at a later date?"

"As you see fit," he replied. "A gentleman does not carry cash, naturally."

"Naturally..." She scribbled something on a torn piece of paper and thrust it into a supermarket carrier bag half-full of such notes. Daniel somehow doubted Scacchi would ever hear of it again.

"Wear your badge always," the woman warned. Daniel pinned it to his shirt and, at Scacchi's beckoning, followed him into La Pietà, pausing by the iron gate that led to the oval hall, listening to the murmur of young excited voices in a dozen different English accents.

Scacchi watched him. "It doesn't matter, does it?" he asked eventually.

"No," Daniel replied. "I don't care if Vivaldi wouldn't recognise a thing. I can still feel his presence."

"Or of those who came after and believed in him so much they placed his presence here, straight out of the ether. Either way," Scacchi mused, "it's all the same. Reincarnation has always seemed to me the silliest of ideas. Yet I do think there is something in the notion that a fragment of a person survives, like dust on a carpet. We breathe it in, consuming each other and the dead of past centuries while perhaps picking up a little of their stain upon our characters."

A cello was being tuned. Two fiddles joined in.

"I'm not good enough," Daniel said immediately. "These people are in a different league."

"Nonsense!" Scacchi said reproachfully. "You told me in your letters you played regularly and had taken examinations."

"And that is true, Scacchi. But exams and talent are not necessarily the same thing."

"Oh, come. It's just a little fun. Some playing. Some theory. Some composition. You can compose a bit, I trust?"

"A bit."

"Then you'll be fine. See the strutting cockerel over there?"

The old man pointed out a short figure in black shirt and trousers, with a head of abundant dark hair and a small imperial, like a misplaced moustache, beneath his lower lip.

"Guido Fabozzi," Daniel said. "I have seen him on television."

"Been the boss for the last four of these things. Since the incident…"

Daniel saw the look on the old man's face. Scacchi had let something slip. "The incident?"

"There was a…problem. But that was ten years ago now. Nothing you need worry about. Fabozzi is a good man, for all his pomposity. I'll have a word with him. Make sure he goes easy on you."

"No! I stand or fall by my own efforts. Please."

Scacchi seemed to like that. He touched Daniel lightly on the shoulder. Then he cast his eyes around the church again, found a figure in pale colours on the far side of the nave, and pointed him out.

"And there you have the great man himself. Hugo Massiter. Lord of all he surveys. We work in the same trade, though I doubt he'd acknowledge as much. No time like the present!"

They crossed the floor of the church, nodding politely at the sea of young faces there, until they stood beneath a large and impressive ceiling painting, which Scacchi announced as Tiepolo's *Triumph of Faith*. Hugo Massiter was a man of around fifty, Daniel judged, dressed in a curiously anachronistic fashion: light shirt and trousers, blue neck scarf, and a pair of expensive plastic-framed sunglasses pushed back onto his glossy forehead. He was engaged in a one-sided conversation with a slim girl in a white shirt and jeans who listened intently to his animated speech. Scacchi held back for a moment, allowed Massiter to recognise their presence, then walked forward and embraced the man.

"Signor Massiter," he said, smiling broadly. "You grace our city with your presence and your generosity once more, sir. How can we express our gratitude?"

"Oh, Scacchi," Massiter replied, "there are ways and ways. Something to sell, perhaps? I have a particular object in mind. We must speak of it."

Scacchi shook his head. "I regret I have nothing of the calibre you rightly expect. I merely deal in baubles these days. But who knows?"

Massiter introduced the girl he was speaking to as Amy Hartston, aged eighteen, from Portland, Maine. Scacchi bowed. Daniel took her soft hand and, awkwardly, shook it. She had long blonde hair tied back in a ponytail, a constant smile, and the blank, vague prettiness Daniel had, against his own wishes, come to associate with a certain breed of American student.

"I don't recall you from two years ago," she said to Daniel in an odd accent, American, but with a genteel flatness not unlike old-fashioned upper-class English.

"I wasn't here. I've never visited Venice before."

"Wow." She seemed amazed. "You live in England and you've never been here?"

"Not everyone has the advantage of a rich and generous father, my dear," Massiter declared.

"He's glad to get rid of me for the summer vacation," she grumbled. "This is just camp under another name."

Massiter beamed. He seemed, Daniel thought, much too disengaged, much too pleasant, to be the owner of a large and successful company working in the aggressively competitive world of art sales. "Ah, the young," he said. "Never explain. Never apologise. Never feel grateful."

"About sums it up!" Amy Hartston agreed cheerfully.

"Hmmm," Massiter grunted, then said, "May I?" Without waiting for an answer, he picked up her violin case, gently opened it, and removed the instrument inside. Daniel Forster blinked at what Massiter held up for all to see in the poor light of La Pietà. It was an ancient fiddle, unmistakably Italian, probably of the early eighteenth century.

"This," Massiter announced, "is what I seek, Scacchi. Well, almost, anyway. You recognise it? No peeking at the label, now."

The old man took the fiddle and held it in his hands, inspecting the instrument minutely from top to tailpiece. The violin had a shallow belly and a narrow waist. In the yellowish artificial light it seemed a light chestnut colour, with some marks, a few old, a few more recent, perhaps the result of a clumsy owner.

"I hate these parlour games," the old man complained. "One should not rush into a judgement."

Massiter was unmoved. "Oh, come on, Scacchi. It's easy enough for a man like you."

"Hmmm," Scacchi murmured. "I would prefer a look in good light, and with a glass, but without that I shall hazard a guess. Cremona, undoubtedly. There is no sign of Saint Theresa, so it cannot be Andrea Guarneri, though it has his feel to it. But that narrow waist. It must be the son, Giuseppe, I think. Early eighteenth century ... perhaps 1720 or so."

Amy's eyes opened wide. "Unbelievable. How do you do that? To me it just feels like a great fiddle."

"And it is," Massiter said. "Though not of the highest order. I seek something rather better. From another Guarneri."

Scacchi surveyed him, his face full of scepticism. "You mean Giuseppe del Gesù, I imagine? But, Massiter, you know there are so few of those in the world. If one were to come onto the market, everyone would know about it."

Massiter snorted. "The open market, yes. But we play the game, Scacchi. We know there are rules and rules. Sell like that, and there are taxes to pay. And a commission to a dealer like me. The instrument I have heard of is one of his beauties, big and bold, worth a fortune, and with a canny seller who's reluctant to show his or her face. Funny, that, eh? You, I imagine, have heard the same rumour. Now, don't deny it."

Scacchi demurred. It seemed to Daniel that the old man was incapable of deception in the face of Massiter's iron-grey stare.

"You hear such nonsense on the streets, Massiter. We both know you cannot believe a word."

Massiter's right arm stole around Scacchi's shoulders, then squeezed, quite hard, the flesh close to his neck. "Of course. But you will alert me should a little bird sing, won't you? My money's as good as any man's."

Scacchi took one short step backwards to detach himself from Massiter's grip. "Daniel here is my guest and part of your school for the duration. If you have anything to say to me, or I to you, perhaps we should communicate through him. I am too feeble these days to be disturbed by the telephone."

Massiter stared at Daniel, as did Amy Hartston. Daniel had the feeling he was being judged.

"Very well," replied Massiter with a sudden, efficient smile, before turning his attention completely to the girl. "And as for you, my dear, I should be grateful if you would join me for dinner at the Locanda Cipriani tomorrow. They have sea urchins and bass ravioli and the finest mantis shrimp you'll ever taste. Afterwards I'll show you some very fine devils."

"Cool!" the girl answered, eyes glittering.

Massiter clapped his hands lightly. "My launch leaves at seven. And you..." He peered at Daniel. "The name again?"

"Daniel Forster, sir."

"Would you care to come along, Daniel Forster?"

He looked at Scacchi. The old man shooed him on. "Good Lord, Daniel. The only way the likes of us will eat at that place on Torcello is if someone else is paying the bill!"

"But the work, Scacchi?"

"There is always time for work. You are here to enjoy yourself too."

"Then it's agreed!" Massiter announced with some finality. "Both of you, bring your fiddles and some notes you intend to submit for the composition section. This circus costs me plenty, so I may ask you to play for your supper. Now...!" He clapped his large hands again, loudly so that all in the airy, oval church might hear. "On with the show, children! *Avanti! Avanti!* Play as if it were your last day upon this earth!"

14

The taste of mud

What an unattractive trait jealousy is! I report to you,
honestly, about the people I meet, and the next thing
I know, your letters are spitting viper's venom from the page.
Did I react like a madman when you told me about that
handsome, flashing-eyed Spaniard you met by the banks of
the Guadalquivir? Let us have a little perspective here, sister.
We are currently spectators in our respective worlds, children
who have by accident flitted into some fancy costume ball
where we scarcely belong. Would you have me tell you pious
fairy tales that are as dull as ditchwater?

Still, if you wish a break from the "lovely Rebecca," as you
describe her (no, I won't argue with that), you shall have it,
though it disrupts the thread of this narrative for no good
reason other than your own vanity.

The day after our visit to La Pietà (which I shall chronicle
for you next), I attended with Uncle Leo when he joined
Mr. Delapole at Venezia Triofante. This is one of those
fashionable coffee shops where the city seems to spend
inordinate parts of the day stirring small cups of a muddy
brown fluid that looks as if it has just been dredged from the

bed of the lagoon. I imagine there is no coffee in Seville. It is a creation of the East brought here by the Arabs apparently, who are forbidden by the Koran to consume it themselves and so sell it on to us in order to rot good Christian brains and teeth. Almost every doorway in St. Mark's piazza now leads to a *botteghe de caffè*. They may soon convert the basilica into one, too, I imagine. You have no idea what geography has spared you.

The Triofante is the most acclaimed coffee shop of them all, though quite why is beyond me, since they all look the same: what I take to be the appearance of an anteroom in some obscure French royal palace, all mirrors and ormolu and chairs that don't quite fit your bottom. Perhaps the attraction is the self-opinionated owner, one Floriano Francesconi, who lords it over the room, ejecting, on a mere whim, anyone he dislikes. Talk about the personal touch. I don't know why the silly man doesn't just name the place after himself and have done with it.

Mr. Delapole had more than us in tow, sniffing at his wallet. We were joined by an odd young French chap called Rousseau, who claims to be on a brief visit to the city but, according to the worried Gobbo, would not be averse to a job on the Englishman's payroll either. Gobbo clearly sees Rousseau as a threat, which is somewhat risible, since they could scarcely be more different. Monsieur Rousseau is a pleasant enough cove, I think, but seems incapable of small talk. Every twist and turn in the conversation must always lead to some obscure allusion, effusive allegory, or mildly outrageous statement, all designed to demonstrate to the world that here is one very clever fellow indeed. I try to like him, because he is a bright chap, but I have to confess it's very hard work.

Mr. Delapole listened to a stream of his French babble for

a while, then waved his hand for silence, fixed our uncle with a penetrating gaze, and announced, "I find myself drawn to a musical career. I was thinking of writing an opera, Scacchi. Would you care to publish it?"

"Sir!" Leo almost jumped out of his seat with glee. "An opera! I had no idea your talents ran so wide."

"A man's talents run to many things more than he knows," Rousseau interjected. "Why, I was only trying my hand at the English pentameter the other day, and I think I could give that Shakespeare fellow a run for his money. . . ."

"Oh, do be quiet," Mr. Delapole said in a cheery tone that could not possibly give offence. "We all know about *your* talents. It's mine I'd like to discuss. An opera, Scacchi. How much for a couple of hundred quire, or whatever you call them?"

"Sir!" cried Uncle again, but this time trying his best to look mortally offended. "Money is the least consideration here. The House of Scacchi merely seeks to defray its expenses and make sufficient profit to pay the Republic's all-too-frequent levies. What matters most to us is the quality of the work which bears our imprint and how it may add to the greater sum of human knowledge. Our title cannot be simply bought; it must be earned."

I thought of the hours I had spent that morning setting a few pages of *The Manifold Mysteries of the Rhinoceros of Madagascar* and reached for my little cup of bitter mud. I was wrong. Coffee does have its place.

"The trouble is," Delapole mused, "opera is so . . . *common*. Perhaps something smaller. A concerto for solo violin, for example, I reckon I'm up to it."

Leo placed his cup slowly on the table. "A favourite of my own, sir, since you know I once wrote the odd page too."

"And presumably," Delapole added, with a canny eye, "there is the economic argument. Fewer parts, less paper. Makes sense."

Leo stared downcast at his little demitasse. "In a world more sane than publishing, perhaps. Paper is but a small part of our costs. The setting, the proofing, the years of skill required to spot that single errant crochet on the stave..."

"Hmmm." Delapole seemed undecided. "Perhaps I'll write a book instead, then. But that would be in English, and you, for all your skills, could not be expected to master such a tortured and difficult tongue. No, I'd have to send to London for that."

An awkward silence fell upon the table, penetrated, of course, in very few seconds by a piping French voice. "It is not merely the notes that matter, my friends," Rousseau declared. "Vivaldi is a fine musician, but I think his popularity has other sources too. It is the theatre of the thing, monsieur. The thought of all those delightful ladies, hidden from view behind screens where they produce sounds of such ethereal, sensual wonder. La Pietà is a bordello for the ears! That's it! I shall note down those words in my little book the moment I get home!"

We all looked at the man. I do not profess to be much familiar with matters of romance, but unlike Rousseau, I think I am able to enter into a conversation about, or even with, the sweeter sex and not suffer some minor form of apoplexy (yes, I know, dear sister, R... is an exception, but I vowed not to introduce her into this portion of my narrative). The very mention of the word "bordello" appeared to place our French friend in a state of extraordinary agitation, puffing and panting, cheeks red and a rash of sweat clinging to his flabby upper lip.

Delapole leaned over and whispered just loud enough for us all to hear, "Perhaps they are naked behind those shutters, Rousseau. Have you considered that?"

The Frenchman shuddered and gave out with a whinny that would have done justice to a six-week-old foal.

"But, sir," Gobbo interjected, "if you think about it, women are standing there stark bare all the time, aren't they? It's just the clothes that get in the way."

One may as well join in this nonsense. "By which token," I suggested, "the players behind the screen in La Pietà must be, to all intent and purpose, naked. Since we cannot see them at all, their garments, if there *be* garments, are as irrelevant as the shutters behind which they . . . perform. A naked woman now in bed in Peking is no less naked because we cannot see her."

"And by that token"—Delapole grinned, catching the ball I had so loosely thrown him—"the world is positively brimming with unclad beauties. Look how many are in this room! If only we possessed the wit to remove those *opercula* from our minds that prevent our worshipping them in all their fleshy glory!"

Rousseau's eyes fairly popped out of his skull. His head revolved on its stalk trying to take in each lady in the café (most of whom were old, an inch deep in powder, and bedecked in more clothing than you'd find in a bishop's wardrobe after a rich man's funeral).

"I think, I think," he gasped, "that I shall retire now. I have but a short time in Venice and there are many sights to see."

We watched him go, smirking cruelly to ourselves. It was an unfair trick, but Rousseau is like an old dog who hangs around the back door, begging to be kicked. One day even the kindest of folk will take a boot to him just because he asks for it so importunately.

"Concerto it is, then," Uncle Leo announced, a tremor of hope in his voice.

"It's finding the time, dear chap," Mr. Delapole replied lazily. "So little to spare. So much to do."

Shortly afterwards we walked to the *molo* and caught a gondola back to Mr. Delapole's rented house, Ca' Dario, as fine a Venetian mansion as you might enter (and most definitely deserving of the term *palazzo,* though mysteriously it, too, remains mere Ca'). I sat in the back with Gobbo. The brief experience of Rousseau-baiting had, I regret to say, whetted his appetite.

"You know folk at that church, the one with the music?" Gobbo asked, prodding me with a conspiratorial elbow.

"We print material for Vivaldi from time to time."

"Good," he said, and leered in the most obscene of ways. "I reckon our French friend deserves a little entertainment before he quits this city for good. You, Mr. Scacchi, shall be my impresario."

The gondola turned into the great bend of the Canal. Ca' Dario bobbed towards us on the left, a small mansion, and one with a little tilt to it (no shame in that when you've spent 250 years with your toes in the Venetian mud).

The afternoon heat was fading. It was a splendid view. I thought of Reb— Ah, but I made a promise.

15

Dust and parchment

LAURA INSISTED ON JOINING DANIEL FOR THE FIRST sortie into the bowels of the derelict warehouse next door. He was initially grateful for her company, if a little disconcerted by her mode of dress. During the day she wore a white nylon housecoat buttoned down the front, the kind favoured by shop assistants. It seemed to him a uniform, a statement that said: *however much you make me part of this family, I remain a servant.* She served breakfast in it. She wore it to hand out the evening glasses of spritz, which always arrived after the last chime of six from the bell of San Cassian over the *rio.* It was an object behind which she could hide, just like the sunglasses which were almost permanently fixed to her face the moment she left the house.

Their rooms were both on the third floor. Laura seemed to occupy most of the rear; he was in the small bedroom that sat next to the warehouse, the third window on the right as seen from the front. Each morning they met on the landing and exchanged pleasantries. Each time, too, he was unable to quell some odd discomfort at her presence, not least because of the uniform. It was the middle of summer and at times unbearably hot. Laura's solution to this problem was to go naked beneath her housecoat except for underwear, then bustle about her business with a constant physical activity. A simple act—passing a glass, picking up a plate—was apt to reveal a small segment of tanned skin and a glimmer of bright white fabric.

In the cellar the pristine housecoat was filthy within minutes, which did little for her temper.

"I appreciate your help," he told her. "But I really don't want to put you to the trouble."

"You mean you don't want me here?"

"No," he replied with some firmness. "I meant that I am being paid to sift through all this filthy junk, and you're not. I'm grateful, but it really isn't necessary."

She threw a pile of ruined eighteenth-century news sheets to the floor. Almost everything of any promise appeared to be damaged by floodwater. Daniel's hopes of sifting gold for Scacchi from the cellar had begun to fade after only fifteen minutes' investigation. They had found two more electric lanterns; the four lamps now cast a reasonable amount of illumination but revealed little except dust and ruined parchment. Aladdin's cave seemed bare of anything that had not been rendered useless by the passing of time and the insistent, seeping waters of the lagoon.

Laura walked over, stared him crossly in the eye, and folded her arms. "What is your problem, Daniel Forster?" she demanded, turning to shaky English, as if this would hammer home her point. "Are you uncomfortable being around me?"

"No! It's just that I am used to working on my own."

"Pah! What kind of skill is that? Are you to be a solitary man, then, Daniel?"

The arrow struck home. He was aware that there was a shyness in him, with good reason. He was only now emerging from "the sick years," the time spent flitting between college and the small bedsit they had rented when his mother's illness and their poverty coincided. There was a hiatus in his life which set him apart, though he was not yet ready to explain as much to Laura.

"It is," he said a little testily, "a question of method."

"Method! Method! What retentively anal English bullshit is this?"

"Logic, Laura. And that's *anally* retentive, by the way." She had, now he came to think of it, annoyed him. "Look," he complained. "You walked in here and threw yourself all over the place. Picking up a sheet in that corner, cursing it, then wandering right across the room to do the selfsame there."

Her eyes flared. "And why not? Look at this mess!" The cellar was huge and littered with piles of ancient documents, machinery under wraps, and empty wooden boxes. It was hard to walk in a straight line for more than a few feet. "Watch me," she announced. "I'll find Scacchi's treasure."

Then, her white housecoat getting filthier by the second, she raced around, snatching pages from each pile as she passed, leaping on heaps of documents as if they were stepping-stones, bumping into the misshapen corpses of mysterious machines, screeching nonsense as she went. Daniel watched her, feeling helpless. He had thought only of the hurt inside himself, never suspecting that some mysterious agony lived in Laura too. Finally, she bounced too hard into the large shape of the old press, yelped with pain, and fell to the floor, surrounded by her collection of pages.

He walked over, held out a hand, and persuaded her to sit on the nearest pile of ruined documents. She was covered in dust and crying. The tears made long, straight streaks through the dirt as they travelled down her cheeks. He sat next to her, placed a hand on her shoulder, and, ridiculous as he knew it to be, felt guilty that he had in some way provoked this outburst.

"It's useless," she said, forcing back the sobs. They both stared at the papers she had collected, all grey, mouldy pages and smeared ink. "There's nothing here. We waste our time, Daniel."

He offered her a clean handkerchief, which she snatched, wiped across her face, then rolled into a tight wad inside her fist.

"I'm sorry. Is it so important to him? To find something to sell?"

"So it seems."

"But why?"

Daniel peered into her face. The anger was, he realised, directed at herself, not his sudden uncalled-for coldness. Laura was just as desperate as he to find Scacchi's treasure.

"I don't know. I am sorry. I should not take out my disappointment on you." She looked at him with frank, intelligent eyes.

"Don't apologise. It's frustrating for both of us."

She shook her head. "Of course I must apologise. You must not let people treat you so."

"You may treat me how you like. I am grateful to be here, Laura. It is . . . the most exciting thing that has ever happened to me."

Her expression changed, from contrition to puzzlement. "Oh, Daniel. Is there so little for you at home that you find our small lives so interesting?"

"No." He hesitated. "I mean, yes."

"Your mother?" she asked. "You loved her very much."

"Of course. And when she was ill, she would talk about Venice, of how happy she was when she was at college here. I believed . . ."

He felt surprised that this sudden, candid conversation was revealing something to him too. "I think that was why I chose Italian history as my field of study. Why I wanted so much to be here."

Laura placed a finger on her lips, thinking. "And you studied so hard to please her, I imagine. To make her feel she would leave something worthwhile in the world."

The accuracy of her insight took him aback. There were times, many times, when he wished to escape the dismal flat and the reek of illness. Yet he was incapable of abandoning her; that had occurred once in her life already, with the father he had never known, and the cruelty of the act never left them.

"I love my work. It is like . . ."

"Like another world, into which you may retreat." She smiled. He was speechless. Laura placed her fingers softly on his cheek, the sort of gesture an elder sister might make to an errant sibling. "Poor Daniel. Trapped in daydreams, like all of us around here."

He stared at the mess of rubbish on the cellar floor. "Is Scacchi in a daydream?"

"He is desperate," she replied mournfully.

"But why?" Daniel wondered.

"Don't ask me. I am just the servant around here."

The irked, slightly peevish tone of her voice suddenly made her seem much younger. "I think you're a lot more than that, Laura, and you know it."

She swore, one of the odd, coarse Venetian curses he was coming to recognise. Then she wiped her face with the handkerchief again, gave it back to him, becoming the adult Laura once more. "The truth of it is, he's old. They're both very sick. Perhaps there is nothing more to it than that."

"But surely he can get some help with the medicine if he has no money?"

"It's not medicine. I don't know what it is. He seems determined to make some final bargain, as if something were unfinished. *I don't know!*"

Daniel surveyed the cellar. The dusty room seemed to be laughing at them.

"I've had enough of this," Laura announced. "There's dinner to cook. Don't waste your time. Give me those clothes. I'll wash them."

"No. I won't give up. I owe it to him. Besides, I believe he's right. There is something here. I can feel it."

His sudden persistence amused her. "Daniel! Where's your English logic now?"

For once he was the one with the scolding look. "I thought you disapproved of that?"

"*Touché*. But that does not alter the fact that this place is full of junk."

"Of course it is." Now that he considered the matter, it was obvious. "Scacchi told us so himself. He said all this was taken down here when the upper floors were used for warehousing. It was dumped on the floor because it was largely worthless even before it was damaged. They would surely know the tide would flood in here."

Laura threw up her arms in exasperation. "There! You have it. Now may we go?"

"Not at all," he replied. "If there is something of value, it would predate that time and, furthermore, be in a place where it was obvious the water could not reach."

"Pah! Mysteries! Mysteries!"

He came to her, clasped her hands in his. "Think, Laura! You are the Venetian. If you wanted to keep something safe in this place, above the water level, where would you choose?"

Laura stared into his eyes, not trying to release herself from his grip. She was, he believed, thinking rapidly and logically about the point he was struggling to make.

"Well?" he demanded impatiently.

"These are bare brick walls!" she replied with a sudden smile. "How could one hide something of value in a room like this?"

There was an idea running around her head. He knew as much from the bright, amused glint in her eyes.

"Perhaps..."

"Perhaps nothing! Supper time approaches. I have food to cook. You must remove those filthy clothes for me to wash. Come!" An insistent hand pushed him towards the stairs. "Come!"

"Laura..." Her sudden haste disturbed him. "*What about the treasure?*"

"Fairy stories," she barked. "Smoke and mirrors. Leave it to the servants, Daniel, and another day."

16

Scacchi's gold

THERE COULD BE NO MISTAKE ABOUT IT. DANIEL HAD seen Laura take Scacchi quietly aside after breakfast, pass him a sheet of paper, then nod discreetly in his own direction. Shortly afterwards, the old man threw a feeble arm around him and read out a list of minor errands: some paperwork from the city council, some stamps from the post office, a repaired piece of cheap glass to be picked up from a workshop on Giudecca. Laura had engineered him out of the house quite brazenly. He would spend the entire morning hopping from *vaporetto* to *vaporetto* while she pursued some secret plan in the cellar.

"But, Scacchi," he objected. "I am here to work. On your library."

"Plenty of time for that. You will miss lunch, I'm afraid, so pick up a little snack somewhere. Not too much, mind. Don't forget you have a dinner date tonight, either. Massiter is not a man to be ignored."

With that he was shooed out of the house with Laura's list of tasks, each set down in neat, intelligent handwriting, in his pocket. He returned, laden down with shopping bags, just after two and had hardly set them down in the hall when she was upon him. Her hair was matted with dust and cobwebs, her white uniform now almost completely soiled. She wore the widest smile he believed he had ever seen on a human being.

"You look like the Cheshire Cat," he noted a touch sourly.

"Stop speaking riddles, Daniel," she replied, bemused. "I have been hunting. Do you not want to see what I have found?"

"I am cross with you, Laura. You schemed to have me out of the house just so you could have all this to yourself."

She batted him with her right hand, sending a cloud of murk across his clean shirt. "Oh, poppycock! You said yourself I got in your way. I have merely prepared the ground on which your brilliance may shine. Come! The ancients are listening to music upstairs. Let's not disturb them until we must."

She passed him a lantern and he followed her down the stairs into the cellar, which seemed at first glance to be in the selfsame dismal jumble he had seen the day before.

"So?" she asked with a grin. "Let us test your suitability to be a Venetian. Where would your chosen hiding place be?"

Daniel glowered at the infuriating room. There was not a single storage place set above ground level. If the cellar had been used for keeping items safe from the depredations of the lagoon, the necessary cupboards had long been removed.

"It's impossible," he murmured.

"What do you mean, 'impossible'? You must begin to understand us. If a Venetian had something of value in here, he wouldn't leave it in plain view. There's a water gate there, Daniel. Any villain could steal in and take it."

"Then where?"

She took the lantern from him and swept the room once more. "In the walls. *In the walls!* Come."

He followed her to the rear of the room. "Here," she said. "The front has no partition. The sides are solid too. But at the rear we go into that mess of houses behind, and anything might be possible."

She placed a hand on the brickwork and worked her way along the damp surface. "Four hours I have done this, Daniel. Feeling for something."

"And you found it?"

He saw the joy in her face and knew the answer. She walked to the last third of the wall, a good four feet above the floor, took his hand, and placed it on the masonry. Here the nature of the mortar between the ancient bricks changed, becoming paler and floury in texture. She dug at it with her finger. The material came away like dry sand. Without a word, Daniel went back into the centre of the room and picked up an old crowbar he had brought with him to open any stubborn crates.

"I saved this moment for you," she said triumphantly.

Not caring about the grime and cobwebs, Daniel kissed her quickly on the cheek. "You are a magnificent woman, Laura. I hope Ca' Scacchi can stand this."

"*Avanti*, Daniel!"

She stood back and he set to the wall, carving away the mortar. After twenty minutes of hard work, when the hole was judged to be sufficiently large, they held the lantern close to the entrance and peered inside. The artificial light revealed a package wrapped in ancient brown paper, tied with string, and set quite deliberately on a stand of bricks to keep it above the water level.

He reached in and grasped the object, untied the string, removed the brown paper, and turned the light on the first page. It was written in a spidery, backward-leaning hand and said simply, *Concerto Anonimo* and, in Roman numerals, the year: *1733*. Daniel flicked through the pages rapidly, setting up a cloud of dust.

"What is it?" Laura whispered.

"Patience," he replied, and sat down on a dusty pile of papers to examine their discovery, his mind racing. Even from a cursory glance he realised there could be only one explanation, extraordinary as it was. "I think we have found the composer's score for a violin concerto. The original manuscript, before it went to the copyists."

Laura shook her head. "But it is anonymous. Why hide it?"

"I don't know." Daniel scanned the music, written in the long-dead composer's curious hand with an extended, sloping slant that seemed to suggest the notes had been dashed out in the heat of creation. At first glance the piece had perhaps a touch of Vivaldi to it. He had once sought out copies of the composer's originals in the college library. The hand looked nothing like this.

"Come!" Laura ordered. "We must tell him!"

They rushed upstairs with their discovery and found Scacchi and Paul in the front room, dancing in each other's arms to some light jazz on the stereo.

"Spritz?" Scacchi asked hopefully. His skin seemed more sallow than it had earlier in the day.

"Later," Laura announced. "Daniel has found something."

"*We* have found something," he objected.

She waved at him like a mother ticking off a silly child. "No matter. Tell us, Scacchi. Is this what you want?"

The old man's dark eyes came abruptly to life. The two men ceased dancing and came over to the table to examine the sheaf of pages Daniel had spread out there.

"I can't read a note of music," Scacchi said. "Is this valuable?"

Laura prodded the old yellowed page gently with her forefinger. "Of course it's valuable! Why else would it be hidden?"

"That is female logic," he complained. "It is anonymous. It says so. Do you recognise it, Daniel?"

"No. But it appears to be a full score for a concerto for solo violin. See! The date says 1733."

"Vivaldi?" Paul wondered hopefully.

Daniel shook his head. "I don't think so. It's similar, but why would Vivaldi write anonymously? And this is not his hand. I know it."

"Still," Scacchi said hopefully, "something from that time, something fresh, would have value, surely?"

Daniel had to agree, though he could not hope to guess at a price. "It must. This seems well-done from a first glance."

"Good!" Scacchi declared. "And you have the perfect way to start a small whisper about its discovery. Tonight, with Massiter, who may well be an ideal buyer."

Laura looked at him severely. "You cannot ask Daniel to take something as valuable as this and wave it under the Englishman's nose. Massiter will snatch it from him straightaway and throw the poor boy over the side of his boat as fish food."

Scacchi scowled at her. "Don't be so melodramatic, Laura. Of course he shouldn't take the original. You can copy out a few pages of the solo in your own hand, Daniel, surely? Massiter asked for some composition. Tell him this is it."

Daniel demurred. "This isn't my work, Scacchi."

"Just a ruse, lad, to whet the appetite. Massiter's probably smart enough to see through it anyway."

"Pen!" Laura shouted. "Paper!"

Paul brought them to him. Daniel stared at the white sheet and the ancient pen.

"Oh, come," Scacchi said, urging him on. "It is such a small thing. I am not Mephisto, Daniel. Nor are you Faust."

Daniel reached for a ruler and, in thick black ink, began to draw the five lines of the stave.

The Red Priest

Santa Maria della Visitazione—or La Pietà, as everyone seems
to call it—is a crumbling piece of stone a little way along
from the Doge's Palace. They say the place is so feebly built
that one day it will be pulled down entirely and replaced
with something more fitting. The Venetians must have
magnificence, you see, particularly in such a prominent
location.

We stood on the doorstep in silence. Until now this was a
prank. Had the city militia caught us, what reprimand might
there have been for a Jewess who forgot to wear her red scarf
and her foolish companion? A few harsh words for Rebecca
and a clip round the ear for me. But to walk over the
threshold of La Pietà was very different. The Hebrew would
be entering Christ's Church, and not for penitence or some
instant conversion, either. Would God strike us down on the
very steps? Would we be damned for eternity for some gross
insult against the Lord's house?

I cannot answer for the latter, but on the first I have to
disappoint you. When we finally summoned the courage
to march through the gloomy rectangle of La Pietà's front

porch, we were greeted by nothing more than the sound of stringed instruments scratching their way through a piece of middling difficulty. No claps of thunder. No roars from on high. We entered the nave of the church, and there sat a small chamber orchestra, mostly girls in dark cheap dresses, with Vivaldi waving his stick over them.

I must admit I expected rather more of the famed Red Priest. For one thing, the red hair is long gone—the poor fellow wears a dusty white wig to cover his bald head. True, there is a vivid scarlet frock coat, but his face is bloodless and pasty and his eyes forever squint crossly at the page. I peered at that high pale forehead, thinking about the miracle of creation (individual, not divine). Somehow all this wondrous music had escaped such a humble frame and ventured out to capture the world. For a while, anyway. They say Vivaldi has had scant success since he wrote *The Four Seasons* eight years ago and must now travel as a journeyman conductor to Vienna and beyond to pay his bills.

We stood in the shadows for a while until he rattled his little stick on the stand and waved silence over the small band of players.

"You," he then yelled in our direction. "You're late."

Rebecca walked out into the light, her small violin case at her side, and I was amused to see an expression of admiration steal its way over Vivaldi's face. Rebecca has this effect upon people. I slid into a pew, the better to observe proceedings.

"Where are you from, girl? What use are you to me?"

She bowed her head modestly. "Geneva originally, sir. I cannot answer for the other. You must be the judge."

"Hmmm. I know men in Geneva. Your teacher?"

"Only my late father, who was a carpenter by trade."

His face sagged quite noticeably. "Very well, then," he grunted in a most miserable fashion. "Play something. Let's get it over with."

Rebecca opened her case and took out a rough-looking instrument stained a rather disgusting shade of reddy-brown.

"Did he make that, too, girl?" Vivaldi demanded. "Must be the ugliest-looking instrument I've ever seen."

She gazed at him with a firmness of purpose I found quite admirable. "He did, sir, and would have bought me something better if we could have afforded it."

"Ye gods," the old misery sighed, and placed a skinny, withered hand over his chin.

I could not take my eyes off Rebecca, for a variety of reasons. Something in this exchange amused her greatly. I felt already that she would best this grumpy old priest.

"A study we used to play, sir," she announced sweetly, then raised her rough-hewn bow and brought it down on that ugly lump of wood like an angel felling demons with a sword. Well! You may guess what occurred next: a miracle. She wrung from that battered old thing such tones of sweetness, such surging passages of passion that I thought at one point our great composer might faint upon the floor in a swoon!

True, some of this was show (and what is wrong with that in the circumstances?). She dashed through scales, note perfect and at a flashing speed. She double-stopped, then treble-stopped, up and down the neck. A slip of a folk tune fell in here, some baroque finery there. Slow passages, fast passages, light and dark, loud and quiet, they dazzled us with their technical skill and yet carried a great sense of feeling too. I am no fiddler—having listened to Rebecca, I now doubt I am a musician at all—but I know genius when I hear it. Vivaldi was right about the instrument, which was not worthy of her. But none could doubt Rebecca's brilliance, and it warmed my heart to see it wrung some emotion and generosity out of the old man, too, for when she finished this astonishing exhibition, the priest rose to his feet, broke into a broad, ingenuous grin, clapped his hands like a five-year-old, and yelled, "Hurrah!"

Rebecca, with that knowing smile still upon her closed lips, quietly placed the instrument back in its case, then looked at him and said, all innocence, "I hope I may be of use to you, sir. In some capacity."

"Good God, girl!" he exclaimed. "You're just the wonder I need."

"Thank you." She said this, I am happy to report, with a touch of firmly demure honesty, which Vivaldi took, I hope, as a small reprimand for his doubt in her.

"But what was it? I recognised Corelli. And some common studies. The rest?"

"I don't know, sir. Things my father taught me." She blushed when she spoke. I did not understand why.

The old priest clapped his hands. "No matter. Shame about that damned instrument of yours. Nevertheless, you are welcome to my little band of ladies." At this the rest of the group, an odd-looking assortment, much like a bunch of nuns who had newly abandoned their wimples, smiled at her and clapped their hands by way of greeting. "Your name?"

"Rebecca." My heart raced. A sharp look of panic had risen in her eyes. "Rebecca Guillaume."

"A pretty name for a pretty face," Vivaldi said pleasantly. "A shame that none shall see you."

"Sir?"

Vivaldi pointed to the large gilt shutters that ran along each side of the nave. "This is a church, Rebecca Guillaume.

Not a music hall. Can't have 'em ogling the orchestra when they should be listening to the tunes. You play behind these golden eyelids, and I'm afraid they'll stay tight shut while the audience swoon over your efforts."

At this her head went to one side, as if to lean upon her shoulder, and I found myself perplexed once more. It was quite impossible to judge what she was thinking.

"Now . . ." Vivaldi announced, beaming from ear to ear. "To the new pieces!"

With that he distributed a score among the orchestra, explaining it carefully, instrument by instrument, with the skill and attention one should expect of a master (none of the "Print that right, lad, or I'll boot your backside out of the window straight into the stinking canal" that I get from Leo). Rebecca's presence moved the old man greatly. He threw himself into the music, becoming quite absorbed as they practised it passage by passage, change by change, until the whole began to emerge from what was, at the beginning, mere chaos. They played for almost three hours. The light was failing when we went back outside. I was anxious to return Rebecca to the ghetto before the guards pulled up the drawbridge and kept the world safe from Jews for the night.

We walked onto the jetty and set up a brisk pace to catch the first gondola. I sought some sign of happiness in her face. She had just been praised by the greatest musician in Venice and welcomed into his band of players. None was there.

"Rebecca," I said as the boat swung into the *volta* of the canal and the leaning form of Oliver Delapole's rented home, Ca' Dario, with its odd rose windows, came into view. "You've made your mark this day. You play like an angel and he knows it."

"Yes," she replied in a low, fierce tone. "An angel that stays locked behind shutters where none may see. I've just swapped one prison for another to let someone else take the glory."

Her anger startled me. "I don't understand. It's such an honour. . . ."

"What? To be shut away like some caged bird? Who does this condescending priest think he is?"

"Vivaldi. More than a musician. A composer. A conductor. An artist who towers above men."

Those dark, penetrating eyes bored straight into me. I felt quite naked before their power. "And you think I can't compose? Or conduct? You think I don't want to stand in front of the orchestra like him and watch your mouths open in wonder when they do my bidding?"

The white arch of the Rialto grew larger before us, humanity swarming over it.

"He wonders what music I play, Lorenzo? *Mine.*"

I sat in the rocking boat, above the greasy waters of the Grand Canal, unable to marshal my thoughts. Rebecca was opposite me, on the narrow seat, and leaned forward to grasp my knee and whisper anxiously in my face.

"But there I'm doubly cursed, aren't I? Not just a woman, but a J—"

There was nothing else for it. As gently as I could, I covered her mouth with my hand, shocked by the damp sweetness of her lips. Her eyes seemed, for an instant, frightened. Then I saw understanding there. No one is more free with gossip than a gondolier. If we continued in this vein, someone would be feeding the lion's mouth tonight.

"Our stop is soon, cousin," I said loudly, then, when her

eyes told me she understood, removed my hand from her lovely mouth. "We must count our blessings and get on with the job."

Ten minutes later we ducked into an alley by the ghetto and she put the scarlet scarf over that mass of curls once more.

"And there's more," she hissed before we went back into the fading day. "It's impossible anyway. I hoped to persuade him that I might perform in the afternoon alone, but Vivaldi said I must play the evening concerts or none at all. I can never get out of the ghetto at night. I am a Jew, so it is my jail."

For a moment I thought she might cry, but her composure held and I wondered unkindly whether she was playing with my emotions. Then she added slyly, "Tell me, Lorenzo. Has a Jew no eyes? Hands, organs, dimensions, senses, affections, passions? Don't I eat the same food, hurt with the same weapons, suffer the same diseases? Am I not healed by the same means, warmed and cooled by the same winter and summer, just like a Christian? If you prick me, don't I bleed? If you tickle me, don't I laugh? If you poison me, will I not die?" Then, most seriously, "And if you wrong me, shall I not seek revenge?"

My own expression mirrored her earnestness. "Of course," I replied. "And I am but a humble farm boy from Treviso. Shall I not read an English playwright, too, and steal his wit for my own purposes when it suits me? And if you are ever false with me, Rebecca, then Heaven mocks itself. I'll not believe it."

We stood in that dark, cramped alley, so close our hands almost touched, feeling like two clowns, not knowing whose turn it was to laugh and whose to make the jest.

"You are an odd one, Lorenzo," she whispered, eyeing me with that curious, crooked expression of hers.

"I shall take that as a compliment and make the same remark to you in return."

She snorted and, briefly, she took my hand. Her touch was warm and soft and delicate, and a sensation stole over me which I have never before encountered. "And I made you risk so much. All for nothing."

At that I had to laugh. "Nothing? Rebecca, I . . ." Oh, dear. There I was, briefly tongue-tied again. "I wouldn't have been anywhere else in the world this afternoon. As for what happens in Venice of an evening, let me think a little. It's easier to hide secrets in the dark than in the day."

"But . . . ?"

"No." I was adamant. "One thing at a time."

In silence, we dawdled back to the ghetto. I stopped at the bridge, with an ill-mannered guard who watched her walk across the drawbridge, then noted, "Five minutes later and that little kike would have been in deep shit, boy. Not that I'd mind an hour or two in the cell with her, eh?"

I refuse to follow the city fashion and carry a small dagger in the waistcoat. If one chooses where one walks, there is, I believe, no need of such a weapon. Nor do I much fancy the idea of wearing some hidden jewellery designed for no other purpose than to wound my fellow man. Nevertheless, at that moment I fancied I had just such a blade inside my jacket and, in my imagination, I withdrew it, slowly stuck the swine in the chest, then heaved his bleeding corpse into the canal.

"Yes, sir," I answered lamely as this regrettable daydream played in my head.

Then I walked back through the dark and narrow streets of

the city, over the bridge, back into San Cassian, where the whores stood around the *campo* whispering filthy come-ons to any who chose to hear. When I walk I think. By the time I opened the door to Ca' Scacchi, I knew how it might be done.

The Grand Canal

AFTER SOME FRANTIC SCRIBBLING AND A SWIFT SHOWER, Daniel was downstairs in Ca' Scacchi, ready to catch the *vaporetto* to San Marco, six pages of solo violin tucked inside a clear plastic envelope. Laura joined him, dressed in jeans and a red T-shirt, hair swept back behind her head.

"Night off," she said. "And tomorrow too."

"Ah."

Scacchi and Paul wished him well. Then he and Laura walked to the canal, caught the boat, and sat together in the stern. For once she did not wear the sunglasses. In some odd way he felt this was a victory for him.

"On a date?" he asked hesitantly.

Laura glared at him. "What an impertinent question! I am going to see my mother. As I do every Wednesday, if it's any of your business. She's in an old people's home in Mestre."

"I'm sorry. Is she ill?"

"No. Merely old. I was a late child."

"I was being presumptuous."

"True."

"I thought there must be a man."

Her green eyes opened wide. "A man! Daniel, do you not think that Scacchi and Paul are enough men for one life? Furthermore, I seem to have acquired a third child of late, and one who can be just as infuriating as the others. You think I am short of men?"

"Oops," he said softly, smiling at the water. Her anger, which was clearly feigned, was amusing. Laura loved Scacchi and Paul. She enjoyed his own presence, too, he believed, which disturbed him mildly. He had avoided relationships in the past. There had been other cares: his mother, studying, and the part-time work he was always seeking to pay his way. When he thought about the kind of woman he hoped one day to meet, he always had the same image: of a person around his age who carried a fiddle case from concert to concert and shared his interest in old books and music. Someone from a similar mould, not a delightfully eccentric servant, and one who was older too.

"Oops," she repeated with a wicked gleam in her eye. "And what kind of English word is that?"

A tourist, a burly, bearded man in his late fifties in shorts and a tennis shirt, several cameras laden round his neck, stared at her.

"*Oops!*" Laura bellowed at him gleefully. The fellow got up and walked to the middle of the boat. They both laughed.

"And since we are now allowed to ask personal questions, Daniel Forster, you will kindly tell me about yourself. There is, I assume, some English rose of a girlfriend back home? Come. Tell me."

He was aware that he was blushing, vividly. Laura's face fell.

"I am sorry," she said. "I forgot. You looked after your mother. It was for so much of the time?"

"A lot," he replied. "And I never regretted a moment."

Laura watched the water and said without looking at him,

"And is this when your life begins, then? With the crazy strangers in Ca' Scacchi?"

"Perhaps."

She folded her arms and, determined to steer the conversation elsewhere, murmured, "I suppose this American girl is pretty. The Locanda Cipriani. I have lived here all my life and been there just once."

Daniel thought about Amy Hartston. "She's very pretty," he said. "In an American way."

"I know," she hissed. "Perfect teeth, perfect hair, perfect ass. Always smiling. Always polite." The bad English accent returned. " 'Ave a nice day!' "

"I think that may be stereotypical."

"Huh!"

"And I hope," he added, "she can play the violin better than me." He waved the plastic envelope. "Because this stuff is hard."

She picked up the paper and looked at his neat, upright rendition of the notes on the staves. "Doesn't look too hard."

"Oh, doesn't it? You know about these things?"

"No. But it's just a few sparrow droppings on the page, isn't it? Not like those spiderwebs you see them staring at in the concerts."

He sighed. "It starts like that but soon quickens. In any case, I shall let you in to a secret about music. Sometimes, dear Laura, the slowest parts are the hardest. There is, you see, nowhere to hide in all those quiet spaces."

She regarded him closely, thinking. "There are occasions," she said eventually, "when I don't know what to make of you. What a very mature and perceptive thing for a young man to say. Furthermore... Oh! Oh! See, Daniel! Tell me the name of that house, please."

Laura was pointing at a small palace on the starboard side of the boat. Daniel stared at it. This was not one of the buildings he recognised, yet it was undoubtedly remarkable. The narrow building sat crookedly a little way down from the Guggenheim gallery, a small pink-and-off-white oddity, with three rose windows set off-centre to its right and a skin that appeared tattooed with smaller glasswork. Three rows of arched glass ran from the first to the fourth floor. A set of inverted funnel chimneys topped the flat roof.

"I haven't a clue," he said.

"Hah! So much for education! That is one of the oldest on the Grand Canal. Even after all these years I stop to look at it every time I go past. Ca' Dario. Fifteenth century. There's a rumour it's cursed. Plenty of murders and suicides over the years."

"And is it?" he wondered. "Cursed?"

The corners of her mouth turned down in a wry gesture he was coming to recognise. "It gave me nightmares. When I was a child."

Daniel studied Ca' Dario. It was unfair that the mansion was dwarfed by the palaces around it. The design was unusual and interesting. "How could a house like that give you nightmares?"

"I was a child! And it was doubtless a dream. I was coming back from confirmation, in my sweet white dress, standing in the back of the *vaporetto*, feeling the most important person in the world."

She hesitated.

"And?" he asked.

"It was Carnival. I looked up at a window. There. On the second floor. The long one second from the left." The boat was moving steadily past the house now. "There was a face. A man, holding up his hands. I thought he was screaming."

"What did he look like? Young? Old?"

"I don't recall. It was a dream, probably."

"Or the house *is* cursed."

She laughed, thinking he humoured her. "I don't think so. Though Woody Allen nearly bought the place a couple of years ago. Now, *that* would have been scary."

"You're a wicked, sharp-tongued woman, Laura," he observed. "Can one visit it?"

She shook her head. "Private house. Mind you, I believe your friend Mr. Massiter maintains an apartment in the neighbouring palace. Perhaps he will let you peer in from there. With your pretty American girlfriend, naturally. ''*Ave a nice day.*'"

He decided he would not rise to that particular bait. The *vaporetto* rounded the end of the canal, with the great grey slab of Salute to the right. Laura stood up, scanning the jetty, and he followed suit.

"Massiter's not arrived yet," she said, pointing to a walkway beyond the public stop. "He'll pick you up there, I imagine, where the taxis dock. The manners of the man. Why couldn't he come for you?"

"I'm grateful in any case."

She gave him a fierce look. "Grateful, grateful. You spend too much time being grateful, Daniel. No one does anything without a reason, not even Scacchi."

"But..."

It was too late. In true Venetian fashion she had elbowed her way through the crowd. The sunglasses were jammed on her face once more. By the time he reached the pavement, she was a distant figure, marching off towards San Marco.

Daniel waited. Ten minutes later a sleek, polished speedboat docked exactly where she said it would. Hugo Massiter sat in the open back, sharing a bottle of champagne with Amy Hartston. As they left the jetty, Daniel, too, held a glass of the exotic liquid in his hand, feeling as if his world had suddenly expanded.

He looked back at the departing San Marco shoreline. There, standing in the small park, was the tiny red-and-blue figure of Laura watching him go, believing, he felt sure, she was invisible in the distance.

An evening on the lagoon

AS THEY PASSED THE ARSENALE AND BEGAN TO HEAD
out into the open waters of the lagoon, Hugo Massiter
refilled their champagne glasses and bellowed over the roar of
the engine, "Dimitri?"

The young boatman at the front of the craft, tanned and tall,
his eyes hidden behind large black sunglasses, turned to peer at
them. "Boss?"

"Fast as you can."

Dimitri shrugged. The vessel's nose lurched skywards. Amy
Hartston and Daniel Forster found their backs thrust deep into
the leather bench seats and immediately broke into foolish
grins.

Amy wore a pale evening dress cut low at the neck, and looked
enticingly elegant, older than her years. Massiter was dressed in
cream slacks and a pure white cotton shirt. The sunglasses had
been replaced by a captain's cap, complete with blue anchor at
the front, which sat at a jaunty angle on his head. Daniel had
never been so close to a wealthy man before. Hugo, as he insisted
on being called, was not what he expected. He seemed too
relaxed, playful almost, to be real. Nevertheless, Daniel found

his presence, and Amy's, exciting. His life had grown larger since he'd arrived in Venice. Everything which preceded it now seemed oddly muted and two-dimensional.

The boat lurched northwards, bouncing off the swell, through the channel marked by buoys which ran between the busy, built-up island of Murano to the left and Sant' Erasmo, a low green oasis of vegetable gardens, and the home of Piero, to the right. Daniel recalled his last trip on the lagoon in the *Sophia*, meandering across the grey water with three sleeping men, a dog at the tiller, and Laura, mysterious Laura, who had hidden herself on the San Marco waterfront simply to see him go.

"Something's wrong?" Amy asked over the roar of the boat and the crashing of the waves.

"No," Daniel replied. "I was just thinking how unexpected all this is. I came here simply to catalogue a library."

Massiter offered them a plate of bruschette spread with tomato, porcini, and anchovies. "Life would be so tedious if it were composed only of the expected," he said. "A library?"

Daniel abruptly realized he needed to be on his guard. He suddenly wished Scacchi had advised him in greater detail about how to deal with Massiter. It was curious that the old man had given him so little guidance. It seemed he expected Daniel, for all his naivety, to shape the course of any dealings which might ensue.

As circumspectly as he could, he explained the history behind his trip to Venice and his special interest in the Republic's printing presses. Scacchi had offered to pay a little in return for sifting through some old documents which would otherwise, he said, be thrown away. Daniel expressed his surprise and gratitude at discovering he'd been enrolled for the summer school.

"And you've found something?" Massiter asked immediately.

"Not yet," Daniel replied, and was surprised to discover that on this occasion he lied quite easily. "The documents were left in the cellar, and most seem to have been affected by water."

Massiter shook his head. "What a waste! But you see, Scacchi is merely a dealer in antiques. We've done a little business with each other before—at arm's length, as he insists. I never get a dinner invitation, you know, or even a call for drinks. The antique dealer's weakness is that he sees value only when it is thrust in front of him. To think he may have had a treasure beneath his very nose and let it rot for want of a little attention."

Daniel was not willing to accept this harsh criticism, even if it was true. "Signor Scacchi has been a good, kind man to me. Without him I would still be in Oxford looking for some menial job to pay the bills for the summer." *And alone*, he nearly added, *drifting through a monochrome existence.*

Massiter waved his hand in apology. "Of course, of course. I meant nothing personal. Your loyalty does you proud. Now, Amy. A little about you, for Daniel and to refresh my own memory."

She smiled vacantly and told, in a few sentences, of growing up in Maine, of her father who was "very big" in "real estate," and how summer in Venice was the highlight of her year.

"But your college?" Daniel wondered.

"Strictly for rich dumb girls. Which I am. Make no mistake."

"Ridiculous," Massiter said sternly. "Amy has played here since she was a spotty twelve-year-old brat, and every year her rise in stature amazes me."

"Yeah. Right. They love the idea of some girl player being the star of this thing, Daniel. Ever since that kid got murdered—the young ones say her ghost still haunts La Pietà. Used to believe that myself."

Massiter turned to face the water. Daniel detected some concern in his manner.

"I'm sorry," Daniel said. "I don't know about this."

"Really?" Amy asked, suddenly animated. "This was before my time, but it was some story. The poor kid was being chased by the creep who was the school leader. Turns out he attacked her after the final concert and *murdered* her. Then he killed himself when the cops were closing in. She was quite a player, too, they say."

Massiter drained his glass and refilled it immediately. "Her name was Susanna Gianni, and she was, my dears, the finest violinist of her age I have ever heard. To think I picked that damned Russian for the job. There's not a day goes by when I don't reproach myself for it. If it weren't for me, Susanna would be alive today."

His grey eyes seemed damp. Amy placed her hand on his knee. It seemed, to Daniel, an oddly adult gesture. "Hugo. I'm sorry," she said. "I didn't realize it was so personal. You can't blame yourself for what someone else does."

"But I do, I'm afraid. Even after ten years. Still, this isn't a subject for now. Look. We arrive."

The island was quite close. The tower of the campanile was visible several hundred yards inland from the *vaporetto* jetty. The speedboat slowed to a crawl, made a sharp right, then entered the mouth of a narrow canal thick with algae. Massiter swatted a mosquito, looked at his watch, and ordered Dimitri to moor the boat temporarily a little way from the restaurant, in a solitary location next to a vegetable field.

"Damned if I couldn't get a table till nine. What cheek! Still, you can play for your supper now, instead of later. Come! Instruments out! Let me hear these pieces you've invented for me."

Amy pulled a face. "Jesus, Hugo. Do I have to? I hate composition. I'm a player."

"And an excellent one too. The best we have this year, Amy. Fabozzi told me so himself."

"Maybe," she replied. "That doesn't mean I can write."

He stared at her, seeming offended. "You mean you didn't bring anything?"

She reached into her bag and pulled out a printed manuscript. "I've got some Vivaldi. The *Seasons*. We never play it in the school. I thought it might make a change."

Massiter looked horrified. "Good God, girl! If I want to hear that one more time—which I never shall—I'll go to the nearest pizza parlour. I've a good mind to make you starve by way of punishment. Women!" His temper was up.

"Perhaps," Daniel suggested, "I have a solution."

"I hope so. Or none of us shall eat tonight."

Daniel picked up the plastic envelope with the six sheets of handwritten music inside. "Amy, it would be a great compliment if you could sight-read what I've written."

"Why?" Massiter asked. "Can't you play it yourself?"

"Not terribly well," he admitted. "I never professed to be a great violinist, Hugo. Just because you can hear something in your head doesn't mean you can reproduce it with your fingers."

"Musicians!" Massiter raged. "Most stubborn creatures on earth. Well. You heard, my girl. Play, or it's back to town and no supper for the pair of you."

"Gimme," she said sullenly, and snatched the pages from Daniel's hand, then sat, for a full five minutes, reading through them. Massiter calmed down a little. Daniel listened to the buzz of insects and the gentle movement of fish bobbing for flies, wondering, with no small amount of rising panic, if he had played his hand correctly. Amy's expression changed as she worked her way through the pages. She became more serious and absorbed. When she was done, she turned to him and asked, "What is this, Daniel? What's it meant to be?"

"A violin solo," he replied stupidly.

"I *know* that. Give me the context. It sounds eighteenth century, almost like Vivaldi, but not quite. And it's part of something much bigger, I think. *What is it?*"

Massiter regarded both of them intently. Daniel understood why Scacchi found it difficult to reveal anything but the truth in the face of those staring grey eyes.

"I imagine it to be a solo passage in something like a Vivaldi violin concerto. In between the *ritornelli*. I was playing with the form. Trying to write something which matched the occasion."

Amy squinted at him. "I'm to imagine what the rest is, I suppose? Without hearing it in my head, it is damned hard to work out how this fits in."

He cursed himself. He had chosen the first obvious violin flourish he could find and never, for a moment, considered the need for context. "That would be fine," he murmured.

"Fine?" She was bemused. "How can you write the middle of something without at least dreaming up the beginning, if not the end? I don't understand."

Massiter had relaxed into the corner of the boat. "Music or starvation, my dear," he said. "What'll it be?"

"Brits!"

She passed the sheets to Daniel, asking him to turn the pages for her, took the Guarneri out of its case, stood up, and, after a moment's consideration, began to play. The rich, full tone of the slim fiddle rang out over the drone of mosquitoes. Massiter closed his eyes and listened, utterly still. Daniel found the notes chilled his blood, gaining several new dimensions over the passage he had scanned in his head as he wrote them down. It began with the long, slow, stately grace of a dirge, then, through a series of turning, quickening changes, moved up the scale gradually, relentlessly, until the solo closed in a rapid, majestic, ringing display of double-stopped fury. If he had to apply a single word to the passage it would, he believed, be *resurrection*. The music started in the realm of the dead and ascended, with a certain steady pace, to a world full of life and colour and movement.

Amy sat down and gave him a frank look. "How did I do? Be honest. It's your music."

"You were wonderful," he stuttered. "Marvellous."

She shook her head. "Wow. That stuff's amazing, Daniel. Can I keep these sheets? Can I work on them?"

"Of course."

"Here. Sign it for me. I can sell it if I'm ever broke."

He held his hands awkwardly on his lap, palms down. "I don't have a pen."

Massiter was watching him like a hawk. He picked a tortoiseshell fountain pen out of his shirt pocket and held it out. "Here, Daniel," he said with a wan smile. "Use mine."

With a shaky hand, and hating himself all the while, Daniel scrawled his name on the first page.

"That was stunning," Massiter said. "On both your parts. Now, let's eat."

It was a feast, as Massiter had promised. They devoured a succession of small plates, sharing each: sea urchins and soft-shelled crabs, shrimp and lobster, pasta stained with squid ink, John Dory served whole, with the mark of Saint Peter's thumbprint still on the side, and monkfish as fat and sweet as scampi. Massiter uttered a few deprecatory words about the Veneto whites, then picked a firm, flinty Alto Adige from the South Tyrol to go with the fish. They drank two bottles, with a grappa each at the end, and talked of Venice and colleges and food, anything but the music they had just heard.

When the meal was done, they walked round to the little basilica. Massiter bribed the caretaker to let them in and turn on the lights, then revealed, with a proud wave, the famous Doomsday mosaic. Daniel was impressed to see, just as Piero had promised, a small dog in one corner which might have been ancestor to the legendary Xerxes, duckhound and helmsdog extraordinaire. Afterwards, with the night well fallen, they went outside and stared at the stars: a perfect lagoon evening, with the sky a soft, dark blue above them.

The caretaker hung around, waiting for more tips. Massiter eyed the campanile and suggested they make the long climb to the top. From there, he said, the lights of Venice would wink back at them from the horizon.

Amy sat on an old stone throne outside the basilica, sighed, and said, "No way am I climbing up that thing. You guys go ahead. I'll wait here."

And so they did, climbing the winding interior of the tower together, each with a flashlight. From the campanile they surveyed the small, enclosed world of the lagoon like gods, feeling as if they could reach out and touch any point: the near island of Burano, the lights on Murano and San Michele in the mid distance. And, beyond, the church towers of the city itself.

Daniel had drunk too much wine to be worried. He smiled at Massiter and thanked him. The older man leaned out of the open arch and stared at the black waters. Then he spoke, with a new seriousness in his voice.

"You're Scacchi's tool," he said. "You know that, Daniel. Surely."

Sobriety fell down from the sky in an instant, and with it the certain knowledge that he would not be able to leave this high tower without telling Massiter at least some of the truth.

"I don't understand...."

Massiter clapped him lightly on the shoulder. "The music, lad. It's not yours. It can't be. The old man's fishing. Does he know what it's worth?"

Daniel said nothing.

"Look," Massiter continued. "It's clear you didn't write it. It's clear, too, from what I have heard, that it may be outstanding. Now, tell me what Scacchi wants and we'll talk."

"I don't know," he replied honestly. "Beyond money."

"He must want plenty of that to play these games. Why doesn't he just pick up the phone and call me?"

"He's ill. I can offer no better explanation."

Massiter scowled. "So I'd heard. Poor chap. Well. What is it, then?"

Daniel took a deep breath. "It's the composer's original score for an entire violin concerto. Like Vivaldi, but not like him too."

"Who did write it?"

"I have no idea. It's described simply as 'Concerto Anonimo' and dated 1733, which puts it contemporary with the close of Vivaldi's career. But it can't be him. Why would he write anonymously?"

Massiter gazed at the stars and the blackness. "Is it all that good?" he asked eventually.

"I believe so."

"And it's yours? Not stolen? I know Scacchi's games."

"The work was found in Scacchi's own house. It's his. I think, too, that it is truly wonderful. I hadn't realised quite how good until Amy played it. But then you felt that, too, didn't you, Hugo?"

Massiter laughed. "Oh, yes. What a tale! This city never stops surprising me."

"You'll buy it?" Daniel asked hopefully. "I think Scacchi will be amenable to a quick arrangement."

Massiter shook his head. "It's a jolly story, but what, in all honesty, is the thing worth? We could pay some tame scholar to say it's Vivaldi's, I imagine, but you seem to think that ruse won't last. Scacchi could get some small sum from a university, I expect. The musicologists will adore it. But it's well below my horizon as it stands, I'm afraid."

Daniel could hardly believe what he was hearing. "But it's marvellous music, Hugo. You said so yourself."

"Absolutely! Scacchi could come to some arrangement with a publisher to have first pick for its transcription and earn a few royalties down the line. But you see the problem? The composer, whoever he was, is long dead. There's no real copyright. Once it's in some college, anyone can pick it up and turn out editions by the score, not paying a penny to a soul. They will, believe me. There's no such thing as an honest academic. No. There is perhaps ten thousand dollars for it on the nail as it stands, and the selfsame over the next five years in residuals. Nothing more."

The logic of Massiter's argument seemed unshakable. "There's no other possibility?" Daniel asked.

Massiter held up the torch and shone it in his face. "Of course there is. Look, this is not the toy I had in mind to buy this summer, as you and Scacchi well know. I'd a fancy to own one of those big fat Guarneris again. But I'm as open to a little game as the next man. What we do, Daniel, is *dissemble*. How do you think the world goes round?"

The night was growing chilly. Part of Daniel wished to be on the ground, yet another side of his character needed to hear what Massiter had to say. Scacchi was desperate for money. Here, too, was life, full of experience and excitement. There was a selfish reason to play this game, not just the practical needs of the old man. "I don't follow," he declared.

Massiter sighed, as if dealing with a child. "Think of the problem. No one knows who wrote this. No one, in truth, owns the thing. If it's made public as it stands, the worth of it lies merely in the intrinsic value of some old paper. Agreed?"

Daniel nodded uncertainly.

"So what we need," Massiter continued, "is to make it something a man might possess. Might own, and sell if he cares to. You provided the answer yourself. Ask Amy. She knows who wrote this concerto. *You.*"

An owl screeched in the black air beyond the tower. Massiter took him by the arm. "Listen. It's simplicity itself. Tomorrow, I have a word with Fabozzi and tell him we have a change of plan. I'll ask him to abandon the current programme and focus on a single work. A new one. Written by a brilliant prodigy who has emerged out of nowhere. One Daniel Forster. Each day you copy something from your original and bring it to him. The school rehearses your masterpiece. At the final concert we debut the work for the world. Think of the publicity! Think of the acclaim! You start the summer a penniless student and end it a celebrity. Not rich, true, but who gets rich out of music?"

"I am not that person, Hugo."

"What are you worried about? That the real one will come back and haunt you? Besides, even if you don't write another note, it's a pretty thing to put on your CV. Have a little fun for once, Daniel. Don't be so stiff."

"It's illegal, surely?"

"Oh, come. Who's been robbed? Not the author. Nor those who pay for the work afterwards. They still get the same music, Daniel. Or will it sound different because your name is on the cover?"

"No. It's just…"

"Wrong?" Massiter dared him to repeat the word.

"Yes." Daniel felt ashamed. His naivety was embarrassing sometimes.

"Perhaps. That's for you and Scacchi to judge. To me it seems there are simply two possibilities. This work comes into the world and earns you a little money. Or you give the thing away. Let me make a proposition. This is small beer for me, but I find the possibilities of the game amusing. Let us say you claim authorship, as I suggest. I, privately, come to an arrangement to collect what royalties may come to be associated with the title over the years. In return, Scacchi gets, let's say, fifty thousand dollars now and a further fifty at the end of the summer, when everyone's feeling very pleased with themselves. You can treat with him for your cut. After that, it's all mine—whatever small residuals ensue, and the original manuscript too. Could be very embarrassing if that got out. Wonderful offer. The risk is mine entirely, and frankly the upside is marginal even if it does take off. We're talking about music, Daniel, and no one ever makes any real money out of that. This isn't for selfish reasons, you understand? I am, in all honesty, the philanthropist with deep pockets. But then, what's new?"

The small square space at the summit of the campanile was, for a moment, silent.

"Think of it," Massiter said, his grey eyes shining in the dark. "All my money in Scacchi's sweaty fist by tomorrow if we're agreed. You must admit. You're tempted."

Daniel tried to weigh the possibilities. The night swam in front of him. "A hundred now, fifty after," he said.

"Seventy now, fifty after. Not a cent more."

The old man needed the money, he told himself. None of this was for his own purpose. "Done," Daniel answered. "Provided Scacchi agrees, of course."

"Oh," said Massiter, smiling from ear to ear, "he'll agree. He knows a good price when he sees one."

Daniel took Massiter's outstretched hand and was surprised to discover that, unlike his own, it was completely free of perspiration and as cold as stone.

20

On the Jews

Institutions have rules. It is their undoing. The ghetto is no exception. Rebecca had explained to me how this particular prison had come about. When the Venetian Republic decided to welcome Jews again into its midst, it did so with conditions. One was that they stuck to certain trades, mainly banking. Another was that they lived where they were told and consented to be locked up there each evening. For this the city needed some kind of fortress, so a small island in Cannaregio formerly used as an iron foundry was selected. It was known as *gheto,* from the term for casting iron (and I still do not know where that extra T came from).

Nothing in Venice can be quite that simple, of course. We have three breeds of Jew, if you please: Ashkenazim, from Germany; Sephardim, from Spain; and the Levantines, who have found their way here from the East. Rebecca is an Ashkenazi; her family originally hail from Munich but fled when the city authorities accused the Jews of poisoning the wells and causing plague. Life was not much better in Geneva, where they ended up. The Ashkenazim were the first Jews allowed back into Venice and, as luck would have it, remain the least trusted. The Sephardim, though they continue to speak a language entirely of their own in addition to Hebrew and Italian, seem to have some sway with the city. The Levantines behave almost like true citizens of the Republic; since most come from Venetian territories, such as Corfu and Crete, they are, to a man, deemed to be good servants of the state. Consequently, the Sephardim and the Levantines live mainly in their own, more recent ghettoes, where the restrictions on trade are somewhat more lax, though the rules on the wearing of yellow badges and scarlet scarves continue to apply, as does the law against usury.

I knew none of this, of course, assuming simply that a Jew was a Jew was a Jew. In truth they are as varied in their ways as the rest of us, with their own idiosyncrasies, their likes and dislikes, their prejudices and dogmas. Perhaps the Ashkenazim tell Sephardic jokes, much as the Venetians make up ribald stories about the *matti*, the crazies from Sant' Erasmo, the island in the middle of the lagoon where everyone, word has it, is mother or father or brother and sister to everyone else. I rather hope so. We are merely human, after all.

Each community has its own synagogue—the Ashkenazim own that curious ark-like wooden structure I mentioned, next to and above Rebecca's house. The demand for living space means there is no room for these places of worship on the ground. Instead, they must be built several storeys above the warrens of small rooms where the ghetto people live, cheek by jowl, sometimes as many as ten to each quarter. And with a temple on the top!

How do Rebecca and Jacopo manage to maintain a single room of their own in this sea of Jewry? His position as a physician helps, I imagine, since his services seem greatly in demand throughout the city, particularly when it comes to female illnesses. Yet I think there is more to it than that. They are different still from the Ashkenazim I see on the stairs when I visit, and that is not simply because they have lived here for little more than a year.

Most of those in the ghetto wish merely for more space. They have no desire to enter the outside world for anything other than business. The Levis, I suspect, harbour broader ambitions. For them the only way to establish their true identity is to see how they might rise in the society beyond those three drawbridges. It is an impossible wish, as you may have gathered. That does not make it burn any the less fiercely. They are also openly sceptical about their own and everyone else's religion, which must, I imagine, make them distant from their neighbours. Thank God the Jews are so sensible they have no inquisition or burning of witches, for if they did I suspect Jacopo and Rebecca might well be first on their list. You should see the colour rise in Jacopo's cheeks when he discusses the efficacy of prayer and votives as a way of curing the sick. He seems to have a point too. Why should a candle hold such power? And if it does, why will it wield it only on those of a particular religion, curing only the devout while ignoring the Protestants, the Jews, and the Arabs or whoever? For him there is, I suspect, only one god, and that is Science, a haughty master, and a little too close to alchemy were we living in a less enlightened time and place.

But back to those rules, and the obvious flaw in their structure. No one is allowed out of the ghetto at night *except* for physicians (what practical folk we Gentiles are—when it comes to our survival, we'll let the Hebrews race to our aid every hour of the clock). For Rebecca to escape for her performance at La Pietà, she need only don the heavy disguise of Jacopo's robe, wear his yellow badge on her shoulder, then let me summon her at the gate for an urgent appointment. The drawbridge falls, I engage the guard in conversation so she need say nothing, and, when we are back in that dark labyrinth of alleys beyond the ghetto, she may throw off the costume, become a lady musician on her way to the concert once more, please Vivaldi and his audience, then assume the guise when I bring her back home.

I used Leo's absence, haggling as he was with Delapole over something or other at Ca' Dario, to race over to the ghetto the following morning and explain my plan. Rebecca listened with shining eyes full of hope. To perform behind La Pietà's dusty shutters was better than not to perform at all and would, at least, diminish greatly the chance of her being recognised.

Jacopo shook his head and said, "You've been going to the commedia dell'arte too much, Lorenzo. This is not some story in a playwright's head. It is life. And death or ruin if we're found out playing such pranks, not just on the state but the Church also. There are vengeful men in that palace up the canal, and the basilica too."

"This, Jacopo," I replied with as much iron and determination in my voice as I could muster, "is Venice. A malleable world. Everything here concerned with our lives will take on the shape we make of it. If you fail to understand that, you may as well stay locked in the ghetto forever."

He gave me a sharp look for no good reason. I might have sounded forward, but I was merely telling the truth. Each life has crossroads, moments at which fateful decisions will be made, whether we like it or not. To shirk these waypoints in our destiny is to make a decision in itself, and one we'll likely regret not long after.

"You're a brave one, lad, and your heart's in the right place," he declared. "But is it worth the danger for an evening's entertainment? One step wrong and there'll be a betraying note in one of those finely polished bronze cats the Doge loves so much, and the next we know we could all be arguing for our lives."

Rebecca saw how we agonised, then reached out and took each of us by the wrist. "Please don't ask me to make this decision for you. I have no right to ask anything of either of you."

Jacopo leaned forward and chastely kissed her on the forehead. "Such a ladylike way of putting it, dear sister. So tell me. This Vivaldi? This place? They merit the risk?"

She shook herself free of him, fighting for some way in which she could say this next thing with a shred of impartiality. "Brother, you know the answer, because you feel it just as much as me. Beyond these walls *there is life!*"

Jacopo Levi studied me, seeking an answer. Our joint decision went beyond music. For Rebecca these hours in La Pietà represented freedom, where she was no longer bound by the twin iron chains of her sex and her race. Jacopo, too, shared in that moment, for he adored his sister more than anything on earth.

"I suggested this course of action, Jacopo," I told him. "Why ask me where I stand?"

"Of course," he said with some reluctance. "Then it is up to me. Well . . ."

Rebecca gazed at her brother, trying not to appear too hopeful. "There is no need to rush this, Jacopo," she said softly.

"Rush?" he wondered. "And things will stand differently tomorrow?"

Neither of us answered. He reached forward and drew up our hands together. We clasped each other's wrists in amity and determination, then Rebecca, tears starting to well in those dark, almond eyes, broke away, snatched off a chain from her neck, and gently placed it round my head. I found the object attached to it: a small silver figure, six-pointed, like two triangles turned against each other, which they call the Star of David.

"Would I make a good Jew?" I asked, feeling the points of the emblem and wondering how many Hebrew necks this had embraced.

"There is no such thing as a good Jew or a good Gentile," Jacopo replied. "Only honest men and honest women. Until the world learns that, we'll all be living in a sorry place."

"Amen," I said without thinking, and we found ourselves gripped by a fit of the giggles.

The third way

A T DANIEL'S REQUEST THEY ASSEMBLED AROUND THE dining table at nine. Laura had placed pastries and cups of *macchiato* on the table for the men. She sat quietly sipping an orange juice, uncomfortable for a reason he could not guess. Daniel finished his coffee in two straight gulps. He was, he realised, rapidly becoming addicted to this halfway house between the harsh, tiny fix of espresso and the milky bulk of the cappuccino. It was part of a rapid process of assimilation. At times he even found himself starting to think in Italian.

He explained the events of the previous night and Massiter's offer. Scacchi whistled when he disclosed the terms. The air made a peculiar noise as it travelled through his false teeth. The old man looked particularly yellow this morning, Daniel thought.

"You let this girl play the piece?" Laura asked. "Why? You mean she's better at it than you?"

"Yes. *Much* better. The best player in the whole school, according to Fabozzi."

"And if you'd played it, he would never have known."

He was unable to understand whether Laura was trying to criticise him or not.

"I can't say."

"Then we might as well have gone straight to the Englishman and offered him the thing on a plate," she observed.

Scacchi tore a croissant in half and nibbled at a small portion. "It's a good price, Laura. I thought we might generate a little excitement by putting around some rumour about the work's existence, then setting those who desire it against each other. But Massiter knows more about this particular world than I. His logic seems irrefutable. Furthermore, even if the piece is successful, it could take many years before it earned the sum of money he seems willing to place on the table this very day."

Laura's green eyes opened wide. "The Englishman is asking you to commit fraud!"

Scacchi shook his head. "That's a very narrow interpretation of the facts, my dear. Under the *thesauri inventio*, I have every right to the object, since it was found on my property. That surely includes the right to dictate how it's brought to market."

She threw up her hands in disgust, uttered an arcane Venetian curse, and turned to Daniel, pleading. "Don't even begin to consider this, I implore you. I know you think this is some grand adventure, and we're all players in it. But what Scacchi suggests is criminal, and you must surely know as much."

"I had not realised you possessed a legal mind," Scacchi observed crossly.

Daniel tried to interpret the expression on Laura's face. It was not anger; it was concern—for all of them.

"I think I'm old enough to make up my own mind," Daniel said, hoping to calm the temperature.

"All children say things like that," Laura moaned, still staring at him.

Scacchi tapped his hand lightly on the table, as if to bring the meeting to some kind of order. "I'm asking for nothing more than a small white lie."

Paul shook his head. "Hey. Let's cut the crap, Scacchi. If Daniel puts his name on the thing, we're screwing people. Period."

"We're making them pay an appropriate sum for a great work of art," Scacchi insisted. "And who's to say the rightful owner did not leave his music with the thought it might enrich whosoever found it?"

"Who's to say it wasn't stolen in the first place?" Paul insisted.

Scacchi would not budge. "That's irrelevant. Now that Massiter has pointed the facts out to us, do you think there is a single hole in his argument? Without copyright for the thing, the amount of money it can earn anyone is marginal, surely?"

Paul sighed. "Probably. You're right about what it's worth with copyright too. The piece couldn't earn the kind of money he's offering in years."

"There," Scacchi announced with a triumphant look. "That's settled, then."

"What exactly is settled?" Laura demanded. "You have not even asked Daniel his opinion of the matter. You simply assume he will agree to this ridiculous idea."

"Daniel!" Scacchi said. "It's your choice. I shall, of course, treat you fairly. Let's say ten per cent. At the end of the summer, when Massiter pays the second part."

Daniel shook his head.

"Fifteen, then," Scacchi offered. "We can do business here, surely."

"I don't want your money, Scacchi! Not a penny of it. You've been generous enough to me already."

Laura's eyes rolled in disbelief. "Please don't pretend this is for gratitude alone, Daniel. That may be a part of it, but I think you are still playing some romantic game in your head. This is not a fairy tale. What Scacchi suggests will make you a criminal, whether you are caught or not."

"I think that is an exaggeration somewhat."

Her eyes lit up. "Really? So what do you think your mother would say on that matter if she were here?"

"You never knew my mother, Laura. You have no idea what she would say."

"I know her son. He wouldn't be who he is if she couldn't see the difference between good and bad. I know—"

"*Laura!*" Scacchi barked angrily. "Enough. He hasn't even agreed yet."

"He doesn't have to. I can see it in his face."

The old man scowled. "It's entirely up to you, my boy. If there's something else, name it."

Daniel was silent, wondering at the heat and the emotion in this conversation. There had rarely been a cross word or a raised voice at home in England, only lassitude and, underpinning everything towards the end, despair. This was the world as he had imagined it: full of colour and life and some enticing uncertainty about what the coming days would bring.

"I don't want anything, Scacchi. If I comply, it's because I wish to perform a service for you."

At that, Laura screeched. "Daniel! If you put your name to this...this supposed *miracle*, you'll be revealed as a liar and a cheat before the summer's through. They'll ask for more music. And you won't have it."

"I've thought of that," he replied. "I shall say the concerto left me drained of ideas, and rather than pull some mediocre piece out of thin air, I intend to go back to my studies and wait for inspiration to strike again. It never will. In five years I'll just be someone else who showed a little early promise and nothing more."

"Now," Paul said, suddenly animated, "that could work. Boy wonders rarely have more than a couple of pieces of genius in them anyway. It's a shame more don't realise it."

Laura shook her head at the three of them. "You're actually going to do this, aren't you? I can't believe it. Well, Scacchi, before he parades himself in front of the world as the prince of lies, would you care to tell Daniel here why, precisely, he's performing this deception? For the life of me, I don't know."

The old man bristled. "And you assume it is your business?"

"I assume you are all my friends," she retorted.

"He will do it because he wishes to," Scacchi said carefully. "Those are the only circumstances under which I would countenance allowing it to happen. And everything will be at arm's length. I've never had Massiter in this house to this day, nor shall I. Daniel can be our intermediary and deal with him elsewhere."

"But why?" she demanded, furious. "Why do you need the money? We've managed to get by so far without some sudden catastrophe. Why now?"

Scacchi stared at her with a deliberate absence of feeling, as if preparing himself for something he wished not to say.

"Well?" she insisted.

He pushed his coffee cup across the table in her direction, then folded his arms.

"Laura," he said slowly, "over the time you have been part of my household I have come to love you dearly, and hope you may feel a little of the same in return. You are the one fixed point in the diminishing lives which Paul and I lead. Without you we would be quite lost, and deprived of a dear friend too. For that I cannot thank you enough."

She stared at him blankly as if she had never heard words like these before.

"Nevertheless," Scacchi continued, "you are a servant in this house. I employ you to do our bidding. Not to tell us our business. There are matters here which in no way concern you, and it is impertinent that you should assume they do. When I wish your opinion, I shall, rest assured, ask for it, and hold what you say in the highest regard. But now I would like you to clear this table. The coffee cups are long cold and these plates are dirty. After which I should like you to go to the fish market and buy some fresh calamari. I've a fancy for squid for lunch, and no one cooks it better than you. On with it! Please. And no more of this nonsense!"

The sudden tears stained her cheeks, a strange contrast with the fury which blazed in her eyes. Laura stood, walked slowly round each of them, collecting the remains of breakfast, then, without a word, left the room.

Daniel listened to her descend the stairs. When he heard the kitchen door close, he turned to the old man, outraged. "Scacchi, I take back everything I said. I'll not do your bidding or tolerate that kind of cruelty. It's undeserved of her and unbecoming of you. How could you even . . ."

Paul rose and patted him on the shoulder. "He's a mile ahead of you, Daniel. He doesn't need you to tell him. I don't know about anyone else here, but I could use a drink."

Scacchi sat mute, desolate, tears in his eyes. Daniel hated himself suddenly for the rush of adrenaline this unexpectedly heated discussion had given him.

Paul went over to the sideboard, picked up a half-full bottle of Glenmorangie, and returned to the table with three glasses. Daniel put a hand over his. "I require an explanation."

They tasted their whisky and listened as the outer door closed with a slam.

"And you'll have one," Scacchi said. "As much as I can."

He gulped the fierce liquid too quickly and burst into a fit of coughing. Daniel watched as Paul patted him lightly on the back. The two men seemed terribly frail, as if a sudden movement could snap their bones.

"You must see a doctor. Both of you," he said.

"This isn't about doctors," Scacchi replied. "Oh, I know you and Laura assume as much, and I'm happy you should think so. Understand me, Daniel, I hated myself for every word I spoke. Laura is as close to a daughter as an old fool like me might have. Without her, I doubt I'd still be alive. But there are matters she should not be involved with, and this is one of them. So swear to me. That you will never, *never* breathe a word of what I now tell you. Let her think this is all for some quack medicine to cure the bitter poison in our veins. Then when it's done, we can all get back to enjoying what remains of our lives and she's none the wiser."

"That's unfair," Daniel said. "You ask me to bind myself to an oath without knowing the cost or the consequences."

"There's nothing in this that harms her in any way. To the contrary. I seek the best solution for us all. Please?"

Daniel said nothing. "Hell," Paul grumbled. "Let's tell him anyway. It's simple, Daniel. We're broke. *In crapola profunda.*"

"I understood that," Daniel answered.

"No," Scacchi said with an ironic smile. "You understood we were short of money. This is somewhat more serious. Five years ago, when both of us were diagnosed with this blasted disease, I never expected we'd live this long. All I thought of was making something of the time we had left. I went to the bank and tried to mortgage this place. Well, the sum they offered was an insult. So, like an idiot, I did what any gentleman did and spoke to a 'man of a certain standing.' You understand who I mean?"

There could, Daniel thought, be only one possible explanation. "*Mafiosi?*"

"A catchall phrase of the newspapers. Not something I would use. But you get my drift. The terms were generous. The penalties for default, however..."

Paul poured himself another glass and, without looking at either of them, said, "Tell him."

Scacchi groaned, as if in despair at his own folly. "In October, the payment becomes due. Since the time I negotiated this arrangement, the price of this kind of property, in this kind of area, has fallen, and Ca' Scacchi is in greater need of repair than ever. With interest, the gap between my equity and the debt they seek repaid is some quarter of a million dollars. Not that either of us expected to have to face it. I believed the insurance and the sale of the house on our inevitable deaths would more than cover the debt and that Laura would enjoy the balance. None of this will happen. If I don't give them the money, they will, of course, kill me, which will be no great loss, I think, except to my dear, gullible Paul here."

"I believe Laura would have something to say about that," Daniel said, astonished. "So might I, for that matter."

"And I think you know none of us as well as you believe," Scacchi declared. "Kindly hear me out. Before they kill me, they will, some weeks before, first kill her, on the assumption that Laura's innocent death will be the most painful spur to my compliance. Should that fail, they will then murder Paul, who has at least the stain of being party to this original arrangement. These are businessmen at heart and murderers only by force of circumstance. Practical fellows. They seek the money they are owed, not revenge, but they will, I fear, have one or the other. I..."

Scacchi's voice broke. He put a hand to his mouth. Paul took away his glass, went to the sideboard, and returned with a tumbler full of water and some pills. Scacchi snatched at them.

"You must go to the police!" Daniel demanded. "Talk to that woman who was here. Immediately!"

The old man shrugged his frail shoulders. "Oh, Daniel. Your innocence is quite overwhelming sometimes. This is Italy. The police would surely investigate. For as long as they could bear interviewing corpses. I believe that policewoman you saw is honest. But she will tell someone who is not. The men we speak of are as close to many in the police as their own family. To complain to the authorities about them...we wouldn't live beyond a week, even if they put us in a cell."

"We've tried every option," Paul said. "Believe me."

"Then what?"

"We seek," Scacchi said slowly, "a creative solution."

"You mean the money from the concerto?"

"No! This is insufficient. But the money from the concerto could be our seed. And from it we grow the crop we require."

"So quickly?" Daniel wondered.

"Oh, yes," Scacchi said. "I am an art dealer by trade. I have my connections. There is an object on the market in the hands of a fool who does not know its value. Massiter has discovered as much too. You heard him talk of this Guarneri? The Giuseppe del Gesù? The selfsame instrument. Unlike Massiter, I know where it is and how much I may pay for it. Between that and its true price lies the solution to our difficulties. With your assistance, I believe it may be ours to sell on to the very highest bidder."

"You're ill," Daniel told the two men. "But you can walk. You can do business. You can think as quickly as any men."

"This is true," Scacchi agreed.

"And this Guarneri," he went on. "It is, I assume, stolen. Otherwise the 'fool' who has it would surely know its true value?"

Scacchi hesitated before answering. "Yes. Let us say it's stolen."

"And this policewoman came here because she suspected you may seek it?"

Scacchi grimaced. "I will be honest with you. She knows there is an object on the market, though not what it is. Who are we to argue with the police?"

"And this is why you asked me here in the first place? Not just for your library? You have known about this violin for some time and sought me out as your route to it."

Scacchi thought carefully. "Nothing is quite that concrete. If I'm honest with you, it was at the back of my mind, should the need arise. Yes. Do you agree, Paul?"

The American smiled. Both of them were, Daniel thought, grateful for this conversation, glad to end the pretence. "Of course I agree, Scacchi. Look, we're sorry, Daniel. We thought we were getting some dumb college kid who'd help us sell some junk from the cellar, then, if we got lucky, run a couple of quiet errands to this guy with the fiddle. We didn't realise you were going to turn out to be so likeable. Or smart."

"Or," Scacchi added, "become a part of us so quickly and so surely."

"Hey," Paul said. "We make lousy villains. We're as sorry, as miserable, and as guilty as hell, and I'll be damned if I am going to make that confession more than once."

Daniel laughed and allowed Paul to pour him a small shot of whisky.

"And we still need you," Paul added. "We could try to do this ourselves. If it's an up day, maybe it would work. But…" He gestured at the two of them. "You can see for yourself."

Scacchi leaned forward, peering into Daniel's eyes. "This is a young man's game, a fit man's game. A meeting here.

Something to carry there. The risk is minimal, and we'll take it whenever we can. But if I can't get your name on the cover of that music, if I can't rely on you to meet this fellow with the Guarneri and see the instrument to ensure he's not trying to gull us, we're lost, Daniel. I will pay for your contribution. Come up with a price."

They waited in silence.

"Think about it," Scacchi said. "But not for too long. Massiter wants an answer."

"I'm thinking."

"Good. You know I tried to tell you, Daniel. I showed you that handsome Lucifer of mine. Don't you think a part of him lives inside me?"

"No, Scacchi, I don't, to be honest."

"As you see fit. But in any case, remember what I said. When the Devil makes you an offer, there are but three options. To do what he asks. To do what 'goodness' demands. Or the third way. To do what the hell you like."

"I recall." Daniel looked at his watch. It was just past ten. The decision was, in truth, no decision at all. To refuse would be to abandon them, and Daniel Forster had been abandoned once before, in his cot, by a father he never knew. From the time he first understood the nature of this act, he had come to believe that there were few greater sins one human could inflict upon another. There was a personal reward in the game too. The dull world of Oxford seemed a million miles distant. He felt, for the first time in his life, that he was shaping the world about him, not watching it slowly fall apart. "I shall require a computer and some composition software. I am not transcribing every last note by hand."

Scacchi looked excitedly at Paul. "Well?"

"I know someone at the university," Paul said. "We can fix it."

"Good," Daniel continued. "This depends, of course, on your meeting my price."

They shuffled awkwardly on their seats. "And that is?" asked Scacchi.

"No more secrets. No more deception. You'll be honest with me, always, or I'll consider everything between us forfeit, including our friendship. And you'll find some way of making Laura happy again, for all our sakes."

Scacchi leaned forward across the table and clutched his hand, his face split by the rictus of a happy grin. "Always. And as for Laura, nothing will give me more pleasure. We are Venetian, Daniel. We are used to these little explosions from time to time."

"Always," Paul repeated. "I'll call about that computer now."

The American headed for the study. Scacchi stayed at the table, pensive, perhaps a little guilty.

"Thank you," he said. "For all of us. Particularly my innocent Laura."

"This changes how I feel about you, Scacchi," Daniel said.

"I can understand that. You feel let down. Deceived. With good reason."

"With very good reason."

"But," Scacchi added, "as Paul said, you are, in part, to blame. Had you been the gullible lad we thought we'd found, none of this heartache need have occurred. You would have flitted in and out of Venice none the wiser."

"And you would have failed, Scacchi. The opportunity for this bargain with Massiter wouldn't have arisen. I think you are, in truth, not very good at this."

The old man nodded, accepting the point pleasantly. "Agreed. While you appear to be developing a formidable and quite shocking talent for such intrigues."

They both laughed. The storm was over. "Ah, and now for

more important matters," Scacchi said. "On Sunday Piero fetches us all for a picnic on Sant' Erasmo. You'll be the honoured guest of Ca' Scacchi's trio of misfits. Bring this American girl too. We should all like to meet her."

"Amy?" The idea was not appealing. "I don't think so. I scarcely know her."

"All the more reason for her to come."

"I don't even know if I like her."

Scacchi gave him a stern gaze. "Daniel. Take this advice, please. You need broader company than this household can provide. Let's not suffocate each other in this place. It is the job of the old to devour the young whenever they have the opportunity. You must do your best to avoid our toothless jaws."

Daniel thought of Amy Hartston, sitting in her elegant dress on the *Sophia*, with Xerxes at the tiller, Piero spouting nonsense, Scacchi and Paul in each other's arms, and Laura dispensing spritz while hissing, "'*Ave a nice day.*"

"Can't wait," he said, bemused.

22

Rebecca receives a gift

Complications! Complications! Before the first evening concert when, nervously, we might try out our scheme, my dear sister, we found ourselves enmeshed in plots of my uncle's making. The negotiations with Delapole continue. Leo decided we must join the Englishman on a boat journey across the lagoon to Torcello with a small party of musicians from La Pietà, Rebecca among them, to provide entertainment along the way.

A pretty group we made too: Delapole smiling benevolently as he handed out money right, left, and centre, to the boatmen, to the players, to just about everyone but Leo. Gobbo wore some shiny finery that made him look like a clown's baboon. Rousseau fluttered about, still angling for a job. Rebecca, without her scarlet scarf, felt sufficiently brave to make her own way to meet us, joining three other female players, plain girls who looked as if they didn't see the light of day much. She cast me a familiar glance and then set her eyes on the water. It was best, we both knew, to keep our relations private in such a gathering.

The summer heat receded the moment our skiff sailed past

St. Mark's and out into the lagoon. It was unusually clear. To the west lay the mountains, still capped in snow, to the north Torcello, and to the east the low, blue flatness of the Adriatic, with scarcely a wave on it, as if the ocean itself felt like dozing on this idle afternoon.

The musicians had struck up some of Vivaldi's lesser stuff as soon as we set sail from the small jetty outside Ca' Dario. Quite why, I don't know, since almost everyone on board talked over them as if they were mere decoration. The priest would have had a fit if he'd witnessed it.

The city receded into the distance. The little band played and played, red Veneto wine flowed profusely, and the party settled into a lazy glow while lounging on the cushions in the stern. Delapole could not take his eyes off the musicians, Rebecca more than any. It strikes me as odd that the Englishman, who's a handsome, amiable fellow in the prime of life, appears not to own some mistress. Perhaps he does and keeps her out of sight. Perhaps there is in Delapole a secret to match Oedipus's sad history. But he wasn't the only one whose eyes were on stalks. Uncle Leo was at it, too, openly admiring Rebecca with something close to lasciviousness.

At around three we entered the narrow canal that leads to the centre of the island. The captain pointed our bow at the tall tower of the basilica. Torcello was the capital of the lagoon before Venice and lost its position only because of the malarial nature of the swamps. Now a handful of peasants and ageing clergy live there, both sets trying to swindle visitors for the odd ducat or two.

We disembarked close to the basilica and, as a group, inspected the place. Rebecca, being in her Gentile guise, was allowed through the door but did not loiter long, and I understood why. The west wall is covered with a vast mosaic depicting Judgement Day. It's a spectacular thing and must make the bucolic locals positively quiver with fear every time they see it. Some very cross-looking devils are busy pushing sinners down to Hell along with every other race on the earth that is not pale-faced and Christian too. She looked at those Saracens and Moors all going to their doom through nothing more than an accident of birth, then excused herself and went outside. When, after a suitable interval, I followed, she was seated on a giant throne hewn out of rock, with some local crone pocketing a coin for allowing her this dubious privilege.

"Do you know what this is, Lorenzo?"

"A chunk of broken Roman stone, like most of the stuff around here, I imagine."

"Don't be so cynical. The good lady tells me it is nothing less than the throne of Attila!"

"Hmmm. And there was me thinking the Hun never did manage to conquer Italy."

"Perhaps it is a prize of war?"

She was so taken by the thought that some element of history might hang around the thing I didn't have the heart to tell her the likely truth: it was just another piece of trickery to bring in the tourists. "Perhaps."

"Hah!" She waved her hand in the air. "I can feel the very power of this rock infect my veins! Behold, slave! I rule from the Caspian to the Baltic! They call me lord from Gaul to Constantinople!"

"Actually," I felt it relevant to point out, "they call you 'Flagellum Dei.' The Scourge of God."

"Then some part of Attila's spirit has been reincarnated in me already! Kneel to your master, villein! For do I not own your very soul?!"

Grinning like a simpleton, I got down on one knee. "Naturally, and I do you honour, great lady. Or is it lord? But if you do not accept the existence of God, how can you believe in reincarnation?"

"Insolent slime! Do you think the human spirit so flimsy it cannot disperse itself a little from generation to generation without some arrogant push from the sky? Why, we're all a witch's brew of everyone who's gone before us, man and woman, mixed together like wine and flesh in a stew. We inhale the humours of our ancestors with every breath. I have the temper of Caesar, the cunning of the Hun, and the vocabulary, on occasion, of a Russian fishwife. Look to your manners, cur, or you'll hear it!"

"And the face?"

She paused over that one. "I don't know. What do you think?"

The words just tumbled out of my mouth. "Helen of Troy. No other possibility."

Suddenly she wore an expression that told me I had destroyed the game. Oh, dear sister! One day I must find the strength to speak out loud the contents of my heart.

I have no idea how your own affairs go—you scarcely mention them in those scraps of paper that are supposed to pass as letters. I don't know whether to wish you this exquisite torture or pray for your deliverance to a saner, more even-tempered life.

"They're coming, Lorenzo."

The party had left the basilica and was ambling back to the skiff, Rousseau twittering away like a canary and stabbing the afternoon air with that long, thin index finger of his.

"Then we had better join them."

There must have been some accidental tone of regret in my

voice. Watching carefully, to make sure she wasn't seen, Rebecca extended her hand and, for one short moment, touched my cheek. "Never despair, Lorenzo. Soon we venture out into the city like thieves in the night. This is no time for the faint of heart. Besides . . ."

She drew herself up to her full height, like some ancient Roman empress surveying her empire. "I have sat upon Attila's throne. Fortune is on our side. We are invincible!"

I set this down now, sister, not knowing whether any will ever read these words after your eyes have scanned them: I doubt I shall ever see Rebecca look so magnificent again. On Torcello, with the golden tower of the basilica and the jumble of rose-tiled roofs behind her, arms folded across her chest, eyes blazing with determination, she looked like a goddess. I could have thrown myself at her feet then and begged for her hand. Instead, I cast a wary glance at the party nearing the boat, who were now becoming interested in our absence.

"We must go, Rebecca," I said with a note of caution in my voice I wished I could remove.

She was right about the good fortune, though. They played for us most of the way back, and Rebecca threw her entire soul into the business, sawing away at that rough-hewn piece of wood to make sounds that by rights should never have issued from such a cheap and unworthy instrument. Slowly, even Delapole's party, now well in its cups, began to realise something was up. The chatter ended, even from Rousseau, and as our skiff zigzagged, chasing the soft breeze across the lagoon with the fiery ball of the sun beginning to touch the mountains to the west, they fell into silence and listened, at last, to the music.

When we rounded the great bulwarks of the Arsenale, so close we could see the fires of the workmen behind the gates toiling on new warships for the Republic, the other players whispered to Rebecca. Modestly, she moved her chair forward in the boat, and as we sailed past La Pietà, she tore into the same exercises and études I had heard her play when she auditioned for Vivaldi.

The power and virtuosity of her performance left us all breathless. We passed Salute and I saw a priest who had come out of the church stand on the edge of the stone jetty, straining to hear the tempest of sound that enveloped those of us fortunate enough to be on the water. Even Uncle Leo seemed moved, though I could not help noticing that while the rest of us seemed entranced by Rebecca's art, it was her face and form in which he seemed most engrossed. He had drunk more than any, and it does not make him more pleasant.

She ceased playing as we pulled into the berth at the front of Ca' Dario. Perhaps it was my imagination, but I heard such hurrahs and applause that I thought the acclaim must come from all around us, from the gondolas on the canal, from the windows of the palaces, the streets and jetties, not just our own party. It made me both proud and nervous.

Delapole stood up in the stern of the boat, a little unsteadily, walked forward, and shook her by the hand in a formal, fatherly fashion.

"You are the very wonder of the day," he said. "Those mosaics and that cathedral are quite gone from my head now. All I hear is your fiddle. What is your name?"

"Rebecca Guillaume. Thank you, sir." She glanced at me, and I could see she realised the possible danger of this kind of recognition. The day was failing too. We would have to hurry to be back at the ghetto before nightfall.

Delapole picked up her fiddle. "I know enough about these

things to realise this piece of firewood isn't worthy of you. Tell me, Rebecca, in an ideal world, what instrument would you choose?"

"One that is most unfashionable these days, sir. A Guarneri, but not by Pietro of this city, though they are very fine. He has a cousin, Giuseppe del Gesù, in Cremona, who makes big, bold instruments that the crowd deem ugly. I played one once in Geneva. It has the bravest, strongest tone you will ever hear in any fiddle."

"Then you will do a rich man a favour, Rebecca Guillaume. It's off to Cremona in the morning, Gobbo. Speak to this Giuseppe. Tell him we have a marvel of a musician here who thinks his big, ugly fiddles are just the ticket, then haggle the fellow to the brink of death."

"Sir!" Rebecca's hands shot to her face. "I cannot possibly accept such a gift. It is more money than our family might make in a year."

"Money, money." The Englishman wafted his hand nonchalantly in the air. "What's it for if you can't throw a little at art and beauty once in a while?"

Leo's eyes positively glared at that. I suspect our uncle thought the cash he'd expected by way of a printing commission was now going in the direction of Rebecca's fiddle.

"No," she said most firmly. "It isn't right."

"Then I shall merely have the thing delivered to you, dear girl, and you can place it on your mantelpiece as a parlour decoration if you wish. Come. We must celebrate inside! Drinks! Tidbits! And I shall demand a song of you, Rousseau, a pretty Parisian serenade."

I made sure she caught my eye then. The sun was half down over San Marco. We needed to be heading swiftly back to the ghetto.

She managed to extricate herself from the party with little difficulty. They were fast on the way to becoming decidedly drunk, except for Gobbo, who was mouthing curses about his mission in the morning. Before we left, Rebecca strode over to him and issued one final instruction.

"There are fakers in the city," she told him. "Make sure you deal only with Giuseppe himself and buy an instrument that has his label on it. There should be the cipher IHS and the inscription 'Joseph Guarnerius fecit Cremone, anno...' and the year of manufacture."

"Anything else you want while I'm there?" Gobbo replied with an ugly smirk. "The odd dress or two? Some nice scent? I bet you'd know how to use 'em."

Quite rightly, she turned her back on him, and we made for the door, followed all the way by Gobbo's beady eyes.

I used what little coin I had to find us a gondola that took us straight to San Marcuola. Then we walked hurriedly for Cannaregio, where, close to the ghetto, she took hold of the collar of my jacket and gently dragged me into the half light of a narrow alley. We stood there peering into each other's face.

"Lorenzo," she whispered. "I will have a Guarneri! I will have a proper instrument for the first time in my life!"

I thought of Attila's throne and wondered if perhaps there was indeed some fairy-tale power hidden in the grey and ancient rock. "You deserve nothing less. But we shouldn't forget there is danger here. For us, and for Jacopo too. We must be cautious."

"Yes, and die of old age in our beds, never having tried to touch the sky! Oh, Lorenzo. There's nothing won in this world without risk. But I promise. I shall be modest and unobtrusive from now on. A quiet, obedient girl."

I laughed. She snorted. I stifled the urge to take her in my arms and said simply, "I think that's wise."

"But I wish the concerto I finished writing last week to be published and performed, Lorenzo. It is very good, I think. Leo may be just the man."

In that dark, musty-smelling alley, the entire world turned upside down and spent a good interval that way before righting itself again.

"A concerto? What are you thinking? They will see through our game at La Pietà immediately if you make yourself more public than you are already."

"I merely said I wished my work performed and published. Not that I should be the one whose name is attached to it. To begin with, anyway."

With that she reached forward, held me very gently, and kissed my cheek, once. "There is much to talk about. And much to teach you. But if we do not get past my jailer soon, it won't matter a damn anyway."

Then Rebecca Levi, also known as Guillaume, brushed past me back into the street. Incapable of rational thought, I raced after her.

23
♣

A balance outstanding

IT WAS TEN IN THE MORNING. THEY SAT AT A SMALL window table in Florian's: Scacchi, Daniel, and the mute, puzzled Fabozzi, all three waiting for Massiter to arrive. The day was grey and overcast. Beyond the glass, tourists posed beneath mobs of squabbling pigeons while the souvenir stands hawked their cheap wares. The price list Daniel had picked up on the table was so ludicrously high it was difficult to take a sip without thinking of the cost.

Fabozzi seemed unwilling to speak without his paymaster. After a good five minutes of uncomfortable silence, the Englishman arrived, puffing and panting, making excuses about the lateness of his launch. Massiter's face, in the sharp artificial light of the café, seemed somewhat older.

"The canal stinks," he declared, having ordered a large espresso and some biscotti. "How anyone lives here year-round, sniffing an open sewer, is quite beyond me."

A party of elderly Americans at the adjoining table rattled their cups and stared. He smiled back at them unctuously.

"Myth!" Scacchi announced. "The stench is entirely modern and artificial. It comes from those blasted factories on terra firma, pumping out their filth day and night. The Grand Canal has not been our *Cloaca Maxima* for many a year and you know it."

Massiter dipped a small biscuit into his coffee. "I once sold a statuette of Cloacina to a Hollywood film producer," he mused. "Quarter of a million bucks. I told him she was the goddess of mountain streams."

Scacchi giggled. "Not sewers?"

"Sometimes in this trade," Massiter mused, "it is prudent to use facts selectively."

"And she was a deity," Scacchi reminded him. "Do you not recall the old Roman prayer?"

He took a deep breath and began to recite in a loud voice which rang around the dainty, gilded room.

> *"Fair Cloacina, goddess of this place,*
> *Look on thy suppliant with a smiling face.*
> *Soft, yet cohesive, let my offering flow,*
> *Not rudely swift nor insolently slow."*

Scacchi drained his coffee and grumbled, "Not that *that* happens much of late." The American party downed their cups and left.

"Oh, dear," Massiter replied. "You must look to your diet, Scacchi."

The old man gave him a sour glance, as if they both knew this was inadequate advice.

Fabozzi, who had been listening to this exchange with open disbelief, reached into his small leather attaché case, took out a sheaf of manuscript, and placed it on the table. "Gentlemen," he said briskly. "If we may talk business? I am now two days into the school, working under new arrangements, and still without a complete score. May someone tell me when I can expect it? And what I should do with it when it arrives?"

They all looked at Daniel. He had soon familiarised himself with the computer which Paul had borrowed, and was steadily turning the scribbled original into a set of separate parts which an orchestra could use. But it was time-consuming, tiring work. He could stand it for no more than four hours at a time each day. By that stage his head was full of notes and soaring themes. It was impossible to go on until time had extinguished some trace of them from his imagination.

"I think you'll have it all by the end of the week, Fabozzi," he said.

"You think?" Massiter asked.

"No. I can guarantee it. But no earlier."

The conductor scowled. "This is an extraordinary business, if I may say so, Massiter. I am employed to run a summer school with the usual curriculum. Then, just as I begin, you change your mind and set me racing after something I've never before seen and which does not even seem complete!"

"Of course it's complete," Massiter said, and patted Daniel gently on the arm. "It's just that most of it's in the head of our genius here. You're getting your parts as they come, Fabozzi. They're good enough, I think?"

"So far they're wonderful! But how can I judge what I have not seen? And why do you not simply send your original manuscript to the copyists to save us all time?"

Scacchi and Massiter exchanged glances. "A reasonable question," the former acknowledged. "Yet, as I understand it, you have an entire movement now for each instrument, and a little of the second. You're surely not worried about the rest? Daniel wishes to produce the individual parts himself. That is his prerogative. Why should he have to put his own precious work out to some jobbing copyists and then have to check every last detail later to see it is correct?"

The conductor grimaced. Daniel was grateful for Scacchi's ingenious explanation. He would have been hard-pressed to lie so convincingly to Fabozzi himself.

"It is difficult for me to discuss these matters," Fabozzi said. "I have here the composer, sitting, watching me from the stalls."

"Could be worse," Massiter observed. "He might be playing."

Daniel had refused this option entirely. He was too busy with the score. Furthermore, he had now worked his way well into the concerto and found even the more modest parts quite beyond him.

"And look at him!" Fabozzi objected. "He says nothing. How do I know if I am doing the right thing or not?"

Daniel took a deep breath. "Fabozzi," he said, "I have listened to what you have done so far and found it so marvellous there is nothing for me to say. All this is as much a surprise for me as it is for you. I came here thinking I was cataloguing a library. Instead, by chance, Mr. Massiter hears a little of my amateur scribblings and decides to introduce them to the school. Perhaps I should have refused. . . . Even now it is not too late."

Fabozzi's face went white. "No! No! I don't suggest this for a moment."

Any plaudits that the concerto attracted would not, Daniel knew, be for him alone. Fabozzi, for all his protests, was well-placed to benefit from the piece.

Massiter shook his head. "I confess I'm bemused by your reaction, old chap. Here you have a new work of no small significance and you'll be the first in the world to conduct it. Is the composer some prima donna screaming at you from the stalls? Does he follow each note, each phrasing, and tear your interpretation of it to shreds? No! He listens patiently and then applauds. What, may I ask, is your beef? Do you want young Daniel here to play the part to which he is, in my view, quite entitled?"

"No! No!" Fabozzi protested. Daniel felt sorry for the little man. It was not an easy situation. "I merely wish for some guidance as to the purpose and the direction of the work."

Daniel smiled pleasantly. "Then let me say this, Fabozzi. I view it as an attempt to imagine the kind of music that might have been heard in La Pietà in, say, the 1730s, if Vivaldi had a son or some star pupil. You can, I hope, hear a little of him in there, and some Corelli too. But there's a sense of change. A move from the baroque towards the classical. If I imagine in my head..."

He paused. He had prepared a small description of the piece in advance, knowing he would face this question at some point. But now, after hours of transcribing further parts of the concerto and hearing the notes run through his head, he was able to extemporise further. "...I rather see someone witnessing the close of one era and the beginning of another. This was, you will recall, the time at which the Republic began its decline. So perhaps I imagine myself as a young scholar working in the company of Vivaldi, learning his lessons, looking at the imminent decay around me, and then inserting a few comments of my own. So you'll find love and admiration in there, and on occasion the anger, the impatience of youth too."

Scacchi and Massiter wore near identical expressions of admiration.

"There," Massiter said. "You can't ask better than that, surely?"

"No," Fabozzi replied honestly. "It's a little to go on. I'm pleased to be associated with your music, you know, Daniel. It's just that I find this method of working somewhat unusual."

"I'm not a great talker," Daniel replied with just as much

conviction. "That doesn't mean I disapprove of what you're doing. The very opposite, in fact. You make it sound better than I could ever have imagined."

The conductor beamed.

"So run along, dear chap," Massiter urged. "The meter's running and I'm picking up the bill. You've plenty to work on, and I'd like that final concert to be a sellout."

"*Sì*," Fabozzi replied. It was not much to go on, but more than he seemed to expect. He rose from the table, edged his way through the tourists in the café, and was gone, out into the piazza, heading back to the waterfront for the short walk to La Pietà.

Massiter beamed at Daniel. "I say. You're rather good at this. Remember all that stuff when the press start to turn up. I'm pulling a few strings already. Good story for a slow news season. I rather thought we might label you the new Vivaldi. The *New York Times* will want a word before long. And *The Times* of London, and *Corriere della Sera* too. But not until next week. No point in jumping the gun before anyone can buy tickets now, is there?"

Daniel felt queasy at the prospect. "Surely they wouldn't be interested?"

"If we wind them up enough, they will," Massiter replied. "A touch of hype, a little exaggeration. Some free flights and a night or two in the right hotel. They thrive on it. Just say what you just said, but at greater length and rather less directly, if you please. Plain speaking will get you nowhere with the arts press. They'll think you're a philistine."

"I agree. You do this well," Scacchi added. "You sounded so plausible."

Daniel gave the old man a sharp look. "I *was* plausible." The work had grown inside him as he transferred it from the ancient pages to the screen of the computer, note by note. Parts of it refused to leave his mind. "What I just said is what I believe to be true. I think that's where it came from. It must be. Yet… there's something else there too. Some foreignness, perhaps. I can't quite put my finger on it."

"You will!" Massiter insisted. "You will!"

"And I don't recall offering to make a public spectacle of myself by talking to the press, either. I want a quiet life when this is over."

Massiter's face became suddenly stern. "It was implicit in our arrangement, Daniel. I made it quite clear that for all our sakes, we must try to milk this thing for all we can. I'll be out of pocket for years in any case, probably forever."

Daniel was abruptly full of distaste for Hugo Massiter, with his odd clothes and his presumptuous attitude. "This 'thing,' as you describe it, is a work of art," he said. "Not some commodity to be bought and sold like a trinket on the Rialto."

Massiter stared at him in silence for the best part of a minute with an expression which was, Daniel believed, designed to inspire some terror. Then he turned to the old man. "You're enjoying your money, I imagine, Scacchi?"

"One always enjoys money, Massiter," the old man said carefully.

"Then have words with your boy." Massiter's grey eyes swept over them both. "There's a balance still outstanding. I'll have what I pay for. I always do."

24

Rousseau's amour

Manzini no longer replies to my letters. I think, dear sister, we must expect the worst. Either the rascal has departed with whatever money there was in our parents' estate or—and I suspect this is more likely—he has discovered there was none there to begin with and saves himself the time of writing to those who will never pay his bills. I hope this news does not come as such a great shock. I expected it for some time and have tried to prepare you for it. We must make our own way in this world. Our parents' only bequest is their character and their learning, both better than any amount of gold that might be squeezed out of the codicil of a will. I hope, too, that you find more suitable food than the rich Spanish stuff you write about. We were raised on plain Veneto fare—polenta and meat—not rich spices and strange vegetables that belong in a Moroccan market. It scarcely surprises me you find yourself queasy from time to time if you insist on eating nothing but that muck.

Now, a tale to lift your spirits! Gobbo has wreaked his vengeance upon Rousseau, and I am ashamed to confess I may give you an eyewitness account. First, however, a warning. There be country matters in this story, the sort we used to hear from that wicked old swineherd Pietro when he thought Pa wasn't listening. If you wish to keep your heart and mind unsullied by some mild filth, I advise you to read no further.

Ah! I do sense, little pen, that our reader has not deserted us! Jolly good . . .

After our journey to Torcello, Delapole's party acquired a taste for music—largely, of course, because Delapole himself announced that it was this particular muse which would henceforth claim his attentions. Leo, to my surprise, was not much put out by this. The House of Scacchi is as capable of printing a bawdy ballad or an entire opera as it may turn out copies of Shakespeare or dissertations on the origins of the rhinoceros. Having detected that Delapole would probably never get down to penning his masterpiece—the rich have much time on their hands but little inclination to intrude upon it with work—Leo now supposes, I imagine, that he can be talked into paying for the publication of some unknown opus in order to bask in the glory when its greatness is realised.

To this end I have played a small game. Last night I pretended that I found Rebecca's score wrapped in paper, like an abandoned baby, on the doorstep of Ca' Scacchi. Accompanying it was an anonymous note claiming to be from a budding composer, currently trapped in another profession, who wondered whether the House of Scacchi might deem his work worthy of a wider audience. If Leo felt this way, the note adds, he should organise the copying of the parts at his own expense (a come-on, of course, to get him to approach Delapole for funds) and organise a public performance. Should the citizens of Venice agree that the work has some merit when they hear it, the composer promises to reveal himself and appeal to their generosity for the future of his career, reimbursing his sponsor twice over for his support and placing with him the rights for all future publication of the piece.

Leo read the note, issued a rude curse about scroungers, and threw the entire package into a dark corner. I shall, of course, retrieve it and meekly play a few notes to see if it whets his appetite. I have heard a little from the strings of its creator; it is wonderful, of course.

Gobbo returned from Cremona with an instrument under his arm. It's an ugly thing, to be sure. Big and muscular, the kind of instrument you expect to see beneath the chin of a farmhand, not the loveliest lady in all Venice. On both sides of the belly it has a sap mark which runs as a singular stain parallel to the fingerboard. This is, Gobbo assures us, a "feature" much sought after in Guarneri's instruments.

Its initiation was at an early-evening concert at La Pietà. Rebecca is sufficiently confident now to attend these events in daylight on her own. On this occasion she managed to make her way into and out of the church without any of us seeing her. Her presence was unmistakable, however. In Vivaldi's mundane programme—I do wish he'd stick to the old stuff instead of forcing these new mediocrities down our throats—the tone of her new instrument rang out like a shining clarion. Whether Delapole noticed or not, I have no idea. Gobbo had informed us all of his plans; the Englishman's mind was no doubt on other things.

Gobbo knew I had been up to something with Rebecca and La Pietà. He's a sly one, though he could not have suspected the scale of our tricks. In any case, he pumped me mercilessly for details about the church, its layout, and what happens before, during, and after concerts. When I had carefully told him what I could, he went into action.

At the end of the concert, after both conductor and musicians had departed, we trooped towards the door. Delapole then took Rousseau to one side, led him into a dark corner, and told him the good news.

"Sir," he says (I imagine this, but it must have been along these lines). "I have received a message and a token for you from one who would renew an acquaintance."

"Mr. Delapole," Rousseau pipes nervously. "I do not know what you are talking about."

"The ladies who played for us on our most pleasant excursion to Torcello. One of them has communicated to me that she thought your face, your form, your learning, all much to her taste, and would be honoured if you might wait here for her arrival. She finds, I gather, the notion of your presence beyond the cruel screen which keeps her out of view most . . . stimulating."

The Frenchman pants. His eyes roll upwards to the dusty ceiling. "Can this be true? Which one?"

"I do not know," says Delapole with a shrug. "No name came with the letter. Only this . . ."

At which point he reaches into his pocket and extracts a single silk garter perfumed with some exquisite Oriental fragrance. Rousseau almost faints upon the spot.

"Come, come, sir," Delapole says with a pat on the shoulder. "You recognise a lady in the very heat of passion. Nothing new for you Parisians, of course."

"Well, yes," Rousseau stutters. "Of course, of course."

"More rumpy-pumpy in a week than most of us achieve in a lifetime, I'll warrant. I wonder you do not populate the entire world with the offspring of your munificent seed."

"Oh!" I think at this point the full import of Delapole's words finally dawned upon Rousseau. This was to be no pretty little flirtation over the coffee table.

"You mean *here*?" Rousseau exclaims. "In the church?"

"Good a place as any. An act of love is an act of God, is it not? And if God sees everything, he'll spot you at it whether it's on his doorstep or in a bawdy house. Besides, in my limited experience of the female—you may, of course, wish to correct me on this—I do find the use of an unusual location may provoke in them extremities of desire which are simply not attained under familiar sheets. I may be wrong, of course...."

"Oh, no," Rousseau assures him. "Spot on, dear chap."

"In that case you are the luckiest man alive, surely. For if this lady is so taken of your person in the public hubbub of a lagoon skiff, why—she'll positively rip the clothes off you in God's house, just a few yards away from the hordes of promenaders out for their evening strolls."

If you may imagine a dormouse squeaking as a naughty child tweaks its tail, you will hear the very sound M. Rousseau emits at this moment.

"Good luck," says Delapole, and pumps his hand in a comradely fashion.

"You are leaving?"

Delapole laughs. "What kind of chap do you take me for? I believe I hear a noise from behind that rood screen over there."

Briskly he walks to the door of the church—in darkness now, thanks to the mean windows set in the roof—slams the ancient wood loudly, then tiptoes to join the rest of us, who have hidden in the shadow beneath the great pulpit that juts out into the nave like a ship's prow.

We try very hard not to giggle. Rousseau stands in the faint circle cast by the light from the dingy rose window, trembling with each sound that comes from behind the screen.

"Mon-*sewer*!" cries a gentle falsetto voice, and I stuff my fist in my mouth to kill the titters. A shape is emerging from the darkness. It is dressed in what appears to be shiny, cheap silk, just about discernible as blue. A veil covers its head. I can recognise Gobbo's disguised form immediately. But the lad is slim enough from the front; with his face and nascent hump hidden, he might have been one of the plainer players from the boat if you didn't share the secret.

"Mademoiselle," twitters Rousseau. "I have only just learned of your message to me. I do not know what to say."

The figure in the silk dress takes one step forward, extends an arm (covered by a silk sleeve, thank God, since Gobbo is a hairy chap), and gestured to Rousseau, indicating that he should approach. "What makes you think I invited you here to say anything, sir? Words are fine, but deeds are better. I had heard that when I plucked my little strings, you found yourself transported to some sweet place of fond imaginings. Perhaps I was misinformed. Perhaps you do not find me attractive?"

He took three strides to face her. "Oh, no. Your talent, your presence, they conspire to make me burst with near ecstasy."

At this point I believe my fist was somewhere deep within my rib cage, and the others weren't doing much better, either. Even Uncle Leo's eyes were filled with tears, and there was such a jogging of elbows, snorting, hiccoughs, and general mayhem I wonder Rousseau didn't rumble us in an instant. Still, his mind was on other matters.

" 'Near' ecstasy, did you say, sir? I would that it were complete before we're done. I've heard you French have tricks that could make us Venetian girls think we are in Heaven itself. Not the 'leap on, leap off, ducat by the pillow' stuff you get from the locals."

His head lolled from side to side and a breathy sigh issued from his throat. Then he said, "I would adore nothing more than to see your face, my sweetness. The thought of the loveliness that veil must conceal tears my heart apart."

"Sir!" hissed Gobbo. "You have your customs. We have ours. In Venice it is unknown for a girl to offer herself thus to a man and reveal her identity before the union is complete. What if we find our coupling is not to our tastes? This way we may make a mistake and leave it behind after."

"I understand." Rousseau nodded.

"Then come here and pay me honour."

We held our breath as the two of them approached each other, Gobbo thoughtfully standing in a shaft of light that gave us an excellent view of proceedings while maintaining his head in shadow.

Rousseau knelt upon the floor. "What would you have me do, lady?" he asked.

"Why, kiss me, sir. What else?"

He rose, lips puckered like a clown, and tried to throw his arms around his silk-clad darling.

"*Mon-sewer!*" Gobbo screeched. "Where are your manners? In Venice a man may never kiss a lady upon the lips until their union has been sealed by the physical pact. Are these your Parisian games? If so, I find them pretty disgusting, to be frank. Perhaps I have judged you wrong here."

"No, no, no. I am merely unused to your customs, lady. What would you have me do?"

Gobbo drew himself up with a harrumph. "What any fine Venetian gentleman would under the circumstances. Make your way beneath my skirts and find that place where the two of us shall shortly be enjoined. Then plant your lips upon it as a token of your devotion."

Rousseau looked hesitant. "This is the way things happen in Venice?"

"In all the world save France, if I'm not mistaken. I'll quench your bestial Gallic hungers once we have the etiquette out of the way, sir, but first things first. It's only proper."

"Very well," the Frenchman mewled, and got down on his knees. Then, gingerly, he dug his head beneath the hem of Gobbo's dress.

What occurred next remains something of a blur. There was so much incident crammed into so little time, and, for the life of me, I cannot recall who screamed first: Rousseau, when his head made its way north beneath the cover of Gobbo's dress, seeking joy and finding horror; those of us in the party, who could stand this jest no more and needed to screech like lunatics before our lungs exploded with the strain; or Father Antonio Vivaldi, who at that moment chose to return to La Pietà, perhaps in search of a sheet of music he had left behind, and found instead a ribald commedia dell'arte taking place before him.

Gobbo, with his talent for improvisation, was on top of things in an instant. He moved forward into the light, holding Rousseau's head tightly beneath his dress all the time, and let Vivaldi screech his fury and outrage till his voice began to run hoarse.

"Get out, you scum!" cried Vivaldi, then crossed himself and panted like a fawn at the end of a hunt. "Leave this church at once, or I'll fetch the beadles and have you all horsewhipped!"

Gobbo scooped up his frock, revealing Rousseau cowering beneath its folds with his face next to what I may only describe as an upright physical organ not normally to be viewed in public on hallowed ground.

"But, Papa! *PAPA!*" roared Gobbo, his voice now back to its full, coarse tenor tone and oozing hurt reproach. "Have *pity*! The froggy has yet to play upon my little piccolo!"

Well, the rest is confusion and chaos. We took to our heels and fled, Rousseau east towards the Arsenale, while the rest of us ducked and dived through the back alleys of Castello, crippled with laughter, short of breath, and tortured, in my case, by a well-deserved stitch. I believe it says much of Venice that a twenty-year-old male servant of unsurpassable ugliness was able to dash through its backstreets wearing a blue silk dress and cackling like a madman, yet none gave him so much as a second glance.

The following day we heard that Rousseau had packed his bags and scuttled back to Paris, promising revenge upon Venice, which he now regards as the very anteroom of Hell. Oh, well. I tried very hard to like the chap, but he did make it rather difficult.

Since Leo was in a good mood when we returned to the house, I went down to the cellar, undid the string on Rebecca's parcel, and played him, as well as I could, some of the work. Even with my amateurish hammerings, the power of the music is astonishing. It has all the power and fluency of Vivaldi and makes much use of his *ritornello* idea, employing the same theme, but with endless variations, as bookmarks between passages, some slow, some at the pace of the Devil himself.

Leo, ever the canny one, is of the same opinion. I believe his mind is working, which is, I trust, all to the good.

25

Rizzo's prize

RIZZO STOOD IN MESTRE STATION, WATCHING THE GREY steel luggage lockers, wondering if the prize was worth the risk. The item behind the grey metal door seemed to mock him. He was coming to hate that plain, dusty box and the hunk of wood it contained. Everything else had been of marginal worth, maybe a few hundred dollars. This strangely alluring object, which he had prised from the dead arms of Susanna Gianni, was of a different class. Its value was perhaps even higher than the sum which Scacchi now appeared willing to pay. He could, he knew, take the plane to Rome and try to find a better price, but Rizzo was aware of his own limitations. The only people he knew in Rome were accustomed to dealing in dope and tobacco and sundry containers ripped off from the transport trade. The violin would mean nothing to them. He could spend months trying to find the right outlet, months in which Massiter might finally work out what had happened that day on San Michele. Prudence demanded he cut a deal swiftly with Scacchi and realise what would be, for him, the single greatest prize of his life.

There, too, the instrument taunted him. Rizzo had believed, always, that his chosen trade had a goal, an endpoint. The day would come when he had enough money to open some small bar restaurant near the university, in Santa Margherita. There he could steal legally, from the tourists and the students alike. He could be his own boss. He could mess with the women who came through the doors and waited on the tables. This dream lay constantly at the back of his head, warm and comforting and, until he had snatched the dusty fiddle case from Susanna Gianni's coffin, entirely unrealisable. Ordinary thieving would never pay for it. Scacchi's $80,000 could open two bars, maybe more. Rizzo's days as a crook could be over. Yet, now it seemed close, the idea gave him no cheer whatsoever. He was, and would remain, a murderer and a thief, because that was his nature. The loathsome violin seemed to remind him of the fact. The thing was like some poisoned apple. He felt as if he could die from a single bite.

Rizzo thought of the policewoman. He would have killed her, given the opportunity, and not regretted the act, even though that would, he knew, have set every cop in the city on his back. Now she was probing, searching, asking. He had heard she was working the streets, asking questions about something that had gone missing from a casket on San Michele. Maybe she would get close. Maybe he really would have to kill her. But not if the crazy instrument that started it all was gone from his life.

The station was near empty. It would be easy to take the case, catch the bus to the airport, walk out into the marshes, and dump it there. Massiter would never know. The steady round of work—of thieving and odd errands for the Englishman when he was in town—would always put bread on the table. Then Rizzo thought of the way Massiter had tried, so coolly, so stealthily, to intimidate him in the big apartment overlooking the canal. The one with the weird paintings and floor-length mirrors that might, or might not, have held Fellini's corpse. He thought of

Massiter's cold hand on his mouth and felt the flicker of a rising flame of anger.

"*Bastardo*," Rizzo said softly to himself. He looked at his watch. There was just time to meet Scacchi's man at the appointed place. Not that he planned to walk through Venice carrying a violin case, announcing his perfidy to all. Rizzo marched over to a luggage store and bought a cheap holdall. Then he opened the luggage locker, took out the dusty case, and placed it neatly inside the nylon bag. The smell had gone. It just looked like old junk. But it felt heavy underneath his arm. He imagined the entire world was staring at him, screaming, "*Murderer! Thief! Murderer!*" as he carried it.

He caught the bus back to Piazzale Roma. The ancient Guarneri sat on his knees, deep inside the bag. He stared at the flat grey surface of the water as the bus sped along the narrow finger of artificial land that joined Venice to terra firma.

Rizzo wanted rid of the thing as soon as possible, this very day if Scacchi's man was willing. Not once in his life had he expressed an interest in music or attended a concert. Yet now, watching the tankers and liners manoeuvre towards the port like overweight dancers trying to negotiate a ballroom floor, he couldn't stop wondering what the damned thing sounded like.

26

A fracas in the church

The deception is simple. We become more bold. The guards are so stupid or lazy or both that we have now managed to create an entirely new doctor of the ghetto! Jacopo no longer need lurk inside his room while we flit about the Venetian night. I merely informed the buffoon upon the bridge that I required the services of Dr. Roberto Levi for a nobleman who was sick. The buffoon waved me through without a second thought, Rebecca donned a spare coat, and we bustled out upon our business without a second glance. This is an excellent disguise, for even if the soldiers had their suspicions, who would intervene to stop a physician on his way to tend upon a man of influence? Each Venetian looks to his own first and the state second. We have gulled them completely, and my only concern is that we become so blasé about the deed that one evening Rebecca will throw off her hood, declaring it to be too hot, shake out those lovely tresses, and make open villains of us all.

Last night, after the concert, with Rebecca still every inch the good Gentile, we decided to explore a little before going home. It was a glorious evening, warm but not airless, with a

full moon reflected in the sleek black surface of the Basin as
our gondola paddled past St. Mark's on to the Grand Canal.

She insisted we stop near Ca' Dario, curious about the
place which we had been forced to leave so hurriedly on the
day of the trip to Torcello. We paid off the gondolier at the
Salute jetty and walked the back alleys until we stood in the
small *campo* behind the house. I kept my fingers crossed that
Gobbo would not catch us together, forcing some awkward
questions, but luck was on our side. Together, beneath the
bright light of the moon, we counted the curious chimneys
on the place, eight of them, all funnel-shaped, as is popular
in some of the older palaces. There is a rectangular walled
garden at the rear. To the front, which may only be seen
to much advantage from the canal, the house is most
extraordinary, a narrow, crooked mansion on four floors.
The ground is for storage and transport, naturally. The three
above are almost identical, with four arched windows
running from floor to ceiling on the left, then a single,
circular rose window, and finally another vast glass arch
on the northern end of the building. The entire frontage is
etched and engraved and tattooed after the fashion of an
African sailor, making it shine out among the larger, grander
mansions on either side like a curious jewel found in a case
of lesser stones. It must cost Delapole a fortune, but the
Englishman has, I gather, money to waste. Curiously, no one
seems to have a clue who the true owner is. Dario is long
dead, and some say the place is cursed, since it has been the
scene of two murders at least. As if bricks and mortar might
carry within them the seeds of human destiny . . .

Rebecca's curiosity is intense. I believe she hopes Delapole's
money will help legitimise her musical ambitions in some way.
Leo and the Englishman have cooked up a plan. The concerto

will be performed in La Pietà shortly. Delapole will pay for the publicity, which will attempt to raise some public interest by promoting a fair deal of bunkum about the piece and its mysterious composer. The story goes that the creator is a citizen of a shy and uncertain nature who does not wish to make his (it must be his!) identity known until he is certain the city approves his style. Therefore the work will be played in its entirety, with Vivaldi (for a sum) condescending to direct proceedings. Then the audience will be asked whether the work has merit or merely deserves an early demise in the fireplace. Should they decide the former, the composer undertakes to reveal himself publicly at a later date. In the event of the latter, he will retire to his present trade, never touching the stave again, grateful that the glorious Republic saw fit to pay attention to his amateurish scribblings for even a moment.

It is all nonsense, of course. No one doubts the work will be a sensation; otherwise, why would Vivaldi deign to grace it with his talents? Money goes so far with artists, but it cannot buy their dignity. Rebecca's goal remains the same: to be seen one day as a musician and composer of the stature of Vivaldi or any other city great. Yet, though I do not say as much to her face, I fail to understand how this might be achieved. Even if she manages to reveal herself without disclosing our misdeeds, I wonder if the city will readily accept a woman, and a Jew and foreigner to boot, as an heir to the likes of Vivaldi. Be honest, Lorenzo. I find this hard, too, and I wish it were not so. We grow up with some prejudices buried deep within the blood. Rebecca's vision for herself goes against everything we have been told about the way the lives of men and women are conducted in our society. Still, it will all come out in the wash, as Mother used to say.

We gawped at Delapole's palace for a good thirty minutes, then wandered past San Cassian, where I showed Rebecca my home, from the outside, naturally. Later, we wound up at Giacomo dell'Orio, a squat lump of church that sits in its own square a little way back from the canal. The pair of us wander the night so freely these days that we walked inside the place without a second thought and found ourselves in the company of an ancient warden who was only too anxious to reveal its wonders. There is a fascinating roof, designed to look like a ship's keel, and a selection of columns purloined from Byzantium, I imagine: one with a very ancient flowered capital, and another in smooth antique marble. These Venetians will steal anything, I swear.

The paintings include some passable martyrdoms and one piece, brand-new, being put in place by the creator, which was so ludicrously done we stood in front of it lost for words. The "artist" (I feel this is stretching things somewhat) noticed our interest and asked me what I thought. It appeared to depict the dead Virgin being taken to her grave, with some kind of commotion in the forefront.

"The reference escapes me, sir," I confessed. "Perhaps you could enlighten us."

He was a coarse fellow, with a hunched posture, a pockmarked face, and a somewhat lunatic expression. I couldn't begin to imagine whose palm had been crossed in order to get his work a hanging in a public place. "Why, it is the defilement of the Virgin by the Jew, and how his sin is punished by God on the spot. You see!"

True, next to the deathly pale and rigid corpse of the Virgin was the form of a poor fellow whose hands had been lopped off by some miraculous divine intervention. A very private divine intervention, it appears, since the rest of the funeral party scarcely notice him, and get on with their job of carrying the unfortunate cadaver to its resting place.

"I don't recall this event from the scriptures, sir," Rebecca said sweetly.

"The Bible alone is not a route to God," the madman said very gravely. "Some of us read more widely than others."

"Some imagine more widely than others too," I ventured. "But I fail to understand. Why is this man defiling her? To what purpose?"

"Because he is a Jew, of course."

Rebecca asked, "For no other reason?"

"What other reason would a Jew need?"

"Some surely, sir," I replied. "For wasn't Mary a Jew? And Christ half-Hebrew himself?"

Even in the half dark of the church, I could see some blood suffuse his pockmarks.

"Why," I continued in the face of his growing fury, "would one Jew do this to another? Unless... unless... he does not see this dead white figure as a human corpse at all but believes it to be some child's model in wax or fat, and seeks to steal a little for his lamp. But then why would God strike him down? I am most puzzled."

"Blasphemy!" the madman roared, and I could see the ancient warden at the far end of the nave cast a worried look in our direction.

Rebecca tugged on my arm, but I could not let this point go. "Not at all, sir. If you scrawl a child's doodle on a wall and call it the Virgin, I commit no blasphemy in pointing out it is a child's doodle. The comment is directed at your skill, or lack of it. Not the Virgin herself."

"*Blasphemy!*"

The warden was heading for the side door. Rebecca was

hissing at me under her breath. I know when it's time to leave.

We fled into the night. Just in time too. The soldiers were racing for the church as we turned the corner and disappeared back into the safety of San Cassian, where I might find a gondola and return Rebecca, briefly transformed back into Roberto, into the ghetto.

When we were on that last, familiar walk towards the bridge, she turned to me and said, "You'll be the death of us, Lorenzo. I swear."

"Nonsense," I replied. "The man was a charlatan. Bad art is bad art, and sticking the Virgin in there to stop someone pointing it out is just plain dishonest."

"So when I write a bad concerto, you will boo along with the rest of them?"

"Louder than the rest, in fact, since I, more than most, know how much better you can do."

That snort again. We approached the bridge, she pulled up her hood, and I started to concoct a story once more, not that the guard, who was half-drunk, seemed much bothered.

I saw her to the door. Jacopo opened it and caught the mirth on both our faces.

"Villains, both of you," he said. "They'll be displaying your heads on the waterfront before the year is out."

Rebecca kissed him once on the cheek. "Falling at my feet in gratitude, more like, dear brother, when they realise the Serenissima has another master in its midst."

"Of course." I caught Jacopo's eye. There was something he wanted to say to his sister, but he didn't have the heart. We both knew what it was.

27

An acquisition

THE SELLER HAD SUGGESTED AN EMPTY WAREHOUSE IN the vast derelict shipyard of the Arsenale. Daniel listened patiently to Scacchi's careful instructions, knowing all along that he would extemporise if the occasion demanded. It was, after all, just such a talent for improvisation that had won them the prize of Massiter's money in the first place. Scacchi's caution, Daniel thought, was understandable in one so old. He did not, however, feel bound by it.

"Make sure the fiddle is the true one," Scacchi insisted. "I've told you of the identifying marks. Look at the label too."

"I know," Daniel replied a little impatiently, which won him a reproving look from the old man.

"This fellow's a crook, Daniel. Don't play games with him."

"And he wants the money. We have nothing to fear."

"You never read the newspapers, do you?"

Daniel was baffled. "Why?"

"It doesn't matter," Scacchi said, scowling. "All I ask is this: take care. Now the moment's here, I wish I could do this myself."

Massiter's sum had arrived as promised. It was in cash, large-denomination dollar bills, now hidden safely somewhere in the second-floor bedroom Scacchi shared with Paul. Scacchi was still $10,000 short of the money he owed but believed that with some begging, a short-term loan, and the sale of a few objects, he could raise the balance within a matter of days. The seller was, he advised Daniel, to phone on Friday and, if all sides were agreeable, conclude the arrangement the following day. If everything went to plan, the excursion to Sant' Erasmo would now be a celebration for them all. Provided the violin was the Guarneri Scacchi expected, it was difficult to see what might go wrong.

"I promised to do this for you, Scacchi," Daniel insisted.

"And you're a man of your word, I know. But this fellow isn't. He's a crook out of choice. Not, like us, out of necessity. You should always fear that kind of man, Daniel. I'm not the only Lucifer at loose in this town."

Daniel laughed. The old man seemed to find it a strain to raise a smile.

When Daniel went outside, the afternoon was hot, the *vaporetto* packed with tourists and tetchy locals. Venice could be a crotchety place during the humid, scorching days of summer. There seemed no escape from the power of the sun and the seeping dampness that rose from the lagoon.

As he waited for the *vaporetto*, he was dismayed to discover, seated in the shelter, the policewoman, Giulia Morelli, reading a book. He said nothing and stared at the water. Inevitably, her head lifted and a smile of recognition came his way.

"Daniel," she said, rising to greet him. "How nice to see you again."

"I didn't realise you came here so often."

She shrugged and placed the book in her bag. "The police get everywhere. It's one of our unfortunate habits. Congratulations, by the way."

Daniel blinked, not comprehending, and unable to shake the image of the stolen violin from his head.

"For the concert Mr. Massiter is planning," she said by way of explanation.

"Of course. It's a great honour."

"And so unexpected. I had no idea you were a composer. Scacchi said nothing of the fact when we met."

"It's a small thing, or so I thought."

"Not for Signor Massiter. He sees value in you. How flattered you must be."

Daniel squirmed on the jetty and was relieved to see a boat heave slowly into view. "Yes," he muttered.

Giulia Morelli glanced at her watch. "Has Scacchi bought anything recently? To your knowledge. I should like to know."

"I'm sorry?"

"An item. An antique. It is what he does, isn't it?"

He was aware of the sweat on his brow. "I believe he is retired."

Giulia Morelli laughed. "A man like Scacchi never retires, Daniel. Surely you must know that?"

The *vaporetto* rolled in towards the jetty. He watched a slim girl in the blue ACTV uniform grip the handrail, ready to release it for passengers.

"Where are you going?" he asked.

"Some weeks ago an item was stolen from a coffin," Giulia Morelli said. "The man who saw it stolen was murdered. When I chanced upon the act, I was nearly killed too. So I have something personal here. An axe to grind, as you English say."

"What has this to do with Scacchi? Or me?"

"Perhaps nothing. I don't know."

He watched the stream of bodies leave the boat and dreaded the thought that the policewoman would follow him on board and continue this interrogation all the way to San Marco, where he would, he knew, have to abandon every plan that had been made in order to humour her.

"Please," he said. "Don't think me rude. I have to go to La Pietà. I must discuss some complex business to do with the concert. And I haven't a clue what you're talking about."

Giulia Morelli said nothing. It was time to board the boat.

"Are you joining me?"

"Me?" she replied, amused. "I have no reason to catch the boat, Daniel. I merely saw you leave the house, daydreaming, and walked ahead here in order to talk with you. I've no desire to go anywhere."

"Then what do you want?"

"The truth, naturally. And to warn you. Whatever you think, this is not some game. A man has died. The reason for it, I still fail to understand, but I know this."

He started to walk along the gangplank. Her thin arm held him back with a surprising strength.

"It's dangerous to be innocent, Daniel. Remember as much. Please."

He shook himself free from her grip and marched on the boat, not looking back. Sure enough, Giulia Morelli did not follow him. The plans he had made, which now ran madly around his head, could still hold. He had time to visit La Pietà on the way. The invitation had yet to be delivered to Amy. He was also, though he was reluctant to admit as much, beginning to feel a small degree of proprietorial care towards the work which now, as far as most of the world knew, bore his name.

They had just finished rehearsing one of the slow passages from the opening of the second movement when he entered the church. All heads turned, and he was alarmed to hear a light ripple of applause come from the floor.

"Daniel! Daniel!" Fabozzi yelled from the rostrum. "A word! A word!"

The little man, still dressed all in black, this time with high Chelsea boots on his feet, dashed from the podium to greet him. He seemed elated.

"We're getting the hang of it, dear chap!" Fabozzi cried. "We start to see your meaning!"

"Good," Daniel replied with as much conviction as he could muster. "I listened a little from the door," he lied. "It sounds wonderful."

"*You* sound wonderful!" He had never seen the conductor look so pleased with himself and his players. For a moment Daniel regretted declining the opportunity to join the orchestra. From the look on their eager young faces, Fabozzi was good at his job. "Oh, please, Daniel. Spend some time with us."

"I will. I will. But not until I've given you a complete score, Fabozzi. Which will, at the present rate, be by this weekend. Next week, I promise."

"And we'll hold you to it. Eh, Amy?"

She had walked out of the mass of musicians to join them. Amy Hartston wore a pale-blue silk shirt and jeans. Her blonde hair was tucked back behind her head for playing. Her face was bright and full of life.

"Of course we will. You do want to hear us, don't you, Daniel? I sometimes think you'd like to run away from this masterpiece of yours."

"I'll sit here all day and watch you play," he insisted. "Provided you don't complain when you run out of notes."

"Ah," she laughed. "You have us there!"

Fabozzi looked uncomfortable, seeming to recognise something pass between them. "Excuse me," he said. "I need to look at that passage more closely before we resume. *Ciao!*"

When the conductor was gone, Daniel found himself standing in front of Amy, awkwardly trying to raise the subject of the boat trip. "I was," he said, "wondering..."

"Yes?"

"There is, um... an outing. Some friends of mine. On a boat. This Sunday. Out to one of the islands. Not a very interesting one, I think. You probably wouldn't want to go."

"OK."

"They're not like Massiter. The boat certainly isn't like Massiter's. Local people. I doubt you'd find it amusing."

"I said OK."

He felt sure he was blushing. "Um. Fine, then."

"When? And where?"

"You mean you do want to go?"

She folded her arms and peered at him. "You *are* asking me out, aren't you, Daniel?"

"Y-yes!"

"Then I'd love to come. Now, when? And where?"

His cheeks felt as if they were on fire. "I'll find that out. I'll come back tomorrow and tell you."

"That would be useful. Here." She pulled a notepad out of her back pocket, scribbled a number on a page, then tore it off and handed it to him. "Alternatively, you could always phone. These friends of yours. They do let you use a phone, I guess?"

"Of course!"

Amy Hartston smiled. "Well!" Her self-confidence in these situations was, Daniel thought, unshakable and clearly the result of greater experience. "Here's to Sunday, then. Now, either sit down and listen or run along, Daniel. These notes of yours are on occasion such pigs to play I sometimes think you're Paganini's ghost. For both our sakes, I would like them to sound as convincing as possible."

With that she turned and walked back to the orchestra, who were now busily tuning for the resumption of the rehearsal, flicking the pages of the scores, mumbling, staring intently at the pages. For a moment, Daniel Forster felt a sickening twinge of guilt. The admiration which these people felt for him was entirely undeserved. Yet, he told himself, without his diligent searching and his dealing with Massiter, they would never be a part of the marvel taking shape on the floor of La Pietà. They owed him a debt, even if it was not the one they assumed.

They were so swiftly engrossed in the music that no one saw him leave. Outside, Daniel walked east along the Riva degli Schiavoni. The Campari sign that marked the Lido *vaporetto* stop shimmered in the heat haze across the water. Somewhere beyond the jetty, on the opposite side of the narrow spit of land, hordes of holidaymakers would be lying on the beach, staring at the flat blue Adriatic. The lagoon seemed to contain an entire universe within its borders, most of it, from his point of view, unexplored.

By the time he had reached San Biagio, where his directions told him to leave the waterfront, the only other figures on the street were clearly local: women carrying shopping, men sitting on benches, watching the boats go by, smoking.

He turned left, along the Canale dell' Arsenale. The alley lay after a small bridge. He walked down the cobbled lane and found himself staring at the vast, empty quarters of the Arsenale. The empty warehouse was down a narrow passage which stank of cats. He pushed open the half-shattered door and walked in. There was the smell of strong cigarette smoke and the aroma of aftershave.

Daniel stood patiently in the light of the doorway and, after a suitable interval, called, "Hello?"

A figure came out of the shadow, shared the sun with him, then offered a cigarette. They were about the same size, Daniel guessed, both tall and far from muscular, though the man was older. He had a sallow face, lightly pockmarked, and he wore plastic-framed sunglasses that seemed too big for him.

"No, thank you. I'm Daniel."

The man snorted. "You're giving me a name?"

Daniel ran a hand over his chin, thinking about what Scacchi had said, and about the policewoman too. There was no easy way to recognise a thief, let alone a murderer. "You have the item?"

"That's what you asked for, isn't it? You got the money?"

Daniel shrugged. "I'm just the intermediary. I have to see it's what he wants."

The man threw his dying cigarette into the corner of the warehouse. It spat and sizzled in a damp pool somewhere in the dark. "It's what he wants. Here."

A cheap nylon bag flew through the air. Daniel just managed to catch it. "If this is what you claim, my friend, you should treat it more carefully."

He was back in the dark, lighting another cigarette. "Hey, kid. Don't tell me what to do with my property. If you buy it, you treat it as you like. Till then, shut up."

Daniel said nothing. He opened the nylon bag and took out an ancient fiddle case covered with queer-smelling dust. It was decidedly heavy. He knelt down in the doorway, placed the case on the floor, and opened it. Inside was the most extraordinary violin he had ever seen. It was massive in form, as Scacchi had told him to expect. The sap stains were there, too, running parallel with the fingerboard on both sides of the belly. He held the instrument in the shaft of light and peered through the left f-hole. Inside, black lettering against brown parchment, was the label "*Joseph Guarnerius fecit Cremone, anno 1733,*" then a small cross above the letters *IHS*.

It was, in a conventional sense, ugly, yet it sat in the grip with a lithe, easy grace. This was, he felt, a fiddle to be played, not admired. There was not the slightest doubt in his mind it was genuine.

"Well?" the coarse Venetian voice demanded from the darkness.

"There are many fakes around."

The man snorted. "That's not a fake."

"Are you sure? Do you really know what you have here, my friend?"

The man came out to the door and, briefly, appeared to contemplate snatching the fiddle, only to reject the idea the instant it occurred. Daniel puzzled over this.

"Two questions, Englishman. Do you want it? And if you do, where's the money?"

Daniel had been prepared to dislike this crook, but the depth of his antipathy surprised him. There was something almost insane about the man. The policewoman's warning was perhaps well-meant. Yet it was impossible to escape the conviction that the man was scared, too, anxious to be done with the deal.

"One more test," Daniel told him. Inside the lid of the case there was a bow. He reached down and slipped it out of the holder. The hair was loose and curiously dry. He turned the nut to tighten it, then placed the Guarneri beneath his chin.

The man's eyes flared wildly. "Hey! I didn't say you could play the damned thing."

"It's an instrument. Do you expect that kind of money without me hearing a note?"

The man backed down, sat on a low, dusty bench behind the door. Daniel lifted the bow and played, gingerly, a fragment of a simple Handel sonata.

Long afterwards, when there was time and some much-needed distance from the event, he tried to analyse what had occurred. The primary cause must, he believed, have been the unusual acoustics of the medieval warehouse, with its echoing corners and centuries of damp. The tone of the fiddle was richer and more luxuriant than any he had ever touched. Yet there was something else to the sound it made with those first few notes. The power and strength of its voice rose out of that fat, ugly body like a genie escaping from the bottle. Even with his weak skills, it roared like an angry lion. Played by a true violinist such as Amy, it would surely be astonishing.

He ran through a few bars of the Handel, paused, then brought the bow down hard to crash out a single line from the concerto which now bore his name. A black veil of deep concentration fell upon him. For a second, he imagined himself in a large open room, with strange windows at the front, feeling he was in the presence of the true composer. Yet the mysterious figure was out of sight behind him. He was dazzled by the strange light coming through the glass. Somewhere, past the music, was the sound of screaming. Then his skill and his memory failed him and the queer daydream went with them. The notes died away. He lifted the bow from the strings.

The thief stood in front of him, shaking—with fury, he judged, and with fear also. In his hand, the sharp metal glinting upwards in the sunlight, was a slim blade.

"No more!" the man hissed. "Not another damn thing."

Daniel stared at him briefly, then placed the fiddle back in its home and tucked the bow into its fastening in the lid. He picked up the dusty case and thrust it out in front of him.

"It's a fake," he said confidently. "A very good one, I have to say, and one which may provide the basis for some arrangement between us. But it is a fake nevertheless. Surely you can hear as much?"

The knife slashed through the air a few inches away from his face. "Don't lie to me!"

Daniel waited a moment and then said simply, "You can take it back if you like."

After a while, after every last, faint whisper of the ringing tones of the fiddle had disappeared from the miasmic air of the warehouse, the thief nodded, a small act of obeisance, then wound the knife back on itself and placed the weapon in his pocket.

"Good," Daniel said, and found it hard not to smile. "Shall we talk now?"

28

The saddest loss

I sit in my small room, the third to the right on the third
floor, and stare mournfully out of the window at the square
of San Cassian, listening to the distant whores and drunks
winding their way through the streets. And I can do nothing
but weep and damn creation. There was a brief letter from
Seville this afternoon. My beloved sister, Lucia, is dead. They
speak of some sickness of the stomach. What would the
Spanish know of such things? If she had fallen ill here in
Venice, Jacopo would have set her right with a single
penetrating look and a potion. Now she lies cold in a foreign
grave. I shall never hear her laughter again, nor feel the
warmth of her soft hand.

Why is she dead? Is this God's revenge for the way I have
played hide-and-seek with Rebecca through His houses
these past few weeks? Are these God's rules? Or those of the
men, all wealthy, all worldly, who are His self-appointed
ambassadors in this place? What kind of deity would wreak
His vengeance on two such as us, young, stupid, happy, and
overflowing with the life they would have us believe was His
gift in the first place?

And yet . . . my sister is gone. Some Spanish infection has stolen her precious life. My mind races with possibilities, decisions, actions I might have undertaken which would have meant Lucia would be alive today, smiling as ever, waiting for the world to entertain her. It is all quite futile. Time bears down on us, without mercy, without pause. We have no way of knowing when the jaws of the lion will shut tight around us, and must therefore accept a duty to embrace each hour to the full and let the priests take care of the hereafter. Why should I agonise over whether I have abandoned God? Is it not more relevant to ask whether He has abandoned me, left me alone with my own dark thoughts?

When I was sufficiently composed, I broke the news to Leo. He looked at me queerly. He has had his own losses, I think. Something in his expression seemed to indicate Lucia's death made me his peer, a co-conspirator in some secret whispering about the true nature of our lives. He came over to the table where I was slumped in misery and placed a hand on my back.

"Lorenzo. I am genuinely sorry to hear this." There were no tears in his eyes. Since I gave him Rebecca's music, he has seemed quite preoccupied. "But you must not be surprised."

I felt some mindless, angry heat rise inside me. "Surprised, Uncle? My sister was twenty-one and as strong as an ox when she left here for Spain. Of course I am surprised."

"Yes, boy. Yes, boy." I tire of being addressed as a juvenile. I was about to tell him as much when he said something that quite took my breath away. "But you must know, Lorenzo, it always comes to this. When you love someone, they will leave you, one way or another. Be a solitary man and circumvent the heartache. That's my advice."

There is a point in everyone's upbringing where one

realises that adulthood is not synonymous with wisdom. I think I was a late developer in this field. Leo is a fool, a sour, narrow-minded fool to boot. He inhabits a monochromatic universe where the only warmth and joy are those that come from his own introverted thoughts. He gives nothing and, consequently, receives nothing in return.

And he steals too. I looked at the papers on the table which seemed to interest him much more than my loss. One was the frontispiece to a part for Rebecca's concerto, back from the outside copyists we had been compelled to employ in order to meet Delapole's deadline. In the place where the composer's title would normally have been printed—which I assumed would be left blank in the circumstances—I was astonished to see the name "Leonardo Scacchi."

"Uncle! You cannot do this."

"Of course not," he replied with more than a hint of sarcasm in his voice. "Not immediately, anyhow."

"Not at all! This is not your work."

"No? And who knows that? When someone steps forward and claims title to this, how do we know he's telling the truth? Why this charade in the first place? There's some funny business going on here, I'll bet. Don't assume it'll pan out the way our anonymous joker hopes. Why shouldn't I see what it looks like with my name on the cover? I could have been a musician, too, if it wasn't for this damn claw. There were plenty of corrections needed to that scrappy script that came through the door. Do I get no credit for that?"

Speechless, I left the house abruptly and sat for a while in the parish church, refusing to tell the priest my news for fear of how my temper might receive his predictable show of sympathy.

Instead I crouched silent on a pew for an hour or more, as

if in meditation. These ramblings have lost their purpose. There is no pretty hand in Seville to receive them. I am no longer the amiable, fraternal chronicler, sanitising the truth for my distant sister. Instead these thoughts may work their way inwards to my soul with all their truth, as harsh and bitter as it may be.

So let me admit this to myself now. My sister was not uppermost in my thoughts for long. My head rebelled at the injustice, the impossibility of her death. So I sat in the church of San Cassian and stared at that ancient painting which I once described to Lucia: the schoolmaster being martyred by his pupils. In the darkness I allowed my imagination to rise up, like Lucifer ascending from damnation. Leo was the master, I was the pupil. In my right hand the adze, in my left a sharp pen, the nib cut as sharp as the finest dagger.

How many men are murdered daily in the mind's eye? Millions, I believe, and the next morning they rise and go about their business, oblivious to the agonising fate their midnight selves suffered in another's mind a few hours before. The penknife and the adze. The sword and the scalpel. If Leo could peer into my head and see what wonders I worked upon his scrawny frame that night, he would faint away dead in horror. But no man knows what thoughts run through another's brain. The following day, over breakfast, Leo bestowed upon me quite a fetching smile, then said, "It's off to Ca' Dario and a word with that Gobbo chum of yours. I must keep Delapole in my power, boy. I must have him tight within my grasp."

29

A forced sale

RIZZO CURSED HIS LUCK. ENGLISHMEN SEEMED TO haunt him. The fellow Scacchi had sent seemed at first little more than a youth. Rizzo soon changed his opinion. "Daniel" was not cowed by his threats or concerned about losing the damned instrument. It was as if he recognised Rizzo's urgent need to get rid of the fiddle and was determined to mark the price down accordingly. That scarcely mattered now. Rizzo had listened to him playing the thing and felt like screaming till his eyes popped out. It was then that he decided he would never touch the cursed instrument again. The only question was how much money he might glean from its immediate sale.

"You say you can talk business," he grunted. "Well, talk."

Daniel ceased offering him the violin case and chose instead to place it on the floor between them. "It's of uncertain value. I don't know."

He was, Rizzo thought, not bad at lying, nor as good as he believed. "If you don't know that, then what do we have to talk about?"

Daniel placed a long, pale hand on his chin, a gesture that

reminded Rizzo of Massiter. "I've no idea how we might dispose of it."

Rizzo waved his cigarette in the air. "Your problem, my friend. All I want to know is what you have to offer. Here and now. If we agree a price between us and walk away together? How much will you place in my hand for this thing?"

The young Englishman blinked, clearly thinking. Rizzo wanted rid of the violin at any price, but he wanted his money in hard cash.

"We don't carry large sums out of habit," Daniel replied, lying again.

Rizzo took him by the arm, leaned into his face, and breathed a thick cloud of cigarette smoke between them. "Hey. Let's cut the crap. This isn't my kind of merchandise, right? But it's got a value. You said so yourself. Maybe it's a fake. Maybe it isn't. I don't know. Seems to me some clever guy like you could make it look real if you wanted to, anyway. Then what would it be worth?"

"True. But then we take all the risk."

Rizzo said nothing.

"Say, twenty thousand U.S. dollars," Daniel suggested. "In cash. This afternoon."

"No deal. You want to insult me?"

"Not at all. I'd just like us both to win."

"Yeah." He even talked like Massiter.

"So what do you want?"

"Gimme fifty grand. Cash. We go pick it up now."

Daniel grimaced. "We don't have that kind of money just lying around."

"So?"

"Let's say forty thousand. I think we could scrape that together. If you come with me, we could conclude this within the hour."

Forty thousand dollars. It was still a huge amount. It could set him up in a bar, if he wanted. "That's a real lot of money for a fake, don't you think? Daniel?" He wanted the English kid to understand he knew he was being rolled.

"It's a lot of money," he agreed. "Do you want it?"

Rizzo scowled at the case on the ground. "We get it now? I come with you?"

"Sure."

"You carry it," Rizzo grunted. "I'm sick of the damned thing."

They walked to the Arsenale stop and caught the first *vaporetto* to come along. It was, for a change, half-empty. The two men sat on the hard blue seats in the stern, out in the open air. Rizzo let him have the right-hand place, closer to the waterfront of San Marco. Some note of caution sounded in his head saying that he didn't want to be seen with this odd, devious English kid. But it made no sense. Daniel was the one carrying the violin case, having left the nylon bag in the warehouse. Still, they did not speak. No one could place the two of them together.

Then the boat pulled past La Pietà, and Rizzo's heart briefly stopped. There was some kind of media gathering outside the church, with photographers and reporters and a crowd of young musicians holding their instruments. This was Massiter's show; he should have remembered that. His figure was there, in the middle of the crowd. He could so easily have seen the two of them together. And thought what? That his chosen thief and errand boy was sitting in the back of a *vaporetto* next to some pale-faced kid who happened to have a violin case on his lap. He wasn't going to worry about it. Massiter had his back to them. If he'd seen something, then those icy grey eyes would surely be bearing down on the stern of the *vaporetto* that instant. All the same, Rizzo mumbled something about the heat and went to sit inside, between the kid and the exit. It was crazy to multiply the risks.

They got off at San Stae and walked back towards the Rialto. Rizzo had no idea where the old man lived, though it would be easy to find out. The one time they dealt with each other, it happened through an intermediary too. The English kid had indicated Rizzo was to stay out of Scacchi's house. That was fair enough. But he still wanted to know.

The two of them shared a beer in the tiny bar that sat on the San Cassian *campo*, opposite the church. He ordered a second. Daniel refused. The place was empty.

"I'll go and get the money," the English kid said. "I'll leave the fiddle here with you. Then come back with the cash. You can go check it in the toilet if you like."

Rizzo laughed. There was something faintly amusing about Daniel, as if this were all a piece of amateur dramatics.

"Take the thing. Then come back with what you owe me."

Daniel smiled. "Thanks. It's nice to be trusted."

Rizzo took off his sunglasses for the first time since leaving home that morning. He stared at Daniel. "What's this got to do with trust? If you rip me off, I come and kill you. Don't you get that?"

The kid went a touch pale, then nodded. Rizzo was glad he understood. "Just bring me the money. Then we never see each other again."

"OK." He was out of the door. Rizzo watched him turn left onto the bridge over the narrow *rio*, then he walked slowly to the front of the bar to see what happened next. It was so easy. Daniel crossed the water, then took out a key and opened the front door of a house set next to a small gift shop. Rizzo stared at the tangle of buildings on the corner. The entrance was humble. But it must lead, he guessed, to a large and ancient palace by the side of the *rio*. He did not doubt for one moment that Daniel would return with what he was owed.

He went back into the bar and slowly finished the beer. After fifteen minutes, Daniel returned carrying a Standa supermarket bag with a bundle inside, like a set of bricks enclosed tightly in a black plastic bin liner fastened with sticky tape.

The barman watched them from behind the counter. Rizzo ordered a third beer. Daniel declined.

"As I said," he repeated, "if you want to check it . . ."

Rizzo shook his head. "We're done, Daniel. You can go now."

He left, clearly grateful to be out of the bar. Rizzo took his third beer and sat at one of the outside tables, the bag of money on his lap. The drink was beginning to run around his head a little. He had, he knew, been cheated, but the resentment he felt was purely personal, not financial. It would fade. The money would help.

He admired a young girl who walked past, a picture of Venetian loveliness with long legs and a head of flowing dark hair. Rizzo whistled and laughed as she picked up her pace over the bridge. He felt good. It was too late to find a bank and place the cash in there today, but tomorrow he would do that, and feel very proper and upright as he listened to the manager crawling for his business.

The house intrigued him. He stared at the half-shuttered windows, wishing he could see inside. Perhaps they were playing the newly acquired violin. Perhaps they were working out their potential profit. It didn't bother him. Something told Rizzo the fiddle was a black thing and that no good was going to come of the transaction just negotiated by Daniel.

Rizzo sat outside the tiny bar, slowly getting drunk, idly watching the house. A tradesman arrived with some food. A man from the gas company called to read the meter. A figure left carrying a shopping bag and set out to cross the square. Rizzo wished he hadn't drunk so much. Then he laughed, a mirthless, convulsive laugh that led to a brief choking fit.

The barman eyed him. "What's so funny?"

"Nothing," Rizzo answered. He felt happier than at any time since his visit to the cemetery of San Michele. The violin was gone. In its place was hard money and the scent of change in the hot lagoon air.

30

Alone on the Arsenale

How many secrets can one head hold before it bursts? Too many for me. The human mind is made for deceit, of others and of itself. I make these observations to myself now, since I no longer dare set them down on paper. Looking back, I wonder I told Lucia as much as I did. The Republic has ways of getting its hands on letters. I can only hope that the unspoken reasoning which lay behind my folly—that the ramblings of a nineteen-year-old to his sister in Spain would hold no interest for their spies—proves well-founded.

The game is now set for the concert. Gobbo took me to a tavern off the *rio* behind Ca' Dario and told me what he knew of the details. Leo and Delapole remain the prime movers, my uncle fixing the musical side of matters, while Delapole orchestrates the ceremony and handles the money.

"Why are they doing this, Gobbo?" I wondered, not much minded to drink the sour red wine he had thrust into my hand.

"For my master, it is a rich man's game," he answered. "These are the amusements that keep the wealthy alive, Scacchi. Without them they would die of boredom. As for your uncle, ask yourself. What motivates him in anything? Money, naturally. I imagine he hopes to catch the coattails of whoever emerges as the composer. I don't think Delapole would mind wetting his beak there, either. Being rich is one thing, but the rate he spends it, he needs to make sure he stays rich too."

He was wrong about Leo, though I did not point this out. Gold drives my uncle, but there are deeper matters there too.

"And after the concert is a success?"

"Why," he said, grinning, "they wage this campaign to the very end. The plan, I gather, is to wait until the public is salivating for the composer's identity like a sailor begging to bed a Dorsoduro whore. Then they wait a little longer, just for fun. Finally, they announce another concert—tickets in advance, please—at which the composer will reveal himself as a finale. A bit of good theatre, that's what Venice likes, and my master fancies he can do that to a tee. Much as he feels he could toss off a play or concerto himself if he wanted, but that's the rage today. Old Leo's much of the same mind, and our sadly departed French friend seemed to think there was not a job in the world he couldn't do."

My mind overran with images of what might happen at this planned event. But who could I talk to, other than Rebecca and Jacopo, both of them too close to these issues to see them clearly?

Lucia's death and this web of pretence we have built around us both served to sour my mood. I collected Rebecca as arranged but scarcely spoke after we played our customary subterfuge upon the guard and stole off to La Pietà. For once I could not listen to her play. Instead I walked along the waterfront, to the gates of the Arsenale, and watched the workmen slaving there over ships for the fleet. As they worked

their hellish braziers, the air rang to the sound of curses in
tongues I had never heard before. It was both fascinating and
a little terrifying too. I understood how Rebecca must have
felt when she freed herself, albeit temporarily, of the ghetto.
Venice has, to some extent, become my own prison. I wonder
if I shall ever have the chance to escape it.

I sat upon the quayside, the very picture of misery. Then,
after an hour or more of useless cogitation, I walked back to
the church and caught Rebecca as she left, shiny new fiddle
case in hand, inside it the instrument Delapole had so
generously provided. Her lot in the world has improved so
much in these past few weeks. She must have looked at me
and wondered what was up, for she took my hand briefly,
then led me away from San Marco, back towards the
Arsenale, stopping short of the great entrance to lead me
into a deserted public garden. Here we sat beneath a patch
of fragrant oleander and watched the boats cross the lagoon.
There were a few lights on the Lido, the distant island that is
the barrier keeping out the full force of the Adriatic. The night
air was thick with the scent of the tree's musky blossom.
Chattering swifts cut dark silhouettes against the moon.
I seemed to be incapable of speaking a sentence which
consisted of more than three words.

Finally, Rebecca turned to me, her face earnest and taut in
the moonlight, and said, "Lorenzo. You are my dearest friend.
What is wrong? I have never known you like this."

I am a man. I must not weep. Yet such passions live inside
us all, and we block them out in order to become the very
picture of the modern Christian being, all sensations kept
tight under lock and key, all feelings, all emotions fastened
tight within the heart. When I walk these city streets and see
these pale, chaste faces trapped in the daily round of habit

and duty, I feel myself surrounded by the dead. And in their eyes, a plea that I should join them.

I told Rebecca about my sister's fate, as clearly and with as much detail as I possessed. I spoke of our family and of my love for my sister. And I cried. In grief and choler. I raged upon that waterfront like a madman, cursing myself, cursing humanity. Cursing God. Hers. Mine. Any I might name. The tears ran down my face. I knew madness that night. It was the taste of salt and saliva in the mouth, the sound of blood boiling in the ears, and the empty black hollow that sits inside the chest.

When, finally, my rants subsided, I sat down next to her once more and wiped my streaming face with my sleeve. She did not touch me. I couldn't blame her. I was the one transformed, not her. What woman would like to see a man behave in such a fashion? Once again I misjudged her.

"Lorenzo," she said in a very calm voice. "Your rage is not against fate. Or God. Or Venice. It is against yourself. You ask why you could not save Lucia from this fate. Even though you know there is no answer, the question continues to consume your soul. You feel responsible, and this presumed guilt turns your anger inwards. It is, I think, one of the stations of grief. Jacopo and I are orphans too. Do you think I don't recognise it?"

It was a sane and rational response, and had I been at that time sane and rational, I would have recognised it as such. Instead I said, with a degree of bitterness inside my voice which shocked me as I heard it, "How could you blame yourself for your father's death? Did you taunt God, as I have done these last few weeks? Did you walk into his house and shake your fist in his face?"

"You know that is ridiculous, Lorenzo," she said with a

distinct note of disappointment. "Lucia is dead of misfortune, not some divine revenge."

"I know," I answered. And it was true. Yet in each of us there lurks the demon of unreason, and it never sleeps.

She looked at me oddly. Then she took my arm. "Come," she said. "I shall show you the true face of God and let you decide for yourself."

31

An uneasy state of grace

THE FIDDLE WAS BOUGHT. SOME $30,000 OF MASSITER'S money remained in the house, with the prospect of a further $50,000 before the end of the summer. The additional reserve, Daniel believed, ought to make Scacchi's negotiations with his creditors more flexible. If this was the case, the old man did not mention it. Once the instrument was in his hands, he thanked Daniel in the most sincere of fashions and declared there was no further need for his involvement in any subterfuge. It was essential the instrument's existence be kept from Laura, Scacchi insisted, but its sale had already been pre-arranged. The sums would be sufficient to save their skins. It was now time for Daniel to concentrate on enjoying himself. With a wave of his hand, Scacchi seemed to dismiss the Guarneri and its acquisition entirely.

For Scacchi and Paul, it appeared, the entire episode now lay in the past, unworthy of recall. The two men's health was a little improved. Their temperaments were happy and nonchalant. Laura, too, seemed relaxed and contented. Ca' Scacchi had moved from the brink of catastrophe to a happy equilibrium in a matter of days, largely through Daniel's efforts, as the old man had gratefully admitted once the violin was his.

Yet Daniel found his own mood failed to follow theirs, for reasons he could not explain to them. Giulia Morelli seemed to be developing a fascination with him. She had now approached him twice since her deliberate appearance at the *vaporetto* stop, once when he was daydreaming around the Guggenheim and a second time, more boldly, at La Pietà. On each occasion she had asked no direct questions and, in the gallery, had gone so far as to pretend her presence was accidental. Yet from her tone and the gentle, insistent probing of her comments, it was clear that she suspected Scacchi had engaged in some transaction of late and that Daniel was a part of it.

The last interview had taken place on a pew at the rear of the church while Fabozzi talked quietly to his players only a few yards away. Finally, Daniel had snapped and asked her to continue the discussion outside. There, on the steps of La Pietà, under a bright summer sun, he had demanded an explanation.

"An explanation?" she had answered, amused. "But you know what I seek, Daniel. Some object that has come on the market. And the discovery of those who seek to acquire it."

"But I have told you a thousand times. I know nothing of this. Nor, as far as I am aware, does Scacchi. If you suspect he does, interrogate him, not me."

She laughed. "And what would be the point of that? Scacchi is intrinsically dishonest, much as I like his company. He would never tell the truth. Not if it did not suit him."

"So you come to me in the belief I will. And when you hear it, you dismiss it as fiction."

"Oh, Daniel. Do you know what I see when I look at you?"

"No. Nor do I care."

"I see an honest young man. An innocent young man. One who has become trapped in some world he finds exciting—up to a point, perhaps. But frightening too. And I ask myself why. What frightens you, Daniel?"

"Nothing you would understand. I have this concert in my head. It is a responsibility."

"Ah! The concert. You see, there you puzzle me too. Where does this music come from, Daniel? Please tell me. I'm interested, as a listener, not merely a police officer."

He clapped his hands, drawing the interview to a close. "That, Captain, is enough. If you have anything else to say to me, kindly ask me to the police station. The same goes for Scacchi."

"You can tell him if you like. Of our little talks."

Daniel swore mildly, then turned on his heels and went back into the church. He was grateful, and a little surprised, that she did not follow him.

The concert, at least, seemed on track. The transcription work was done. Fabozzi cooed over the final product. There was every sign that the première would be a considerable success. Daniel had given interviews to several journalists from the international press, flown in at Massiter's expense and kept in luxury at the Cipriani. He made it plain in these brief, vague conversations that there would be no more work from his pen in the foreseeable future. This did not prevent word of the surprising nature and quality of the work leaking beyond La Pietà into the world at large, with Massiter's encouragement, ensuring the night would be a sellout, and followed soon by performances in greater concert halls elsewhere. The risk of discovery was surely small and predictable. Giulia Morelli suspected much but knew nothing. Yet Daniel was troubled by a distant, intangible feeling that all was not as it should be. Nor was this concern self-centred. It was the Scacchi household which worried him. Each one of them seemed to be living in a pleasant daydream set firmly on the border of hubris. Irrational as he knew this to be, it was impossible to shake from his head the idea that another catastrophe, of a different nature, might lie around the corner.

The following morning, Sunday, found them on the jetty at San Stae, waiting for the *Sophia* to crawl down the Grand Canal and pick them up. It had the makings of a hot, dry, sunny day. Scacchi wore a dark jacket, pale trousers, and an old-fashioned trilby hat. Paul was in jeans, a denim shirt, and a baseball cap. Laura chose plain, cheap slacks—the kind, Daniel thought, they sold on market stalls—and a simple cheesecloth top. He and Paul had helped her carry the supplies: baskets of *panini*, sausage, ham and cheese, a selection of fruit, and a brown paper bag of tiny leaves of rocket, chicory, dandelion, and lettuce which, covered in Parmesan, seemed to grace every meal. There was drink too: bottles of white wine safe inside a vast cooler with bags of ice, three litres of Campari, and two of sparkling mineral water. More than sufficient, Daniel judged, to keep six adults in a comfortable state for an entire day.

Scacchi and Paul sat together on a bench. He stood with Laura, watching the traffic on the canal. *Vaporetti* vied with delivery barges and refuse-collection vessels, each dodging the low black shapes of the gondolas ferrying locals across to the *traghetto* stop by the city casino. Laura had been to the hairdresser's and now sported a short, practical cut which curled in at the neck. Daniel had come to believe she dyed her hair yet never once wore a speck of make-up. Perhaps because it suited her, he thought, cursing himself. Sometimes he sought roundabout explanations when simpler answers stared him in the face.

"He comes!" Laura cried. "Daniel! Look!"

The low blue form of the *Sophia* cut a steady, straight line through the canal traffic, the large bulk of Piero upright at the tiller in the rear. At the prow Xerxes stood smugly erect, nose in the air, mouth open, pink tongue lolling lazily to one side. Daniel was grateful to find himself gripped by a sudden fit of the giggles.

"What's so funny?" Laura demanded.

"I was wondering what Amy will make of all this. It will be a little different from our trip with Massiter."

"Amy must take us as she finds us."

Daniel gave her a sharp look. "You'll behave, won't you? She's our star violinist."

She seemed taken aback. "I always behave!"

He did not reply. The *Sophia* was making a sharp cut into the jetty. Xerxes eyed the planking, chose his moment, then leapt with precise timing onto land and began to sniff at the picnic baskets.

"Rope!" Piero yelled. Laura caught the end before Daniel began to realise what was needed, tethered the boat, then helped Scacchi and Paul on board. Xerxes watched the humans clamber onto the *Sophia* with their customary lack of elegance, eyeing this escapade with disparaging canine bewilderment, then sprang in at the last moment. Within the space of five minutes, they were in place, with provisions, turned round in the canal, and setting back towards San Marco, where Amy would be picked up as previously arranged. They had assumed—automatically, it seemed—the same positions they had on that first trip from the airport: Paul and Scacchi together in the prow, Daniel next to Laura on the left-hand side of the boat. Xerxes seemed more interested in the food baskets than the tiller at this moment, but soon abandoned them to be petted by Paul.

They entered the long bend of the canal which the locals called simply the *volta*. The curious mansion Laura had pointed out emerged on the right.

"There's your palace," Daniel said, pointing.

"It's not *my* palace," she objected.

Scacchi overheard. "Explain, Laura. I didn't know you were familiar with Ca' Dario."

"I'm not. Daniel makes up fairy stories."

"But you told me—!"

"I said," she interrupted, "that it was just the foolish fancy of a child."

"Out with it!" Scacchi ordered. "Let's probe your psyche, dear."

She glared at Daniel, blaming him for this turn of conversation. "There's precious little to tell. I was a child. It was the day of my confirmation. I was dressed in white and it was carnival, so everyone was in costume too. The *vaporetto* went past that place and I looked up, seeing in a second-floor window" —she pointed very deliberately—"that one, a face. Which frightened the stupid little girl I was then."

"Ah," Scacchi announced triumphantly. "A carnival figure? The plague doctor, no doubt. Don't be ashamed, Laura. That long nose and those white cheeks scare us all. That's the point, isn't it?"

"It wasn't the plague doctor. Or any of the others. It was something else." She fell silent.

"Well?" Scacchi probed.

"It was a man. With his hands and his face covered in blood. He was staring through the window, looking straight at our boat, seemingly straight at me, screaming. As if he had just witnessed the most terrible thing in the world."

Scacchi raised an eyebrow. "Your confirmation dress wasn't that bad, surely? I know the Venetian ladies like to adorn their little darlings, but..."

Laura reached into one of the hampers, withdrew a croissant, and launched it through the air. Before it could strike the intended target, Xerxes leapt skywards from Paul's lap with infallible accuracy, caught it in his jaws, and began to devour the pastry greedily. The occupants of the *moto topo Sophia* were reduced to an immediate bout of laughter, ended only by Scacchi's weak cry of "Spritz! For the love of God. Spritz!"

"No," Laura replied curtly. "It's too early. And you've been wicked."

"As you see fit," he murmured, and was content when she handed out glasses of mineral water with the admonishment "I don't want Daniel's friend to believe we're a bunch of drunks."

Daniel saw she wished to change the subject, but he wanted one last question answered. "So what do you think you saw, Laura?"

She thought about her reply. "Some carnival nonsense. Or perhaps it was some kind of hallucination. I was a child, Daniel, as I continue to remind you. My mother never saw anything, nor did anyone else on the boat. All they knew was that they suddenly had a screaming girl in their midst."

"Of course." He hesitated. She never spoke of her past. He knew nothing about her life outside Ca' Scacchi at all, it occurred to him. "What did she do, your mother?"

The sharp green eyes flared. "Work."

"And your father?"

"Drink. When he was still alive."

The two men in the prow watched them, seeming uncomfortable, then fell into a low conversation of their own.

"I see," Daniel said.

"Do you?"

"No. I...I'm sorry, Laura. I didn't mean to pry. I just wondered who you are when you're not looking after us."

"I'm just a simple, boring servant, Daniel, who is both lucky and cursed by the fact that my masters appear to be my children too. My past is as dull as the water in this canal."

"And your future?" He felt as if he were pressing her too much, but insisted in any case.

"The present is full of enough cares, don't you think?"

He was about to answer when she pointed to the jetty. They were fast approaching San Marco, and the *Sophia* was headed directly for the landing stage where they had joined Massiter's boat. Amy stood there, not yet seeing them. She wore, Daniel was dismayed to see, a cream silk dress and a floppy white hat to keep off the sun. She looked as if she were prepared to be a guest at a society wedding, not spend a few hours on the grubby planks of the *Sophia*, then disembark to deal with whatever bucolic pleasures Piero had arranged on Sant' Erasmo.

"Oh, dear," he sighed.

She slapped him hard on the knee. "And you ask if I'll behave! You will be an English gentleman, my boy, or I'll want to know why."

"This wasn't my idea," he muttered, then stood up, broke into a broad smile, and greeted Amy from the low-slung *Sophia* as it hacked towards the jetty. Scacchi rose, too, and announced to everyone, including the tourists who lounged by the jetty, "It's Amy Hartston, the famous American violinist. Behold! Applause!" And smacked his leathery hands together until a fair number of those in the vicinity joined in.

Amy's tanned cheeks turned a darker shade. Daniel wished he could see her eyes. She wore large sunglasses of the Italian kind. They did not suit her. He held out his hand and let her step, very gingerly, into the boat, then take a seat opposite Laura, amid the introductions.

"Spritz!" Scacchi declared. "Spritz!"

Laura remained seated, wearing a wry grin, and lightly pushed

Daniel in the chest as he lowered himself to join her. A single flash of her eyes gave him the message. He crossed the boat and sat next to Amy, who daintily arranged the silk hem of her dress around her legs, watched by the puzzled Xerxes. Drinks were duly served.

"Where are we going?" Amy asked eventually.

"To paradise," Piero replied, turning up the little diesel engine until it coughed like an asthmatic donkey. "Away from this festering sore of iniquity and these hard-assed city bastards."

Laura waved at him. "Poppycock. You worked in the city when you were younger, Piero."

"Yes," he admitted, "but only in the morgue. Therefore, I dealt with dead people who were, to a man and a woman, very decent and unobjectionable. The living, on the other hand— Hey! *Pisquano!*"

A water taxi roared away from the neighbouring jetty, sending up a swell which tipped the *Sophia* to near forty-five degrees. They clutched for handholds. Xerxes barked angrily. Amy's drink spilled down the front of her elegant dress.

"Shit!" she hissed with a sudden vehemence.

Laura reached into her bag, crossed the boat, and motioned for Daniel to return to the other side. Then she set about dabbing at the fabric with a damp tissue, clucking all the while. It did not work. The dress now possessed a long, broad stain, the colour of bright blood, running from Amy's navel to her knees.

Daniel saw the sullen fury in her face and watched the way she let Laura, who had so quickly assumed the role of servant, try to help. La Pietà moved slowly past behind him. Sant' Erasmo lay on the horizon, a long, low finger of green.

He finished his drink and, for no reason at all, found he could not shake from his head the image of Giulia Morelli and her incessant questions. Daniel took the pack out of Laura's bag and, for the first time in his life, began to smoke a cigarette.

32

In the eaves of the ark

The bells of San Girolamo marked twelve as we slipped back into the ghetto. The Jews must retire early. There was scarcely a light in any window and not a sound in the building as we climbed the stairs. Jacopo was out on his rounds, ever the busy physician. The night remained passably hot. Rebecca threw her cloak onto the chair by the fireplace, then took my own, gripped my hands tightly, and looked into my eyes.

"Lorenzo," she said. "Where do you think this God is that has nothing better to do with His time but peer down upon us like some base spy? In every church? In every bedroom? Watching us now? Is this all He is? Some servant of the state with wings and all-seeing eyes?"

"Of course not."

"Then what? Some divine thorn to prick our consciences and make us ever aware of our own shortcomings?"

"You mock me. I think I should go."

She continued to cling to me. "If you like, Lorenzo. But I had something to show you. One of the oldest gods of all, and I hoped that if you saw Him for what He truly was, perhaps we'd both be the better for it."

I said nothing. Rebecca wore the black dress of the concert musician, with a circular neckline and a slender silver chain around her throat. Her face was more serious than I had ever known. She had the benefit of just six years over me, but at that moment I felt like a child in the company of an elder.

"Come," she said, and took my hand. "Be brave. Don't look down. You won't fall to hell, but you will go six floors down to the ground and you won't much notice the difference."

I followed her to the large sash window at the side of the room. This gave onto the corner of the square, the jumble of buildings surmounted by the wooden ark of the synagogue which she had pointed out to me on an earlier occasion.

"Be as quiet as you can so none shall hear us. And mind your footing. Follow me all the way."

With that, she threw open the window, lifted a leg, and was out of the house onto a tiny, flat tiled roof no bigger than a balcony. I followed and stood there, with nothing to hold but her arm, and we swayed, just for a moment, in front of the great black maw of space an arm's length in front of us.

"Be calm," she whispered in my ear, and then reached round for a handhold, found it, and beckoned me to follow.

This cannot have been the first time Rebecca had made this journey. On some occasion during the day, she must have sat in the square, stared at this shambling collection of gutters and roofs, and even, at one point, a small external ladder—used, I assume, for maintenance—marking down each point, fixing the route she would take when she decided to tackle this queer little peak, like a mountain goat consumed by curiosity. Tentatively, not once looking down, I came on behind, trying not to clutch for her hand too often, slipping once or twice, then seeing her anxious face, alabaster in the light of the moon, peering at me from above.

After two or three minutes which seemed, in all truth, as long as an entire evening, I dragged myself up and found her sitting on a tiny wooden balcony close to the peak of the wooden ark. There was a small leaded window. Through it came the yellow, waxy light of distant candles.

Rebecca put a finger to my mouth and said, "Shush. There are men inside. But they won't be there long."

We waited until we heard the sound of a door closing, then she slipped open the window and we prised ourselves through, half falling into a corridor that seemed to squeeze itself beneath the eaves of the building. There was a narrow walkway on the wall side. Opposite was a line of plain wooden benches, and, in front of them, large shutters running almost the length of the floor, which opened onto the room beyond, much like those of La Pietà behind which the musicians hide. The "nave" of the synagogue, though, was one floor below us, as I discovered when I opened the nearest shutter and stuck my head through into the central hall. It was like being thrust into the kind of fantasy one finds in dreams where dimensions are quite out of joint. I felt at one moment like a child peering into some rich, ornate doll's house, and the next a pygmy who had crawled upon the roof of some hidden cathedral, bare wood on the outside, full of golden riches beneath the skin.

"This is where you worship?" I asked Rebecca, who sat on the bench, arms folded, awaiting my reaction.

"Where *they* worship," she replied. "Women are not allowed. We must wait up here, watching through the shutters, unseen, not worthy of their thoughts. The Hebrew God is a busy one, Lorenzo, at least for the Ashkenazim. Don't ask me if it's the same for everyone else. He has only time to talk to men, and prefers a bearded rabbi above all others."

I looked at the place. It was beautiful, but so different from anything I had seen elsewhere in Venice. Then it struck me. "There are no paintings, Rebecca. Where are all the glorious martyrdoms? Titian and Veronese would starve if they were born into a Jewish state. What would they do?"

"False idols, Lorenzo. We must allow no graven images in our temples. There are a few paintings if you look, though. And I gather that's unusual."

I craned my neck and saw she was right. Around the walls was a collection of small landscapes.

"There," she said, pointing to one. "Moses leading his tribe through the Red Sea."

I screwed up my eyes to follow her finger. "But there's no one in it."

"I told you. It isn't allowed. Also, we mustn't depict God, either. Or utter His proper name—which is Yahweh, in case you're interested. There. I said it."

I felt quite baffled. The place was so unlike any Christian church I had ever entered. Yet it did feel holy, and I couldn't help wondering if one might find the same air of sanctity in a mosque or the temples where the Hindu worship. Could it be that holiness comes not from God but us? Do we make Him after the image we would have of ourselves?

My mind was overwhelmed by both the sacredness and the ordinariness of these surroundings. Here, Rebecca pointed out, was the ark where the laws were kept. Here, the eternal light and the raised platform from which lessons were read, much as they are from a Christian pulpit. This was the seat of the daily round of ritual which the Hebrews used to explain their place in the world, why men lived and died, fought and loved, just like anyone else who walked the earth.

Rebecca sat close, watching my face avidly as I scanned

this holy temple, wondering what it meant to me. I wore a plain white shirt, the neck open. It disclosed the Star of David she had given me. She reached forward, took it with her hand, and was flattered, I think, that I wore it.

"Do you think God's here, Lorenzo?" she asked. "Do you think He is hiding behind the Torah, His face like thunder, all because two hapless mortals happened to walk where other men said they shouldn't?"

"No," I said honestly. She was right, of course. My grief had eaten into my mind. Lucia was dead because of some accident of fate, not the actions of her foolish brother. "But God is with us, I think. Not your God or my God, but something more simple, and more complicated. I don't believe we are like the animals, Rebecca. When I listened to my sister sing to me in my bed, when I watch you play in La Pietà . . . Whatever Jacopo says, I don't believe our lives can be written down as numbers on a page. I don't think love is an affliction of the blood, like palsy. We are more than we seem, and we build these places to try to explain our bewilderment at our imperfect state."

"Jacopo," she murmured with a gentle laugh. "He is my brother, and I love him dearly. My impetuousness mirrors his caution. But one day a woman will trap his heart, and then his pretty theories will fall down like bricks in a child's toy castle."

I felt well, I felt whole. Rebecca had healed me. And why not? The Levis were a family of physicians.

"Thank you," I said, and gingerly, with the soft, remote tenderness of a brother, I kissed her pale, warm cheek. She did not move. The temple was silent save for the erratic sputtering of the lamps below.

"Here is another piece of God," she said, and quickly, with not a moment's hesitation, unfastened the back of her dress, letting the black fabric fall open to expose, in the half light that came through the shutter, the fullness of her breasts, the colour of a marble statue in a rich man's palace, and as smooth and perfect too. "Here."

She took my hand and pulled it towards her, splaying the fingers. They came to rest upon this warm and lovely place. I felt her life pulsing beneath my touch. I felt the tightening of the tender rosebud trapped lightly in my grasp, heard the sudden short, halting breaths sucked between her teeth.

I brought my hand to her hair and, slowly, wishing that we might both record every moment of this for eternity, kissed her open mouth, our lips pressed firm together, our breathing as one.

She broke away, an urgent look on her lovely face, then stood up and, in one swift movement, pulled her dress over her head, clutched it modestly to her chest for a moment, then bent down to lay it carefully on the bare wooden floor as if to make a bed for us. I swear that at that instant I felt as if I could die. My lungs were starved of breath, my blood refused to course its natural path.

"Lorenzo," she said, and tugged at my shirt, twisting open the buttons with a flick of the hand. "Lie with me now and I will remain yours always."

I started to babble ridiculous sweet nothings, and she laughed, silenced me, and bade action. I threw an arm around her naked back, feeling the gracious form of its curves. Her body pressed hard against mine. I disrobed and, wrapped around each other, we wound slowly to the floor. Thus, in the narrow corridor on the first floor of the Ashkenazi synagogue, on the island ghetto of Venice, I left my childhood behind and entered, willingly and with much joy, the adult world.

Afterwards, in the most unforeseen of locations, while setting a line of type or walking alone across the Rialto, a detail of that encounter would appear in my head out of nothing. This act is a blur of passion, a string of confused images and sensations. I recall the shock of feeling Rebecca's tongue probing my mouth. I remember the sudden alarm and just as sudden passion that followed when, with her guiding hand, I found that secret part of her and discovered, beneath the luxuriant locks, the unexpected well of heat and dampness within.

That night shall live with me always, whatever the future holds for the two of us. Rebecca threw open the shutters of the world for me, and I can never remain the same hereafter. But one image remains uppermost in my mind. Ecstasy and agony walk hand in hand in this act, much as they do in life itself. At that point when our two bodies moved in such tight rhythm that we might have been a single creature, I opened my eyes, anxious to see her face in the moment of rapture. It remains an image I find both hypnotic and shocking. Eyes tight shut, mouth half-open, she had the look of the dead upon her. The long moan that issued from her throat might have been her last breath upon this earth. The French call this the little death, with much justification. I watched her so and found my own cries rising to mingle with hers in that narrow, ill-lit corridor, on the clumsy pile of clothes that scarce hid the hardness of the boards beneath.

I saw my love at this instant of rapture, and her face made me think of Lucia, distant Lucia, dead Lucia. Here was Rebecca's most important lesson. That when life is as ephemeral as the beat of a butterfly's wing, these moments of wonder give us reason to exist. And that, in itself, might be a gift from God.

The eel contest

PIERO INTRODUCED HIS VISITORS TO THE ESTATE slowly. He showed them the small vineyard and let them taste his homemade wine, which was brash and young, but very drinkable. There were fields of artichokes and broad beans. In a corner of the plot sat a patch of Treviso chicory sown for the winter, solid red hearts growing fat on the rich island soil.

They ate and drank, perhaps a little too well. Then Piero announced the "entertainment" and, bucket in hand, lurched to the small channel that ran inland from the lagoon. They watched him busy himself there, then walk to the cottage. In a few minutes he returned with the bucket, which was now full to the brim with what looked like black water. Beneath the surface, creatures moved, long, sinuous bodies circling, half-hidden.

"Squid ink!" Piero declared. "You see how it blackens the water. I caught them myself! And the eels too!"

Amy gave them all a worried look. "Before we go any further, let me say, here and now, I am not eating that."

Piero stared into the murky bucket. "No, no, no! This is not about eating. This is the *gara del bisato*!"

Daniel saw the growing bewilderment on Amy's face and translated. "The eel contest?"

"*Sì!* You come back in October, after we harvest the grapes. That's when we do it proper. But now I show you. Watch!"

Piero walked forward, knelt, took a deep breath, then thrust his head almost completely into the bucket. The black water boiled with frantic bodies squirming around his scalp. Bubbles frothed on the dark, inky surface. Xerxes sat patiently by his master's side, watching the show as if it were the most natural act on earth.

After an unconscionable period with his face in the water, Piero finally emerged. Gripped tightly between his teeth, wriggling to break free, was a large eel. Piero's jaws had it firmly by the middle. With a bizarre, fixed grin on his face, he turned his head slowly so that everyone in the party might see. They spoke not a single word. Then he went back to the bucket, opened his mouth, and let the stunned eel fall back below the churning black surface of the water. Piero wiped his mouth with his sleeve, took a long gulp of wine, then beamed at Amy and said, "Now you."

"Not for a million bucks."

"Scacchi?"

The old man opened his mouth and pointed at his very yellow, very false, teeth. Piero made a small gesture, accompanied by a sympathetic noise. Paul shook his head. Laura stared at Piero, aghast, but a little intrigued too.

"And you wonder why they call you '*matti*'?" she declared. "I thought this was all a myth, Piero."

He bristled. "It is a tradition. I guess you city folk aren't up to it, huh? You just want to bob for apples."

Laura swore gently, walked over to the bucket, and did her best to tie back her short hair.

"No!" Amy cried. "This is disgusting!"

"Listen. If this bumpkin can do it, so can I."

"Not easy," Piero said slyly. "There's a trick. You want the bumpkin to tell you?"

Laura uttered a curse of such vulgarity Daniel was glad Amy seemed not to understand, then, without another word, pushed her head into the bucket. The surface writhed once more. Her auburn hair turned a darker shade with the ink, making Daniel believe, in an oddly disconnected moment, that this was perhaps its true colour.

She emerged, gasping, choking. There was nothing in her mouth.

"I told you there's a trick," Piero said, gloating. "You want me to tell—"

"Shut up!" She plunged back into the inky water again, was there for no more than a few seconds, then emerged. In her lips, struggling maniacally, was a large, powerful eel. Piero leapt into the air, shouting with glee. Scacchi and Paul, who appeared fascinated by this turn of events, applauded heartily. Daniel joined them. Amy simply stared, aghast.

Laura dropped the eel. It missed the bucket and darted off into the dry grass, looking very much like a snake. Then she stood up and waved her arms in the air, yelling nonsense, triumphant. The black water stained her skin and hair. She looked like a fake minstrel whose make-up was running. The applause grew louder. Piero sang, very briefly, an unintelligible dialect chant in which the only recognisable word was *bisati*, after which Laura sat down, picked up a teacloth, and wiped her mouth.

"What does it taste like?" Daniel wondered.

"Slimy. Don't take my word for it. Try yourself."

"No!" Amy almost screamed at him.

Daniel considered the decision. It was, in some way, a question of taking sides. "I'll do it," he said firmly.

Scacchi looked at him. "There's no need. It's just one of these crazy island things."

"Please..."

Piero, sensing his determination, put the bucket back on the ground. Daniel walked over, knelt in front of it, and stared at the surface, which moved occasionally with the ripple of the creatures below. It was impossible to see precisely what lay beneath. There could be just a couple of eels or an entire clan.

"There is a secr—" Piero began to say, but Daniel didn't wait. He breathed deeply, then sank his head into the water, eyes closed, mouth open, trying to work out what Piero's trick might be. The water was icy cold. Soft, slimy shapes brushed against his cheeks. Once, a narrow, powerful body bumped against his lips. He tried to seize it tentatively with his teeth. The eel was free in an instant, and no more came close before the need to breathe forced him to the surface, gasping, shivering.

Amy had turned to one side, refusing to watch. The rest couldn't take their eyes off him, Scacchi most of all. It was irrational, but in some way the old man seemed worried.

Daniel stared up at Piero and gasped, "Tell me."

"You have to bite, Daniel," the big man explained. "Not gently. Not like some aristocrat picking at his food. Eels are the most slippery things in the universe. You have to bite them like you want to eat them; otherwise, they'll just get straight out again. It's all or nothing."

Laura had understood this instinctively, he realised. This was what set him apart from the lagoon people: his sense of distance, his unwillingness to engage himself fully in the sport of existence.

Daniel pushed his head back into the water, mouth open, jaws ready to seize, knowing Piero was correct. The creatures taunted him, touched his cheeks with their sleek, greasy bodies. Then one, a large one, brushed against his upper teeth and he gaped wide, biting, biting, until he sank into its flesh, holding on as tightly as he knew how.

He broke surface, opened his eyes, thrust his arms above his head. The fish struggled in his mouth with an astonishing strength, curling its long body into his hair, around his ears, struggling to be free. Daniel jerked himself upright with it still in his jaws. The city's outline stood in the distance with the sun starting its downward journey to set behind the mountains. He opened his mouth, let the eel tumble to the ground and disappear. Its aftertaste, of slime and mud and grit, was disgusting. Laura was by his side in a moment with a glass of spritz. Daniel gulped at it and found, between the bittersweet drink and the taste of the eel, some odd resonance.

"Magnificent," Laura said, and gave him a firm pat on the back. There was, he thought, an edge of sarcasm in her voice. "You and Piero are now blood brothers. Clearly you will make a Sant' Erasmo *matto* any time. And a composer too!"

He choked a little, laughing, and found his head swamped by the idea that he might take this peculiar woman in his arms and, still tasting the mixed flavours of live eel and Campari in his throat, kiss her with a sudden, fierce passion. The notion was utterly bizarre, yet enticing too. Perhaps eels were hallucinogenic.

Something turned in his stomach, a dim, deep, bilious rumbling. Daniel belched, then, realising what was happening, raced to the small channel. When he was by the water, he began to vomit with a violent rapidity. He sat down and watched the proceeds float slowly away on the sluggish tide. His head was still spinning from the drink and the bizarre encounter with the eel. Something nudged at his knee. Xerxes' face, comically concerned, stared up at him. He patted the dog's damp fur, laughed, and closed his eyes. When he opened them, Laura was there, alone, rifling her bag for mints.

"Do you feel better now, Daniel?"

"Only physically. The rest of me feels as embarrassed as hell."

"Oh, dear." She handed him the sweet. He took it gratefully.

"I'm sorry."

"For what?" Laura asked, astonished.

He looked back at the rest of the party, who were now packing the picnic away, preparing to return to the boat. "For behaving like a fool."

"Silly boy. You are too conscious of yourself, Daniel. You don't honestly believe Amy thinks any the worse of you for this, surely?"

The idea had never occurred to him. Something else was on his mind, though he was unwilling to admit it.

"Daniel," she said, suddenly very serious. "I've some advice for you. It is time for you to learn how to hold on to something real. This game you're playing with Scacchi isn't enough." She hesitated. "You need to find out what it's like to love someone. There. I have said it."

He felt the heat rise to his cheeks and wondered what he looked like. He gazed at her hand on the ground and considered reaching for it.

"I know," he said, not moving. "And I—"

"Good," she interrupted. "This secret life you pursue is unhealthy. Even Scacchi tires of secrets after a while. Tomorrow, he says, he has one to share with me. I am grateful for that. You three have been cooking something up in my absence, and I should like to know what it is."

There was only one secret Scacchi could mean, and that was

the existence of the elusive fiddle which had now, he assumed, been sold on to some new owner. Daniel could not understand why Scacchi would choose this moment to reveal it.

"And furthermore," Laura continued, "Amy is so nice. So interested in you, Daniel. *You*. Not this music you are supposed to have written."

"But..." His mind whirled.

"Good," she declared, smiling, and patted his damp head before rising to her feet. "Then it is agreed. Tonight you will take her home to her hotel. Go into the city with her, Daniel. Escape from us for a while."

"*Laura!*" he cried. But she was gone, back to the boat, where Xerxes now sat at the tiller, ready to depart.

34

Questions of authorship

Venice loves a mystery, and it has taken this one to its heart.
Here are some of the theories bandied around the
coffeehouses, though no member of the Venetian public
outside the rehearsal room of La Pietà has yet heard a note
of the work.

The mysterious figure is none other than Vivaldi himself,
attempting to revive his flagging career with a little
showmanship and a new name on the frontispiece. Or the
German Handel, who has not been much heard of in the city
since his *Agrippina* made an apparently sensational debut here
more than twenty years ago. Handel now lives in London.
The gossip says he smuggled the new work into Venice to test
the water for his return, fearing the English taste for Italian-
style opera is somewhat on the wane. The German doubts
the lessons he learnt at the knees of Corelli and Scarlatti will
pay his English rent much longer. There is, I am told, a satire
on his style called *The Beggar's Opera*, which is much in favour
there.

After these two comes the real nonsense. The composer is
a local gondolier who learned his talents singing for his

supper while paddling the Grand Canal (find me a gondolier who knows a sharp from a flat and I'll place a pile of ducats in front of the Basilica after breakfast and expect to see them there at supper time). The work is a lost *opus* of Corelli's, recovered from his tomb when his cadaver was exhumed during building works in the Pantheon in Rome. A churchwarden in Santa Croce is telling his drinking friends he wrote the piece on the parish organ after the nightly flock went home. A man has heard from another man, whose impeccable sources must never be revealed, that a half-blind watchmaker with a tiny stall on the Rialto has painstakingly assembled the work note by note over many years, knowing he suffers from a terminal disease and impending deafness. Now this poor soul desires nothing more than to hear his creation played in La Pietà by Vivaldi's gorgeous band before expiring, content in the knowledge that he has bequeathed to the world a musical masterpiece which will live forever.

Finally, the most ridiculous of all. That it is some nobleman in the city—perhaps even Delapole himself—who has hitherto hidden his signs of musical greatness and now plays this game to make the grandest entrance of all. Furthermore, he will, when revealed, shower upon the city both financial and musical riches that shall restore the Republic to its former glories, cure the palsy, make the Grand Canal smell sweeter than a Persian whore's bosom, etc., etc.

I listen to these fairy tales, nod sagely, and keep my peace. Once, when Gobbo and his chums were making merry with the rumours in his local tavern, I was tempted to interject an even more outré theory: that it was written by a woman. But then they would have thought me mad. Female fingers must work at nothing save the roles we give them; 'twas always thus and always will be.

So I smile and play the ignoramus. Only Rebecca and I know the truth. She has not told Jacopo, even, for fear of worrying her brother further. While we stay mute, the industry around her artistry grows. Pages for the various parts appear from the Scacchi presses, some even set by my clumsy hand. On the frontispiece, where Leo covetously tried his name, there is nothing but blank space beneath the plain title copied from her own manuscript, *Concerto Anonimo*, and the year.

When I stare at this bare white lacuna, I see it filled by Rebecca's face. In the thickets of elder bushes that cover the flat, unkempt wasteland in the northernmost part of the city, above the ghetto, where none may see a pair of ardent lovers retire of an afternoon. And in her room, where we steal when Jacopo is out, and writhe together naked beneath sheets that come to twist around us in our labours, like swaddling clothes for infants who toss and turn in the grip of deep, enrapturing dreams.

Here are Rebecca's true mysteries. The dark glitter of an eye, the turn of her hip, the soft, full weight of her breast. These are secrets that live beyond words or the tones that even she may pluck from Delapole's gift. It seems a lifetime now since that first night, and still I wonder she should reveal them to such as me.

Encounters

THE SOUND OF A STRING QUARTET DRIFTED ACROSS the water from San Marco. It was evening now and the bands were out in the square, playing for the tourists. The *Sophia* had meandered back across the lagoon at a sluggish pace, fighting the tide. The moon was a bold silver disc set in velvet, tugging at the water with some mystic, invisible power.

The journey had been made mostly in silence. Daniel sat next to Amy all the way, at the urging of Laura. The farewells at the taxi jetty were muted. The men were tired, Laura busy at the tiller. Daniel and Amy walked into the piazza and drank two cups of espresso outside a café a little way on from Florian's packed patio. They listened to a jazz quartet crucify Duke Ellington note by note and watched the tourists taking photos of each other. Then they ambled through the shopping streets, into the quiet residential quarter that sat on the lower northern edge of the canal before it made the turn for the *volta*.

Daniel stopped on the front steps of the Gritti Palace. It was not simply that he deemed it wise to go no further. The hotel peered down at him from another world, one of luxury and riches, one where he did not belong. He was aware of his mud-caked jeans and the taste of grimy water in his mouth. He knew, too, that his mind was confused, torn between two possibilities, each of which might be ridiculous.

Amy watched him, a little nervous. "Are you coming in?" she asked. "Just for a little while?"

He shook his head. "Looking like this?"

"Daniel! My old man's paying close to four thousand dollars a week for a suite here. I can walk through that door naked if I feel like it."

He hesitated. "You're on your own?"

"This is the first year they let me come by myself. Even two years ago I had to put up with my mom. At the age of sixteen. Can you believe that?"

He could, and the thought made him feel old. Yet it would be rude to refuse. He wondered, too, what Laura would say if he arrived early at Ca' Scacchi.

"Just for a little while," he agreed, and then they walked into the Gritti Palace, ignoring the raised eyebrows of the staff, trailed their muddy feet across the carpet to the lift, and rose four floors to Amy's suite. It was ten times the size of Daniel's bedroom. There was an expensively decorated lounge, with windows overlooking the canal.

"I need to clean up," Amy announced, and headed for the bathroom. The sound of running water came soon after. He found the second bathroom, tore open one of the hotel's courtesy toothbrushes, and tried to scrub the taste of eels and worse from his mouth. Then he walked back to the window. The hotel stood opposite the Punta della Dogana, the very tip of Dorsoduro. The vast shadow of Salute sat a little to its right. He was just able to see the curious shape of Ca' Dario, like a giant medieval doll's house sitting crookedly by the water's edge. There was a single light in the front first-floor window. Daniel thought about

Laura's daydream and the carnival, with its masks and costumes. To be anonymous in the Venetian night would be to embark upon an adventure, like biting into a writhing, struggling eel. Life required adventure from time to time, and decision too.

The bathroom door opened. Amy came out, carrying a bundle of dirty clothes, threw them into a linen basket, then walked over to the fridge. She took out a bottle of Stolichnaya vodka and two chilled glasses from the freezer, poured a couple of shots, then brought them over to the window. The spirit was so cold it looked semi-liquid in the tumbler, sitting there beneath a taut meniscus. Daniel tasted it and choked instantly. It was like iced fire.

She was now wearing nothing but a hotel robe. Her blonde hair was still wet, tied back behind her neck.

"What are you looking at?" she asked.

"The canal. You've got a great view."

"Yeah."

He wondered if she had ever stood at the window in all the time she'd been there.

"Look." He walked to the far left of the long pane and she followed him, standing in front as he pointed. Not thinking twice, Daniel softly placed a hand on the damp gown covering her shoulder.

"Down the canal. Past Salute. You see the small house? The crooked one? With the tall windows?"

"Sure. So what?"

"Don't you think it's unusual? Attractive?"

"I guess so."

Amy leaned back against him, rolled her head up so that her damp hair fell beneath his chin. "Dan?"

"Yes?"

"Wouldn't you like to clean up too? We got pretty dirty out there. A first date to remember. I'll say that."

"It was," he agreed, and said no more. She pulled herself away from him and turned round. He was pleased to see there was no anger in her eyes, simply the need for an answer.

"I was going to shower when I got home," he said. "When I have clean clothes."

She winced, with a touch of sourness in the gesture. "I don't normally do this, if that's what you're thinking. I'm not given to..." She didn't want to say the rest.

"I never thought you were, Amy."

"Then what's the problem? Is it me?"

"*No!*" he lied. She folded her arms, a gesture he was beginning to recognise. "This is too quick," he added. "Too sudden."

"I'm only here for another nine days. What is this? The Middle Ages or something?"

A *vaporetto* sounded its horn on the canal. Daniel wished he were on board, safe in the stern, alone. "I just—"

Her temper broke. "I don't get you, Dan. It's like there's two people inside the same skin. One of them writes this music and it sounds so grown-up, so confident. As if the person who wrote it knows pretty much all there is to know about everything. And then there's you. I don't know who you are."

"I'm sorry."

"Do *not* apologise!"

He disposed of his empty glass, moved forward, and touched her hair. "No, Amy. I must. You're wonderful. When I look at you...when I hear you play the violin..."

Her face turned upwards to his in a motion meant to tantalise. Whatever ardour he was beginning to feel vanished in an instant. She still wore the traces of a teenager's hurt snarl. Her open mouth pouted towards his, expecting to be kissed. He retreated awkwardly, half a step back.

Amy glowered at him. "So why don't you want to touch me?"

"Because it's late. We're both tired. We've both had too much to drink. Also, I've a lot of things to think about. Things I can't discuss with you just yet."

The scowl grew more fierce. "But you discuss it with *them*, don't you?"

"I don't know what you mean."

"The weirdos, Dan! Those guys on the boat. That woman. Jesus, what kind of freak show was that?"

"They're my friends," he replied icily.

"Oh, come on! You're not one of them, Dan. You're one of us. Me. And Hugo. You realise that, don't you?"

"As I said," he repeated, "they're my friends."

She walked over to the bar and shot a refill into her glass. "Don't be naïve. If they let you in, it's only because they want to. Oh, will you just go! Please."

"As you see fit," he replied automatically.

"No." She stepped in front of him before he reached the door. "There's one more thing you've got to know. I decided that day when we met in the church. Not because of you, but because my head's waking up in this place and I start seeing things I should have seen a long time ago. All that crap they fed me at school. All that stuff from my folks. I'm out of that prison. This is my big chance to start growing up, and I thought it might be with you. No matter. Plenty more fish in the sea. Can't get Hugo off the phone."

"Hugo?" He was outraged, on her behalf, not his.

"Yeah. Old enough to be my dad. Thought I'd say it for you."

"Oh, Amy." He found his hand straying to her damp neck.

"Don't touch me, you bastard!"

"I'm sorry."

"More apologies, dammit. *Will you go?*"

He was unaccustomed to seeing hatred in another's eyes. The quiet, predictable blandness which consumed his life before

Venice now seemed to have deserted him entirely.

"Why the rush? That's what I don't understand."

There were tears in her eyes, and he thought he knew why. She had seen the shock in his face, how moved he was by her sudden fury with him.

"I'm eighteen, Dan," she said quietly. "I have lived my life in this rich kid's cocoon, and it is *so cold*. I want someone to love. I want someone to *love* me."

He touched her cheek, touched the tears. She didn't pull away. "I don't know anything about that, Amy. I just know you can't demand it. You have to wait for it to happen."

"Wait?" she spat back at him. "Like some old maid? Like that Laura friend of yours? What's she waiting for? Because it's not coming. Not from anyone. She's just growing old drying dishes, turning into a spinster a little bit more every time she looks at her watch."

Daniel took his hand away from Amy Hartston and felt a sudden urge to be out of her presence. He did not know the answer to her last question, which had, he now realised, been nagging him long before Amy put it in words.

"When we meet again," he said, "let's forget this happened."

He made for the door, listening to the torrent of angry words behind him. Hugo Massiter's name seemed to play a very large part in them. He wondered why she thought this would hurt him, what power she believed there might be in those few syllables. It was impossible that she knew of the arrangement about the concerto. No, Amy threw the name at him as a rival, which meant, he believed, that she misunderstood both his feelings and those of Hugo too. Massiter had a slyness of his own, but that did not, Daniel believed, extend to seducing teenage girls whom he must have known, albeit distantly, since their childhood. It was impossible. It had to be.

36

The dancing lesson

THE NIGHT WAS WARM AND HUMID. FEELING THE NEED to walk, Daniel turned away from the *vaporetto* stop and strode north, finding the narrow passage to the Accademia bridge, the single crossing over the canal before the Rialto, and climbed the steps. He stood in the centre of the gentle wooden arch, watching the traffic on the canal, thinking of Amy's last remark. Then he set off on the long walk to San Cassian, past the Frari, where, close by in San Rocco, the eyes of Scacchi's Lucifer would now be shining in the dark, through the backstreets of San Polo, until, by guesswork and accident, he found himself in the small *campo* of San Cassian. The old church looked less of an ugly hulk in the dark. The square was deserted. If it were not for the electric lights in the windows, he could have been in the Venice of two or three hundred years earlier. This was, he believed, what had made his mother come to love this city, and pass on the feeling to her son: the hint of ghostly footprints in the dust, a sign of successive generations puzzling over their lives. And such power in the dead. When he looked at the paintings in San Rocco or listened to that tantalising music which now, unfairly, bore his name, he found himself in awe of those who had walked these streets before. His own imprint seemed so tiny by comparison.

He stopped in front of the bar where he had passed the ransom over to the mysterious thief. It was now closed and shuttered. Venice went to bed early. Then, his mind still working, he walked the few paces over the bridge and let himself into Ca' Scacchi. The loud, uncompromising sound of big-band jazz came from the front room on the first floor. He peeped cautiously around the half-open door, not wanting to be seen. Scacchi was seated on the sofa, looking exhausted, watching Paul dance, slowly and elegantly, with a phantom partner, making certain and accurate steps upon the carpet.

Slowly, feeling weary after the long day, he went upstairs. The music was so loud it drifted along the stairwell, filling the house, even on the third floor. He walked towards his bedroom. A noise behind made him turn. Laura stood there, looking bright and sober, back in her white uniform, back on duty.

"Daniel?" she asked, full of concern. "Why are you home so early?"

He paused on the landing, and for once, Laura seemed surprised by the set of his face. "Enough!" he declared. "I'm back, and that's all there is to it."

"I thought," she said, not quite smiling, but not entirely neutral either, "that perhaps you and Amy...She is so very nice and pretty. And talented too."

"I have never once, Laura, given you the slightest reason to believe that I wish anything between Amy and myself. Yet you insist..."

Her green eyes, all sudden innocence, laughed silently back at him.

"You seem upset," she said. "Would you like something? A drink?"

"No! I've had quite enough to drink for one day. For an entire month, as it happens."

"Tea, perhaps. The English like tea, Daniel."

"I'm aware of that." The idea of tea was irresistible. "Yes, please. Tea."

"I have a little kitchen. We should not disturb the gentlemen below. As you may hear through the"—she broke off and brought her voice up several decibels to produce a deafening yell down the staircase—"*floor, they appear to be having a party all to themselves!*"

He followed her into a large, tidy apartment which had a faint smell of perfume. The walls were plain white; the furniture was modest. A small hob and a microwave sat at one end of the room, next to the sink. A neat, square table with four chairs filled the centre, with a sofa by the wall. An open door disclosed, in the dim light of a lamp, a double bed covered in a flower-patterned quilt. Scacchi's music rose through the floor with an insistent thump.

"Earl Grey or Darjeeling?" she asked.

"Um. Earl Grey." He sat on the low cream sofa and watched her busy herself at the hob.

"What is the Gritti Palace like?" she asked.

"Large. And grand."

"Is that all there is to say about it? Amy has a suite, I gather. It must be wonderful."

"It is . . . not to my taste."

"Ah." Laura went to the table, stirred the pot briskly, and came back to sit next to him, two mugs in her hand. Downstairs, the music grew in volume: a big-band stomp. They could hear Paul's wry laughter. Daniel did not, for one moment, wish to think of what might be happening. There had been noises in the house before which suggested the two men, in spite of their condition, remained vigorous when the occasion arose.

"Do you like jazz?" she asked, clearly unwilling to address the subject of Amy any further.

"I can't say I've listened to it very much."

"Listened?" There was a glimpse of tanned skin behind the buttons of her white coat when she spoke. Daniel began to wonder if this was a mistake. "Jazz is for dancing, isn't it?"

"I don't know."

"Come!"

She put down her mug and beckoned him to his feet.

"I can't dance, Laura."

"Excellent! I've found something I can teach my clever Englishman!"

"I cannot..."

She tugged him upright with both hands and dragged him to the centre of the room. Downstairs, as if on cue, the music changed to a sprightly tune. Laura held out her arms. He walked forward and found himself in her loose embrace.

"Move," she commanded.

"How?"

Her hair was newly washed and fragrant. She gazed at him, full of life, demanding action.

"Like this."

She took them in a gentle arc, leading. He tried to follow, tripped over her feet, and found himself starting to giggle. They came to a halt by the table. There was a look of amused consternation in her gaze.

"Daniel," Laura noted gently, "I know that the English are not known for their sense of rhythm and grace. But you're a famous composer in the making. You should at least *try*."

"Oh, don't," he sighed miserably. She saw the sudden worried expression on his face.

"I'm sorry. I shouldn't have made that joke." They stood

unmoving, each with a hand on the other's shoulder, the second to the waist. Daniel had never been this close to her before. Laura's face, half-crooked, staring up at him, was exquisite. There were delightful lines at the corner of her mouth when she smiled. The contrast between her and the girlish Amy could not have been greater.

"She plays those notes, Laura, and thinks they're mine. It's the music she wants, or the mind behind it. Not *me*."

The sound ended downstairs, then was replaced by a slower song. They made small, random movements around the floor.

"I don't believe that for one moment. Though you deserve as much. I warned you all about this deception and got bawled out by Scacchi for my pains."

"He was thinking of you, Laura," Daniel answered, treading carefully. "I believe you're the dearest thing to him, dearer even than Paul."

Her eyes darkened. "If that's so, why has he kept secrets from me? No. I must not complain. Tomorrow, he says, we will speak frankly."

"Good…" He decided to change the subject, boldly and abruptly. "How old are you? If I may ask."

Her eyes sparked, out of surprise, not anger. "I'm not yet thirty, and shall remain so for many a year."

"Oh."

She waited, until it was plain that he would go no further. "Daniel. When a man asks that question of a woman, it's customary he makes some comment in return, not stay as silent as the grave."

"You don't look a day over twenty-four."

"Liar!"

"No. I mean it. Sometimes you don't, anyway. At other times…"

"What? Forty? Fifty? The measure of your compliment is diminishing by the second!"

"I didn't mean it to. I think, in all honesty, Laura, that you're a chameleon. You take the shape that suits you, be it maid or cook, elder sister or..." He checked himself. "I would never put you at forty, not even when you're determined to be your dowdiest. Thirty-five at the most."

She held her delicate nose in the air, as if sniffing something bad. "I have never, Daniel Forster, danced before with a man who has called me dowdy. Least of all one who comes caked in lagoon mud with the stink of *bisato crudo* upon his breath."

The urge to kiss her was growing wildly at the back of his imagination. Somewhere deep in his head, he could picture them already, as if he could separate his mind from his body and become a camera on the wall, next to the small picture of the Virgin and Child hung above the microwave. Downstairs, the music stopped. Daniel and Laura came to a halt, still clinging loosely to each other.

"But to return to my former point," he continued briskly. "Amy's determined. If she doesn't have me, she'll have someone."

"Ah. I understand. This is Venice as the 'city of romance'? A wonderful cliché. The Americans fall for it all the time. *'Ave a nice lay!*"

They laughed, and he believed that she held him just a little more tightly.

"It's obligatory to fall in love when one visits Venice," Laura continued. "You foreigners have believed as much ever since you invented that thing called the 'Grand Tour'."

"I know," he replied absently, lost in deliberation.

"Ah. I see. You're pensive. You're thinking: Who's this woman servant to speak of such things? What would the likes of her know of the 'Grand Tour'?"

Daniel felt as if he were standing on the edge of some tall cliff, staring down at the perfect blue ocean, wondering whether to leap. He moved his hand from her shoulder, slowly, gently pushed back the chestnut hair from her neck and touched the soft, warm flesh there. She froze. The room seemed so full of silence he could hear both their hearts beating.

"No," he replied. "I was thinking that at the heart of all clichés there must lie some truth; otherwise, they wouldn't be clichés at all. That one may fall in love here. And that I have."

Laura's head fell forward until she stared, silently, at his chest. He moved his fingers slowly to her cheek and ran the side of his thumb upwards, to the corner of her hidden eye. A tiny drop of moisture met him there. As if embarrassed by its presence, his hand moved on and found her hair, which slipped between his fingers like silk.

"Daniel." Her voice was low and without emotion. He wished he could see more of her face. "I'm an idiot. I didn't invite you here for this reason. Nothing was further from my thoughts."

"I know," he said, and, as tenderly as he knew how, kissed the curve of her cheek, tasted the single salt tear there, heard the slow intake of her breath.

"I'm happy alone," she announced with some finality.

"As was I."

He danced his fingers lightly across her cheek, amazed by the softness of her skin. Laura's face came up to look into his. There was something akin to fear in her eyes.

"This can't possibly be right."

"I agree. Probably not."

She smiled at him, and he was overwhelmed by her beauty. "What has come over you, Daniel?"

"Determination," he replied. "And wasn't it you who said I was here with a purpose? To save you."

"I have no need of being saved! I …"

He bent down, and, with the precise, steady motion of a clockwork mechanism, their mouths met. His hands fell around her back, felt the taut, perfect curves of her hips. She touched his waist, reached down, slowly withdrew his grubby shirt from under his belt, and placed her palm on the warmth of his pale body.

They paused to look at each other, keenly aware that there was time for turning back. Her mouth was half-open; her eyes never left his.

Daniel reached forward and unfastened the top button of her white nylon housecoat, then methodically worked on those below. The front fell open. She shrugged the clothing off her shoulders and stood there, the perfect bleached underwear making a strange contrast with her flawless, tanned skin.

"It's been a long time, Daniel," she said. "I'm frightened."

"We've been waiting for each other, Laura. Can't you feel as much?"

She said nothing. He persisted. "You do believe that, don't you?"

"I don't know what to believe." She moved her palm upon his chest, feeling the beating of his heart. "The other night I had a dream. I was back on the boat, outside Ca' Dario."

"And?"

"When I looked up at that window, Daniel. I saw that man again *and it was you*. In agony. With your hands covered in blood. Screaming."

"Then we both dream of each other, Laura."

The corners of her mouth turned upwards. There was a hint of yearning in her face. She picked at the shoulder of his shirt, removing a small clump of grass and mud.

"I would like to remember this night, Daniel Forster," she

announced primly. "But not for your smell. To the bathroom, dear. This instant."

He obeyed, feeling no need to hurry. When he returned, she was in the bedroom, beneath the flowery quilt. The room was illuminated by the single lamp. He slipped naked into the bed and was immediately in her arms.

"I'm not an ... expert," he whispered.

"And you think, because I am older, I am?"

"I don't know. And I don't care."

She rolled above him, holding his face in her hands. "Remember me, Daniel," she said.

"Of course! I ..."

She placed her fingers over his mouth and reached down with her free hand, moving with a certain intent which would in any case have silenced him. Delicately she poised herself over him, searching for the correct arrangement of their bodies, then lowered herself slowly. The metal springs of the cheap double bed began to sound to their mutual rhythm. Words disappeared from their heads, replaced by a more elemental conversation conducted with feverish hands and probing tongues. And after endless turns and changes, he heard the rising tone of her voice, felt himself forced to join in. In this sweet, damp delight, they lay together for an age, locked together like a single creature. Then the ardour returned and the night seemed to consist of nothing except two bodies, one pale, one darker, searching for, and finding, some nameless heaven.

He did not recall removing himself from her arms. Some inner drive told him this must not happen. That he must sleep with her tight within his grasp, because to do otherwise would be to invite her to step outside his world and enter another where he could not follow. But it was difficult, that night, for Daniel Forster to distinguish between reality and dream. It was as if two worlds had mingled in their coupling and, with the same feverish determination, mated so perfectly that he could not detect the seam.

Then he jolted wide-awake in the clammy bed and found himself alone, head ringing with the memory of a terrible sound. The little alarm clock beneath the bedside lamp read 3:15. The noise returned, and with a growing sense of panic, Daniel recognised it. Somewhere below, Laura was screaming in utter terror.

He dashed for the sofa, dragged on his jeans, and raced downstairs, mind going black with fear.

She was in the second-floor bedroom which Scacchi and Paul shared, wearing her white housecoat again. It was covered with blood, the crimson stains running the length of the front. Her face was bloodied, too, and in her hand she held a long kitchen knife dark with gore.

Paul lay on his side on the floor. His hands were wrapped around his stomach, which was rent by a large, gaping wound. His eyes were wide-open, glassy. Scacchi sat in a chair in the corner of the room, clutching his chest, staring into nothingness.

Daniel looked at her and said, "Laura. Give me the knife. Please."

She no longer recognised him. He watched, his mind blank with horror, as she slumped to the floor, clutching the weapon to her chest as if she would kill any man who might try to take it from her.

Outside, a distant siren wailed. Daniel stared at the weeping figure on the floor and felt his world fall apart.

37

A concert to remember

It was a fine afternoon. A faint wind blew from the northeast across an empty lagoon, and so the air upon the promenade was as sweet as any Venetian might expect of a summer day. Whoever took the proceeds of the gate—Delapole, in the main, I gather—must have been delighted indeed. Every one of La Pietà's four hundred seats was sold. The tall double doors to the church had been thrown open to entertain those who could not find, or afford, a ticket. The orchestra sat far back behind its shutters, and the airy interior swallowed up most of the sound they made. Still, this was about more than music. The prospect of a new master in the city seemed appropriate to the local mood. The Republic's fortunes may be on the wane, as Rousseau once warned us. Beneath this manifest grandeur, it is not hard to see the presentiments of decay, like marks on the face of a beauty just passing her prime. The city cries out for genius and hopes the mysterious composer will provide it.

We were late, and that because of the most extraordinary argument between Leo and Delapole. The Englishman, with Gobbo in tow, arrived at Ca' Scacchi just before noon, smiling at first, making pleasant enquiries about the arrangements Leo and Vivaldi had made for the afternoon. My uncle answered politely, if with little grace. He has, I think, difficulty in maintaining good relations with those who sponsor him. While he desires their money, he hates them for making him so dependent upon their favours. This is a circle Leo may never be able to square, I think, as he knows full well himself, and that makes him madder still.

So, when Delapole asked for copies of the various musical parts, Leo took pleasure in being able to smile for the first time during this interview and shake his head firmly. "No, sir. That I cannot do."

"Why not?" asked Delapole. "It's my money that paid for it."

"Of course," Leo agreed. "And most grateful we are for that, though I think you will more than recoup your investment from the admissions. But this music is not mine to give. It belongs to its creator, who entrusted its care to me. Until I have some instructions from him, it shall remain in my custody, not hawked around the streets like penny gossip sheets."

Delapole's face, normally the picture of English restraint, flushed bright red with fury. "This is ridiculous, man. I am the fellow's patron. I deserve a little for that, surely."

"If he so decides," Leo replied with a wry smile. "It is quite out of my hands."

"Then what will happen to the musicians' parts once the concert is over?" Delapole demanded. "You will surely let me have one of them."

"To be burnt, sir," Leo announced in triumph. "Every last one, and the plates too. As a publisher of repute . . ."

Gobbo coughed very purposefully at this point, and I admit I had trouble keeping a straight face. It was clear that Leo was being intentionally annoying while also creating further work for himself in the future, when the music would have to be copied, set, and printed once again.

". . . it is my duty to protect the rights of those who choose me as their conduit to the public at large. Should our maestro so decide, I will print this music by the million and hand it out to beggars on the street. But until I have instructions . . ."

"I have scarcely heard such nonsense, Scacchi. If you burn these parts, then what remains of the work?"

"Why, the original, sir. Nothing more, since I doubt a genius who chooses to keep himself anonymous has sent his manuscript out for copying himself."

"And where is that now, precisely?"

Oh, how Leo loved this. "In my safekeeping, of course. Where none may find it."

Delapole picked up his walking stick, a fine wooden one with an ivory head, and banged it on the table in our modest office. I rather think he would have liked to hammer it on Leo's skull and frankly couldn't blame him. Delapole is a generous man—as Rebecca already knows. It would cost nothing, and break no great rule, to let him have some paper for his scrapbook. "You play games with me, Scacchi, as if I am some London popinjay. You mistake me greatly."

Leo opened his arms wide and extended his palms as if to say *But what else may I do?* "Come," he urged us. "We will be late for this momentous occasion, Mr. Delapole. Let us bask in this unmerited glory and see what news ensues. This work is no *succès d'estime,* I assure you. It will please the cognoscenti and the masses too. Once that becomes apparent, our mysterious musician will surely want the world to know his name, and pay you due homage when he does."

"Harrumph."

The English make that noise sometimes. Most puzzling. Delapole's temper was receding. I suspect he felt more hurt than offended. The rich do not like being gulled. Leo would do well to watch his step.

So we walked to Delapole's gondola and edged our way through the fleet of vessels on the canal, past St. Mark's, then on to dock at the jetty outside La Pietà. Venice was in a festive mood. A little stage troupe had set up a makeshift platform some way down from the church steps and upon it played the usual cast of brightly coloured characters: Scaramouche and Pantaloon, Punchinello and Harlequin. Harmless, ribald fun for the masses who milled around the waterfront. Here was a seller of sweetmeats, here a fortune-teller. Boats of all kinds thronged the lagoon, fighting for somewhere to disgorge ever more souls onto the seething pavement. Young and old, rich and poor, crooked and honest, comely and hideous, Venice was on show for the world to see, in all its colours: the vermilion of fine silk dresses, the coarse grey weave of a sailor's jerkin, black and white in the Harlequin's blouse, a pigment like the yellow gold of the sun in the tresses of the gaudy street women working their trade beneath the Doge's long, thin nose.

I confess I smiled at this. To think that Rebecca had prompted such commotion. If only they knew . . . Then Leo pushed his way through the throng, crying, "Ladies, gentlemen! The Englishman Delapole, who favours us with the means to hear this wonder, would kindly have you let him pass and reach his seat."

That put up a hearty murmuring in the masses. "Aye, these English aren't so bad." "A gentleman, no doubt, to grace us with this debut here when he might so easily have thought of his countrymen's ears." "Three cheers for Delapole, I say!

Hurrah for our English benefactor!"

This last, of course, came from Gobbo himself, fetching up the rear. Soon the hurly-burly was full of applause and commendations. Delapole's pale, handsome face rose above it all, beaming with pride. Hands were thrust through the pack to pat him on the shoulder, hats waved, carnations flew through the air. Then he waved a handkerchief at them, muttering the words we've come to expect of the English, "Jolly good! Too kind! Oh, really, too kind!"

Leo was right. All it took was a little adulation, and his resentment was gone. We pushed through the doors and found ourselves in the nave, where the audience was already seated, every head turned to mark our arrival. The players no longer sat behind screens. They were on the low marble platform in front of the altar, the very picture of a small chamber orchestra, dressed uniformly in black, arranged in a gentle arc. They sat meekly, looking very young. Rebecca was in their centre, the focus of everyone's gaze. My heart leapt inside my chest. We make ourselves conspicuous; we court disaster. This game now lurches beyond our control.

Vivaldi was in front of the players, naturally, baton in hand, turned to the audience, his grey face quite expressionless.

"See," Leo whispered to us. "So great is this work that Vivaldi himself feels jealous. He puts the players on show in order that their beauty might distract us from the notes."

Delapole waved to the pews at the front which had been reserved for us. "Enough talking, sir," he said in a loud voice so that all might hear. "Let us take our seats so that Venice may judge whether we waste her time or not."

A low swell of applause ran through the audience as we walked forward. I sat at the end of the pew, next to Gobbo, and tried not to look at Rebecca. She seemed entirely

absorbed by the event and I think failed to notice me at all.
Perhaps this was deliberate. This was not the Rebecca I knew.
Her hair had been brushed so that it might appear as straight
as possible, then tied back behind her head. There was a
patch of rouge on each cheek. She looked, for all the world,
like any mute, obedient player from a provincial orchestra.
I puzzled for a moment, then understood. She would never
have taken this risk had she known Vivaldi would parade the
orchestra to the world with her as its point of focus, as the
soloist. She had come expecting to play behind shutters,
then, when forced to perform so publicly, made this effort to
disguise herself to avoid the awkward questions that might
follow her detection. Yet there was not a scintilla of
nervousness in her demeanour.

Vivaldi cleared his throat; the audience became silent,
followed in degrees by the crowd beyond the door. Then he
spoke.

"Fellow citizens," he said. "This is a most unusual
occasion. I am not used to directing the work of others, nor
do my players spend much time on any pieces but my own.
So I apologise, to you and to our anonymous composer, for
whatever mistakes and omissions we may make when we
perform. Our English friend . . ."

Delapole nodded modestly.

". . . has been kind enough to offer his patronage for this
event in order that we might pass judgement on a work the
provenance of which is quite unknown to us. Perhaps its
author is in this room now. I have no idea."

I watched Rebecca closely. She did not even blink.

"It scarcely matters. These are notes upon a page,
remarkable notes, too, I think; otherwise, I would not be
associated with them. How remarkable, you must judge.

Not, I hope, out of curiosity, applauding for no better reason than to see the author make himself public, but out of honest appreciation of this concerto's faults and merits. We are, if you will, invited into a room to witness a painting which is unsigned or taste a vintage which has no label. Is this Veronese or a third-rate copyist? Does one taste a fine vintage of Trentino or a glass of Lombardy muck? I can offer you no guidance, save to say that I think it is worthy of your consideration. Furthermore—"

"Oh, get on with it, man," someone cried from the door. There was a murmur of agreement. Delapole whispered to Leo, more loudly than he realised, I think, "The fellow is scared of playing it, surely. Does he think it will sink his reputation or what?"

Leo said nothing. He could not take his eyes off the orchestra and, I fear, Rebecca. Vivaldi understood he could dally no longer. He waved his hand once in the air. His players rose at his bidding. Thus did *Concerto Anonimo*, the first public work by Rebecca Levi of the ghetto, make its public debut, and none but two in that room knew who had written it.

This was like no concert Venice—or any other city, I'll warrant—has ever witnessed. Rebecca stood in front of her fellow players, straight-backed, with dark, determined eyes, half watching Vivaldi for guidance (though I doubt she much needed it and wished instead she could both play and conduct the entire proceedings herself, and lecture the audience on the finer points of the piece simultaneously).

I listened, rapt, as the music I had so amateurishly tried out on our old harpsichord found its true home. At times Rebecca's instrument flew with the speed and agility of African swallows, around themes and inventions that wove in and out of each other, soaring and diving, taking directions none could predict. Then she would settle into deep, slow passages, simple on the surface yet laden with dark sonorities that defied their apparent effortlessness. Finally, she embarked upon a cadenza, one I took to be improvised, since Vivaldi did nothing but raise a single eyebrow and merely let her play her heart out, searing the air with the resonant tones she wrung from Delapole's most excellent gift.

When the music ended and she sat down, there was for a moment utter silence. I looked at Delapole. He wore the fondest expression I have ever seen on a man. The tears rolled down his cheeks for all to see. Even Leo seemed quite awestruck by what he had heard, and stared at Rebecca—as did most of the room—in open admiration. I caught her eye briefly. She seemed frightened, all the more so when the peace was shattered by a growing roar of applause—cheers and clapping, wild whoops, and cries of "Encore! *Encore!*"—that threatened to bring the flimsy roof of La Pietà down upon our heads.

Vivaldi let this racket run for a minute or more. I was dismayed to see that all the while he regarded Rebecca in the most intense way. Then he waved his arms for silence and announced, "I would give you more, sirs, but it is not mine to give. I think Venice has issued its opinion. It only remains for our hero to make himself known to us, that we may worship him the greater."

If I am not mistaken, there was a note of irony in that last comment. Vivaldi looked like a broken man. He had not simply lost his crown; he had, albeit unwittingly, abdicated. Still, he could not take his eyes off Rebecca, and I was not the only one to notice. Leo had a queer expression on his face. I closed my eyes and tried to savour Rebecca's moment of glory. Yet all that came was the presentiment of some dread turning upon this dangerous road of ours.

38

A brief investigation

MASSITER SCOWLED AT THE POLICE TEAM WHO WERE scouring the room in which Paul had died. Daniel felt giddy and ill. It was now eight in the morning. The unconscious Scacchi had been removed by ambulance boat to the Ospedale al Mare on the Lido, where he remained critically ill. Laura had left for the police station in the early hours—to make a statement, they said. Ca' Scacchi seemed empty without their presence, even though twenty men and women were now examining its every corner in the search for information.

"Damn, damn, damn," Massiter murmured. He seemed, Daniel thought, genuinely shocked by the attack. In the hard morning light he looked older, almost frail. "Such luck," he murmured.

"I don't understand, Hugo."

"I know the police, Daniel. They phoned me when this dreadful event occurred. I am helping by being here, aren't I?"

"Of course," Daniel replied without thinking.

"Well, that's something, then. I never knew the American, but Scacchi I thought of as a friend, you know."

The relationship between Scacchi and the Englishman seemed

more complex than that, Daniel believed. "I am sure," he said.

"And they send this…crew! I don't know a single one of them."

The police wore dark clothes and seemed singularly obsessed with the house, not its occupants. A quiet, sallow-faced man had interviewed Daniel for half an hour, appearing bored with his own questions. It was as if they knew the answers already and simply sought confirmation. Daniel had lied on several fronts, telling them that he had been in his own bedroom when he was woken by the sound of screaming and that there was nothing of great value that appeared to be missing. Yet they were examining every cupboard, every drawer, even in the adjoining warehouse, and had yet to find an ancient fiddle, a fading manuscript, or the stash of dollars Scacchi must have secreted somewhere. These items were, Daniel knew instinctively, gone from the house.

Finally, to his dismay, Giulia Morelli had arrived and announced she was to take charge of the investigation. The policewoman had nodded gravely to him in the living room and said nothing before disappearing about her business.

"They were robbers," he said firmly, as much to himself as Massiter. "Whoever it was stole the manuscript, Hugo."

The older man scowled. "Damned good job you'd copied it. Or we really would be in trouble. Is there anything else missing?"

Daniel stared at him. "A friend of mine has been murdered. Another is at death's door. I don't, to be frank, much care about the manuscript. I want the person responsible for this found."

Massiter seemed offended. "That won't help Scacchi. Or get the music back. There was something else, wasn't there?"

"I don't know," Daniel replied testily. "Scacchi liked his secrets."

"And the money?"

"I already told you. I don't know!"

It was possible, Daniel believed, that Scacchi had somehow tried to swindle the very criminals he had sought to satisfy by acquiring the Guarneri in the first place. He had assumed the fiddle was gone from the house, though Scacchi had never discussed the matter as soon as the instrument was in his hands. Perhaps whatever money he had raised had already been spent elsewhere. But on what?

"They must know the manuscript is gone," Daniel said firmly. "I shall tell them."

Massiter seized his shoulder and hissed in his ear, so loudly that Giulia Morelli, who was on the far side of the room going through the contents of a desk, turned to look at them. "You must do no such thing, you little fool! Tell them about the music and we're both exposed as frauds."

"I don't care, Hugo."

Massiter's face grew hard and threatening. "Then learn, Daniel. The pair of us are signatories to contracts which name you as the author of this piece. If you tell them the truth now, we could both face criminal charges. Being foreigners, we would, I imagine, find ourselves in the dock in an instant. You're a minnow, but imagine the pleasure they'd get out of bringing me down."

Daniel shook himself free of his grip. "I thought you had friends."

"Venetian friends," Massiter replied, calming down a little. "Fit for fair weather only."

Giulia Morelli had gone back to examining the papers in Scacchi's desk but kept half an eye on them. Massiter was right. He was trapped by the deception. They both were, which was, he suspected, why Massiter had rushed round to Ca' Scacchi after hearing of the incident.

"Well?" Massiter asked.

"All right, I won't tell them," Daniel said. "Not that, anyway."

Then, abruptly, he left Massiter's side and crossed the room. The woman detective put down a sheaf of letters written in Scacchi's ornate, flowing hand.

"When can we see Scacchi?" Daniel asked, aware of Massiter scurrying to his side.

"I'm afraid he is in a coma."

"You know each other?" Massiter asked immediately.

"I am Captain Morelli." She seemed fascinated by his presence. "I've been to your concerts, sir. Every one of them. This year Daniel here is the marvel, or so the papers say."

Daniel grimaced. "The papers..."

"I'm sorry," she said. "This is a shocking event. I should not have mentioned lighter matters at this time. But you will still go ahead with the concert?"

"Of course," Hugo replied, butting in. "Scacchi would have wanted as much." They had already begun to talk about the old man in the past tense.

"Good," she said with a brief smile. "I think we're almost finished here. I'm sorry for the inconvenience. And also for your grief. I didn't know the American, but I've always enjoyed Scacchi's company. I will pray for his recovery."

"And you found something?" Massiter asked hopefully.

She shook her head. "Nothing. This is an old house, but there is little of real value in it. I think many things must have been sold over the years. You can see nothing missing, Daniel?"

"Nothing I'm aware of. But robbery must have been the motive."

Giulia Morelli's eyes narrowed. "Why? What was there to steal?"

"I don't know," he answered quickly.

"And where's the evidence? There are no broken windows. No forced doors. If this was a robber, then Scacchi or the American must have let him in."

Daniel tried to think quickly. "There is something I must tell you. I don't know if it's important or not."

The policewoman nodded at him. "Something that was not in your statement? I read what you said. It seemed quite straightforward. You were in bed. You heard a noise. You found what you found."

"It's not about me." He was aware of Massiter's presence close by his side. "Scacchi owed money. He borrowed from some men and was worried what they would do to him and Paul if he failed to repay them."

"Some men?"

"Criminals, I believe," Daniel admitted.

She seemed amused. "Scacchi knew criminals? I believed he was some kind of art dealer, like yourself, Signor Massiter."

"Not quite in my league," Massiter sniffed.

"Nevertheless..." the woman continued. "He dealt in objects of a certain history and gave them value through his actions. Like most art dealers, I imagine. Let me be honest with you. As you surely know, Daniel, we're not entirely unfamiliar with Scacchi. We're not fools."

"Then you know the kind of men he would have dealt with?" Daniel asked.

"Of course! And I would be aware, I think, if any of them had reason to be angry with him. There's no advantage in keeping quiet about debtors in default. A little gossip enhances the pressure upon them to pay and serves to deter their counterparts should some punishment be necessary."

"Then," he added, "you have it. You can speak to these people. You can find out who his creditors were."

She cast him a condescending glance. "I did that shortly after I came here. This house has the smell of penury about it, but I can find no evidence Scacchi owed anyone a cent."

"That's not true! He told me so himself!"

"And this man never lied?" Giulia Morelli waited for his answer. Daniel was lost for words. She turned to Massiter. "You don't remember me, sir?"

He peered at her. "Sorry. No."

"No reason to. I was barely out of college. Ten years ago, when there was that tragic case of the girl violinist. What was her name?"

"Susanna Gianni," Massiter replied softly.

"Correct. You have a good memory for some things. I worked on that case. I was there when you were interviewed. I was much moved by your grief."

"It was a great loss," Massiter noted. "I had been thinking that perhaps I should dedicate this year's concert to her memory."

She shrugged her shoulders. "But why now? After so many years? She is forgotten, surely?"

"Not by those of us who knew her," Massiter said archly.

"Then perhaps you should have a private meeting and remember her for yourselves. Not force her name upon a new audience who have never heard it. The poor girl is dead and should stay that way. Sometimes these cases have a degree of finality about them which we should respect. You do remember that aspect of the matter, don't you?"

Massiter shuffled on his feet, then looked at his watch. "I miss your point."

"My point is this. The Gianni girl is murdered, and for a week every police officer in Venice searched everywhere to discover her killer. Then, in an instant, it becomes apparent. We find this dead conductor of yours... and he has confessed! Can you imagine how much gratitude my superiors felt towards this man? One minute, chaos. The next, order—and not a penny to be spent on a trial, either."

"It was," Massiter said bleakly, "a dreadful summer."

"Yes," she replied. "And yet I learnt so much then, sir. I learnt that wisdom is synonymous with simplicity. That to seek secrets and conspiracies simply muddies water that is clean to begin with. The first solution is usually the most...apposite. Yes, I believe that is the word."

They were both silent. There was something in this woman's manner, half-joking, half-threatening, which made them wary.

"Gentlemen." Giulia Morelli leaned forward and touched Daniel on the shoulder. He could smell perfume on her skin. Her white, perfect smile shone at him. "You do agree with me, don't you? Why turn stones unnecessarily and let all manner of black creatures scuttle around our feet as a consequence?"

Daniel felt incensed by her tone. "I want the person who did this found. I want him brought to book."

"Of course!" The woman was clearly laughing at him.

"I want—!"

"Please," she said firmly. "You already have what you want. We have the culprit. We will lay charges in a few days, I imagine. Shortly after that we will be in court. Domestics...always the problem."

"What?"

"You saw it yourself? She was holding the knife. It's covered with her fingerprints."

"This," Daniel said, voice rising, "is ridiculous. Laura was one of the family. They loved each other."

"Families," Giulia Morelli said. "So many reasons for arguments. Money. Passion. Hatred. She's in the women's prison in Giudecca. You may see her. I have no objection."

He felt like taking this woman by the shoulders and shaking her until she saw sense. He felt like screaming at her, knowing all the time that this was what she wanted.

"You are," he said, fighting to keep calm, "so mistaken about this. Scacchi will recover and tell you so himself."

"Perhaps. But in the meantime, go talk to her yourself," she insisted.

"Daniel," Massiter said, taking his arm. "Best leave this now...."

"*NO!*"

She stood in front of him, almost smirking, possessed, he knew, of some precious piece of information she was waiting to disclose.

"Well?" he said. "There's something else?"

"It is simple, Daniel. Like all great mysteries. The housekeeper has confessed. Here, when we took her statement. And again at the station. She gives no motive. She is a little insane, perhaps. Who cares? *She has confessed.* Now, what could be more convenient than that?"

Unmasked

After the concert we fell into sunlight, blinking like captives
who had spent a day beneath ground, locked in some fairy
cavern. Delapole was the hero of the hour. The crowd was
determined to make Rebecca the heroine, too, but she had
fled unseen. I searched for her in vain and all the while felt
my nerves fray at the possibilities. What if she had been
recognised in spite of her attempt to alter her appearance?
What was going through Leo's mind? And, most of all,
how had we given her the gift she most earnestly desired,
and deserved, without bringing the world falling down
around our heads?

Two hours later, back in the house, with Leo gulping
down wine and looking like a hyena that has stumbled upon
a fresh corpse, my worst fears were confirmed. He beckoned
me to sit at the table, fixed me with a cheery glance, and
asked, "So where will it be for Vivaldi now, do you think?
Not a chap who likes to stand in someone else's shadow."

"I have no idea, Uncle. It depends who the composer
is and whether he will produce new works. Perhaps he is
old...."

"Old! Old! Did that sound like an old man's music? Why, someone's trying to rewrite the rules beneath our noses, and none over the age of thirty would dream of doing that."

"If you say so. But I wonder how many people would notice such a thing. They just hear delightful music, well played, and ask no such questions."

Leo grinned slyly. "Perhaps they should. I asked Vivaldi a question."

The blood froze still in my veins. I said nothing.

"I asked him why he stared at the nicely disguised violinist I had sent him—Rebecca 'Guillaume,' I believe he called her. Why, she seems to think herself a rosy-cheeked Gentile these days."

I answered this after some decent pause for deliberation. "I believe neither of us should dwell on the issue of the Levis, Uncle. Or we might both find ourselves incriminated."

In an instant his hand shot across the table, grabbed my collar, and dragged me over the food and drink until I was no more than an inch or two from his face. He was surprisingly strong, and I was so shocked I didn't resist.

"Don't play with me, boy! I talked to Vivaldi and asked him how long it took her to learn her part. He gave me that supercilious look of his and said, 'Why, Scacchi. It must be a miracle indeed. A day or two, no more. It was almost as if she knew the piece *before* I gave her the notes.' "

He flung me back into my seat, where I remained, desperately trying to see a way around this inquisition.

"Do you think I'm a simpleton, Lorenzo? That manuscript you found 'left outside the door'? And all the time you and the pretty thing have spent together."

"I don't know what you mean, sir."

"Hah! She's the one. You know it full well. And let me tell

you something. She can never claim authorship of that music. She can whine and plead and throw herself at the feet of the Doge himself, and the city will still tear her apart the moment it realises Rebecca 'Guillaume' has been duping them all along. Jewesses do not write music or taunt the Church in this world. Her only hope—for her music and her survival—is to throw herself on the mercy of one who will invent some subterfuge that keeps her hidden."

It was obvious who Leo had in mind for this role, and I knew already what kind of master he made. My mind whirled.

"And you," he snarled. "You call yourself my flesh and blood, and still go along with this deceit. One glance from a pretty Hebrew face and it's to hell with all your loyalties, eh?"

The painting in the church across the *rio* came into my head once more. I marvelled I had once found it incomprehensible that an apprentice might harbour thoughts of murdering his master.

"Is there anything more you require of me, Uncle?" I replied.

"What do you have to offer?"

"Nothing, sir."

"Then off with you. I'll speak to the Levis myself and see what may be done. As for your excursions with the lady, I think you may forget them. There's plenty of work for you here. Start by sweeping out the cellar, for one thing. And mind the rats don't bite. You stay within these doors until I say you may do otherwise."

With that I retired to my room to watch the evening strollers in San Cassian and let my fury dissipate like smoke into the night. Leo is like the spider. He throws his web in dark corners, watches from the shadows, then pounces when his victims are ensnared. Yet in this vain confidence lies his undoing.

I listened while, two floors below, he drank wine, talking to himself, with the cold, metallic sound of his empty laughter echoing from time to time around the room. The red Veneto grape is my uncle's only bedfellow these days, and when this affair is consummated he sleeps. After midnight I heard the sound of snoring and was gone, out into the night, out to the ghetto.

40

The captain makes progress

GIULIA MORELLI SAT AT HER DESK IN FRONT OF A neatly stacked pile of reports, thinking about Ca' Scacchi, Daniel Forster, and what had happened some weeks before in the apartment in Sant' Alvise. All were, she felt, somehow linked. It was the third event—her nearness to death in the small, dark room—which enlarged her personal stake in discovering the thread which tied them together. The memory of that moment, of being on her knees opposite the dead caretaker, wounded and waiting to follow along the journey he had made, haunted her. It was, she felt, an imposition, a ghost. One that required exorcism, by whatever means were appropriate.

Scacchi's housekeeper was lying; that much was obvious. So were both Englishmen, though in the case of the younger she found it impossible to grasp the reason. She had been inside his bedroom, seen the barely ruffled sheets there, and compared them with the tangled mass of fabric that was the woman's bed. It was not hard to guess where he had really spent that night. Was the housekeeper lying to protect him? That seemed impossible. He was too convinced of her innocence, too anxious for Scacchi to recover sufficiently to exculpate her from the attack.

Massiter was a different matter. His name appeared in every one of the files on her desk, each as inconclusive as the next. That he partook in smuggling illicit objects could not be doubted. They had intelligence from myriad sources to suggest this was the case. But there were rumours, also, of tax evasion and outright fraud. Massiter's name cropped up in too many conversations for its appearance to be coincidence. Yet not a shred of evidence had been found against him. Even so, an ambitious detective had, some four years earlier, gained authority to search his apartment near Salute. He came away empty-handed and now pushed a pen in Padua.

Massiter had friends everywhere, friends who stood in the dark. He would, she assumed, be constantly forewarned of any impending action against him and act accordingly. Nevertheless, some soft Achilles' heel must exist, and she knew where it lay. If the rumours were correct, there had to be some lockup or small warehouse in the city or Mestre where he was able to store his contraband goods before moving them on. The hapless detective whose career now ebbed away in Padua had ransacked the city records, looking for some *magazzino* that had Massiter's name on the deeds or rental contract and found nothing. Still, this illicit Aladdin's cave must exist. Massiter dealt in real objects, solid artefacts. They could not be spirited through the city on wings.

She walked to the window and watched the crowds heading for the station. It was a close summer day. The city swarmed with tourists. Somewhere beyond the glass, no more than a mile or two from where she stood, must lie all the answers. And some, too, to questions which no one had asked for years. Giulia Morelli returned to her desk and opened the final file, the one marked "Susanna Gianni." She recalled the way the records clerk had looked at her when she asked for it. This was a case which had lost none of its potency for those who had been touched by it. She could not forget that brief week of frantic activity a decade before when, for a short interlude, it seemed a vicious killer might be loose in the city. Then the sudden sense of finality which resulted from the discovery of the conductor's body. She had been in the party which visited the Gritti Palace to look at his corpse. The room was so tidy, the position of the dead man so perfect. She had looked through his luggage and found some mild homosexual pornography and a phone number which proved to be that of a gay pimp in Mestre. She had opened his wardrobes and smelled the heavy, cloying scent on his clothes. Later she had spoken to those who had known him and confirmed what she already understood to be true: that Anatole Singer's sexual tastes did not lie in women of any age, least of all a lovely teenager who had blossomed beneath his care.

But she had revealed none of this for a good reason, one which continued to haunt her. She had been there when they searched the conductor's suite, had seen what was found and what was taken away. She had followed in the footsteps of the captain in charge, old Ruggiero, who was now comfortably retired to Tuscany. She had watched him catalogue every last item and seen the report book before they left the hotel. There had been no suicide note. Every one of them knew as much; every one of them acquiesced when Ruggiero later produced it from nowhere and declared the case closed. She had never once taken a penny in bribes or as much as a free drink from a neighbourhood bar. Yet, through that single act of acceptance, Giulia Morelli continued to feel as stained as the grubbiest of Veneto cops whose palm stood open, always.

She stared at the typed report in front of her and started to read it again, even though by now she felt she knew it by heart. Almost an hour later, when her head was beginning to ache from the pointless effort, there was a knock on the door. One of the uniformed sergeants stood there, looking wary.

"Yes?"

He shuffled, uncomfortable in her presence, as so many of them were. "You said you wanted us to trawl for something on that killing."

He had a file in his hand. She felt her spirits rise a little. "I did."

"We picked up some cheap little hood lifting an American's wallet in San Marco this morning."

"Well?"

"When I asked him if he knew anything about what happened at the Scacchi place, he went white. *Really* white. Like he couldn't believe it. There's something there. Hell, I don't know what."

She walked to the door, took the file, and followed him down two flights of steps to the interview room, reading all the way.

"You know this man?"

"Rizzo? Sure. Minor league. Pickpocket. Errand boy."

The sergeant was about thirty, tall and straight-backed, with a plain, pale face. He looked trustworthy. The new crop always did.

"Did he have any ... associations?"

"Not that I'm aware of," he replied. "He doesn't belong to any of the local packs, if that's what you mean."

It wasn't, but she let that pass. "So what else do you know?"

"You mean apart from him going white like that? You need something else?"

She just stared and waited for an answer. The sergeant shrugged. "When we picked him up, he had a bankbook in his pocket that showed he'd deposited forty thousand U.S. dollars just on Friday."

They stopped outside the interview room door. "Do you know where he was around three-thirty this morning?"

He smiled at that one. "Oh, yes. Here. We picked him up at three trying to roll this guy in San Marco. Odd. This jerk looks more professional than that. Maybe something's worrying him. This is some small-time neighbourhood jerk. He doesn't go around breaking into big houses and killing people. It's beyond his imagination."

"Is he married?"

"Complete loner. He's got some fixed-rent place near the old ghetto. Nothing there except a few things that'll never get back to the owners, wherever they are. Hey, it's not a big deal. If it weren't for the money and the way he came over all queer, I wouldn't even have bothered you."

She touched the sleeve of his shirt and was amused that he almost jumped at her touch. "Thanks anyway. I'm grateful. Are you going to charge him?"

"You bet I'm going to charge him. Why do you think we do this? For the pleasure of their company?"

"I was just thinking..."

"Yeah, yeah. I know what you were thinking."

"If it makes sense to wait awhile. Let him think he's trading something..."

"*If*... You make the case to me. You tell me why I should let him go."

She nodded. There was a decision here she would one day have to face: finding someone to trust, someone with whom she could share her ideas.

"What's your name, Sergeant?" she asked.

"Biagio."

"Well, thanks." Giulia Morelli pushed open the door and walked into the interview room, took one look at the man, waved at the cigarette smoke that made the atmosphere opaque, then strode to the window and threw it open, letting in the faint smell of fumes from the nearby car park. She stared at the grey landscape until she had stopped trembling. She had trained herself to ignore instinct. Facts were all that mattered. Yet, crazy as she knew it to be, Giulia Morelli found it impossible to shake the idea that this was the killer she had last met in the Sant' Alvise apartment. Then it came to her. There was the stink of that dread room in Sant' Alvise: cheap, strong cigarettes, African maybe, and the rank odour of sweaty fear. Such a small fact, and one which meant nothing in law.

"Put that out," she barked at the figure on the other side of the table.

"What?"

She reached over, grabbed the cigarette from his mouth, and stubbed it out on the plain plastic top of the table. Rizzo looked shocked.

"Hey!"

She stared into his eyes. It had been dark in the apartment. She had never looked closely at the figure that hovered over the caretaker's dead body. Nevertheless, there was the smell, and something about his presence too. She was sure it was him.

"You remember me?"

He scowled. "Never had the pleasure. So what is this?"

There was time, she knew. As much as she wanted. There was no point in tackling the issue head-on. "Are you deaf as well as stupid?" she barked. "Forty thousand dollars in the bank and you try to roll some American in full sight of a couple of cops. Jesus. If there was a law against being dumb, you'd get life."

Rizzo's narrow eyes opened a little wider. There was an expression of relief on his face, and she understood why. He had been expecting to be quizzed about a murder, and found himself faced with a simple mugging instead. The man was off guard.

"You listen to me..." he objected. His voice had a coarse city croak.

"*All in good time!*" He went quiet when she yelled at him. She looked at the sergeant. "You've got his possessions. Give them here."

Biagio smiled, enjoying the show, then brought a red plastic tray to her. She picked up the bankbook, glanced at it, then threw it on the floor.

"Bitch!" Rizzo screamed. "That's my money."

"It's going to buy you a lot in jail," she hissed.

Rizzo held out his hands to the sergeant. "Look. I give in. Take away the crazy witch and bring me a normal cop. The American just asked for it. OK?"

"No such luck," she said, then picked up his mobile phone, one of the tiny ones the young liked so much. She pressed the button. It burst into life with a beep.

"What are you doing?" he asked quietly.

"Calling my cousin in New York. You don't mind, do you? These things are just so pretty you have to play with the buttons. Oh, look! You're not such a loner at all!"

Rizzo's eyes were back to being slits again. He looked pale. Not quite the white shade the sergeant had spoken of, but she got the message anyway. "What do you mean?" he asked.

She shook her head. "These uniform people. They go all over your flat and think you're just some solitary, antisocial scum. Just because you don't know anyone and the only girlfriends you've got live in those magazines you keep by the bed."

He didn't say anything. Deep in her head Giulia Morelli let a little whisper run around the long, dark corridors there, one that said: *Get lucky, get lucky, get lucky.*

"But we know different, don't we? Look. This loner's got four people he loves so much he keeps their numbers right there all the time just so he can call them when he feels like it."

She pointed the face of the phone at him. "Who are they, Rizzo?"

"Relatives," he grumbled. "Friends."

"Right." She looked at the numbers and tried to keep hoping. The first two were in Mestre. The third was in Rome. Only the last was local.

"Do you think we should call them?"

"If you want. My folks live in Mestre. They're divorced. Two numbers, OK? And I got a friend in Rome."

"And the last?"

He didn't reply. She pressed the key, waited for a few rings until someone answered, then killed the call without saying a word. Rizzo was grinning at her.

"Listen," he said. "I like pizza. You call, they come. Real cheap too. I can recommend it, though I guess you cops never like to pay for anything, do you?"

She listened to the sound of traffic outside the window and wished there were a better place to work. It was the absence of cars that made her stay in the city. Then she stabbed at the buttons again.

"You had pizza last night, Rizzo."

"Maybe." He'd turned surly again.

"No, that was a statement. Not a question. Look." She turned the face of the phone to him again. "It shows the last ten numbers you dialled. And when."

"Right." He was pale once more. She tapped at the keys, listened to the call go through, then once again hung up without speaking.

"Bank," she said, then dialled again.

Rizzo swore and glanced at the sergeant. "This is private, man," he moaned. "There are laws about this stuff."

"Wow," Giulia Morelli said gleefully. "You bet too? All that money's not enough for you, Rizzo? You still have to play the horses? That is sad, surely. It shows an undue obsession with material objects."

She looked at the list of numbers again. Rizzo's social life was not wonderful. There was only one other unique entry. The rest were repeat calls to the bank. She pressed the button, listened for a good thirty seconds, then hung up. Giulia Morelli pulled her chair up to the desk, put her elbows on the blue plastic, and smiled.

"How do you know Hugo Massiter?" she asked. "What do you do for him?"

His head jerked from side to side. "Who? I don't believe this woman. What kind of stupid game do you think you're playing?"

"How do you know Hugo Massiter?" she repeated. "What do you do for him?"

He slammed his hands on the table. She didn't blink.

"Enough," he said. "Just charge me or let me go. I don't care. I just want this bitch out of my face. Trying to play these stupid tricks."

She keyed the number again and held the phone between them. They could both hear it ring twice, then make way for the click of an answering machine. Massiter's suave voice recited an unimaginative excuse for his absence. She waited until the message was close to the end, then, a moment before the beep came, said, "I'll just leave a message and ask him to join us all here, Rizzo. So we can clear this up right…."

"*No!*" he screamed, and dashed the phone from her hands. The sergeant was over in an instant, wrapping his arm around Rizzo's neck. She wondered why he bothered. Rizzo wasn't violent. He was just scared. As scared as anyone she had ever seen.

Giulia Morelli got up and walked to the corner of the room, picked up the phone from the floor, then killed the call. When she returned to the table, the sergeant had let go. Rizzo sat, head down, glowering at her through narrowed eyes.

"Want a coffee?" she asked.

"No," he grunted.

"Beer? Orange juice? Prosecco?"

"Nothing!"

She nodded at the sergeant. "Fetch some coffee. I can handle him for a while."

Biagio grunted, then walked out of the room. She sat down opposite Rizzo. He was sweating. She felt fine.

"Just say you remember me. That's all."

"You're a crazy woman."

She shook her head, put her bag on the desk, then reached inside and retrieved her small police handgun, the one that had wriggled out of her grip in Sant' Alvise.

Rizzo stared at it. Giulia Morelli lifted the gun and turned it in her palm.

"My hand doesn't shake anymore," she said. "I ought to thank you for that. Maybe I could save you, Rizzo. Understand?"

"Fu—"

In an instant she was out of the chair, reaching across the table, grasping his greasy head, holding it tight as she jammed the nose of the gun into his cheek.

"Don't speak," she said. "Just listen. I don't want you. I don't care about you. Maybe I can even forget about what you did that day. It depends on what you do now. What you say."

She took the gun out of his face. The barrel left a mark on his cheek, a circle of disturbed flesh. Giulia Morelli sat down and smiled.

"Before he comes back, Rizzo. Tell me you remember me.

Then we have something we can work on. Something that might keep you alive."

Rizzo stared at the door, waiting for it to open. He was shaking.

41

The prison

TOURIST DOLLARS RARELY CROSSED THE WATER TO Giudecca. The narrow promenade where the *vaporetto* stopped was filthy from construction work. Old mattresses, supermarket trolleys, and plastic bags littered the pavement. Dorsoduro sat across the canal, another world, affluent and remote. Daniel glanced at the familiar shoreline, examined the map, then headed west, towards the ugly red brick monstrosity of the Molino Stucky. After five minutes of dodging bags of rubbish and workmen's barricades, he turned gratefully away from the waterfront, following a narrow *rio* populated by small private craft. A modest wooden bridge led over to the Fondamenta delle Convertite and the former monastery which was now part of the prison service.

He stopped for a moment and looked at the oval sign over the white marble entrance. It read: *Istituti Penali Femminili*. A small video camera was hooked over the arch on a swan's-neck clasp. This was a place he had never expected to visit. Even now, a day and a half after the strange and terrifying incident in Ca' Scacchi, he continued to feel that he was walking inside a dream, one which would disappear if only he knew how to press with sufficient force against the dull, persistent inertia which held him in its folds. At times, when his mind seemed incapable of grasping the full extent of the events shaping around him, he hoped this was some momentary nightmare, a brief second of reverie between rolling out of Laura's bed and landing on the floor. The jolt never came. He had sat for an hour watching Scacchi's unconscious face in the Ospedale al Mare that morning, praying for answers. He had spoken to the undertakers about the shipment of Paul's body to an ancient mother in Minneapolis, as the American's will had requested. He had listened to Massiter's urgent pleas, half-begging, half-threatening, and sat through the first entire performance of the concerto in rehearsal and found himself both awed and chilled by its strange, relentless power. Dreams did not contain such details. They occurred only in the unavoidable harshness of reality.

He ran his fingers through his hair and briefly found himself wondering about the state of his clothes. Laura always examined him, he realised. He constantly sought her approval, even now. Then he let the single grey eye of the camera record his presence, announced himself at the counter, and waited to be called. Fifteen minutes later he was summoned to a small room with a single window barred with a twisted iron grille. She sat at a low table. A woman guard stood in shadow in the far corner. Laura wore a plain blue shift. Her hair was tied back severely behind her head. Her skin was pale and perfect. Watching the uncertainty in her bright, nervous eyes, sensing the flux of emotions she felt in his presence, Daniel Forster knew then, more surely than at any time in the past, that some kind of immutable bond existed between them.

Her hands were pressed flat on the table. He reached out and touched them. Slowly, deliberately, she withdrew her fingers from his.

"Don't, Daniel," she said softly.

The sense that he was in a dream returned. In his head, he was helping her to her feet, they were walking out of the door, out into the hot afternoon sunshine, out into a new life which had no past, only a bright, never-ending future.

"I miss you," he said finally.

She turned her head to face the wall, and he saw there a single tear resting in the corner of her eye. The guard coughed. Outside, a boat passed noisily along the *rio*.

"You saw him today? How is he?" she asked.

"He is unconscious."

She turned and stared forcefully at him. "All the time? He has not woken at all and spoken to the police?"

This sudden practical turn in her manner offended him for some reason. "He has not come to and told them you have gone insane, if that is what you mean. He has had more than one stroke, they say. They don't know if he will speak again. Why are you doing this?"

Her eyes flashed at him, accusing. "Think of Scacchi, Daniel. Not me. I should have protected them."

"I'm sorry, Laura. I don't know what to say. I don't know what to do or think. I feel as if I'm going mad, because I understand nothing. *Nothing*. And you're not there to help me see through the mist. You make the fog yourself. Why, please?"

She sighed and relaxed on the hard prison chair. "Will he never recover?"

He said nothing, merely bowed his head. Laura closed her eyes. A thin line of tears ran down each cheek.

"You owe it to me," he pleaded. "You owe it to him. To explain. To tell them the truth."

She seemed affronted. "I owe none of you anything. I loved Scacchi. Perhaps I love you, Daniel. I simply don't know. But I'm not in anyone's debt. And you've always understood less than you believe. You weren't there. How do you know I haven't told them the truth?"

"How?" He very nearly laughed. "Because I recall sitting on Piero's boat, when I was younger, when I was a different person, hearing you warn me very seriously that you loved those men, both of them, and would be obliged if I either learnt to love them, too, or affected as much. Now you say their blood is on your hands. I know you're lying, Laura, and I don't understand why. This is madness."

"We mustn't meet again, Daniel," she said in a low, firm voice. "Never. It's as painful for me as it is for you."

"Laura!"

"I will tell them. The prison people. I'll say they must not allow you admission. I will not see you again. In this place, or anywhere else. You must go now, go to this concert of yours. Forget about us. Make the most of your life. Find the people who are like you. Talk to Amy. Anyone." She moved forward until her head was back in the light. He had never seen such determination in her face. "If you stay here, you will be devoured for sure. And I'll hate your memory for refusing my advice. I say this to you out of love, Daniel. Go, and do not look back."

The vehemence in her voice chilled him. "I deserve an explanation," he murmured.

"It is a dangerous thing to ask for what one deserves," she answered primly. "You may whisper for angels and find yourself dancing with demons. Listen to me. Their blood is on my hands. When I wake in the morning, I see their faces staring back at me, I hear their voices rattling around my head. This is my hell, and I do not wish to share it. Now, go!"

He reached forward and seized her hands. "I will not abandon you, Laura."

She snatched her fingers from his touch, stood, and was immediately transformed. A stream of vile curses flew from her lips like acid spittle. Her hands waved manically in front of her face; her arms windmilled through the air.

The slumbering guard woke up amid Laura's insane screeches. Daniel stayed on his seat, waiting for his head to burst. The woman in uniform came over and tapped hard on his shoulder. "You'd better get out of here, mister. If she carries on like that, I have to do something and it's not nice."

He refused to move. Laura retreated to the corner, shrank down into a small blue shape on the floor, hands around her legs, face buried in her lap, like a child. He heard her sobbing; he closed his eyes.

"Mister?"

The guard's hand lay heavy on his shoulder. Daniel Forster rose from the chair.

"Laura?" he said, close to tears. She did not budge, making only a rhythmic, meaningless sound.

He walked outside, out into the hot afternoon, sat on the edge of the grimy canal, stared at the rubbish in the water, lowered his face into his hands, and began to weep.

42

A *fateful argument*

"Lorenzo!" It was late. She seemed tired, pale, and out of sorts. "You take such risks."

There was something foreign in her expression that took me aback. Rebecca was changed somehow.

"I had no choice. We must talk."

She calmed a little, presuming my urgency came from love, not necessity. "So. What did you think of it?" she asked. "Vivaldi, praising my efforts like that. *My* efforts. And the audience!"

"I thought . . ." This was a time to choose my words carefully. Perhaps she had ideas of her own that might circumvent any plans Leo could in the meantime concoct. "I felt they gave your work no more than the honour it deserved. And that they will not be patient when it comes to learning the identity of the artist who penned it."

"No." She seemed somewhat downcast at that last thought.

"Do you know what to do next?" I asked. "The more you hold back, the greater the frenzy will be for someone to claim authorship."

"I hoped Jacopo would have some notion. Instead, when

I found the courage to tell him the truth, he just looked at me as if I've committed some sin. He senses danger more keenly than most. He was like this before we fled Geneva, and it probably saved our lives."

"You might flee?" I strode across the room immediately, fell in front of her, and placed my arms upon her lap. "Do not talk of running, Rebecca. I will not listen to that."

"Would you have us stay here and face the peril, then? Some love for me that is, Lorenzo."

These were rash, cruel words, and I could see from her face how distant they were from her true thoughts. Something was wrong between us, and I could only guess at what. I touched her soft, pale cheek. "I will lay down my life for you, Rebecca, and sacrifice our happiness if that means you prosper. But do not run too easily. And if you do, I pray you'll let me lead the way."

She drew back from my touch as if this were a promise she had heard before. I assume Rebecca is as new to love as me. I assume too many things.

"Jacopo says it is impossible. They would not accept a woman and a Jew as author of such a work even if I came to them as pure as driven snow. If I stand up now and reveal myself, I risk their derision first and then their anger when they discover how I have deceived them. With luck none recognised me in the church—damn Vivaldi for putting me on show like that. But if I enter the public eye, the game's up. For all of us. There'll be a ticket in the lion's mouth before nightfall, and we'll be talking to the Doge's inquisitors in the morning."

I held her hands tightly. They did not stir in mine.

"Well," she said coldly. "Tell me I am wrong."

It came to me then. If love requires a set of proofs, then one of them is this: that neither party may lie easily to the other. But if a set of proofs be required, is this truly love?

"No," I answered. "You are not wrong. I wish I could honestly say the opposite, but Jacopo sees the situation as it is. There must be a place in the world where you may hold your manuscript in your hand and walk with it freely into an adoring hall. But Venice isn't it. Nor anywhere else I know."

The truth, they say, may hurt. She withdrew her hands from my tender grasp. "Then what are we to do, Lorenzo?"

"Stay calm. Stay quiet. We have a few days yet."

A bitter laugh, a sound I had not heard from her before, rang around the room. "And will the climate be much different three, four days hence? Of course not. This is all my doing, and I have dragged you and Jacopo down with me. What a fool I've been. To think that talent's all you need in this world and that if you have sufficient of it, your sex, your race, your ancestry, all these things become invisible to the masses. They judge us as much on who we are as what we may do. If I were the Doge's harlot, perhaps things might be different, but a poor Jew stands no chance. This is a Gentile's world, and one for men at that. I should have known it all along."

Her dark eyes were full of anger and resentment. How could I blame her? Rebecca sought glory through her work, but more than anything, I think, she searched for some sense of her true identity in a society which would deny its existence.

"Don't judge us all by the crowd," I said. "There're some who'd help you, love, and maybe more elsewhere."

"Who?"

"Vivaldi, for one. I saw the way he watched you in the concert. Do you think he doesn't know?"

"No. I assumed he didn't."

"I suspect you're wrong. You played like a giant. You knew that work inside out. How was that possible?"

She realised there was some truth in my words. "And he will keep this secret to himself?"

"He has. Otherwise, we wouldn't be here now."

"Then let's hope he continues in this vein." She seemed nervous. "There is more, Lorenzo. I can see it in your face."

"Leo."

"Your uncle?"

"He saw it clearly, too, and sought my confirmation. I denied it, naturally, but he doesn't believe a word. You'll hear from him before long, and that was why I came. Beware. Both of you. I know my uncle better than most. He is not to be trusted."

She gasped, surprised. "Trusted? Lorenzo, it is thanks to your uncle that I first found my place in Vivaldi's orchestra. Thanks to him that I gained an introduction to the Englishman, without whom that violin over there would still be in some Cremona workshop. He has done me many favours."

"I don't deny that. But Leo fancies himself a musician too. He would steal your glory for himself given half the chance."

"That I cannot believe."

"He thinks he has the only copy of your concerto in existence."

"Of course he has!" She spoke as if exasperated with a child. "Do you think I have the money to copy it, even if I had the courage? And why bother? I can re-create every note from my head, and probably improve a good few along the way."

We had never argued before. It was only much later, when this scene replayed itself over and over in my head, that I understood how little logic ran on either side.

"You do not know him!"

"And you do? I think you hate to be any man's apprentice, and colour your view accordingly."

"I have seen the way he looks at you!"

She laughed in a kind of triumph. "Well, now we have it. This is the true reason for your hatred, and a sorry one at that. You will spend a great part of your life in misery, Lorenzo, if you seethe with fury at every man who steals me a glance. What would you have me do? Put on a veil like the Moslems? Isn't that scarf you Gentiles make us wear enough?"

Her anger did me a great injustice. "I came to warn you. Leo is not what he seems."

"Find me a man who is," she said quietly, and stared deliberately out of the window into the night.

"Rebecca . . ."

She rose and walked away from me. "I am tired, and this argument wearies me. It is too childish to occupy my time."

At that the redness flooded into my head. I stood upright and regarded, with a growing fury, the back she had presented to me. "As is my love, no doubt. So let me do us both an act of kindness and remove it from your presence."

She fairly shrieked and wheeled around to face me, eyes brimming. "Lorenzo! Don't say such a thing. Isn't it enough that the world tortures us without we torture ourselves? A woman may have cares and worries you cannot guess at. Sometimes they make her speak the very opposite of what is in her head. If I were to tell you that I, that we . . ."

Then she hesitated and fell silent, and her reluctance infuriated me. I recognised neither of us in this conversation. We had been transformed by events, although I was too stupid to understand as much. And so I did the manly thing and hid my weakness through a show of so-called strength. I retreated from her imploring arms and made for the door. "You know my opinion, Rebecca," I heard myself say, not recognising the means by which the words formed in my mouth. "I have nothing more to add."

Then I was out the door, ignoring her calls for me to return, bounding down the staircase like a madman. When I awoke the next morning, with an aching head from the wine I downed upon my return, I found Leo in a sweet and happy mood, dressed in his best finery, thinking of his meeting with the Levis, no doubt. Before he left, he despatched me to the cellar with instructions on what to clean and what to move, what to throw out and what to dust off, and even an order for some amateur attempt at masonry to repair some feeble brickwork in the wall. I listened, watching his eyes, thinking how covetously they would soon regard Rebecca's form, knowing how foolish I was to let such considerations occupy space in my head at a time when I had other matters on my mind.

It was easier when Leo had gone. I abandoned the cellar and searched the house. Sure enough, I found Rebecca's music safely deposited behind a painting of ancient Athens that covered up the canal-side wall of the great room downstairs. Leo must have had a space cut out of the brick to provide such a hiding place. More fool him.

I took the score, trying not to feel her presence through the ink upon the page, and deposited it safely in a hiding place which Leo had inadvertently suggested. The concerto was in the cellar, safe from all. Leo hated rats. As with magnets, like repels like.

Then I left the house and began to walk to Ca' Dario, thinking of how this interview with the Englishman might fruitfully proceed. If Rebecca were to gain a benefactor, it would at least be one she might trust.

43

Music in the dark

C A' SCACCHI SEEMED EMPTY SAVE FOR GHOSTS AND
the lingering scent of Laura. When Daniel could stand the
loneliness no more, he left for La Pietà, where the second full
rehearsal was due to begin at five in the afternoon. The city was a
teeming throng of people, surly locals pushing their way
through the *vaporetto* queues and a sea of aimless tourists forever
stopping without reason in the most awkward of locations. He
was acquiring the local contempt for visitors. Yet he slipped
through the mass of bodies like a phantom, unseen, as if he lived
on a different plane, wondering at times if the spark of madness
which seemed to have infected Laura was now racing through
his own veins.

There was a small crowd outside the church, trying in vain to
talk their way into the rehearsal. The woman on the door
recognised him and was immediately on her feet, barring his
entrance.

"Signor Forster?" She seemed distraught. "What has happened to Scacchi? They tell such stories in the papers. I can't
believe a word of it."

"He's very ill."

"You've seen him? May I too?"

"Of course. He's in the Ospedale al Mare. But..." Daniel held out his hands, an Italian gesture, which he realised instantly.

"He'll not live?" the woman asked.

"I don't know."

"I'll go. And I'll say a prayer for him tonight. He's a good man, Mr. Forster. You remember that, whatever else anyone says. He wanted to do something for you. But I think you understand as much."

Daniel wondered whether he did comprehend fully Scacchi's motives. Laura had warned him against such naivety.

"I think it would be good if you could visit him," he told her.

"Who knows if he can hear me or not? Doctors. Pah! And that woman of his. The one they say was responsible?"

"I don't know," he said, feeling evasive.

"It's rubbish. I met her sometimes, when she could bear to bring herself out of the house. She would no more harm Scacchi and his friend than she would hurt you or me."

He thought of Laura's histrionic ranting that afternoon. It was an act, and they both knew it.

"I agree," he said.

"She'll be free! I shall go to the stupid police and tell them myself!"

The small crowd was growing restless. One Japanese couple tried to sneak through the door, only to be halted by a stream of Venetian vernacular.

"Off with you! Off with you! Buy tickets for Friday or be gone."

The Japanese man scowled at her. "We're not here Friday."

"Then wait for it to come to you," the woman responded. "It will, surely, if it's as good as they say it is. Ask the composer yourself. Signor Forster?"

The crowd began to murmur and flock around him. Daniel felt the heat rise to his cheeks, found himself apologising, and then, with a sudden urgency, made for the door. Inside, the church was cool and dark. The first movement had just begun. He found a chair to the right of the entrance and sat there in shadow, letting the music absorb him, wondering again what strange provenance the work might have had.

It lasted close to an hour, though he soon lost what little sense of time he possessed. Heard now in its entirety and played by musicians who were becoming familiar with its themes and nuances, the work astonished him. It was bold and dexterous, but its true power lay beyond the technical. For most of the time he listened with his eyes closed and found himself swept along by the swell of its coursing emotions. The music ranged from slow, stately tragedy to quicksilver passages of shimmering beauty and life. It was like the best of Vivaldi but overlaid with something younger and more modern. When it became more widely known, the concerto would, he felt sure, rise rapidly to the status of a new classic, sought after by violinists of a greater stature than Amy, though she performed superbly throughout. With that realisation, too, his mind became more determined than ever. There would be a time when he would reveal his deception, however Massiter felt about the matter. Even if he disappeared entirely from public view after Venice, the knowledge of the sham would remain with him always. He could not, in all conscience, shoulder the deceitful burden any longer than was necessary. The consequences were immaterial. He had played the Venetian game, to the tune of both Scacchi and Massiter, for too long.

The rehearsal came to a close with a show of fireworks from Amy, who tore into the final passages with a verve and resolve that astonished him. Their argument in the Gritti Palace now seemed to exist in another lifetime. He could not countenance the idea that there should be any lasting rift between them. When the final note sounded, Amy sat down, drained, to a round of applause from her fellow players. The entire orchestra seemed exhausted by the work, too, as if they were mesmerised by their own efforts.

He felt a hand on his shoulder. It was the woman who manned the door, asking him to take a call. When he returned, Amy was placing her fiddle in the case. He caught up with her as she emerged into the soft early-evening light. The lagoon was busy with *vaporetti*. A larger ferryboat was departing for Torcello. Across the water, the Campari sign was prematurely lit on the Lido. It was an exquisite evening.

"Oh, Dan." She looked at him with a mixture of grief and pity. "I don't know what to say. I read it in the paper. Hugo told me he went round after it happened. It's unbelievable."

"I know." She had found the apposite word. "It's quite unbelievable."

"How are you? How's your friend?"

"Laura's in prison."

Her eyes grew wide with astonishment. "Laura? I meant the old man. How can you think of her? After what she did?"

The childishness never stayed hidden for long, though he cursed himself for such a stupid mistake. "She didn't do anything, Amy. She loved both of those men and couldn't harm them, not for anything. You were on the boat with us all. You know that, surely?"

She folded her arms tightly across her chest and sighed. "Hugo told me she had admitted it. And that the police plan to charge her. Why won't you face facts, Dan?"

"I'm more than happy to face facts, if only I could find some."

"Then why would she confess to something she didn't do?"

"I think because she blames herself for what happened somehow and feels desperate to take the responsibility, for some reason."

"But that's crazy!"

"Yes. It is. Perhaps that's your answer. She loved those men, Amy, Scacchi in particular. In some way I don't comprehend, I believe they saved each other and, as a result, felt some kind of pact between them."

"And now he's unconscious, Hugo says. He can't even tell them what happened."

"No." He stared at the Campari sign across the water and thought of Scacchi in Piero's boat, with Xerxes at the tiller, and the constant flow of laughter and spritz.

"What do you mean 'No'? He'll recover?"

Daniel sat down on the steps. She joined him, bemused.

"No. I mean he's dead. They called me while you were playing. They found him at four o'clock this afternoon. His heart must have failed suddenly. They hadn't expected anything to happen so soon. On Friday I must bury him on San Michele."

"Christ," Amy said softly, then folded her arms around his shoulders and pulled her warm face into his neck.

"I wanted to be there," he said to himself. "That's the worst part. If he was to die, I wanted to be with him at that moment. I feel cheated somehow."

She pulled back and looked into his eyes. "Dan . . ."

"And I feel lied to. As if they all saw me for a fool."

"A fool? Didn't you hear what we were playing in there? No one can think you're a fool."

He could see Amy was taken aback by the sharpness of his expression. She withdrew her arms from him and wiped her damp face on the sleeve of her shirt.

"Tell me that before you leave," he said. "Not now."

"I don't…"

"Please, Amy. Be patient with me." He watched the familiar figure in white shirt and pale trousers approach along the promenade. "Or ask Hugo what I mean. I gather you're close."

"Meaning what, exactly?"

"You said it yourself," he said coldly. "He seems interested."

She stood up, deeply offended. "Enough! I don't give a shit how big a deal you think you are, Dan. You act like a complete jerk sometimes."

Massiter strode up the steps of La Pietà towards them. He bowed politely to Amy, then nodded to Daniel. "I heard the news. It is a great loss, Daniel. Scacchi was my friend."

"Quite."

Massiter's grey eyes held no emotion. Daniel could not prevent a single fevered thought running through his mind: that the death of Scacchi and Paul stemmed, in some mysterious way, from the pact they had made with Massiter. That this could be some kind of cruel justice which had yet to reach its close.

"I would like to honour him, Daniel," Massiter continued. "I would like to make the concert on Friday his memorial."

Daniel shook his head in puzzlement. "I thought you planned to do that for the girl, Hugo. How many memorials do you want?"

"Yes. I hate to say it, but that bitch of a policewoman was right. Susanna Gianni is long dead and buried. Scacchi's in our hearts now. We should mark that moment."

"Why do you do this, Hugo?" He was no longer cowed by Massiter. Daniel wondered what had wrought that change in their relationship.

"What, precisely?"

"The school. The concert. The whole *performance*. What do you get from it?"

Massiter seemed intrigued by the question. "I can't paint, Daniel. I can't write. I can't play a note of music. But don't you see? In a sense, I own it all. Is it so hard to understand? I like my name on the things I admire. I like to see that little line of print that does me proud." He ceased to smile. "And I like to know you're all in my debt."

Amy shuffled uncomfortably beside Massiter. They were close already, Daniel thought. The moment would arrive when she would become one of Massiter's possessions, too, just as he had.

"I'll make the concert in his memory, Daniel. You may have your name on the music, but I pay the players. I rent the hall. I have my rights."

"Of course." Daniel nodded.

"And it will be a revelation!"

"A revelation," he agreed. "Quite."

Then, without a further word, Daniel Forster walked down the steps of La Pietà and turned right, into the backstreets of the city and the narrow labyrinth of alleys which would, at some point and after many wrong turnings, deliver him to the empty shell of Ca' Scacchi.

44

An interview with the Englishman

I entered by the tradesman's door at the rear and found Gobbo in the kitchen, taunting one of the maids. He took one look at me and abandoned his pursuit.

"Good God, Scacchi. You look like you've spent the night on the tiles, and I know that's not your style. What's up?"

"I would like to see your master on a matter of some importance."

"If it's money, chum, forget it. Our Oliver's quite sick of Venetians hanging round his purse. Some blackguard got away with the cash from that concert of his. There's the city's thanks, eh? Pat him on the back one moment, rob him blind the next. Couldn't have come at a worse time, either. He put off getting funds from London because of that. Now the banks are getting sticky and we've all manner of locals asking to be paid."

He stared at me with a chilly expression. "If that's what you've come for, some debt he owes to Leo, you're not going through that door. Friendship ends when the master starts throwing the pots around. I'm not getting my arse kicked just to see you present another bill upon the table."

"It's not for money, Gobbo. At least not demanding it. In fact, he might even turn a penny or two out of what I've got to tell him."

"Really?" He was an ugly fellow, particularly sneering like this.

"Yes. Really. Now, get along there and tell him I need ten minutes of his time and not a penny of his money."

With that he was off, through the door which led to the front of the mansion and the first-floor room that, with its view of the canal, served as its principal meeting place. I waited, enduring the maid's childish smirks, and then was summoned through into the vast, mirrored space I had last seen on the day of our trip to Torcello. Its magnificence seemed to have waned somewhat over the weeks. The glass could use a clean. The furniture looked old and marked. Rented premises are never the same as property occupied by the owner, I imagine. With just the three of us in it, this hall seemed empty and cold. Only the noise of the canal beyond the windows added a little life to the scene.

Delapole looked at me cheerily. "Scacchi! Not seen you since the triumph, eh? What a performance! Shame some thieving local saw off with my gains. I could have used that. I've a house in Whitehall, an estate in Norfolk, and God knows how many lumps of sod in Ireland. But tell that to one of your oh-so-worldly bankers and I might as well be offering collateral on Lilliput. You read Swift out here, I imagine?"

"It takes a little while for the translation, sir. Though I have heard much of him."

"Damned good stuff, not that I understand it all. One verse hits the mark, though."

He waved an arm in front of him, like a gentleman taking a bow, then recited:

"A flea hath smaller fleas that on him prey,
And these have smaller fleas to bite 'em.
And so proceed ad infinitum."

It was a humorous line and even brought a smile to my face.

"There," he said, pleased that he had amused me. "That wasn't hard, now, was it? Mind you, I think I'm not a flea, but the very dog—the *original* dog—upon which the first flea fed. At least I can find no blood to suck, try as I might. It's bread and water till that envelope gets here from London."

Gobbo raised an eyebrow at me from the corner. Delapole is neither as impoverished nor as credulous as he wishes to appear, I think. No aristocratic fop could make his way alone through Europe for three years or more, as I understand he has, without a brain in his head. At least I hoped so if we were, together, to outwit my uncle.

"Well then, young Scacchi," he demanded. "I am at your service."

I had rehearsed these words in my head as best I could beforehand. This was a tricky path I sought to negotiate, and one with steep chasms on either side.

"Sir," I began. "I wish to speak alone, if you permit."

"What? Not in front of your friend here? Why, I think he will be quite offended."

Gobbo did look shocked. Perhaps I shouldn't blame him.

"It is not that I mistrust anyone, sir. But I believe what I have to say is best confined to as few as possible."

"Oh," Delapole objected. "Two sets of ears are scarcely more than one. Young Gobbo knows things about me that would set your hair on fire, lad, and never has he betrayed a trust. If he can't hear it, neither can I. For if it requires action, then who should I turn to but my manservant?"

He had a point there. "As you please. But first let me say that I bring this news to you reluctantly. It pains me to reveal it, and in doing so, I place myself and one I admire at your mercy. You have shown yourself to be a good and generous man, Mr. Delapole, and I would not presume on these admirable qualities more than I have already."

He cast a weary eye out of the window at the traffic on the water. "It's obvious you're not a Venetian, Scacchi. Three whole sentences there and you didn't ask me for money once."

"It is not your money that I need, sir. It is your advice and wisdom and impartiality. For I fear a grave injustice is about to be done which will harm one you have already honoured with your kindness."

His pallid English face looked intrigued at that. He took a tall dining chair at the old walnut table which formed the centrepiece of the room and waved both Gobbo and me to join him. Once seated, I took a deep breath and told my tale, as accurately and as clearly as I knew it, withholding only those things which I deemed irrelevant, the most important being my own relationship with Rebecca Levi. I also left, for the moment, the matter of her race.

As I fell into the rhythm of my exposition, I relaxed a little, seeing on Delapole's face, and even Gobbo's, some shock at my revelations. Both had marvelled at Rebecca's virtuosity in La Pietà; to learn that she wrote the selfsame marvel astonished them. When I told them how Leo had held on to her single manuscript and sought to bargain with it to his advantage, Gobbo gave out a low whistle.

"There," he said with some self-satisfaction. "I told you

that man was a bad 'un, Scacchi. You can see it in his weasel eyes. No one treats his own blood like he treats you, especially when you're new orphaned and left in a place like this."

"You did tell me, my friend," I agreed. "And I listened to you. But he is still my uncle, and I his apprentice. It is his right to treat me so, and if this were simply a matter of his attitude to me, I would not trouble you with my worries. I cannot, though, sit by while he wrongs another, and one whose talents are so great."

Delapole was puzzled. Rightly so, for I had left out the crucial element in my tale, and without it nothing made sense. "I don't see it, Scacchi. It's very odd, I'll admit, for a young girl to produce such stuff as this. Raises a few issues, I'm sure, particularly with the older generation. But what's to stop her standing up and riding the storm? She wrote it. Presumably there's more where that came from. There'll be a few catcalls, naturally. Vivaldi gets his share of them these days. Why doesn't she just take a deep breath and get on with it?"

He gazed at me across the ancient, polished table, and I knew I hadn't judged him wrong. Delapole could cut to the heart of matters when required. The English foppishness was a façade behind which lurked a canny brain.

"Because it is impossible. She is a Jew, though none outside her circle know it, save for me and Leo."

The long, sallow face regarded me with puzzlement. "A Jew? Good God. Are you sure, lad? Being English, I'm not so good at these things. If they don't wear a badge or that thing on their head, I'm damned if I can spot them. Why, I swear I could strike up conversation with a Negro in the dark and never know and—"

"I am sure, sir. Every night when she has played for Vivaldi, under the name Rebecca Guillaume, I have secreted her out of the ghetto on false pretences."

Gobbo groaned. "Oh, Scacchi. You are in it now, up to your neck."

Delapole seemed mystified. "But is this such a problem? So, she's a woman. So, she's a Jew. Damn fine player as well, and quite a beauty too. We're not living in the Dark Ages. What difference does it make?"

"Maybe none in London, Master," Gobbo groaned. "But this is Venice, and the Doge has his rules. They live where they're told. They stay behind their walls after nightfall. They keep out of our churches lest their presence defile the place. To break those rules is to defy the Doge, and we all know where that leads."

"I still don't understand," Delapole persisted. "It's such a little thing in the face of such talent. Why, it might add a little colour to the tale. A touch of melodrama never did any artist harm."

We said nothing. He looked at our faces, and it was our grim silence that finally convinced him. "Very well," he admitted. "I accept your interpretation of these facts. There are times, Gobbo, when I miss my native soil. A spot of English practicality would do you folk no end of good. I deem it somewhat amazing that Venice should find itself possessor of, apparently, the first great woman musician the world has known, and thinks the best way to deal with this news is to throw her in prison, then start spouting mumbo-jumbo and throwing incense in the air. If I'd wanted Spanish habits, I'd have gone to Spain."

Gobbo looked sideways at me. Delapole did not appreciate the gravity of the position. The Doge was impartial in his interpretation of the law. He'd throw a loose-tongued Englishman in jail as quickly as a Hebrew impostor if it suited him.

"I think, sir," Gobbo said carefully, "it would be best if we keep this matter to ourselves and not make light of the Republic's justice outside these walls. You are a celebrity in this city, and that makes you an easy target for the gossips."

At that the Englishman grew very cross. "Oh, so that will be their gratitude, will it? To scrawl my name on some false charge and drop it in one of those stupid leonine pisspots, eh? By God, they should not do down this poor girl so cruelly. You blame your uncle, Scacchi, but let me tell you, without the city on his side, he'd never dream of acting thus. This place is rotten as a pear, and that's what leads him on."

"I agree, sir," I answered, nodding. "But what is to be done?"

"Tell me," he replied. "What's old Leo's game?"

"To claim he is the composer when the moment arises."

"A week today is when we're set for the revelation," Gobbo interjected. "It was supposed to be sooner, but Vivaldi's playing up about the dates. I believe he sees it as his nemesis. Can't put it off forever, though. Three o'clock at La Pietà. Quite a commotion that will be."

"Before that," I continued, "I fear Leo will offer Rebecca some arrangement. He will take the credit—and the money. In return, her secret remains safe with him and she gets a little income, perhaps. I don't know. The cards are all in his hand."

"That they are," Gobbo agreed glumly.

"And what of the girl?" Delapole asked. "What does she think?"

"I am not sure what she thinks, sir."

"It is her decision, Scacchi. If Leo comes up with some compromise she finds satisfactory—she continues to compose in freedom while he picks up the plaudits—there's nothing we could or should do."

"I agree, sir. But knowing Rebecca as I do . . ."

Those pale-blue English eyes never left me.

". . . I do not doubt for a moment that Miss Levi will have all the glory or none. She has risked everything to smuggle her art out of the ghetto. Even if she were to sign such a covenant, I fully believe it would of itself stifle her such that she might never write nor play again."

"Hmmm." He stood up and walked over to the window. We watched him. Delapole was the master here. Both of us depended on his guidance. Gobbo fetched me a playful punch upon the arm as if to say *It will be all right*.

We waited for his decision. After a full five minutes, he returned to the table, sat purposefully in his chair, and regarded me.

"A wise man should think twice before crying 'injustice' in a society which is itself unjust. I am a foreigner here, and one who has already paid his dues, as it were."

My heart sank, though I could not argue with his logic. "I only seek your counsel, sir, nothing else. It is your foreignness that draws me here. If you were a Venetian, then my name would be heading for the Doge's clerks the moment I left this room, and Rebecca Levi abandoned to her fate alone."

He smiled. "You've got a fair turn of phrase on you, lad, I'll say that. Even saw off that twittering peacock Rousseau once or twice, and he was no fool."

"I thank you, sir. I shall not think one iota the less of you if we never speak of this again."

"Oh, come." His hand reached across the table and patted

mine in a gesture which was almost paternal. "You *are* a serious fellow, Scacchi. Do smile a little now and then."

My heart was pounding. "You'll help me, then?"

He glanced at Gobbo. "Between the two of you, make an appointment with the girl. In daytime, please. No more subterfuge on my part. Until I know her thoughts, it's impossible to proceed. But yes, Scacchi, I'll do what I can, pathetic and misguided as it may be."

The Englishman clapped his hands. "There! Another smile! We'll cure this melancholy yet, young Scacchi. Gobbo, buy him a drink around the corner. I need some solitude. There's many a solution to this puzzle. It requires only some thought and prescience on our part."

He stood up. We did likewise. "Sir," I said, bowing. "I will always be in your debt. As will Miss Levi."

"If debt is friendship in another form, I think I must be both the most loved and loving man in all the world. Now, be off with you. And cheer him up, Gobbo."

Which he tried to do, after his own fashion, by leading me into one of the low taverns by the *rio* and introducing a couple of his lady friends. They were both pretty, with large eyes and straight black hair, scarlet dresses, and a ready manner.

Gobbo took me aside for a moment and said, "Come on, Scacchi. I think we'll get this ride for free. Both find you comely."

"I don't wish to offend," I replied. "My mood isn't up for it, Gobbo."

"Your mood. Your mood. Well, there goes my sport."

"I'm sorry."

"Huh." He stared at me. "I hope she's worth it, my friend. Your little Jewish mistress could kill us all if Delapole steps too far out of line."

I finished my wine and went outside. It had been a satisfactory morning. I had no intention of spoiling it by feeding Gobbo's curiosity. Soon there were more immediate matters to occupy my mind. When I returned to Ca' Scacchi, Leo was at his desk, waiting for me. I would not, I vowed then, allow him to beat me again. But he had a more subtle form of punishment.

"Lorenzo," he said mock pleasantly. "I despair of you, I really do. All I ask is a simple task, that you remain at your office, and it goes undone. And now, being the generous soul I am, I intend to reward you with an adventure."

The look of triumph on his face depressed me greatly. If he had found the time to speak to Rebecca, he had no intention of revealing the outcome to me.

"An adventure, Uncle?"

"There's a magistrate, Marchese, in Rome. He thinks his memoirs may make a little light reading for the masses. You shall fetch the manuscript for me and I'll consider it at my leisure."

"*Rome?* Uncle, that is a good two days away by coach. There is much to do here."

"There is indeed, but given your showing this morning, I doubt you'll do it. So, Rome it is. Two days out, two days back. One day to discuss my pricing structure and editorial requirements with Signor Marchese. If you get a move on, you'll be home for the big day. When *all* will be revealed. You wouldn't want to miss that, now, would you?"

I couldn't speak. He had me trapped. If I refused, I would be ejected from his household as a faithless apprentice and lose what little standing I had to aid Rebecca.

"Come along, boy. You must take the boat to Mestre and get the evening coach. Miss that, and God knows when you'll return."

I dashed to my room, filled my bag, then took the papers and the pitiful pile of coins Leo gave me. And so my body departed for Rome, leaving my mind and heart in Venice. In the Ghetto Nuovo, to be precise.

45

Shapes in the mirror

THE APARTMENT SEEMED TO BE MADE FROM GLASS. AMY
Hartston swayed gently, half-drunk. They had eaten at Da
Fiore: fried soft-shell crabs with polenta, turbot, and lobster,
and an excess of flinty white wine. She stared at her reflection in
the huge window overlooking the canal. *Vaporetti* crisscrossed
the water with only a handful of late-night passengers on board.
A lone gondola carrying a handful of tourists made its way to
the Accademia bridge, an accordionist crooning from the prow.
Something about the sight disturbed her. She was becoming too
familiar with Venice, too entangled in the city. Her head swam.
She felt concerned, for herself, and for Daniel too. The last,
strange interview outside the church made her fear for him.
There was a darkness in his eyes which betokened more than
simple grief.

She turned and looked at Hugo Massiter. He was pouring two
glasses of cognac from a decanter that sat on a stark, modernist
cabinet, all smoked glass and satin metal. Her boast about
Hugo's interest in her now seemed remote, childish. Yet some
determination remained inside her: she did not wish to leave
Venice as she had arrived.

He walked towards her with the drinks. In the mirrors that ran around the walls, his shape was multiplied over and over again. She felt she was surrounded by Hugo Massiter, swallowed by his powerful presence.

She took the glass and gulped the contents. Her head felt heavy. He grasped her arm, and they walked back to the window. For some reason she could not comprehend, she was disinclined to look out at the canal again.

"What is it, Amy?" he asked pleasantly.

"I don't know."

"Ah," he replied, as if her answer said everything. "I understand."

"You understand what, Hugo?"

"You regret accepting my invitation to come here. You think it was the wrong decision. Beautiful young girl. Decrepit old man."

"No!" He was teasing. He had to be. Hugo was well-preserved for his age.

"Then what?"

She sat on the pale leather sofa, feeling it gasp beneath her. "I don't know precisely."

Hugo laughed lightly. "But of course you do, my dear. You simply don't want to talk about it. Or do you?"

That was a sign of age, she thought: Hugo's perception, and his refusal to hide it for fear of offence.

"I'm concerned about this music, Hugo. The concerto."

He blinked, bemused. "You think there's something wrong with it? You don't like the way Fabozzi is doing his job?"

"No! It's wonderful. We all know that."

"Then what?"

She took a long drink of the brandy, relishing the way that for a brief moment it appeared to clarify her thoughts. "I don't believe Daniel wrote it. It's impossible. He's a fraud. And it's eating into him more and more. He's falling to pieces, Hugo. Right in front of our eyes. Surely you can see that?"

Hugo shook his head and sat down next to her. "What are you talking about? Daniel's upset by Scacchi's death, as one would expect. It doesn't mean he's a fraud."

"This is more than Scacchi's death." She liked the certainty she detected in her own voice. "I knew before that happened, though I didn't want to face it. In a way I even knew that night we went out to Torcello and he first pulled out those sheets. Daniel couldn't have written that piece. It's not inside him. He wants to run away every time he hears it."

Hugo peered at her. "You really believe that?"

"I *know* it."

"Then who did write it, Amy?"

"Search me. Perhaps someone stole it. Perhaps that's why Scacchi was killed."

"The housekeeper..." he objected.

"I met the housekeeper, Hugo. She didn't kill anyone. She just went crazy after it happened."

He refilled their glasses. "This is most upsetting. Whether there's any truth in it or not, we must not allow it to interfere with the concert or your own future."

"To hell with that! It's Daniel I'm worried about. You heard him."

Hugo was lost. Sometimes, she thought, he was too trusting. "I don't understand."

"This thing is eating him up. Dan's not that kind of person, and with Scacchi gone, there's no one to pull in his reins."

He stared at her, uncomprehending.

"He's going to spill the beans, Hugo. He said as much. A revelation. If you want my opinion, he's going to let this thing run its course—he wouldn't want to harm any of us—then, when the concert's over and done with, he'll get it off his chest."

Hugo Massiter fell back on the sofa with a sigh and said, "Well..."

She watched him, wondering for a moment if his open disbelief could begin to raise doubts within her. Yet she knew that Daniel was lying. His deceit explained everything she had come to understand about him, including, ironically, his innate honesty.

"Hugo," she said. "You must help him. He's in hell over this. You have to get him out of it."

He grimaced. "If you're right, he's committed fraud. He's signed legal contracts for the work on the basis that he is the composer. Some of those people won't take kindly to being told otherwise. They've paid out money already. The police will be involved. He could be looking at jail."

"And if he doesn't let it out, it will kill him. Please, Hugo. I hate seeing him like this. Talk to him. He can let us all down gently after the concert, talk to the cops, clear it all up. But he has to share that secret with someone. It's tearing him to pieces."

"Very well." He nodded. "I'll speak to him. After Scacchi's funeral. You think that would be an appropriate time?"

"Great!" She kissed him lightly on the cheek, tasting the scent of some expensive aftershave. Hugo Massiter stared at her with an expression she was unable to decode.

"I never envy the young, you know," he said. "You fill the most precious part of your lives with such pain and anguish over nothing at all."

"I don't think this is nothing at all. Claiming ownership of a work like that. And Scacchi's dead, remember."

"True. But what are these things to you?"

"I like Dan," she said, astonished by the question. "He's special in some way. He's got... integrity."

"But you just said he was a fraud."

"He is. It's the fact he has integrity that makes him so bad at it."

Hugo shook his head. "So many complications. The young..."

"Right," she replied, half-laughing. "And you never went through this. You were grown-up the moment you entered the world. And you never fell in love? Got your heart broken? Stayed awake all night with that guilty thought that wouldn't leave your head?"

A curious expression crossed his face. "Not when I was your age. I just travelled. And lived, dear girl. Living is everything, you know. Nothing else matters."

There was an invitation to probe here. She hesitated before taking it. "But..."

Hugo looked warily at her. "Do you really want me to tell you?"

"It's your choice. I'm not forcing anything."

He sighed, then said, "I was nearly married once. I was about to become engaged. I believed everything would be perfect in my world. Then it fell apart, and every day I wonder why."

A film of moisture appeared briefly over his grey eyes. Some other Hugo Massiter had appeared before her: vulnerable, pathetic almost.

"I'm sorry," she said. "I shouldn't have asked."

"No. But having asked, you should listen. Perhaps I'm like Daniel. I keep these secrets too long, though this is ours, Amy. You must tell no one, please."

"Of course."

He took a deep breath, flaring his nostrils, and looked deeply sad. "I was due to become engaged to Susanna Gianni. The girl who was killed ten years ago. You spoke of her when we went to Torcello."

"What? Oh, Hugo!"

"I know," he said coldly. "She was eighteen and I was forty-one. What could I have been thinking of? They would all have said that, wouldn't they? If they'd been given the chance."

"I didn't mean that," Amy objected. "Not at all."

"No need to apologise. They *would* have said it. Even her mother, who knew my intentions, naturally, though the money seemed to make up for everything else. Susanna was perfect, you understand. She would have played the greatest houses. We would have been the happiest pair."

"Did anyone know?"

"I thought not. We were discreet. We amazed each other and knew that we would one day amaze the world. So we kept ourselves secret. The Sunday after that last concert, we planned to issue an announcement and be gone before the paparazzi arrived. But that damned conductor knew. I realise as much now. He coveted her from the start, I think, and somehow lured her away when the concert was over. I waited and waited, and she never appeared. Then the next morning…"

He stared at his hands. "And there you have it, Amy Hartston. One old man's secret which he expected to take with him to the grave. Instead I tell it to you. Explain that, please."

She took his hands, which were warm and smooth and soft. "I can't," she said.

He touched her cheek lightly. She did not move.

"Is that why you have these things, Hugo?" she asked, looking at the apartment. "All these possessions?"

"Perhaps," he replied. "In London I have a Tiepolo of Cleopatra. It is perhaps the most beautiful object I own. But it is still an object, Amy. It is lovely, but it has no warmth, no life. As I said, life is everything."

He traced a finger on her cheek.

"Do I remind you of her?" she asked.

"Not in the slightest," he answered immediately. "She played better than you ever will. But you're more beautiful. You have more confidence and character, I think. Susanna was a blank canvas who demanded, always, that I decide what should be there on the surface."

Her mouth felt dry. Her head ached a little. "Was that good or bad, Hugo?"

"Neither. That is what she was. You are what you are. I can admire and love both."

"We cannot—" she began to say.

"The world is what we make it," Hugo said, interrupting, then gently moved his right hand to the neck of her evening dress, pressed his fingers down, and cupped her breast through the loose fabric. "You've never been with a man, Amy, have you?"

"No," she replied, her breath now shallow.

"Good," he said firmly. He removed his hand from her breast and ran his fingers down the front of her dress, reached down beneath her knees, picked up the hem and lifted it, exposing her legs. Slowly, as if performing some kind of examination, he moved both his hands between her thighs, rubbing his thumbs on the soft skin there, reaching upwards until his fingers touched cotton. Then he lifted the evening dress further until it exposed what his hand felt and, with a gentle circular movement, slid his thumbs beneath the elastic, probing.

Amy sighed, not knowing herself what the noise meant. Hugo's feverish fingers worked at her. He removed them and, in a single movement, lifted her in his arms. He held her like a child, staring into her eyes as he carried her into the bedroom, where every wall seemed a mirror.

She saw their reflection in the glass, watched it all the time as he lowered her on the bed, then tore at his own clothes until he knelt by her, face suffused with red. She had seen a boyfriend naked once before, and refused his invitation. Hugo was, by comparison, huge, almost terrifying in his size.

She looked at him. "Hugo," she said. "You must wear something."

"I believe not," he said, and took both hands to the front of her dress, then tore the thin fabric apart in a single vicious gesture which jerked her body off the bed. She struggled out of her underwear, fearing he would rip that from her too. His head came down to her shoulder. She felt his teeth bite sharp and hard into her neck, and cried out softly from the pain.

"Hugo," she repeated, pulling at his neck so that he could see her face. "I'm frightened."

"You've nothing to fear. With me, you never will."

She wanted to cry. She wanted to run from the room. Amy remembered the previous Saturday, when she had offered herself so openly to Daniel and he had refused, setting these events in train.

Her head fell down on her chest. She refused to look him in the face. "I don't...want to," she said quietly.

His hands moved again, fingers poking, searching, entering.

"Oh, but I do, my love," he answered. "Now, if you please..."

46

The Roman magistrate

I stayed with Marchese on the Quirinal, a little way down from the palace where the Pope was in residence, fleeing the heat and malaria of the Vatican. With my mind in such turmoil, I was grateful to discover I had a genial host. Marchese occupied a small patrician mansion with his wife and a single manservant, Lanza. Marchese was elderly, with a stooped back, an awkward gait, and a shock of white hair. Yet his eyes were as bright and sharp and querulous as those of a child. For all his cheery demeanour, I suspect few villains had found their way past this chap in his prime.

I arrived late at night, after two days, each of ten hours, on the road, and was grateful to be offered a bath, fed a good meal, then despatched, exhausted, to bed. The Marcheses had never had children, I'll warrant, since both master and mistress fussed around as if I were their offspring. It had yet to dawn fully upon me that I was in Rome, with all its sights and possibilities, for I climbed into a comfortable divan on the second floor and fell immediately into a deep and dreamless sleep, waking only when a cock crew and the sun, bright and warming, fell through the curtains.

I spent the morning scanning through Marchese's manuscript. Leo had his limits—we would not publish absolutely
anything. It took only a little while to discover that this
particular commission would pose no problem, and could
even shift a few paid copies. As a writer, Marchese possessed
a slightly rambling fashion, though nothing which a spot of
editing couldn't improve. But he had flare. While there were
dull patches, which I skipped, there was much of interest in
these tales of city low-life.

Most of those who pay the House of Scacchi to see their
names in print do so out of vanity. That smudge of ink upon
the page bestows immortality in their own eyes, I imagine,
though if they saw the sorry pile of unsold volumes in our
cellar, they might feel differently. Marchese did not fit this
description. His purpose, as he explained to me, was to set
down his methods of investigation in the hope that others in
his trade might learn from them and, over time, find better
ways of bringing the guilty to book. To him the law, as it
stands, is a random process. On most occasions some
hapless victim is first sought out, and only then does the
search begin for evidence by which to establish his
culpability. Marchese believes the first step should be to
establish facts and wonder where they lead, not follow the
gossiping throng to wherever it happens to point the finger
and arrest the first person with a guilty look on his face. I did
not say as much, but this seems to me an idea that is too
revolutionary for the Italians, who have hot blood and a
thirst for instant satisfaction. The Germans or the English,
perhaps, could stomach the slow and painstaking practice
which Marchese recommends. I doubt it would satisfy many
of those who hang around the side entrance of the Doge's
Palace when a plot's about and the old man's temper's up,

counting those unfortunates who go in, then noting how few
come out again.

Each chapter had some melodramatic title: "The Tuscan
Fragment and a Spray of Camellias." Or "How an Egyptian
Cat May Bark at Midnight." The magistrate had, however,
a higher intent than mere entertainment. He wished to
inform his readers of the process he described as "forensic
mechanics." He also believed that by setting down personal
characteristics of the scoundrels he apprehended, he would
dispel the notion that they were wicked by nature or
choosing, a separate species altogether from the average,
honest citizen who walks the streets.

"The greatest delusion," Marchese declared, waving a fat,
wrinkled finger at my face, "is the belief that this world must
be divided into black and white, the sinner and the righteous.
Nowhere is there evidence for such a nonsensical notion.
Each argument has many facets, each individual a panoply
of traits, some praiseworthy, some obnoxious, and most of
them inherited, I suspect. It is how each man selects—or has
selected for him—a particular version of events and set of
characteristics that makes the difference. I am as close to
being a murderer as you. Only fate, a lack of temptation,
and, I hope, a certain steel within our character save us from
the scaffold. Always beware those who would tell you this
world falls into two camps—good or bad. They are either
fools or, worse, manipulators seeking to enhance their power
by gulling those poor, sad folk among us who crave some
distant enemy to explain their present plight."

He sniffed the air. A most delightful aroma was making
its way out of the kitchen. A mountain of meat and potatoes
and two small jugs of wine later, we were back in the
armchairs. I felt sated and sleepy, and glad, too, that he had

taken my mind off events in Venice. Whatever was happening with Rebecca and Leo, however much progress Delapole had made in heading off my uncle from his vile plans, nothing I might think or do in Rome had any consequence.

"Money," he said, and I covered my cup as he swung a flagon of grappa my way. "I'll pay the going rate and nothing more. I know you Venetians are the very Devil when it comes to negotiations."

I had no mind to haggle with this lovable old chap, though I doubted he was short of a bob or two. So I cast aside the inflated price list Leo used as an opening gambit and, to foreshorten matters, gave him the real one, which was, in all honesty, as cheap a deal as he might get of any Venice publisher.

He slapped me gently on the shoulder. "Oh, come, Lorenzo. There's always space for bargaining in these affairs. How much for cash on the nail, eh?"

I waved my hand, beginning to feel sleepy from the food and drink. "As I said. This is the price, sir. We should waste no more time on these matters."

He looked at me and sighed. "Do you know? I cannot decide whether you are the most uncharacteristic Venetian I have ever met, or the most cunning of them all."

"I am a country lad from Treviso, not the city. I lack the wit for all this mental juggling."

"Hmmm. Now, that I *do* doubt. You've been juggling with me all the time. Thinking of one thing back home while you dealt most professionally with me here."

I said nothing. I was not to be drawn.

"Very well, then!" He rose from his chair and held out a hand. "Let us put the sordid matter of capital behind us, shake upon this contract, then take a whiff of putrid Roman air. It's boiling hot out there, my son, but I'll not let you go without a few of the sights. What do you say?"

I took his outstretched hand. Marchese was the first man of Rome I had ever done business with, and a true Roman he was at that. "I say it will be, like everything else in your company, the greatest pleasure."

And so we found our way around the greatest city on the face of the earth. With Marchese as my guide, always keen to point out a landmark here, a piece of crumbling statuary there, Rome came alive. I walked with Caesar and Augustus, trembled at the presence of Nero, and stood silent before the Colosseum. I felt like a child in the presence of a generous, kindly uncle who possessed the key to the most wondrous secret garden in the world. By the banks of the Tiber, the old man showed me the former site of the wooden bridge of the Ponte Sublicio, which Horatius and his comrades had so bravely defended against Lars Porsena and the entire Etruscan army. Then he led me to Tiber Island, a ghetto for the city Jews, who had been there under curfew since Pope Paul IV had them herded behind its walls, under pain of death, some 170 years before.

At this last I became thoughtful, which he mistook for tiredness (the old man's stamina, in spite of his lameness, never seemed to wane provided he paused now and then), and so we returned to the Quirinal.

In the house we chatted idly. Old Marchese scarcely took his eyes off me. Eventually he put down his glass and said, "Lorenzo. Your mind is not entirely upon our conversation."

"I am sorry, sir," I replied. "There are personal matters with which I need not trouble you. I apologise if I seem distant."

"Sometimes these things are best discussed with others."

"Sometimes. But not on this occasion. Were it otherwise, be assured I would not hesitate to discuss them with you, since rarely have I enjoyed so much congenial company in one day, and with someone who began it as a stranger and ended, I hope, a friend."

"I should be most offended if you regarded me otherwise. To prove as much, I shall ask you, as a friend, to settle one last quandary which you may resolve at your leisure, in bed, on the coach back to Venice, or later as it pleases you."

He went to the bookshelf, took out a thick volume, then reached behind it and retrieved a sheaf of paper. When he brought it over, I could see it was written in the same careful scrawl used for the manuscript I had read that morning.

"There is a missing chapter in what I showed you, Lorenzo. Not all my cases were successful, though that is not why I withheld this one. I had wondered whether I should show this to anyone. I still do not know if it is fit for the light of day. You must help me. Read it, and I shall abide by your decision."

I took the pages, then rose and said good night to him and his wife. The day had been long. Tomorrow's journey would be tiring. Yet in bed, in the quiet, small room on the Quirinal, I found sleep difficult. I drifted, half-dreaming. Images from ancient Rome assaulted me: Caesar dying beneath a rain of bloody blows; Caligula murdered by his bodyguard; the head and hands of Cicero, butchered by Augustus's men and displayed for all to see upon the speaker's platform in the Forum.

Then these ancients disappeared, and in their place I saw Rebecca, naked, pale-faced, and frightened, her hands covering her modesty, apparently unable to speak. We were in her room in Venice, as if it were still the scene of our last meeting when we had argued, and she, I believe, wished to reveal something but lacked the courage or opportunity. I opened my mouth, but no words appeared. Her eyes pleaded for my aid. I was unable to walk towards her. Then, with an effort that made the tears tumble down her cheeks, she lifted a single, white hand from her body, showed me the palm, and uttered four words: "*There is no blood.*"

I awoke, shaking, as if in a fever.

It was impossible to sleep. Seeking something to distract my confused mind, I reached for Marchese's manuscript, lit a candle, and began to read.

An hour later I understood the dream and much, much more. With cold dread in my heart, I raced along the corridor to hammer on my host's door, demanding entrance.

Hard questions

GIULIA MORELLI SAT OUTSIDE THE CAFÉ IN THE SQUARE of San Cassian, watching Biagio squirm on the hard plastic seat. The sergeant was off duty, out of his uniform, and, moreover, in the company of a detective.

"You look uncomfortable," she observed. "Relax. I don't bite."

He swore. "I can't believe I agreed to do this. What's wrong with your people?"

"All in good time," she answered. "You know why I feel like this?"

"Yes," he groaned. After the interview with Rizzo, she had probed him about his background: college in Rome, his home city. Venice was an accident. There were no relatives. Biagio could not be a part of any clique, not unless he had been recruited since his arrival two years ago, and that seemed improbable. She had to trust someone. He seemed the best option.

"When I have the evidence," she said. "When everything is so obvious it can't be stopped. Then I can move with some hope of success. If I raised any suspicions now, I would be halted the moment I mentioned the wrong names. Then we'd both regret it."

He nodded and cast a sour eye at the ancient brickwork of Ca' Scacchi across the *rio*. Biagio could be trusted, she felt. But that did not mean he was a willing participant.

"The English kid isn't going anywhere," he noted. "We've been sitting here for an hour. He hasn't even stuck his head out to get some breakfast."

"You're right," she agreed, and wondered what that meant. If the newspapers were right, Daniel Forster was a brilliant musician. His first composition, a masterly re-creation of a Baroque violin concerto, by all accounts, would receive its première at La Pietà the following Friday. Yet he behaved as if he were adrift in the city. The deaths of Scacchi and the American had affected him; of that she had no doubt. But there had to be more to his lassitude than simple grief. She had set Biagio to tail him. He reported only one visit to La Pietà, on Monday evening. Daniel Forster had spent almost the whole of Tuesday inside Ca' Scacchi, making just a single phone call, and that to the undertaker (she had discreetly placed a tap on the line). He left the house once only, to buy wine and some precooked lasagne. It was now eleven in the morning on the Wednesday. The moment she assumed would be the greatest achievement of his life was only two days away. And he was behaving like a recluse, as if the palpable excitement now building around La Pietà—which was reflected in the growing presence of the international media—were nothing to do with him.

"We could sit here forever," Biagio moaned.

"I agree." She had hoped to be able to follow Daniel in the street, catch him off guard, away from what he surely now regarded as his home territory. Biagio was right, though. Daniel Forster seemed to have retreated behind the shell of Ca' Scacchi for good.

"Come," she said, then threw some coins on the table and left the sergeant struggling to keep up as she strode across the small bridge to the old mansion.

He answered the door looking a mess: hair dishevelled, eyes red. His breath stank of wine. His eyes refused to meet hers.

"What do you want?" Daniel Forster asked.

"To talk to you."

"I've nothing new to say."

"Perhaps not. Perhaps we have something new to say to you. May we come in?"

He nodded and, with obvious reluctance, opened the door. They walked upstairs into the living room, which overlooked the *rio*. The dining table was now littered with dirty plates. Two empty bottles of wine stood in the centre. He beckoned them to sit in the deep armchairs by the dead fire.

"You're missing your housekeeper, Daniel," she observed. "This place has the smell of a lonely man about it."

He stared at the mess on the table. "True. I still . . ." He glanced around the room as if it were some kind of cruel illusion. "I still find it difficult to believe they won't come back."

She thought about going upstairs, looking to see if the twisted, matted sheets were still there in the large bedroom at the back. There was no need. Nothing had changed in the house since she'd last seen it. In all probability the bloodstains were still on the carpet in the bedroom.

"The funeral is at San Michele on Friday, I gather," she said. "Only a few hours before your concert. You must compose yourself for that. The living should allow grief to consume them only so much. If it oversteps itself, it offends the dead. Or their memory, at least."

"I thank you for your condolences," he replied flatly. "I'll bear them in mind."

"Good." She found herself liking Daniel Forster in spite of his coldness towards her. "Tell me: Who do you think killed your friends?"

His head cocked to one side as if he were suddenly lost in thought.

"I thought you told me the answer to that. Laura. You seemed to think it was an open-and-shut case."

"No!" she laughed. "I merely reported to you what the housekeeper herself said to us. She told you as much herself when you visited on Giudecca."

He cast her a filthy look.

"You don't think those guards are deaf, Daniel?" she asked. "They have ears. They can talk."

"To hell with you."

Biagio—who had, it appeared to her, been intent on keeping out of this conversation as much as possible—wagged an admonitory finger at Daniel Forster.

"Language," he scolded. "In front of a lady."

She raised an eyebrow at the curiously prudish sergeant. "Thank you, Biagio. I believe I can handle this. For what it's worth, Daniel, I don't blame you for feeling aggrieved. You seem to be surrounded by people who have let you down. Who have deceived you."

He looked out of the window. It was going to be another hot, airless day. Perhaps, as a foreigner, he felt the temperature more than the locals.

"Is this going to take long? I was thinking of going out soon."

"Not so long," she replied. "It depends on you. I ask you again. Who killed your friends?"

His head moved slowly from side to side, as much in despair as anger, she thought. "Why do you keep tormenting me like this? You have Laura. Are you telling me now you no longer intend to charge her?"

"Not at all!" She waited until this news sank in. "I signed the papers for her release this morning. She's gone from the jail."

"To where?" he asked anxiously. "Where can I find her?"

"She's a free woman. I've no need to speak to her again. She can go wherever she likes. Perhaps she's coming here at this very moment. I don't know."

He scowled at her again. "Don't play games with people I love."

"Ah," she replied, then placed her hands together and stared at her fingers, thinking, saying nothing, waiting for him to force the pace.

"You said she was responsible," Daniel Forster declared when he could stand the silence no more.

"No, Daniel. *She* said that. Personally, I never believed it for a minute. It would have been possible to charge her with wasting our time. But that would have been cruel. She found these two men she loved on that terrible night, one dead, one dying. She regarded herself as their protector and felt a sense of guilt over their fate, perhaps. But I am a detective. I had to consider another possibility: that she was trying to protect the person who was truly responsible. You, perhaps."

He swore again. Biagio shuffled in his chair but was quiet.

"If you think I'm guilty, arrest me."

"No, of course you're not the one," she continued. "How could you be? You were in bed with her that night. Why would either of you get up and stab her master and his boyfriend just after you made love? Again, what was the reason?"

"You're fishing," he murmured.

"No. I merely looked at the sheets, Daniel."

He reached for a packet of cigarettes on the coffee table and, with a fumbling hand, lit one, took a couple of puffs, then coughed.

"Do you enjoy this?" he asked.

"Oh, yes! Isn't that obvious?"

"But why?"

"Because sometimes—not always, but sometimes—we manage to put things right. We see a kind of tear in the fabric of the world and we manage to mend it. What else should we do? Close our eyes and walk on by? There are so many people behaving like that already, Daniel. Why choose to walk with the crowd?"

He gave up on the cigarette, stubbed it out, and said nothing.

"You're so different from the friend of yours I met that sad morning," she continued. "You hide here, as if the sunlight were your enemy. All the while Signor Massiter is the man about town. A lunch here, an appointment there. Do you know he dined with the mayor the other day? To move in such circles, yet he has not an iota of your talent, I believe, but merely feeds upon it."

"People like Hugo Massiter are . . ." He searched for the words. "A necessary evil."

"Of course. And a successful evil too. You know that young violinist? The American?"

His eyes glinted with interest again. "Amy?"

"Quite. I happened to be taking breakfast near his apartment in Dorsoduro before I came here. She appeared from there very early. With that look. You know? I think . . . But no. Who is one to judge such things these days?"

"You're following Hugo?" he asked.

"I didn't say that. I merely happened to see the American girl leave his apartment. She seemed a little dishevelled. Upset, perhaps. I don't know. You should ask her when you meet."

His eyes lost their shine again. "Perhaps."

"Do you think Signor Massiter has a taste for young girls?"

Daniel Forster sighed heavily. "I've no idea. For what it's worth, I don't really know Hugo Massiter. I never met him until I came here."

"He seems to have pursued an interest in…Amy? Quite successfully too."

"If you say so."

The idea did trouble him, she thought, but not in the way she expected. There was no sign of jealousy, simply concern.

"Tell me," he asked her. "Who do you think killed Paul and Scacchi?"

She shrugged. "Someone with a reason, of course. A person who either wanted something from them or felt the requirement to punish them for some perceived misdeed."

"I told you about the money he borrowed. You called me a liar."

His habit of exaggerating, of straying from the strict truth, was annoying. "No, I said that I had no evidence to support your claim. That does not mean it's inaccurate. Simply unlikely."

"Then who?"

She waited a moment, so that the question would have some impact. The unsatisfactory interview with Rizzo had established only one thing for certain: that Massiter had been anxiously searching for some musical instrument which had come onto the black market. However hard she pressed him, Rizzo maintained his innocence of the superintendent's murder—and his attack upon her. Nor did he shed any light on the instrument itself, although, if she was right, Rizzo himself must have taken it from Susanna Gianni's coffin. None of this worried her. Rizzo could not escape her grasp. She would return to him later, time and again, pressing a little harder on each occasion. And one day he would break, bringing the greater prize with him, for it was this that mattered all along.

"Scacchi handled stolen artefacts from time to time," she told Daniel. "Were you aware of this? Did you negotiate for any such item on his behalf?"

His young face reddened slightly. "He told me he dealt in antiques. That's all."

"Such a catchall phrase! But answer my question, please, Daniel. Did you handle any such object for him recently? This may be important. Do not worry. I am not chasing a thief. I wish to catch a murderer."

"There were some things in the house which he wished to keep hidden," he replied obliquely.

"Are they still here?"

"I can't find anything of value anywhere," he admitted. "I've looked high and low."

"Why did you do that? Did you hope to sell them?"

"No!" He fell silent.

"Then why, Daniel?"

She cursed her impetuosity. His face had settled into a mask. "For my own satisfaction," he said. "I am a musician, not a crook."

"A musician who rarely goes to see his work rehearsed. Will you be there for the première, even? And the party afterwards?"

His eyes were on the window once more. "I'll be there. Have you asked enough questions?"

"No. Have you provided enough answers?"

"As many as you deserve," he replied.

She looked at Biagio. The sergeant was growing restless. He was on duty at three. The interview was going nowhere.

"I rather hoped, Daniel, that you killed them. It would have been so neat and simple, and you know how much the police like that."

He glared at her. "What?"

"You are the one person I can find with a verifiable motive. Apart from the housekeeper, that is, and we both know she wasn't to blame."

There was hatred in his eyes. It surprised her.

"You should deal with matters of the estate more promptly," she said. "Before trying to drown your misery in wine. I spoke to Scacchi's lawyer yesterday. The old man divided his estate into three parts. To his lover, to his housekeeper, and to you. The change was made only a week ago. The lover is dead. The housekeeper immediately withdrew her claim once I told her about it. This leaves you as sole beneficiary of the will."

Daniel Forster's eyes widened in disbelief.

"This house is yours, Daniel," she continued. "And everything in it. With no debts or charges upon it. Scacchi made you his heir, though he knew you for just a few weeks. Now, why do you think he did that?"

The redness had gone from his face. At that moment, Giulia Morelli believed, Daniel Forster was full of outrage and anger towards his dead benefactor, as if Scacchi had managed to pull some mysterious trick even from the city morgue, where he now lay.

"Daniel? Why?"

His mind was elsewhere, a place she could not begin to guess. Then he turned to gaze at her with a fierceness in his eyes she had not seen before.

"Tell me," he said. "When you go home, when your work is finished, do you feel you've added to the sum of good in the world?"

"Naturally. There would be no other reason for us to do this job."

"And how do you define that, Captain?"

"I don't steal," she replied immediately. "I don't take bribes. I don't invent convictions for those I simply suppose to be guilty, or look the other way for those deemed to be beyond the extent of the law."

"So that's how you define goodness?" he asked. "By what you don't do?"

"In this city it is," she replied sharply, wishing on the instant that she had given the question more thought.

Daniel Forster folded his arms and smiled. She stood up, glowered at Biagio, and mumbled some excuse about having to leave. Then she threw her card on the table.

"Talk to me again, Daniel. It would help us both. And on my mobile number only, please. Remember what I said about this city. Remember what company you keep."

Outside, the temperature had risen by several degrees. Venice would soon be unbearable. Her mind was unusually confused. Biagio eyed her quizzically.

"Well?" she demanded.

He shrugged. "I'd been wondering what it might be like, seeing someone get the better of you."

"Now you know. Smart English bastard."

"I like him," the sergeant said. "He seems honest enough."

"Enough for what?" she wondered.

He cast her a harsh glance. "Enough to help us if he can. If he wants to, that is, and has some reason."

Biagio was right. She knew it. Without Daniel Forster they were lost. The suspicions that rolled around her head night and day would lose their momentum. She might not even face the option of a desk in Padua.

"I'll find a reason," she muttered.

But Biagio was in the shadow of a nearby doorway, taking a call on his mobile. The sergeant's face was flushed, and he was cursing rapidly into the handset. He finished and turned to her.

"What is it?" she asked, fearing the answer.

"They found Rizzo this morning. Floating facedown in one of the old docks by the port. Shot once in the head. Last night, probably."

She closed her eyes and wished she had acted more swiftly to pump the truth out of the man. "Damn."

He remained silent, watching her.

"I'm going to pull in Massiter," she said. "Find out what he did last night."

"You can't," he said instantly. "The case has been assigned. You can't go near it without telling them what we've been doing."

"Who's got it?"

"Raffone."

She was outraged. Rizzo's murder had been given to the worst detective in the city, and one who was probably corrupt too. "Jesus. Someone really wants a result there. So what do you think we do?"

Biagio straightened himself up. Giulia Morelli wished she'd sought his opinion before. She took him too much for granted. He nodded back towards Ca' Scacchi. "You got the Scacchi case. You use that. We find some way of leaning on this kid. If you think about it, there's nothing else."

She looked at Biagio. "You liked him, didn't you?"

"Sure," he agreed. "You didn't?"

Daniel Forster had withheld something from her. Of that she was certain. Yet somehow she felt unable to blame him for his actions. It was impossible to believe that some selfish, dishonest motive lay behind them.

"I liked him," she conceded. "But if we have to, Biagio, we must break him. If that's what we need."

The sergeant looked at his watch and said nothing. He was

probably thinking about going back on shift, starting his real work.

"Did you tell anyone?" she asked.

"About what?"

"Rizzo."

Biagio glowered at her. "The jerk was in the station. Do you think there are any secrets there?"

"No," she replied. There were a million ways the news could have leaked out. She had to learn to trust someone. "I'm sorry."

"It doesn't matter," Biagio said. "Listen. I go along with this for the rest of the week. Then either we have something or we give up. We forget about the whole thing. Is that agreed?"

"Naturally," Giulia Morelli lied.

48

The demon who escaped my grasp

Being an excerpt removed from the memoirs of Alberto Marchese, magistrate of the Quirinal quarter, 1713–33, at his request.

AS YOU, DEAR READER, WILL APPRECIATE BY NOW, THE *rogue is a most ordinary species. I have, in my time, despatched more than 200 to the prison and thirty or so to the scaffold. Human nature being what it is, I cannot, I confess, feel much regret for their fates, nor satisfaction, either. Life is much determined by a throw of the die. None of these felons possessed some seed of the Devil in their blood. Born to different parents in another time, they would all have made model citizens, I'll warrant, except perhaps for old Fratelli, who was as mad as a swineherd's hound and twice as dangerous. But anyone minded to strangle his wife, then serve up cooked portions of the dismembered corpse for the relatives who arrived for her own birthday feast, must be deemed lunatic, and therefore not fully human in the first place. Even Brazzi, that light-fingered blackguard with a taste for lifting the purses of tourists on the Palatine, had his finer side, quoting wistfully from Petrarch as I set down his appointment with the axe (a little thievery is one thing, but the fellow should never have stuck that chap from Milan—I know these northern types can be annoying, but murder is murder, after all).*

I can think of only one villain I have encountered over the years for whom I feel the word "evil" is truly appropriate, and it is to my eternal shame that he remains, as far as I am aware, a free man. But this was no ordinary criminal. I cannot give you his real name or history. What I do know is that he is surely one of the most wicked creatures ever to have walked this earth, in that his malevolence was both intentional and directed at the innocent in full knowledge of the pain and injury it would cause. Most malefactors fall into their cycle of criminality through laziness, accident, or, let it be said, necessity. The one I describe here indulged in his devilry—there is no other word—because its performance, and its consequences, amused him. Money, influence, power both sexual and worldly ... all these things were but side dishes for the main course of his pleasure, which was to deceive the world with one face and devour it with another.

Every other criminal I have encountered in this odd career, I could in one way or another understand. Poverty, lust, greed—read the Good Book, they're all there—have driven men to bad since Eve first offered Adam a bite of the apple. Yet this one was beyond me, beyond God in all his wisdom, I'd venture. You will suspect I say this because he was a foreigner, an Englishman at that. You are wrong. This fellow—Arnold Lescalier, as I knew him (though I doubt that bears much resemblance to the name he was christened with, if christened he was)—possessed a streak of evil that ran through his soul with the same unbending accuracy of a flaw despoiling a piece of fine marble. It was appropriate, then, that we first met at the Teatro Goldoni, where a passable pack of players was trying to entertain us with a translation of some ancient piece about Faust by the Englishman Marlowe. It was an amusing melodrama, and would have been all the more so had I known that this articulate, entertaining Englishman to whom I was introduced at the interval could have passed as inspiration for the theme. The doomed

*doctor on his way to Hades, you think? Ah, no. For all his faults, Faust
was human throughout. Mr. Lescalier, I believe, had more in common
with Mephistopheles, the Devil's cool and calculating aide-de-camp, who
would smile while slitting your throat, then steal your soul as it departs
your bleeding carcass and stop it up in a bottle for his master.*

    *None of this was apparent when we met, naturally. All I saw was a
pleasant-looking Englishman, perhaps just past thirty, with fair hair, a
querulous, deceptively blank expression, and the kind of foppish clothes
the travelling aristocrats prefer when visiting Rome: all silk and finery.
Mr. Lescalier appeared the sort of fellow who might wear two kerchiefs
in each sleeve and never dare to blow his nose in public. The one hint to
the contrary, which I should have noticed, was his manservant, an
unspeakably ugly little native whose name I never discovered. I
assumed that it was the servant's coarse worldliness which saved his
ingenuous master from being torn apart by the Roman hoodlums.
Their story was that Lescalier was the bastard son of a rich English lord
who had sent him to Europe for an education. The means to gaining this
seemed to be to apply money to all in sight in return for admittance to
their circle. Lescalier loved painting, sculpture, music, dance, everything
that Rome had to offer. He had, he told me, travelled through Paris,
Geneva, Milan, and Florence before arriving in our fair city, and while
all had their finer points, none could touch Rome. There was, I later
discovered, some truth in this. An Englishman named Debrett (strange
how the chap chose these French-sounding titles) had fleeced a score of
nobles in Milan before decamping, and I heard reports of similar
behaviour in Geneva by a scoundrel called Lafontaine.*

    *Mr. Lescalier cast a spell upon all he met that night. The ladies wished to
mother him. The men regarded him much like a younger brother newly
arrived in the city, in need of guidance and protection from its cruel
realities. Before the evening was out, he had invitations to dinner at six of
the best tables in Rome (I declined to join the game for no other reason than
embarrassment—my humble home could not hope to match those he now*

had in his appointment book). Lescalier swept through the cafés and dining rooms of the city like a whirlwind, and it was not until a good seven months after that we discovered what tragedy and wreckage lay in his wake.

It was January of my last year in office, 1733, the year in which I now write. I was woken at three in the morning by a rapping on the door. The weather that night was vile. Soft snow, as cold as the grave, swirled from the night sky, and a bitter wind chilled the bone. There was nothing I wished more than to stay snug in bed. I kissed my darling Anna and told her to go back to sleep while I dealt with the visitor. It is a magistrate's lot to be at every man's beck and call, night and day. There is no reason why this burden should be shared with one's wife.

Downstairs was someone I recognised immediately: the chambermaid of the Duchess of Longhena, a handsome young woman utterly devoted to her mistress. The poor child was quite hysterical, in floods of tears, babbling nonsense, throwing her hands to her cheeks. Longhena, a fat, unlovely, and wealthy widow of somewhat flighty nature, lived three streets away down the hill, on the very border of my jurisdiction. I had never liked the woman, to be honest, and lately she had seemed more gross than usual. She had gone to pieces since her husband's death and, so the street gossip had it, taken to entertaining young men indiscreetly (the sin being in the indiscretion, of course, not the act itself—this is Rome, after all).

I sent Lanza into the kitchen for some grappa for the girl and made her sit down. When he returned, she drank it in one, then, after a further minute of sundry sobs and moans and trembling, calmed sufficiently to be asked the obvious question.

"It is late, girl," I said. "What is the meaning of this?"

She turned upon me eyes full of grief. "Oh, sir. It is my lady. She is dead, and horribly too."

"Dead?"

"Murdered, sir. By one she thought loved her more than any other."

"Lanza!" He had our coats all ready, and scarves and hats to keep *out the cold. Thirty years this man has been by my side, and never once has let me down. "Come, girl. We must see what you are talking about."*

"Sir!" Her eyes were wide and open and glassy with tears. "I cannot. Do not make me go back in that room again. I swear I'll die."

"Nonsense," I roared, impatient to be on with matters. "If there's a crime here, we must see for ourselves, and I shall hear how you discovered it. How else will we find the villain? Come!"

Lanza took her arm and, with the hapless girl wailing more loudly all the time, we ventured out into the night, where we fought our way through the gale and sleet, down the icy cobbled streets, struggling to remain upright. In spite of the weather a small crowd had gathered at the iron gates to the Longhena mansion, muttering darkly about murder and revenge. The night watch had yet to make their way to the scene. I announced my presence and pushed through. The house was very grand, on three floors, with a small Palladian entrance. The front door was open. From inside came the faint light of a small chandelier. With one hand on my dagger, I strode across the threshold and listened for activity. Some felons are late to quit the scene of their misdeeds. It is best to be prepared.

The great mansion was quite empty. Not a sound came from anywhere. Lanza followed on behind with the servant girl, who was now hiccupping and sobbing in that rhythmic way that sometimes betokens the onset of mania. If only I had listened more. Instead, suspecting intrigue (servants figure in crime more than one might expect), I turned upon her.

"Where are the rest of them, girl? The cooks? The servants?"

"All gone for the night, sir. Like the lady asked. She said she wanted me here alone when she met him, and I wasn't to let on I was around, neither. Just hang about in case I was needed. And he was done so quick, I ran for my life!"

I have, I imagine, no need to tell you who this "he" turned out to be. "Where is she, then?"

"No . . . !" She gazed terrified at the staircase, then fell to the floor in a huddle and covered her face with her hands. I have seen many a similar

show from villains seeking to escape detection. Justice requires an iron
hand if it is to be impartial. I ordered Lanza to drag her to her feet if
necessary and follow me up the stairs.

Human blood smells like no other. We climbed two floors to the top of
the house. When I reached the landing, I could recognise the stink. At the
end of the corridor, in what I took to be the lady's main bedroom, was a
dim light leaking past a half-open door. On the icy draught of night air
that came towards us—through an open window at the front, I
suspected—was the stench of murder. I have seen enough dead bodies in
my time to view this dread task with equanimity. Without another word
I walked down the corridor. Lanza forced the girl to follow, her screams
rising until, at the door, she fell to the floor and clutched my knees.

"I beg you, Signor Marchese. For the love of God, do not make me
return to that place!"

I am the very cynic in these matters. I must be.

"If you are innocent, child, what do you have to fear? If your lady
has been done a wrong, you should help us find the perpetrator, not
stand in our way."

Her face went rigid and there was the unmistakable cast of contempt
in her eyes. "Find the perpetrator, sir? Would you lock up the Devil?"

"If I could throw my shackles round his ankles."

There was a movement at her chest. I think it may have been the stirrings
of grim laughter. "And you think he'd sit in your cell and await his fate?"

Her strangeness annoyed me.

"Come," I ordered, and Lanza lifted her bodily, then the three of us
entered the bedroom of the late Duchess of Longhena.

I have watched the axe sever a man's head from his shoulders. I have
attended the scene of the vilest of low crimes Rome has to offer. Nothing
had prepared me for this sight. Lanza let go of the girl, went faint and
pale, then dashed to the fireplace to vomit freely into the dying embers.
The poor child knelt on the floor and buried her face in her hands,
making the kind of howling sound one might expect of an animal

coming face-to-face with the knife in the slaughterhouse.

She was right, of course. None should have entered that room and hoped to come out sane. The Duchess of Longhena, or what remained of her, lay naked on the bed like a small white whale beached in a sticky sea of her own blood. The woman's throat had been cut from ear to ear, giving her face the appearance of a carnival clown sporting a false smile. Her belly had been ripped open from the breast to the groin, the fat flesh thrust aside to expose the internal organs, and these then torn from their fastenings and scattered around the bedroom much as an angry child might launch its toys at the walls of the nursery.

I remained calm in the face of the girl's mad chanting and the continued heaving of Lanza in the corner, though this was a false show of reason. Somewhere at the back of my head, the real Marchese shrieked and howled along with her, as if in some locked room of my imagination. His was the true vision of this scene: a cruelty and violence that originated beyond the normal world we inhabit. Yet I must remain the magistrate always, and so contain my sentiments.

I took one step forward towards the bed. By the side of the mangled corpse lay something small and red, a familiar shape, though not in these circumstances. I bent and saw, on the bloodied coverlet, the tiny, perfect form of a human child, its head held forward as if in concentration, its eyes tight shut, tiny fists clenched, legs drawn up to its stomach. The cord still protruded from its belly. I took note of this scene, trying to calm my thoughts, and was aware of a hand upon my back. It was the girl, drawn to the bed, for all its horror. I looked at her crazed face and wondered how she might fare in the asylum. Our eyes returned to the collection of flesh upon the stained white satin and the tiny corpse there, surely the oddest victim of human brutality one might ever hope to find.

We stared at this still miniature of the human miracle for a moment, and then the universe turned turtle on us. For it moved. In one short, convulsive twitch, its limbs jerked into life, and the eyes, still covered with sheen, like those of a lizard, blinked briefly open. A bubble of *mucus and blood emerged from its lips. Then the child, a male child, born of the Duchess of Longhena by some bloody parody of the Caesarean manner, died before our eyes.*

I fell to my knees and found myself, without thinking, struggling in vain for prayer. Two lives had ended on these bedclothes: one tired and wasted, the other so short it was impossible to imagine how God's grace had touched its brief, bloody blink of existence.

When I rose, my head a maze of conflicting thoughts, the girl stared at me, not weeping, not shouting anymore. Her face was full of hatred and I knew why.

"I did not . . . understand," I stuttered.

"This is the Englishman's doing," she replied without emotion. "My lady called him here to tell him she was with child. She asked all but me to go away, wanting some solitude in which to break the news."

"But why . . . ?"

The room felt steeped in some mad, incarnate rage. It bore down on us all; its weight sat achingly on our shoulders.

She was looking at the bed again, no longer afraid. "I cannot have this poison in my head forever," she said to no one in particular.

My mind was wheeling in too many directions. I did not see what was happening until it was too late. She walked over to the half-open window, threw up the sash, and, without a word, flung herself out into the night air, two storeys aboveground. I recall the nauseating sound of her body as it met the marble terrace below. It took all my resolve not to follow her. That night I stood in the presence of evil and its stain touched me. The irony was that I had met it many times before and never recognised its true face.

Lescalier had impregnated the Duchess, of course. He had, it transpired, been having affairs all over Rome. A priest or some kind of doctor might be able to tell me why it was the news of the child which unhinged him. It could not have been planned, though my investigations proved beyond doubt that even without this casual murder, the Englishman would soon have departed Rome. His modus operandi seemed to be consistent with that adopted in the other cities where I traced him. First, he appears as a wealthy, innocent visitor, spreading around the riches he has stolen from his last port of call to gain some favour. Then, when he is embraced by all who matter, he becomes the thief and the rogue: borrowing, stealing, seducing at will, until the net of deceit becomes so broad and encircling that it begins to tighten around his neck. At this point, he flees, and a few weeks later another English aristocrat, with another counterfeit name, appears in society somewhere else in Europe. Curiously, in Paris and Geneva, too, he is thought to have killed, both pregnant women, one who was entirely innocent and merely happened to meet him in the wrong circumstances. What demon in a man's topography could make him hate so much the notion of motherhood? I cannot begin to imagine. Faced with such horrors, I find the complexities of the human beast beyond my comprehension.

So he escaped me as he escaped my counterparts elsewhere. Should he return to Rome, he will stand trial. But I doubt that will happen. This man is too clever. He deceives us by appealing to the better part of our nature, our generosity, our love of art, our proclivity for welcoming the charming stranger. That makes for a much more cunning villain than your average rogue.

Still, if he is brought to justice somewhere, I shall buy myself a ticket for the trial. And when a lull occurs in the proceedings, I shall remember the most horrific sight I witnessed that evening: the shattered body of that poor maidservant lying upon the marble terrace of the mansion of the Duchess of Longhena, all through the pompous stupidity of an old Roman magistrate who put the letter of the law above the need for simple human compassion.

With that image in my head, I shall abandon my lifelong devotion to so-called justice, take out my stiletto, walk over to the dock, and carve the bastard's guts out on the spot.

I doubt you will print this, my publisher friend. Yet, of all the tales I have to tell, it is, I submit, in some ways the most edifying.

Sant' Erasmo

THE MORNING FERRY FROM THE FONDAMENTE NUOVE crawled across the expanse of lagoon at a snail's pace, depositing Daniel a good fifteen-minute walk from Piero's smallholding. The Adriatic shimmered a weak shade of grey on the eastern horizon and sent a welcome breath of air across the neat rows of vegetables that lined the footpath.

Daniel had waited in the house for an hour and she had not come. Giulia Morelli said she had been released the day before. If she planned to return to Ca' Scacchi, she would surely have done so already. Her comments in the jail seemed plain enough. She must have known where he would be. So she would have fled elsewhere, to the elderly mother in Mestre, perhaps, or some nearby relative.

To Piero's, even. He tried to imagine seeing her in these verdant green fields, much as he had done on the day of the boat trip in those final moments before their world had disintegrated. He recalled her standing triumphant after the ridiculous game with the eels. He remembered, too, the taste of the fish in his own mouth and the way she looked at him after he braved the inky bucket of squirming bodies. It was at that point that he had committed himself to the city and, as a consequence, to her.

The cottage grew larger on the horizon. There was no female figure outside, beyond the artichoke field, where the green, flowery heads nodded in the light wind. Only Piero, hacking at some wood on the spare ground with Xerxes by his side, seated, nose erect, staring at his owner in admiration. Daniel shouted a greeting. The dog's head turned and a loud bark rang across the still of the island. Piero looked up. It was impossible for Daniel to discern his expression from this distance. Even so, he felt Piero seemed disappointed.

The dog bounded up to him, leaping at his thighs.

"Get down!" Piero shouted testily. He was covered in wood shavings from the object he had been carving in the garden. "Damned dog."

"It's all right, Piero," Daniel said, extending a hand. The huge man took it with some reluctance. His skin bristled with wood chips.

"I don't mean any offence, Daniel," Piero said. "But why are you here? There must be so many things to do in the city, what with the funeral and this concert I keep hearing about? What can concern you in this backwater?"

"A friend, I thought," Daniel replied carefully. "One who reminded me of happier times."

Piero nodded, accepting the reproach. He went to the rough outdoor table, pulled out a plastic bottle, and poured red wine into a couple of paper cups.

"Here," he said. "To absent companions."

They drank and there was, Daniel realised, some palpable distance between them. It occurred to him that Piero was Scacchi's cousin and had not been mentioned in the will. Perhaps this was some source of resentment on his part.

"I wanted to talk to you," Daniel said. "About so many things. I don't wish any misunderstandings, Piero. I didn't write that will. I didn't even know it existed. Tell me what you want from Scacchi's estate and you'll have it."

The thick brows knotted, and Daniel realised, on the instant, that he had made a mistake. "Money? You're offering me Scacchi's money? What need do you think I have of that, Daniel?"

"I apologise. It is just ... You didn't seem pleased to see me."

"No." He downed the wine and poured himself more. "I hate deaths. I hate everything about them. I worked with the dead once. You won't see me on Friday, not on San Michele. I know that place too damn well. But look here. I was going to send it. Now you can save me the trouble."

He went back to the makeshift bench and pulled from the nest of shavings a small piece of dark, stained wood and placed it on the table. "I carved this for Scacchi. He would have hated the thing in life, but now he's dead he can't stop me. Promise this will be in the coffin. That old man needs all the help he can get where he's going."

Piero's work was an intricate cross carved from a twisted gnarl of olive wood.

"Of course," Daniel said. "It's beautiful."

"It is an idiot's offering to his smart-ass cousin. Who knew me to be an idiot all along. Scacchi would have thrown it in the fire and then complained it burned meagrely."

Daniel felt the smooth wood and thought of the long care that had gone into the piece. Piero was correct: Scacchi had had little time for the mundane. "I'll place it there myself. I promise. And I hope you'll reconsider your decision. I'm no expert on funerals, but I feel you may regret not being there."

"No. The person is gone with that last breath. Why say goodbye to a carcass? I have Scacchi where he belongs, in my head, still alive there, where he will remain until I join him. I have no need of a funeral to convince myself he is dead. But you must go, Daniel. You are young. For you it's different. And..." Piero wrestled with the words. "This is all so *strange*. Scacchi gone. The American too. For what?"

He required an answer, which was impossible. "I have no idea," Daniel admitted.

"Ah! I'm a cretin. Why should you? Scacchi was a difficult man. He wound himself in mysteries and dealt too often with people best left alone. I know. Sometimes I was his errand boy on those excursions, more fool me."

Daniel said nothing. Piero scanned his face closely.

"So he treated you the same way too, eh?" he asked. "Don't deny it, Daniel. We were all, to some extent, Scacchi's playthings. I loved the old man, in the way one loves a dog that never behaves. But when he wanted something, we were all merely pawns upon his chessboard, and there, I feel, lies the answer to his death. He has cheated someone, no doubt, and for once pushed too far."

"Laura..." Daniel began to say.

"Laura! What fools the police are! To put her in jail like that. Do they have a brain in their heads?"

"She confessed, Piero. What else do you expect them to do?"

"Think about what they are hearing, for a start. Do they believe everything some villain tells them? Of course not. Yet when some poor woman whose head is mad with grief makes up this kind of cock-and-bull tale, they swallow every word and put her in prison. And all the while the real crooks swan around the city free as birds. You wonder why I live in Sant' Erasmo? It is to distance myself from the stupidity that rains down upon you, day and night, in that place across the water."

Daniel placed his paper cup on the table and held his hand over it when Piero tried to pour more wine. "Where is she now?" he enquired. "I need to talk to her."

"I have no idea. Why ask me?"

"Because you're her friend. You know her. This is important, Piero."

"*I have no idea!*" His angry voice boomed across the low, flat fields. Xerxes' ears fell flat to his head as the dog scuttled off to the corner of the clearing. Daniel said nothing. Finally, Piero apologised.

"I shouldn't have shouted, Daniel. My nerves are frayed. You ask these questions and assume I have some answers. I have no more than you."

"Where could she be? She said she had an elderly mother in Mestre."

Piero cast him a withering glance. "A mother in Mestre? Laura was an orphan, Daniel. She came straight from the home to work for Scacchi many years ago. There was no mother. A man, no doubt, and why not?"

"But she told me!"

"Your capacity for belief astonishes me, boy. I wonder you manage to walk the streets of that place without having the clothes stolen off your back."

"Then who is she? Where might she be?"

"Daniel, Daniel. How many times must I tell you I do not know. Besides..."

Daniel waited. Piero seemed unwilling to go on. "Besides what?"

"You care for her, I think. More than the care of a friend. Is this correct?"

"I believe so. I believe she feels the same way towards me."

Piero took a swig of wine, then spat on the ground. "This

tastes like piss. The wine has turned this past week. The world has turned too. Oh, Daniel! How can it be true that Laura loves you? She's not mute. She's not deaf or blind. If she cared to contact you, she could, surely. Yet she's gone. With no news to you or me. What does that tell you? Are these the actions of a woman who has a care?"

Daniel suppressed his anger. "It tells me she is frightened, perhaps of the men who killed Scacchi. Perhaps she seeks to protect me from them for some reason. I don't know. That's why I must talk to her. If she tells me to my face that she wishes to see me no more, then so be it. But I can't leave it like this. I will not."

"You have no choice. I can't help you. She will not." Piero watched the dog slumbering by the canal and sniffed the salt air. "Perhaps it's in the atmosphere. That poison they push into the sky from all those filthy factories in Mestre. It's driven us all mad. I thought, that day we came here, that you were one of us. I saw the way you played our little game. We all loved you. Scacchi more than any other. But we were wrong. Every one of us."

He turned and took Daniel by the shoulders. "You don't belong here," he said. "When your business is over, go home. You won't find any happiness here. Only misery or worse. Go, while you are still able."

Daniel stared at the man in front of him who now seemed a stranger. "If I didn't know you, Piero, I would have interpreted that as a threat."

"No. The very opposite. Sound advice from someone who cares for you. Who does not wish to see you wasting your life chasing ghosts, clutching at thin air. Will you listen? Please?"

Daniel closed his eyes and tried to think of some way through this maze. Piero was right. There were ghosts in the air: Scacchi and Paul laughing on the wind, Laura standing in front of him, staring in bemusement at the eel writhing around his face. And Amy, sad, lost Amy, who had been abandoned from the start.

"I'll heed you, Piero," he answered. "Next week I shall leave Venice, for good."

Two vast arms swept around his body. Daniel found himself gripped to Piero's massive chest. When he let go, Daniel saw there were tears in the huge man's eyes.

"If it were in my power to turn back the clock," Piero said. "If this poor simpleton could give anything to make things other than as they are…"

"No," Daniel replied, shocked by this sudden turn of grief. "You've done everything you could to help me. I'll always remember you, always the best times, on the *Sophia*, in our little party."

"Boy!" Piero gripped him again, and this time the tears flooded down his cheeks.

Daniel disentangled himself somewhat, wondering all the while how Scacchi might have handled such a situation. "But there is something you must promise me, Piero."

"Anything!"

"That you'll remember me as I am. Not as others may paint me."

Piero slapped him on the shoulder and poured two more cups of the sour red wine. Then he turned to watch the nodding heads of artichoke and the dog, who was awake again, tail now wagging hopefully, at the corner of the clearing.

"I know you, Daniel," Piero said, not looking at him. "I'm not such a fool as some think."

50

A *hurried return*

I could not have blamed Marchese if he thought me mad. At four in the morning, with the sun beginning to rise over the city, I began to tell him, in a stream of tumbling words, of the man I knew as Oliver Delapole and he as Arnold Lescalier, the scar upon the cheek which confirmed their joint identity, and why I must return to the city on the instant. The magistrate listened to me patiently as I laid out my case as openly and honestly as I dared. It was imperative Delapole was stopped and apprehended. But in doing so, I had to ensure Rebecca and her brother escaped the Doge's net, too, for reasons Marchese could not hear.

As I might have expected, Marchese saw the lacuna in my tale in an instant. "This concerns you greatly, Lorenzo. The man is a beast, no doubt, but not a common rapist. I do not see why you should worry yourself at a simple meeting."

"The Englishman may be able to make demands of her," I offered lamely. "And she is vulnerable."

"*Vulnerable?* You made her sound a strong character to me."

"Sir, I recall the way he looked at her when we met. He

finds her attractive. Given the opportunity, he will use any means he can to press himself upon her."

"Ah." The old man's face spoke volumes. "You and this lady, then . . . ?"

"Please, my friend. I do not have the time to gossip. I love this woman, and that is all there is to say."

He placed a finger thoughtfully to his cheek, and I realised how formidable a foe Marchese must have been to those he had pursued. Nothing escaped his attention. "Yet Lescalier . . . Delapole . . . whoever he is . . . This man will meet many women in the course of a week, Lorenzo. We must report him to the authorities, of course. But I think you should be content that having done no harm we know of, and still unaware we have him in our sights, he will play the part of the English fool a little while yet. Unless . . ."

I buried my head in my hands, unable to speak.

"Lad," the old man said, and there was now a note of impatience in his voice. "I cannot advise without the facts."

He was right. I was acting like a child. I thought of our last meeting and the way Rebecca had struggled to tell me the truth and, in the end, failed to summon the strength, dismayed by my own coldness. I thought of the dream. Her single outstretched hand and those four words: *There is no blood*.

"The facts . . ." There were none, only guesses, yet they had now achieved such solidity in my head I knew them to be true. "I believe the facts are she is with child. *My* child. And the picture that repeats itself in my head is that she uses this in order to resist his advances, with consequences we may both imagine."

The old man's complexion turned quite pale. He gripped me by the arm. "Good God, Lorenzo! Are you sure? For this changes things mightily."

"I believe it to be so, and that she wished to tell me before I left, and instead fell into an argument because I—I—urged her speak to the Englishman for help upon a private matter!"

He groaned and a look of hard determination came upon him. "A child . . . Well, you know how much he thinks of that. At least you believe you do, though what I set down on that paper was but a tenth of what I saw and learned. Had I told all, none that read it would sleep again for fear that he might pass their door. This man is the very Devil himself. We must stop him!"

"But how?" I pleaded.

Marchese had the plan already set in his head. "It is more than three hundred miles by coach from here to Venice. I shall take the first seat I can find, and be lucky to reach there after midnight tomorrow evening. Can you ride?"

"I grew up on a farm, sir. Show me the saddle."

"Excellent! My neighbour keeps a decent nag. I'll pay him well for it. You'll take the mountain route by Perugia to Ravenna on the coast. Then ride to Chioggia. See if you can get a boat there. With luck you'll beat me by a good six hours or more."

I followed him to the door, where already he was yelling for his neighbour to get out of bed and ready the horse. It was a fine Rome morning, with a light breeze and a few wisps of feathery cloud in the sky. A perfect day to ride like the wind. A dark, bearded face appeared at an upstairs window next door and threw a few half-hearted curses down at us.

"Come, Ferrero," Marchese bawled back. "Out of your pit and help a man do justice in this world!"

Soon the fellow was with us in the street and, to his credit and that of Marchese's, too, did just as he was told once the magistrate barked out his orders. As the bell of the Pope's summer palace tolled six, I was ready to depart and eager to face the road. Before I could, though, Marchese gave me some final, earnest advice.

"Lorenzo," he said. "When you arrive, go straight to the watch or a magistrate. Tell them this lady of yours may be in grave danger and they must ensure her safety. Tell them, too, that a magistrate of Rome follows on to confront this murderous villain with his deeds and set the wheels of justice in motion. Once they hear me speak, and see my papers, his head's upon the block, believe me."

I looked into his eyes and said nothing. This situation was too complex to offer answers. I could not do as he said, not until Rebecca was safely out of the clutches of both Delapole and the city. He saw my hesitation and seemed, for the first time, afraid.

"Listen to me, son. I know this man. I have seen his handiwork. Tackle him alone, and he'll skin you alive on the spot."

"Yes, sir" was all I said, then leapt into the saddle and spurred Ferrero's lean piebald mare down the street.

As I rode I laid my plans as best I could. It was out of the question that I should go to the watch and alert them to Delapole's past before Rebecca and Jacopo were clear of the city. Until Marchese arrived with evidence, they would more likely believe a supposedly moneyed English aristocrat than two Jews and an orphaned apprentice who had all but deserted his master. With his cunning, Delapole could have turned the tables on us instantly, revealed the nature of our all-too-real crimes, then fled with whatever loot he had beneath his arm. My first aim must be to find Rebecca and keep her safe, then help her flee before this precarious fabrication of deceit tumbled around our heads.

At Chioggia I left the panting horse and talked my way on board one of the fishing skiffs that sail each hour from the port across the lagoon to dock at the fish market on the Grand Canal and unload their catch. On their way they could drop me on Cannaregio's southern limit, near San Marcuola, and from there I could be in the Ghetto Nuovo within minutes. With these instructions issued, I found a resting place in the back of the boat, fashioned a makeshift bed out of my jacket, and fell sound asleep to the lapping of the waves against the little vessel's hull.

When I awoke some two hours later, we were wending our way down that broad, busy waterway I had come to know so well. A few yards to my right and a little further on, I could have strolled into Ca' Scacchi and asked my uncle how he fared. Delapole's relations with him must have reached a pretty state too. As had mine. Whatever future lay ahead, it was not as a Venetian printer's apprentice.

The small sail that had taken us across the lagoon was now furled, so we made our way through the mass of vessels by oar, ducking and weaving. We passed the narrow channel of the Cannaregio canal. My heart stirred at the thought of Rebecca's presence nearby. Then the boat hove into the jetty by the church and the captain bade me farewell with a friendly curse and a thump on the back.

I leapt the short distance to the landing and found myself on solid ground once more, as solid as it gets in Venice. Then I strode through the tangle of back alleys until I came to the bridge where I had first entered the world of the Jews. The guard yawned and waved me past. Once out of sight and across the *campo*, I took the steps to Rebecca two at a time. To my amazement, the door to their home was half-open. I pushed it back and saw Jacopo as I had never witnessed him before. He was slumped at the table, a flask of wine in front of him, eyes glassy, quite drunk.

"Well!" he cried. "What do we have here?"

My heart froze. He was clearly quite alone. I walked into the room and closed the door behind me.

"Jacopo. Where is Rebecca? It is vital that I see her."

A bitter laugh was my only answer. Then he picked up a spare cup on the table and poured some wine into it. "Vital, eh? Not so quickly, lad. We've time to make a toast, eh?"

I brushed aside his hand. Jacopo's eyes were full of hatred. I could feel my well-made plans begin to crash to the floor.

"Where is she? Please?"

"*Please?* Oh, come on, Lorenzo. A toast. Rebecca and I have found good fortune at last. For, within a matter of days, we'll be on the road once more, like little lapdogs, following that English friend of yours. She writes the notes, he puts his name upon them, and I just follow in their wake. So generous of him to talk that out of her, don't you think? Although he had a little weight behind his elbow."

He spoke in riddles. "I don't understand," I said. "You plan to leave so soon?"

"We are Mr. Delapole's new household, don't you know? To supply whatever he needs, and I fancy that's more than fame and fortune. He's got a roving eye, that one."

I took him by the shoulders. "He is not the man he seems, Lorenzo. We cannot let him near her."

"Oh! Now Delapole is not the man he seems. I thought that was your uncle. With whom, I have to say, I negotiated a fine agreement before your man got in the way. Old Leo would have done us proud: to publish and stay quiet, until she found herself able to make her authorship known. A penny-pinching chap, perhaps, but an honest one, Lorenzo.

You judge him wrong. And *in his place* . . ."

I thought for a moment that he might strike me. Yet Jacopo was above that, even in his present condition. Instead he grasped me roughly by the collar and pulled my face in to his. I could smell the wine stink on his breath.

"In his place we now have the Englishman," he said. "Who knows everything about us and will reveal it all unless we do his bidding. Oh . . . damnation!"

He launched the pewter pot against the wall and cursed me vilely. "What gave you the right?" he demanded. "To barter with our lives this way?"

"I thought Leo might take her from me," I answered, not entirely honestly, and needed immediately to correct myself. "I believed he might have thrust himself upon her in return for his patronage."

Jacopo stared at me, incredulous. "Leo! He lives in his dreams, Lorenzo. Can't you see? And besides, if my sister thought that was the price of her deliverance, who were you to decide otherwise?"

This question outraged me. "I am the one who loves her!"

"Hah!"

"I am the father of her child," I said quietly.

His face reddened with fury, then he seized the mug he had poured for me and claimed it for himself. "This madness gets worse with every moment. Be gone, Lorenzo. Your presence offends me."

"Delapole is a villain and a murderer! We must not let her near him."

"A little late for that, lad. I have not seen her since we visited him, at your suggestion, two days ago, and listened to every order and instruction that he laid down as the price of staying outside the Doge's clutches. Perhaps she packs his trunks for him, Lorenzo. Yes, I think that is it. She is his *housemaid*. For tomorrow he reveals himself as owner of the muse, and soon after we all depart for different climes, I know not where."

My spirits sank. Such images ran through my mind. "She would not willingly give in to him . . ." I began to say.

"Oh, child!" He was now furious. "Your innocence is more galling and more dangerous than a thousand criminals combined! Do you still not know us, Lorenzo? Do you still not realise what we are?"

I wished to stop up my ears. I wished to be out of that room, and stood up to leave. His powerful arm dragged me down.

"You will listen even if I have to pin you down upon the floor! How do you think we fled Munich and survived when so many others perished? And did this same trick in Geneva? What separates us from all those other Hebrew families in this ghetto? Our looks? Our manners? Or our history?"

This small, dark room now seemed oppressive. Its drapes and hangings threatened to close in and stifle me.

"You are drunk, Jacopo," I said quietly. "You should sleep, and speak again when reason has returned to your head."

"Reason never leaves me," he answered bitterly. "I would not dare allow it. So tell me. How do you think a woman, a fair one at that, escapes a room of soldiers come to kill her? How does a pair like us throw off our pauper's cloak and fit ourselves out in velvet?"

"I will not hear this!"

He grabbed me by the shoulders and spat the words into my face. "You will listen to every word! What do you think I dispense on these night visits to the middle-aged ladies of the Republic? Just a potion? Or a little comfort after, bedding

painted matrons? Lorenzo, we are the very picture of
practicality. We'll earn our living as best we can, in what
small space you Gentiles allow. And when that doesn't work,
we'll whore our way out of trouble and scurry for the next
stop on the road. Though I had hoped this was an end of it."

These words rang true, for all their hated resonance.

"If Rebecca sees an opportunity between the sheets with
your Englishman, that is her decision. Not yours. Or mine.
Necessity is a harsh mistress, Lorenzo. You heed her words or
pay a hefty price."

He had said his piece and not enjoyed it. Jacopo Levi
regarded me with the sullen misery of drunkards everywhere,
loathing himself as much as he loathed me.

"All of this may be true," I answered. "But I cannot wait to
hear it. I have intelligence of this man from Rome, Jacopo. He
is a murderer, of the most vile kind."

"Your fantasies are fast becoming tedious, lad," he
murmured. "Be gone. I had fancied myself a little longer in
this city and resent the fact that you have changed my plans.
You are a meddler and a fool and think you may excuse both
by being well-meaning in your intentions. You bore me. Go. I
have drinking to do."

"Jacopo—"

"Go! Before I lose my temper and do something I'll
regret!"

So I left him there, with his black thoughts and his wine
and his emptiness. The sun was almost down when I began
to make my way through the streets. Night stole upon Venice.
The moon's face shone from the filmy black surface of the
canals. I slipped through the darkness like a thief and raced
south, to Dorsoduro and Ca' Dario.

51

An eventful interview

H E HAD CHANGED. GIULIA MORELLI SAT NEXT TO
Daniel Forster in the upper hall of the Scuola di San Rocco
and tried to make sense of the situation. She had left a message
on his answering machine that tantalised deliberately, holding
out the promise of some kind of offer. She expected him to
respond, but not so quickly or with such apparent determination. The doubt and misery which she had seen in him the
previous day were now gone.

She followed his eyes and gazed at the paintings in the
corner of the hall, feeling all the same that the game could still
be hers. "I love this place," she said. "I could sit here for hours.
It's as if someone painted the entire history of the world on
these walls."

"You really think that?" He seemed surprised.

"Sure. A policewoman can like paintings, Daniel. Music too.
You'll get me a ticket for the concert, won't you?"

"I thought you didn't take bribes."

"True!" she laughed. "You're very sharp today. Your eyes
aren't red. I think you're no longer living in the bottom of a
bottle of cheap *rosso*."

"The wine has turned this past week," he said obliquely. "I'll have tickets left at the door. Just the one?"

She shrugged. "That's all I need, Daniel. I'm a solitary sort. You're kind."

"It's nothing." His eyes seemed fixed on the painting, though it was one of the less conspicuous ones, a work she had never much noticed before.

"What are you looking at?" she asked.

"The room," he lied. "Why do you really like this place?"

"As I said. Because it feels as if there is an entire world in here. All the emotions. Every story there's ever been, for good and evil."

His gaze stayed on the canvas in the corner.

"Tell me about that one," she asked.

"It's the Temptation of Christ. You haven't noticed it before?"

She stared at Tintoretto's two figures, refusing at first to believe him. But there was nothing else the work could be: there was Christ in darkness and doubt, and Lucifer with the rocks in his extended hand.

"No," she said, surprised. "Not really. There are so many bigger works here. And…" Giulia Morelli paused, needing her words to be precise. "It's odd. It is Christ who is in the shade and the Devil in the light. A handsome Devil too."

" 'The Venetian Lucifer,' Scacchi called him. He warned me that we would meet one day and I should face a choice."

There was something important here. "Did you meet his devil?"

"Perhaps," he replied. "Perhaps I'm in his company now."

"Ah," she said, pleasantly impressed. "So that is why we meet here, not at Ca' Scacchi?"

"No." He wore an ingenuous smile and Giulia Morelli felt once more that Biagio was right: Daniel Forster was an honest man, if rather more slippery than she had first imagined. "To tell the truth, I was just tired of being in that big, empty house, waiting to hear another voice. And I love this place, as you do. As Scacchi did. These faces talk to you after a while."

She said nothing, waiting.

"And you have, I think, something to tempt me?" he guessed. "Or so you hope, judging from your message."

She made a noncommittal noise. "We both want the same thing, Daniel. To find whoever murdered your friends. I've some ideas in that regard, but no evidence. I could arraign you, of course, and try to force you to assist."

"As you see fit," he replied dryly. "Scacchi had little regard for the police. I should tell you that."

"He had good reason to wish to avoid us from time to time. What else would you expect?"

He shook his head, unconvinced. "It wasn't that. Scacchi was ambivalent about moral matters. That made it impossible for him to deal with anyone of a similar mind, and I imagine you must by definition fall into that category. The law isn't black and white here, is it?"

"Some of us try to make it that way," she insisted.

"Perhaps. But you do Scacchi a disservice if you think he disliked the police simply out of self-interest. You served him no purpose. Since he was unable to define his own position, he relied upon the certainties of others to define it for him. That was why he liked me, I believe. Why he adopted me, almost. What he took to be my steadfastness, my relentless sincerity, allowed him a pillar he could lean on, depend upon. For a while, anyway."

He could not stop looking at the painting. She was unable to see the emotion in his eyes.

"And he was wrong," Daniel added firmly. "Utterly wrong. Which is why we are here."

"We should talk about this," she said. "At length."

"No," he insisted. "Like him, I have nothing to gain from you."

"So you've found the woman? The housekeeper?"

She had his attention then. The two figures on the canvas were entirely forgotten.

"Come, Daniel," she continued. "She's not returned to Ca' Scacchi. You've no idea where she is. You need to speak to her. You need to understand why she has abandoned you."

"That's a personal matter," he replied coldly. "None of your damn business."

"I wouldn't argue with that. Yet we can help each other here. In return for your assistance, I can point you to where she may be found."

He stared the length of the hall, seeming to weigh her offer. "Tell me now and I'll help you."

"No! Do I look a fool?"

"So much for trust!"

"Oh, Daniel. Don't work so hard at being exasperating. You're a young man in love. It's written all over your face. If I tell you what I know, everything else will be forgotten. My case. This concert of yours that has the whole city on the edge of their seats. Everything. Both of us might lose more than you think. Have you thought of that? She *confessed*, Daniel. There was a reason."

He turned away from her and stared at the opposite wall. "She lost her head. She was mad with grief."

Did he really believe that? She held it out as a possibility, too, much as the idea grated. "Perhaps. Neither of us knows."

His eyes went dead. "Then you haven't a clue where she is, or surely you would have dragged this from her. Please. No more. I'm tired of these games."

Giulia Morelli reached into her bag and pulled out the

376 ♣ David Hewson

photographs she had retrieved that morning from the files and the morgue.

"This isn't," she insisted, "some 'game.' There are three men dead now, not two. And one more, sometime before you came here, who was connected to this case, too, I believe. There's no reason to think they will be the last. The Venetian Lucifer isn't just some paint on canvas. He's real. He's here. He's around us now. He breathes in our ears, he laughs in our faces. You see this man?"

She passed him the photograph of Rizzo from the files. It was two years old, taken the last time he had been pulled in for some minor theft on the Lido. Daniel looked at it with no perceptible interest. Giulia wasn't fooled. He knew this face.

"Just some little crook who, from time to time, wound his way between the legs of this demon of ours," she said, not expecting a reaction.

She handed him the second picture, taken on the pathologist's slab the previous day. There was a black, bloody hole in Rizzo's temple. His dead eyes stared at the camera.

"That's what he looks like now," she said, watching Daniel's face.

Daniel Forster went white. She wondered if he might throw up.

"You can deal with the devil who did this. Or you can deal with me and, when it's over, try to make your peace with Laura. If you're still alive."

He didn't flinch. His eyes were back on the wall again.

Angry in spite of herself, she took hold of his chin in her hand and forced him away from the painting, forced him to look in her eyes.

"I've no more patience for this, Daniel. I've no more time. Choose now, please. And choose wisely."

52

Striking a bargain

DANIEL SAT IN HUGO MASSITER'S APARTMENT, WATCHing his multiple reflections in the glass. It was eight in the morning. An hour later they would both walk into the press conference Daniel had demanded. At noon they would attend Scacchi's funeral. The concert was at eight, with a party afterwards.

The previous evening Daniel had caught one of the late-night stores in Castello and, with money found in one of Paul's jackets, bought an expensive suit in dark-blue linen, with a matching white shirt and a black silk tie. His hair was now cut in a neat, tight business crop. Massiter raised a single eyebrow.

"You look too commercial, Daniel," he objected. "Like a broker. Not a composer."

"I'm sorry. I'm new to this sort of thing."

"Next time I'll come with you and offer a little advice. If you're finally to start thinking about what you wear, a little experience will not go amiss. Please..."

Daniel looked at Massiter's pale-blue suit and pink shirt, thought about the impending funeral, and wondered whether to say something. Then, before he could speak, he was waved to the sofa.

"Well," Massiter said. "Thank you for coming here first. I can't pretend I'm not concerned, Daniel. What's this about? Why the change of mood? What, exactly, do you intend to say?"

"Whatever you want me to say, Hugo. I thought that was the point."

Massiter shook his head. "I don't understand. You've been like a recluse ever since poor Scacchi died. Now, out of the blue, you seem suddenly recovered and can't wait to talk to the press. I'm glad of the former, naturally, but as your principal supporter in this venture, I think I've the right to know what you intend to say."

"Everything but the truth," Daniel replied. "Isn't that what you want to hear?"

Massiter looked at him intently. "Amy seems to think you're troubled, Daniel. She already suspects you're not the author of this piece and thinks you're about to tell that to the world to salve some misplaced outbreak of conscience. Is that the case? Because if it is, I have to tell you we would both suffer from the consequences. You're still due the balance of the arrangement I reached with Scacchi. Fifty thousand dollars. No small sum, as you appreciate, since you negotiated it. More than that, there is, I must repeat, the question of fraud. You've been party to a conspiracy. If you wish to turn awkward on me now, we'll both find ourselves on the wrong end of a criminal investigation. Do you want to go to jail?"

"Of course not," Daniel replied immediately. "Nor would I want that for you, Hugo. You've been kind to me. You were kind to Scacchi too."

"It was business," Massiter insisted. "Make no mistake about that. But pleasant business. I hope you've enjoyed my company as much as I have yours. I hope, too, that you have picked up a little from me. I have much to teach, Daniel. You, to be blunt, have much to learn."

Daniel nodded. "I know. But I'm making progress, aren't I?"

Massiter's slate eyes darkened. "Yes," he agreed. "I believe you are. More than I had expected, to be honest."

"I'm flattered."

Daniel wondered about the nearness of that other house, the one which had fascinated, and terrified, Laura so much. She had said that Massiter could, perhaps, organise a visit to Ca' Dario to satisfy his curiosity. There was, he was beginning to realise, so much that could be gleaned from the present situation. He had been a fool to sit back and wait for the prizes to arrive, as if they were his by right.

"Don't let me down, Daniel," Massiter said. "Or yourself."

He smiled into Massiter's cold face, wondering what it had been like when Amy was here, what means he had used to seduce her, and, most of all, what power his grip still possessed.

"I wouldn't dream of it, Hugo. I intend to milk today for everything I can. I'll make you feel proud of me. Tonight you'll walk out of that concert the hero of the hour. More so even than me, because I'll tell them how none of this would have been possible without you. How you're the benefactor that a true artist—which I am, naturally—requires. But there will be a price, Hugo. Beyond that which we have agreed. You must meet it. There's no bargaining here. I shall exact it. You shall pay and smile at me all the time."

"What?" Massiter murmured.

"After the funeral," Daniel insisted pleasantly. "When my mind is finally settled. Then we'll discuss it, once Scacchi's in his grave."

Massiter glowered, dissatisfied.

Daniel rose and said, "Now come, Hugo. The world awaits us. We mustn't keep it waiting."

A refusal and a surprise

It was almost ten by the time I found the rear entrance to Delapole's rented mansion. The night people were about their business in the narrow alleys that led off the *rio*: pale faces cooing from doorways, shambling figures falling out of taverns to keep them company. I felt weak in this dark and unruly world. Delapole was a tall, powerful man. Gobbo had the twisted, muscular strength of one of those terriers they turn upon a badger's sett, then wait and watch as he tears poor Brock to pieces. If I could only talk myself in and out again with Rebecca by my side, I should be happy. Marchese was on his way, past Padua by now, I hoped. With his help, Delapole would be locked tight away tomorrow, on the very day he hoped to be the hero of the Venetian crowds, and we would be gone from the city.

I rang the bell; a surly maid answered and ushered me into the empty kitchen. In a moment, Gobbo was there, surprised to see me. He sat down at the table and bade me join him, shrugging his shoulders as if to say: *What can I do?*

I refused his offer of a glass of wine. Then he said, "I

thought you might have stayed in Rome a little longer, Lorenzo. On your master's business."

"I think I have no master anymore. You and the Englishman have seen to that."

"Meaning what, precisely?"

"That you have seized her. I spoke with the brother. He tells me she has not returned for two days and that soon you will be leaving the city. Not much left for Leo there, and I'm the one to blame."

"You get this all out of proportion. Seven months we've been here, Lorenzo. Delapole gets bored so easily."

I had to be careful not to reveal how much I knew. "So I imagine."

"No, you don't. Not really. Look . . ." He pushed a glass towards me. I do believe Gobbo genuinely meant me well in some fashion. "Take some advice. You've been playing on the rich man's field, and that's not the place for you or me. Get out while you still can. This is not a game for amateurs, Lorenzo. You'll only end up hurt."

"I placed her in your care, Gobbo. I thought you would save her from my uncle. Now I learn I have simply removed her from a middling fate to one much worse. I learn—"

He banged the table with his fist. "Oh, come on, Scacchi! It's not that bad. She lives. She's fed. She sees the world. She writes her pretty tunes and gets some reward from them, even if the old man's name sits on the cover. It could be worse. She'd get no more from Leo. Less, in all probability."

The two bargains could scarcely be compared, but there was little merit in pursuing that particular argument. "It cannot work, Gobbo! There will be questions from those who can spot a fraud. He will be asked to play. To conduct."

"You think he's not capable? Delapole can make a pretty noise at the keys. As for all that arm-waving stuff... As that French fool Rousseau used to say, it's amazing what you can accomplish—or pretend to—when you try."

"But—"

"But nothing," he interrupted. "You are very slow at understanding people sometimes. It is a dangerous flaw. Do you not comprehend what kind of man my master truly is?"

I did, but dared not let him know it. "An Englishman. An aristocrat. A gentleman, I thought."

"Pah! Let me tell you the tale from his own lips. When he was a lad—ten, no more—his widowed father married again. A painted bitch—they all say that, I imagine. Still, one night, a month after the wedding, he is awoken by the sound of screaming in the house. He sleeps next door to his father, always has, and rushes in. To find this new 'mother,' if you please, astride the old man, riding him for all he's worth, the pair of them bellowing like animals."

Something Marchese had said, about the origins of Delapole's behaviour, came back to me. "What has this to do with us?"

"*Everything!* He died, you see. The old man's heart burst, in front of the lad. Two months later it's apparent she's with child, too—and not his father's, if Delapole's to be believed. Less than a year after, there's a new son in the household. The firstborn one is out on his ear, despatched to some bog in Ireland with a pittance to keep him. You see?"

"I see he feels wronged by this woman."

"No! He feels wronged by the world, and that is why he plays these games. You meddle in them at your peril, Lorenzo. He can scare the wits out of me when he cares to, and there's not many men I can say that about."

There was no shaking him. Delapole had made up his mind: so shall it be. "When do you leave?" I asked Gobbo.

"A day. Two. No more. After the little show we're planning at La Pietà which we had hoped would provide some funds. Not that *that* is going so well. She has no music, would you believe, and says she can't reproduce it all in time for the performance. Unless we can talk the original manuscript out of Leo and race it to the copyists soon, we're in a pretty pickle. We'll have to let Vivaldi play his tunes instead and make some lame excuse for why the sheets are missing. Then find the money somewhere else. They'll all love us for that, won't they? I'm sick of turning creditors away from the door. If we're not gone quickly, we'll be playing this game inside the debtors' prison. I don't imagine you know where he's hidden it, do you?"

"Leo is his own man. Ask him yourself."

"We have. He's as stubborn as a mule. Makes some pathetic excuse about it not being where he put it. As if he expects us to believe that." He finished his glass, then looked at me expectantly. "I have things to do, old chap. Can't stay gossiping all night."

"I need to see her," I pleaded.

He glowered at me. "You haven't listened to a word I've said. Go now. Forget us all."

"One time, Gobbo. Then it's done. I promise."

He sighed. "I don't know why I go along with this. If I do this one thing, will you swear you'll bother us no more?"

"You have my word."

"You'll have to see Delapole too. They're thick with each other at the moment. I'll talk to him first. So there are no misunderstandings."

He left the room. I heard murmuring from beyond, in the

great hall that gave onto the canal. Gobbo returned and
ushered me in. Rebecca sat on an embroidered stool by the
window, her back to me, staring out of the window into the
night. Delapole stood next to her, beaming as always,
looking every inch the kindly English gentleman.

"Scacchi," he said, and beckoned me to join him. "Your plan
has come full circle. Rebecca has found a place in my
household and shall see her talents richly rewarded. In all but
name—though given these cruel times, that is, I fear, inevitable."

I tried to see her face, but she kept it turned away from me.

"I would like to speak with Miss Guillaume alone, sir. If
that is possible."

"Guillaume? Oh, you mean *Levi*? Come. There are no
secrets between us anymore."

"So I see, Mr. Delapole. I would appreciate a moment,
nevertheless."

The Englishman looked down his nose at her and I hated
myself. In the candlelight reflected from the window, I could
see him for what he was: a cold, cruel man who viewed his
fellow creatures as mere playthings, pieces on a human
chessboard, to be moved and sacrificed at will. It amazed
me I had not guessed as much before. He stared at her and
relished what he saw: her powerlessness, I thought. And
her beauty, as if he had trapped a butterfly in his fist.

"Gobbo and I have business," he told me. "An hour, no
more. Then I'll be back. Don't mistreat my generosity, lad.
This is an adult affair, and you'll have no part in it."

I bowed my head deferentially. Then, with an arrogant
smirk, he swept out of the room, with Gobbo in his wake.
She sat with her back to me still. There was no time for such
nonsense. I interposed myself between her and the glass,
bent down, and took her by the arms.

"Rebecca," I said. "Whatever you think is happening here, you must, I beg you, flee. Delapole is the very Devil. I have been in Rome and know his true nature better than I'd like. If you stay with him, he'll take your life before long, and that's a fact."

Still she stared outside at the dim lights and the movement on the canal until the anger began to rise inside me.

"Come!" I gripped her arm tightly and tried to make her move. "We must be gone."

"No!" She broke free and fixed me with a look that was pure hatred. "Why do you torment me like this, Lorenzo? Have I not suffered enough for your jealousy?"

I fell back against the window and closed my eyes. What a fool I was to think I had only to see her in order to win her back.

"Yes," I said, and she did look at me then. "You have indeed, and for that I apologise with all my heart. But believe me, love. This man is a devil dressed in silk. He has robbed and murdered his way across half of Europe, and tomorrow the city shall have the proof of it. Come now and we'll be gone from Venice by the time the watch are upon him."

The cry of "wolf" had been heard once too often. There was contempt in her eyes. "But every man who looks at me is a demon, Lorenzo," she declared. "Every last one. I have got to know our English friend well these last two nights, since he set out clearly the terms upon which Jacopo and I may keep our freedom, and a crumb of our dignity if we are lucky too. He does not seek to kill me, Lorenzo. He has other ideas than that, though I may wish myself dead when forced to accede to them."

Her meaning was plain. "Then come in," I pleaded, "and escape this beast! What reason could keep you here?"

"Because I have no choice! You, of all people, should see that."

"Once we set foot on terra firma, Rebecca, we have all the choices in the world."

"How?" The dead, defeated expression in her eyes chilled my blood. "One word to the authorities and we'd never leave Venice. This is an island, Lorenzo. Forewarned, they would catch us the moment we tried to take a boat. And not just me, but Jacopo, too, whom I have greatly wronged by entangling him in this affair. He thought that we were settled, finally, and hates the idea we'll flee again."

That much I had seen in his despairing, drunken face. Jacopo always was the most cautious among us.

"In Rome," I said, "Delapole murdered a mistress who bore his child, the method of which I would not dare tell you. The same in Paris, and Geneva too. This man is deadly, Rebecca."

Her hand ran through that sea of curls. She gazed at me, nervous, unsure of what to say. "Why should any man do that when all he need do is flee or deny the child?"

"It is in his history somehow. Or his nature. I do not know for certain. I only tell the facts, as they will be revealed when a magistrate arrives tomorrow and demands his arrest. When that happens, we are all in danger, love. Delapole will take whoever he can to join him on the scaffold."

"With plenty of reason too," she replied. "Forgery and blasphemy, fraud—for that fine fiddle is not paid for and has my name on the bill of sale." She hesitated. "And a little whoring, too, when needs must."

She sought to chase me from her sight with this, and make me flee for my own good. "I spoke to Jacopo," I responded. "I know what you have done to survive."

Those dark eyes glittered at me. "You know nothing,
Lorenzo. Of who I am. Or what I am capable of. When you
look at me, you see some perfect lady. You are much
mistaken."

"I see a woman. One who comforted me in my despair.
One who made me see a world beyond myself. One I love,
and who carries my child."

She shook her head. "A child? More nonsense this,
Lorenzo?" Yet there was blood in her cheeks.

"No. I saw you in a dream, in Rome..."

"A dream?"

"...which was, I think, my mind's translation of what
passed between us that last time we met. When you were
troubled and I was angry. You carry my child, Rebecca, and
hide the fact to protect me, when in truth you are the one in
peril."

Her eyes closed. Tears seeped beneath the lids.

"Oh, Lorenzo. If this is true, then all the more reason for
me to take Delapole's offer. What life would we have
together with a child? We would be destitute or worse."

"The life of a man and woman who love each other,"
I answered swiftly. "What else might anyone ask?"

"No!" She sobbed before me, and I felt ashamed. "This is
not possible. If I refuse Delapole's bidding, we are all
doomed. Jacopo and I, and you, too, if you are so foolish
that you stay here."

"I will never abandon you."

"Then," she said firmly, "I shall make you. Please, Lorenzo.
If ever I meant something to you, go now, flee the city and
find happiness elsewhere. For none of us shall discover it
here."

"He will kill you, Rebecca!"

"Then it will be over with, won't it?" she answered severely.

The look on her sweet face horrified me. I fell to my knees and took her hands in mine. "Do not say that!"

Then, as if for the last time, Rebecca leaned forward and embraced me. I felt her damp cheek against mine. I held her tightly, but not tight enough, for she withdrew and wiped away the tears from her face.

"A woman of my kind must learn tricks in order to avoid this fate," she said, not looking at me. "One must make a man happy but prevent the consequence that happiness so easily brings. You made me forget those skills by allowing me to realise there could be happiness on both sides too. And your sweetness and your innocence reminded me that once I came from the same mould. Now we both know the outcome. If I can convince Delapole the child is his, perhaps he'll show a little mercy."

"He'll slit your throat and rip the unborn infant from your body, as he did in Rome."

Her cheeks went pale. "So you say. Then let us hope this magistrate of yours comes knocking for him tomorrow and a miracle saves us from his wrath."

"The only miracles are those we make ourselves, Rebecca! Come with me now. Be safe."

"Safe? None of us is safe as long as he walks free. Tomorrow. If he is in chains. Then we could take to our heels and hope we're out of the city before he points his accusing finger at us."

"Now!"

"I cannot," she replied. "Nor must you ask me anymore. Go, Lorenzo. If there is some God, perhaps he will take pity on us, for all our sins. Quick," she declared. "Before they return and guess what's up. I play at La Pietà at this carnival he's fixed. You may see me there if you are so foolish as not to heed my words."

I kissed her once, fondly, on the cheek and felt the way she withdrew herself from my embrace. Then I left Ca' Dario and walked the city into the early hours, planning, planning, planning. When the bell of San Cassian struck one, I made my way back into Ca' Scacchi, through the dark side entrance of the warehouse, which gave me secret entry. Leo deserved an explanation, and an apology, before he sent me penniless on my way.

I scrambled up the back stairs, went into the main house by the window, and found myself in my old room: the third along on the third floor. The boy from Treviso who, a few short months before, had arrived here excited and unprepared for this new world now seemed a stranger to me. He lived inside my memory, but as another, unfamiliar and unfathomable. I collected a few things I believed would be useful for the itinerant life that would follow whatever transpired the coming day: some clothes, a handful of letters from my darling Lucia, a tiny portrait of my mother. Then I took that silver Star of David Rebecca had given me, which I had removed in anger, and placed it round my neck.

After that, quietly, not wishing to make a sound until I chose the moment, I found my way downstairs. Leo was about, in his cups probably, since this seemed to be his preferred medicine for dealing with adversity.

The fire was dying. A sputtering candle sat upon the table. Sure enough, my uncle was there, a bottle of wine and some glasses before him. He sat slumped, immobile, drunk. This was not an ideal moment for our conversation, but I knew it must take place. I had wronged Leo, imagining him to be that cruel master in the painting across the *rio* in San

Cassian. In truth he was simply a sad fellow struggling to make his way in the world as best he knew.

"Uncle," I said softly, hoping to wake him, and came from behind to place a hand upon his shoulder.

His body rolled, a strange and terrifying movement. Then Leo's face turned sideways and fell to the table, his bloody mouth agape, a yawning space where his front teeth should have been. There was gore in his throat. One eye was now a dark and liquid socket. His right hand, the claw, ended in stumps. I felt some cold inner voice inside me start to scream and knew in an instant who alone could have been responsible for this vile deed.

"Lorenzo," said a familiar English voice in front of me. Delapole's figure came out from a pool of darkness by the fireplace. Gobbo stood with him, eyes downcast, as if he felt some little shame. "Your uncle was an awkward fellow, to be sure. 'I do not know, sir. I do not know' was all the wretched man could squeal, however much we stuck him. And still we lack that manuscript. It is too late now for the copyists. But I will have it. The thing is mine, and I must possess that which belongs to me. Poor Leo said it must be hidden. Now, where could that be, do you think?"

"I do not know," I answered, and backed towards the staircase which lay behind me.

Delapole's face came further into the candlelight, yellow and cadaverous in its cast. He wore a sardonic smile. "Oh, such palpable lies, and told to one who has favoured you so! This Venetian toying with the truth appalls me, lad, and does you no good at all. Why, after I'd removed those crippled fingers, even Uncle Leo convinced me he told the truth at last. What good did it do him, anyway? By that stage he was making so much noise it quite offended my ears. And so I took this out to silence the row. Catch, boy! Catch!"

His right arm moved. Some small object flew through the air and brushed, cold and damp and bloody, against my cheek. I thought of that gory gaping hole at the back of Leo's throat and knew what Delapole had launched towards me. Marchese was right: some demon lived inside this man's skin, and now it was loose upon the earth.

"Fetch him, Gobbo," Delapole said, yawning. "We'll tear it out of that scrawny frame in five minutes and let his corpse confess his master's murder. Such perfect symmetry. Then it's plain sailing all the way to Vienna, I fancy."

The squat, ugly shape of the fellow I once called friend began to move towards me through the shadows, past Leo's mutilated corpse, travelling as fast as a hound closing on a fox. Without thinking, I said a prayer.

54

Public relations

THEY SAT ON THE PODIUM, HALF-BLINDED BY THE lights: Daniel, Massiter, Fabozzi, and, pale-faced and a little scared, Amy, as a representative of the orchestra. Something, guilt or shame, lingered in her face. There was scant time between the press conference and Scacchi's funeral, but Daniel was determined that he would speak with her before he left the room.

The concert had now gained an unmistakable momentum. The tale proved a perfect story for a news business suffering late-summer lassitude. There was the air of mystery, too: Daniel's reluctance, until that day, to be seen in public, and the violent deaths of his two close associates. The reporters sniffed something deeper, Daniel believed, and would, given half a chance, do everything to throw him off guard. There must have been more than a hundred of them in the room, with a battery of photographers forever firing off flashes. As he posed in front of the electric cloud of camera flashes, a polite, static grin on his face, he knew none in the audience could begin to guess what kind of headlines they would be reading before the weekend was out.

Massiter rose and greeted them in a succinct speech of welcome, noting that their location had musical antecedents: Tchaikovsky had composed his Fourth Symphony while staying in the hotel in 1877. It must have preceded *Onegin* directly, coming at the time when his life was beginning to descend into chaos and insanity. Daniel found it discomforting to know that somewhere, in a suite above his head, Tchaikovsky must have agonised over his failed marriage, his homosexuality, and the long, hard work about to begin on the opera. Another ghost flitting through Venice. Another reason why he could never wear the face Massiter hoped to place upon him: he lacked the capacity for self-torture. With genius came, too often, a blight, and that perhaps had been why the concerto which now bore his name had lain hidden, anonymous, in Ca' Scacchi for just a few decades short of three hundred years. There was a human being behind the music, still waiting to rise from the dust.

He made a mental note of that idea and then, as Massiter sat down to light applause, rose on his bidding. He blinked at the ranks of dim faces judging him and knew that the Daniel Forster who had, only that summer, walked naively onto the *moto topo Sophia* at Marco Polo airport would have wilted beneath the heat of their attention.

Daniel found it difficult to remember that person. He nodded modestly at the audience and announced himself as a composer, not an orator, asking for questions which he promised to answer as honestly as he could. For thirty minutes they came, from all directions, some intelligent, some stupid, some simply incomprehensible. In return he fudged, politely thanking Massiter for his sponsorship, Fabozzi and Amy for their support as fellow musicians. The several persistent enquiries about the death of Scacchi and Paul he fielded discreetly, suggesting that they would be best directed to the police.

When an English reporter pressed him on the point, Daniel's voice broke a little, then he paused, before saying simply, "Please—they were my friends. I bury Signor Scacchi today, a man whose kindness towards me has been surpassed only by that of Mr. Massiter here. Without Signor Scacchi, I would never have come to Venice. Without his introduction to Mr. Massiter, I would never have found such a benefactor and come out of my happy obscurity into this dazzling brightness. Indulge me a little at this moment, ladies and gentlemen. When today is over, when you have heard this concerto in full and I have this sad duty out of the way, speak to me again and I'll try to answer your questions as best I can. But for now you must be patient. Judge me by what you hear tonight, not my inarticulate ramblings here."

There was a swell of admiration among them. Daniel was relieved. He had prepared himself for an ordeal full of potential pitfalls.

A woman reporter from one of the big American stations was on her feet, jabbing her microphone at Amy. "Miss Hartston?"

"Yes," she replied, remaining on her chair.

"I was wondering what you made of this. As a musician."

Amy glanced at Daniel, unsure of what to say. "In what way?" she asked.

"You tell me," the reporter continued with ill-concealed aggression. "What does it feel like playing something that's written by someone almost your own age? And yet it's not modern. It's like some ghost from three hundred years ago, if we're to believe all the hype we're hearing."

Amy nodded. "I haven't spoken to Daniel about it."

The reporters went quiet, sensing something but not recognising what it was.

"You never *talked* to him?" The woman seemed amazed. "But he's the composer, right?"

"I..." Amy's eyes sought his, pleading for help.

Massiter rose and clapped his hands. "My dear lady," he declared loudly. "We have Fabozzi, a fine conductor, at the helm of this event. When we discussed how we would handle this unexpected opportunity, it naturally fell to him to direct the orchestra, not the composer. A decision you fully support, don't you, Daniel?"

They stared at him, puzzled, resentful somehow. Daniel nodded. "Naturally. Why should I make life difficult by inter-posing myself between the players and their conductor?"

"Why indeed?" the American woman responded.

"There!" Massiter announced quickly. "Now, to practicalities, please. There will be tickets in the house for those of you who are accredited critics, naturally. And a few more besides which will go into the hat."

Daniel tried to judge their mood. They worked as a pack, he thought, and, like dogs that had been half-fed, their resent-ment for what they had not received far outweighed their gratitude for the few morsels that had come their way. There was an air of nervousness about the concert, which he regretted. Fabozzi and his musicians had worked hard and deserved their acclaim.

Massiter stood and watched them go, then sidled over, took his arm, and whispered loudly in his ear, "Excellent, Daniel! They're hanging on your every word."

"Really, Hugo?" That was true, he supposed. "Perhaps they smell a rat."

The cold eyes stared at him. "Nonsense. They're too stupid to see anything that doesn't strike them full in the face. But let's play safe, eh? Tomorrow I'll spirit you away somewhere, any-where you like. Perhaps a room in the Cipriani for the weekend. Some peace and quiet."

The idea of the palatial hotel in Giudecca instantly brought back another memory, of Laura screaming at him in the tiny room of the women's prison at the opposite end of the island.

"Or Verona?" Massiter suggested. "Wherever, Daniel, but you need these animals off your heels. Think about it."

"I will," he promised.

Amy had stopped at the door, across the room, trying to catch his eye.

"Later, Hugo," Daniel said.

The older man peered into his eyes. "Ah, yes. When we discuss this new price of yours."

"Exactly."

Unexpectedly, Massiter favoured him with a broad, conspiratorial smile. "You're quite the one, Daniel Forster," he declared.

"I'm sorry?"

"All this fey façade, when really you're as tough as old boots inside."

Daniel bowed his head gently. "Thank you."

"Not at all. You could be a good pupil. I wonder whether I need an acolyte sometimes. Instead of the hangers-on."

"But I'm a composer, Hugo. Don't forget that."

Massiter laughed, a short, controlled sound, then patted him hard on the shoulder. "Quite! Now, you'll share my taxi to this miserable event?"

"No. But thanks anyway. I want to walk. I want to think."

"Yes. About your price."

He hesitated. "About Scacchi, actually."

Massiter said nothing and slipped away. Daniel crossed the room and found Amy at the door. She was different now, he thought. She had lost some of the naïve exuberance he had seen in her face when they first met.

"Amy," he said. "I'm sorry. I've been out of things. I should have called you."

"Why?" she asked, refusing to meet his eyes directly.

"Because I owed it to you."

She sighed and stared at the long corridor stretching in front of them. They were alone in the echoing room. "I want to play this thing and be gone, Dan. Don't ask me why, but this all feels so *wrong*. Like I'm going crazy or something."

He placed his arm on her shoulder. "You're not crazy, Amy."

Her wide eyes met his. "Really? I told Hugo you never wrote that piece. You weren't capable of it. Then I see you this morning. I guess that's the real you, isn't it? I just never saw him before. You had those reporters in the palm of your hand."

"Perhaps."

"No, you did, Dan. I don't know why I read people so wrong. I don't know why I read myself so wrong sometimes."

"Be patient," he said. "It'll all work out."

She folded her arms. "It's all worked out already. Hugo and I are an item, in case you hadn't heard. I'm to be a star. Just like you." There was a bitter tone in her voice, directed more at herself than Massiter, he thought.

"We all make mistakes, Amy. It doesn't mean you live with them forever."

"No? But it's all mapped out. He's getting me into Juilliard. I can stay at his apartment in New York. It's walking distance from Lincoln Center, apparently. I'm made, don't you see?"

"That sounds wonderful," he replied hesitantly.

"Sure. All I have to do is screw him whenever he comes around. Not that it's about that, really. That's just him marking his territory."

That last insight seemed remarkably apposite. "Amy. You don't have to do anything you don't want. Your parents—"

"He's talked to them," she spat back. "They think it's all wonderful. Suddenly their dumb daughter's got a career. Some rich, old boyfriend with English breeding too. They don't need the money, but the class...that's priceless."

"Nothing's set in stone."

She glowered at him. "Really? Are you sure you get this? We're both in the same boat. He *owns* us. Like he'd own a painting or a statue. That's what turns him on. Knowing we're there. On the shelf. Waiting for when he wants something. And..."

She swore under her breath. "Jesus, *there is no way out*. He understands when you see a door and just closes it in your face. We're his now. We always will be."

Daniel leaned forward and kissed her lightly on the forehead. Amy stared at him, amazed.

"What was that for?" she demanded.

"For me. And also to say that I'm your friend, Amy. To say I'll help you. Just be patient. And play like the wind tonight, love. Not for me. Certainly not for Hugo. Do that for yourself."

She looked a little like the old Amy then. There was some hope, some innocence in her face. Amy Hartston slowly placed her arms around him and leaned her head on his chest. He could smell the perfume in her hair. It was an old, adult scent. Something Hugo had given her, he thought.

Daniel asked, "What do you plan to do now?"

"I don't know. Go back to the hotel. We're ready. Fabozzi says there's no need for a further rehearsal. We're there."

"I'm sure he's right."

"You're going to the funeral, aren't you?" she asked.

He stared at the floor and said nothing.

"Do you want me to come?" Amy asked. "I only met him a couple of times."

"Then come for me, Amy," he said. "Please."

55

Fugitive from all

Gobbo lunged up the stairs, his face an ugly, determined
mask. I backed a step or two, waited, then drew up my right
leg, retracted it, and kicked as hard as I might. My foot
connected firmly with his face. He screamed with pain and
tumbled backwards into the stairwell. A man must seize his
advantages. I knew this house and the building next door
intimately. Gobbo and Delapole were strangers. I could hide
in places they might never guess at. Better still, when the
opportunity arose, I could be out into the night and race fast
into the Calle dei Morti, then be gone, into the labyrinth of
alleys that is Santa Croce.

These thoughts flashed through my mind as I ran up the
stairs to the second floor, then the third, planning my escape.
Such foolish confidence . . . I should have thought of nothing
more than fleeing, and engineered my route once I was out of
that infernal house. Near the top of the last flight, a few short
steps from my bedroom and that exit route I'd used before,
there was a clatter behind me; a hand rose up and gripped
my ankle. In one swift, agonising movement, Gobbo twisted
my leg and brought me tumbling to the hard wooden stairs.

"Hurrah!" Delapole yelled from far below, hearing the noise. He was not as quick as his manservant and must barely have left the ground floor in my pursuit. Gobbo, for all the force of the kick I'd delivered to his ugly face, had recovered in an instant and chased me all the way until I was in his grasp. As I lay caught like an animal, a short, powerful arm turned me over. A little watery moonlight fell through the single window in the roof above. Blood ran from Gobbo's eye where I had struck him. He gasped for breath. Yet there was something odd in his expression, too, a look of puzzlement, reluctance even, that it had come to this.

"Hold him, Gobbo," the Englishman cried from below. "This will be my pleasure, not yours."

Gobbo stared at me, as much with pity as contempt. "Why didn't you listen, Scacchi?" he whispered, panting. "I have tried to guide you out of danger all along, and every time you do the very opposite of what I tell you."

I moved my neck a little. His hands had me fast. There was no escape. "I follow where my heart dictates, Gobbo," I answered. "As you would if you were your own master, not his lackey."

"There you go," he said mournfully. "Making it worse for yourself again."

"Worse than Rome? And what he did to the Duchess of Longhena?"

His eyes narrowed. He was clearly amazed. "What do you know of this? He told me that he merely defended himself, and that the woman was mad."

"He lies! I have spoken to the magistrate, Gobbo. Your master murdered that woman in the most fearful of ways, ripping his own child from her stomach and placing it by her butchered corpse. These crows come home to roost. That

same magistrate arrives on the night ferry now with a warrant
for your master's arrest. You'll be on the scaffold with him if
you don't look sharp."

Those fat fingers relaxed a little round my throat.

"You lie."

"No. It's true. How else could I know her name? I will not
let him do this to Rebecca."

The sound of Delapole's feet upon the stairs grew louder.
He was beyond the second floor now, coming up directly
beneath us in this last straight, single flight of steps.

"I'll thieve and kill a man who asks for it," Gobbo
admitted. "Women have got no part in my game."

"Tell that to the axeman," I hissed at him, then saw,
beyond his squat body, the first shadow of movement from
his master below.

"You lie!" he snarled, and began to take from his pocket a
short, slim blade stained black by my uncle's blood. This was
my final moment. I breathed in hard, then brought up my
knee to his groin and pushed him back with my one free arm
until the force of gravity threw his balance out of kilter.
Gobbo was frozen there for a moment, hands flailing in the
darkness, struggling to keep himself upright. I wriggled my
right leg free, scissored it into my body, then pushed with all
my force. He cursed me, fell backwards down the stairs,
upon the ascending figure of his master, and both rolled
down, shrieking, back to the second storey, where they
landed in a tangled pile of limbs.

There would be no more opportunities. I cleared my head
of all thought and rushed into my bedroom, climbed out of
the open window and into the warehouse next door. From
there I scuttled down the stairs four steps at a time, left the
warehouse at water level, and then, fearing they might see me

if I took the small bridge over the *rio* where the deliveries were made, slipped fearfully into the black slime of the lagoon.

In all my time in the city I had not entered this noisome liquid once. It was cold and had a viscous quality quite unlike the ocean. The smell was vile, that of the open sewer. Above me, through an open window in the house, I could hear Delapole and Gobbo discussing my disappearance and wondering how they might follow me. The Englishman was furious, bellowing without caring who might hear. "Either we find him, Gobbo, or incriminate him in his uncle's fate. If we don't have him in our hands these next five minutes, it's off to the night watch for you, to tell them of this crime you've uncovered, and how the perpetrator ran off into the night."

So I was condemned either way. The cold of this filthy dowsing did me one service: it silenced the cry of fury in my throat. I swallowed hard, then ducked my head beneath the surface, pushed with all my might, and, staying below the water for as long as my lungs allowed, swam towards the Grand Canal. When I struggled quietly upwards, I was by the small bridge that runs from the Calle dei Morti to the church. I took care to find the support on the northern side, away from Ca' Scacchi, then pulled myself a little out of the water, gripping the stone, and listened. There was no movement close by. Gobbo had many exits from our *campo* to explore. The odds that he might choose mine were slender. I pulled myself from the slime, climbed over onto the narrow bridge, and ran like the wind into Santa Croce.

I knew the rules. I had heard Delapole set them out myself. If I was not his within five minutes, he'd be handing my name to the watch for the murder of my master. So I waited a good

half hour, then doubled back, south of San Cassian, towards
the Rialto, the only way I might cross and head for
Cannaregio, where the boats from Mestre docked. My heart
pounded as I wound through the straggle of villains and
harlots who hung around that place. Gobbo could have
easily caught me there. But he was a servant through and
through, and now would be lying through his teeth to the
idiots of the watch.

Dripping foul water, my jacket pulled up around my face,
I crossed over the Grand Canal and followed that familiar
route, which required only a short northwards detour to take
me to the ghetto. I had no way of knowing where Marchese
might spend the night, but it could not be far from the ferry
jetty. If only I could locate him, I might begin to concoct
some tale that could see us safe through the coming day.

All these possibilities ran through my head. And then
were dashed by the ferryman's grim news. He stared at my
appearance, drenched, dishevelled, like a beggar, and
muttered, "Rome coach is late. Won't see no one from
that till midday at the earliest. Lost a wheel outside Bologna,
so they say, and went right off the road."

I must have looked a sorry sight. When I asked him for
some paper and a piece of charcoal so I might write a
message for a friend, he walked into the nearest tavern and
came back with both.

"What kind of simpleton are you, lad?" he demanded.
"Asking a sailor for something to write with."

I thanked him, then, penniless and starving, joined the
other destitutes picking scraps from the remains of the
Cannaregio market around the corner: a mouldy piece of
bread, a half-devoured apple. I stole some oranges from a
cart, and dashed into the darkness when the trader saw me.

In an alley near the ghetto, I devoured what little food I had. Under the light of an illuminated alcove Virgin, I tore the paper into pieces and wrote—in a different hand, I hoped—a similar message on each. Then, exhausted and half-sleeping, I walked the city, into San Marco and beyond, finding each of those bronze lions' mouths I could remember and making a small offering which might, I hoped, give the Doge's men pause for thought when they read it, and provide us with a chink in the English armour.

The last I posted in the figure close to the palace itself, then, to remind myself of the stakes in this game, I walked close to the dungeon by the Bridge of Sighs, and heard the wails and plaints that drifted out of those high windows with their iron bars. In a dank doorway nearby, I spent the night, sleeping, dreaming. A dreadful dream, too, for in it I saw from behind the silken figure of Delapole stalking the slumbering Rebecca in a half-lit bedroom full of mirrors. He crept upon her stealthily, like some common criminal. Then, brutally, while she fought beneath him like a tiger, he took her by force, screaming like an animal all the while.

When this deed was done and he hung over her still, the saliva dripping from his mouth onto her white neck, he lifted his face and stared into the mirror. There I saw myself, in Delapole's guise. I was the true perpetrator of this act in concert with this devil, who stood behind us both, having watched approvingly, and now applauded with foppish claps of his hands, as if it were some performance on the stage.

I woke with a start, these frightful images still in my head. With them came some lines I recalled from that English play I had once, in my innocence, thought the likes of Gobbo might have read.

The Devil can cite Scripture for his purpose.
An evil soul producing holy witness
Is like a villain with a smiling cheek,
A goodly apple rotten at the heart;
O what a goodly outside falsehood hath!

The sun had barely risen. I trembled, still damp from my
night adventures, although behind those shivers lay something
deeper. In my dream I had, I felt, seen some glimpse into
Delapole's true identity. What was he in his own eyes? For
want of a better word, the Devil. What did he seek? To hold
others' lives in his grasp, to do with and dispose of as he
wished. What Delapole coveted, above all else, was title to that
piece of a man or woman they thought their own. Beside this,
lust and greed and deceit were but everyday sins, practised by
the many. In his own mind Delapole wore these trophies as the
primitives of Guinea sport the heads of the defeated upon their
belts. The more the merrier. Rebecca was not the first; she
would not be the last. His thirst was unquenchable.

I shook this miserable thought from my head and, looking
every inch the ragged beggar, stumbled to the waterfront, not
a hundred yards from La Pietà, thinking of my next move.
The makings of a great day were already obvious. Hawkers
were arguing over their pitches. The familiar scaffold which
Canaletto used was being erected on the Arsenale side of the
promenade, with the painter himself barking orders at the
hapless workmen doing the job. Several completed canvases
were being readied for show to attract commissions, among
them, as I recognised from a distance, that work I had seen
him begin when I was a boy, some months earlier. At first I
dared not look at it too closely, for fear of all the memories
it might provoke.

A soldier hammered a notice into one of the tree trunks used to tie up gondolas by the water's edge. I waited until he had finished, then, to satisfy my curiosity—though in truth I knew what to expect all along—I wandered over and read the poster. It was a call for the arrest of one Lorenzo Scacchi, an apprentice of San Cassian, who had murdered his master most foully the previous evening. A description of the scoundrel followed, one that none seeing me then would begin to recognise. And there was the promise of a reward, from the city's newfound English benefactor. If he could not take my head himself, Delapole would pay the Republic to do the job for him.

I damned him, damned Venice, too, and, in spite of my fears, walked over to see Mr. Canaletto's canvas, taking care to observe that the artist himself was busy roasting a carpenter on the other side of his scaffold. The painting was magnificent, yet cold. Between this frozen moment in time and my present state lay entire chapters of sweetness and misery. All the artist offered was an exquisite testament to spectacle and grandeur. I glanced at the work a final time, then slunk back into the shadows to dream of our escape.

56

An unexpected bargain

DANIEL CLOSED HIS EYES AND SWAYED UNCERTAINLY IN the heat, his head full of the smell of cypress and the chemical odour of the lagoon. They had travelled with the coffin in the funeral gondola, standing in the stern, stiff and awkward. To begin with, he was aware that he wished it were Laura by his side in the black, gleaming vessel. Then, as they crossed the narrow stretch of lagoon that separated San Michele from the city, Amy took his arm and squeezed it gently. Daniel responded in the same way and was immensely grateful for her presence. He did not wish to be alone, and there was business to be done.

As they docked, he stared at the white Istrian stone of the quayside church, almost blinded by its brightness in the fierce midday sun. Behind them Venice went about its business. *Vaporetti* darted in and out of the jetties in a constant stream, a ceaseless movement of life around the perimeter of the city. Ahead lay the red brick outline of Murano, with its dusty furnaces turning out ornamental glass for the tourists. Scacchi must have made this journey many times, burying friends and relatives in the cemetery, where they would rest for a decade, after which their remains were forced to seek some other sanctuary. It was a curious end for a human life, Daniel thought, but one on which Scacchi's will had insisted. It was the Venetian in the old man; he could countenance no other fate.

They left the gondola and followed the coffin, walking slowly in pace with the pallbearers. There was a small group of people waiting on the quayside. Massiter stood alone and had changed into a black suit. Daniel recognised the woman who had handled the admissions at La Pietà and a local shopkeeper who made deliveries to Laura from time to time. And Giulia Morelli, in a black trouser suit, impassive behind thick plastic sunglasses. He should have known the police would attend. Finally, there was a huge figure in a shiny blue suit. Daniel blinked, fighting the light in order to see this man properly, then realised what was missing: a small black dog by his side.

Piero came forward, vast arms encircling him, tears in his eyes. "Boy, boy," he sobbed. "Such an occasion."

The big man looked at Amy, unwrapped himself from Daniel, then pumped her right hand with both of his. "And our American friend, too, Miss Amy. We had such laughter. Then this?"

She kissed him on the cheek and said, "I'm so sorry."

Daniel felt proud of her. They walked on, through an old stone arch, into the cemetery proper, turning right past a collection of shiny coffins half-hidden in the shadow of an open storage room. He had promised himself he would come here one day and rubberneck like the tourists, searching for the more famous inhabitants. But that was a different Daniel Forster. There was now only one memory of moment in San Michele's brown earth, and Daniel swore that whatever happened, he would return ten years hence when, briefly, it resurfaced again. Scacchi deserved as much. For all the old man's cunning and deception—and Daniel was by no means sure he appreciated the full extent of either—he had provided him with a life.

The party left the buildings behind and entered the fields of the dead, where row upon row of small headstones, most of them with a recent photograph on the marble, ran to the perimeter wall at the rear. He glanced at the marker: *Recinto 1, Campo B.* Each small line of graves identified by its row and plot, dug and redug every decade, a continuous cycle of humanity moving through the parched orange soil.

They stopped by an empty grave. The pallbearers manoeuvred the coffin onto the sashes with care. The priest began to speak in a flat, monotonous voice. Daniel closed his eyes and captured the moment: the scent of cypress, the dry dust of the soil, and, overhead, the lazy clamour of the gulls. He felt Amy's hand on his arm and tried, with scant success, not to think about Laura, wondering where she could be, knowing that he could never understand what might have kept her from this ceremony. Behind him he heard sobbing: a woman's voice and that of a man, loud and uncontrolled—Piero, who had seemed so familiar with death from his time in the city and had sworn he would never set foot on San Michele again. Scacchi drew them all to his side, even in the grave.

The priest bent low, picked up a handful of dust, then threw it into the open earth, where it rattled on the lid of the casket. Daniel watched Massiter do the same, feeling no need to join him. Piero was right. The bond one felt with another died with their final breath. These rituals had their place, but they were for the benefit of the living, not the dead. Daniel Forster knew he had no need of them. What stood between him and Scacchi was now frozen in the amber of his memory. Only the future was mutable.

Piero watched him keenly, seeming to approve. Then, when it was apparent the ceremony was over, he made some excuse about needing to retrieve Xerxes from the caretaker and was gone. The other mourners drifted away aimlessly. Daniel waited by Amy's side.

Massiter came over, placed an arm around each of them, and said, "I still can't believe it, you know. The old man was sick. We were all aware of that. But one never really appreciates..."

"What?" Daniel asked as Massiter's words trailed into nothing.

"That it might happen so suddenly. So brutally."

"I believe Scacchi did," Daniel said. "I think he half expected it."

A voice came from behind them. "Gentlemen?"

Daniel turned and scowled. Giulia Morelli stood there.

"Yes?" he snapped.

She joined them and smiled most professionally. "I merely wished to offer my condolences. Nothing more."

"Not much use to Scacchi, are they?" Massiter grumbled. "I don't suppose you've picked up the hoodlums who were responsible for this outrage?"

"No," she replied, taking off her sunglasses and staring at them with intense blue eyes. "But we always have hope, Signor Massiter. Where would a policewoman be without hope, eh?"

They said nothing. Giulia Morelli nodded at them. "*Ciao.* And thank you for the ticket, Daniel. I'll be there. I can't wait."

Massiter watched her go. "Damned woman. Why doesn't she go out and catch someone, instead of pestering the likes of us?"

"It's what she does," Amy observed. "It's in the job description."

"Perhaps." Massiter tapped her lightly on the bottom. "Run along, my love. Rest, please. You're the star performer tonight. I don't want you exhausted. You'd be letting us all down."

She glowered at him but still turned to leave.

"No," Daniel objected, gently taking her arm to stop her. "There is something you must hear, Hugo. It can't wait any longer."

Massiter eyed him. "I believed we were due a private discussion?"

"We are, later. I don't know how to say this except bluntly, Hugo. This nonsense about you and Amy can't go on. For one thing, she's mine. We were together last weekend, though I'm sure she was too discreet to mention it and I foolishly neglected her after Scacchi's death. For another, I simply won't allow it."

He watched a little of the tan drain from Massiter's face. Amy gripped his wrist tightly.

"It's quite wrong, Hugo. Juilliard? Amy needs the inspiration of a foreign college. I'll talk to people at the Guildhall and the Academy in London. She would be much happier there, near me. Not trapped in some apartment in New York."

"I see," Massiter mumbled.

"Don't misunderstand me, old chap," Daniel added earnestly. "I'm not a jealous person. I'm not offended by what has happened between you and Amy, not in the slightest. If you should care to renew your friendship at some stage in the future, it's fine by me. But you must curb your natural greed, Hugo. She can't go along with your ideas. Tomorrow I'll disappear somewhere with Amy. We need to be together. In a few weeks, when the fuss has died down, you and I must talk about this again and make sure our friendship is in no way damaged. I owe you much, Hugo. I admire you greatly. But on this I must be adamant."

Massiter rocked on his heels. "As you are, Daniel."

"Indeed. She came to you on the rebound. That's the truth of it, and you should feel no less flattered for that. I'm sure I'll feel pleased if some young thing flings herself at me when I'm your age. No hard feelings?"

He extended his hand. Massiter took it with a firm, dry grip.

"Of course not," Massiter replied. "You're right. I can't imagine what I was thinking."

Amy ran her hand through Daniel's arm and kissed him on the cheek. He caught her eye, approving her performance. "You're so sweet, Hugo," she said. "It just went too far. Can we still be friends?"

The diplomat's grin, all charm and persuasion, returned. "Of course! This is Venice. We're excused a little madness, aren't we?"

The three of them stood by the grave for a moment, wondering who would speak next. It was Daniel who broke the silence.

"But Hugo's right, my love," he said. "You must go and rest. Tonight you shall amaze us all."

"Yes," Massiter agreed. "Do that and I'll forgive you everything."

They watched her walk down the path, back towards the distant jetty. When she was gone, Daniel turned to Massiter. "You never fought, Hugo. You disappointed me."

The older man watched her go, an avaricious glint in his eye. "Oh, it was too fine a performance. I doubt I could have done better at your age."

Daniel kicked some earth onto Scacchi's coffin. A pair of sweaty grave-diggers were approaching. There was work to be done.

"But you didn't fight? Damn. She wasn't worth that much to you, was she?"

Massiter shrugged. "Amy is beautiful and more talented than she thinks. But to be honest, she bored me somewhat. She is so . . . passive. I like them to fight a little. Don't you?"

Daniel thought about his choice of words, noting them for the future. "But you see my problem?"

"No, frankly."

"I keep looking for the right price, Hugo. You take so much from us. You almost steal our souls. All I want is a little of the same in return. To relieve you of something so precious it gives you pain. I thought that Amy, but . . ."

"You've an excellent bargain," Massiter warned.

Daniel laughed in his face. "What? I've nothing I couldn't have taken for myself, at any time I felt like it. No. It's not good enough."

"Careful, Daniel."

He stared into the grey eyes, no longer in awe of them. "About what? You must meet my price, Hugo. Something precious. Otherwise I'll tell them all. Tomorrow. What's it to me? A little notoriety and a few months in jail at the most. I can never go back to the way I lived before, in any case. You, on the other hand—"

"Don't threaten me," Massiter snapped.

Daniel opened his hands wide. "I threaten no one, Hugo. I only ask for a fair reward."

Massiter paused. He would always want to know the price, Daniel understood. It was in his nature. "What, exactly?"

"Scacchi told me you had a secret place," Daniel said. "His exact words: 'Massiter must own a treasure trove where he keeps his objects of a greater beauty.' "

Massiter said nothing.

"I think," Daniel continued, "that you don't come here for the music alone. You're a merchant, Hugo. You buy and sell. All manner of things. Much like Scacchi, except on a higher scale."

"Say what you want," Massiter grumbled.

"I want a piece of your treasure, Hugo. I want to be taken there and see your objects for myself. When I do, I'll pick the one I desire. That's my price, and then we're done."

Massiter pulled himself away and stared at the grave-diggers, who now stood immobile, leaning on their shovels, waiting for them to leave the site. "I'll think about it."

"Tonight," Daniel said. "After the concert. A few glasses of champagne and then a private viewing." He stared at Massiter. "You're not offended, are you?"

"Not at all," Massiter answered. "In fact, I'm flattered. You learn quickly, Daniel."

"Of course," he agreed. "But then I have the finest teacher of them all."

57

Marchese's entrance

"I've no money, lad. Wave that palm elsewhere."

I tugged hard on Jacopo's jacket and pulled him into the shadows by La Pietà. He had not been hard to spot. That yellow star on his chest stood out a mile, even among the milling masses headed for the concert.

"Hey!" His eyes were bloodshot, his cheeks sallow. Still, he had lost that doomed expression I had seen on his face the day before, when he sought to drown his misery in wine. He peered at me in the darkness of the passage. "Lorenzo?"

A pretty sight I must have looked, a beggar from head to toe. I had dirtied my face—not that it needed much work—and torn my clothes. No self-respecting Venetian pays much attention to a scruffy vagrant. Or so I hoped. "Keep your voice down, brother," I whispered. "I'm a sought-after fellow these days."

He leaned against the wall, face half-caught by a shaft of late-summer sun, then sighed. "Murderer, too, I hear. To think I entrusted her to such a rogue."

"She's with a rogue now, Jacopo. And you know it."

He watched the crowds milling on the waterfront. The

mood was mixed. The public was beginning to lose patience with this game. Delapole had kept his hand over the prize for too long. They were anxious for some swift resolution.

"Perhaps I do. You didn't kill poor Leo, did you?"

It was my time for an exasperated sigh. "What do you think? You've read the details on the posters—as much as they see fit to print, because the truth was much, much worse. Yes. I was there, and they'd have slit my throat, too, if I hadn't run for it. But it's Delapole's handiwork. I warned you."

"Then the game is up for all of us."

"No! You give up the ghost too easily. As I tried to tell you before, there is a magistrate on his way here from Rome, with evidence that will put Delapole under lock and key."

Jacopo's eyes brightened a little. "Then where is he?"

"Delayed. There was an accident on the coach. But he'll be here. When he arrives, we will need our wits about us, Jacopo. The Englishman will surely try to damn us alongside himself."

A spark of hope rose in his face. "Let me talk to Rebecca after they have played. We'll flee then, Lorenzo. I'm ready to leave this damn town now. Not really my kind of place at all."

This was, I knew, impossible. "He's too clever for that, Lorenzo. He'll be watching her like a hawk when she's out in public. Besides, until the watch are after him, he could so easily make us the fugitives, and with little chance of escape. These streets are running over with the Doge's men."

He rubbed his wispy beard. "Then what?"

"What do you do after the concert?"

"He wants me with him and Rebecca at Ca' Dario. To pack, he says. I suspect we'll ship out this evening."

"Then that is where to make our move. They'll surely come

for him there. Before they do, you must find some way to escape the house. Meet me at Salute, and we'll look for a boat to bribe on Zattere."

"You make it sound so simple, Lorenzo. Do you have any idea how sly that fellow is?"

The image of poor, maimed Leo was still alive in my head. "Oh, yes," I murmured. "More than you might imagine."

He was silent.

"What's wrong?" I asked.

"I was just thinking. I remember you when you were a boy."

I gripped his arm. "That was a long time ago, my friend."

Jacopo Levi embraced me then, and I felt the most curious sensation. It was as if I had my arms around his sister. There was in our closeness the same warmth and affection, and some trepidation for the future, too, I suppose. I found, to my embarrassment, tears began to start behind my eyes. Jacopo looked into my face and did me the good service of failing to notice them.

"I am sorry," I stuttered, "to have brought you both to this. To have ruined your lives this way. I will give everything I have to correct it."

He laughed, like the old Jacopo. "Oh, God, what rubbish you talk sometimes!"

I felt wretched. There were no words in my head, only sorrow.

"It's all a game, Lorenzo," he said with a grin. "Never forget that. Besides, I was growing fat and lazy in that ghetto, and Rebecca couldn't wait to get out, as you well know. Man is a sluggish animal at heart. We need to be shaken out of our lethargy from time to time."

"All the same . . ."

"All the same nothing. I tire of curing Venetian matrons one moment, then sealing the remedy by bedding them the next. There's more to life. Besides . . ."

He eyed the crowd on the promenade. Then, with one sudden, determined movement, he ripped the yellow star from his dark jacket and threw it into the gutter. The badge lay there in the dirt, a small, pathetic remnant of his past.

"I have learned one thing from you and Rebecca." He undid his jacket and let his white shirt, open to the chest, show through, as is the style of the Venetian gentleman. "That I walked willingly into that ghetto and helped them turn the key. It is our acquiescence that gives them power over us. We are who we believe we are. Wherever I alight next, I'll be what I damn well like—Jew or Gentile, Swiss or Italian, doctor, quack, or gigolo. If Delapole can do it, why can't we?"

His certainty unnerved me. "I am not sure he makes a good example. Or that any of us can shrug off our inheritance when we please."

"Perhaps not. But if we Jews are such a different race, why must they place badges on our coats to tell us apart?"

In his own mind, Jacopo was beginning to invent himself anew. He answered his own question. "Because it's themselves they fear, not us. The presence in their midst of those who speak differently, worship differently, and—most of all—think differently alarms them. They mark us so we do not taint them with our dissimilarity and, as a consequence, bring this gilded state crashing down upon their heads."

It was cold in the passageway, in spite of the late-summer sun. I shivered a little. Jacopo embraced me once more. I felt a little of his strength, an intellectual vigour, pass into me. Then he was gone, back into the crowd, his jacket half-askew like that of any young Venetian blade, his head held high, black locks tossing in the fetid air that rose from the lagoon.

He was right too. None would have marked him for a Jew unless they knew him. Jacopo's actions were his way of throwing in his hat with us. One way or another, our lives would be transformed before this day was out.

I tousled my hair, pulled my jacket up around my cheeks, then ventured out into the sea of jostling bodies. The concert was due to start any minute. Across the cobblestones, by the waterside, was some commotion. I stretched on tiptoe, anxious to see. There, to my dismay, was the squat figure of Marchese, hand upright through the masses, clutching some parchment. His croaky Roman voice came through the throng. He pushed towards La Pietà, looking as if he were ready to arrest Delapole on his own if need be.

This was too soon. I had expected warning—a troop of guards, one of the city officials at their head, coming to seize Delapole with due ceremony. Rebecca remained in his grasp.

Ignoring the clamour of complaints and the accompanying kicks and elbows, I dashed into the bustle and clawed my way towards him. This crowd was the largest I had ever seen, a thick and surly mass of humanity fighting for a view of the platform on the concert steps, where Delapole now stood beaming, hands behind his back, master of the ceremony.

There was so much noise none could hear what Marchese yelled. I fought my way towards him and finally succeeded in pressing through until I caught his arm and bade him calm down. His face was crimson with effort and anger, his breathing laboured.

"Sir!" I cried. "It is I! Scacchi!"

"Scacchi?"

He tugged me backwards with him, towards the water's edge, where the noise was a little less overpowering.

"You are too soon," I warned him. "You must have the watch with you, or he'll surely flee."

"The watch?" he spat back at me. "Why, they're even more useless here than back in Rome. They're waiting on the captain, who's awash in some tavern, no doubt. Only then will they look at the papers I brought them. And . . ." He stared at me. "What happened to you, lad?"

"The Englishman's doing. He murdered my master and puts the blame on me."

"Then his game's afoot, and he'll not rest until he's done. This girl of yours. You have freed her from his grasp?"

The podium was out of my view. I did not doubt Rebecca was there, as Delapole had instructed. I could only pray that Jacopo would see this through.

"Not yet. That's another reason why you must wait for the watch. I fear he'll take her hostage."

Marchese looked at me as if I were an idiot. "She's hostage already. Don't you understand? Damn that coach. If we'd been here on time . . ."

"Sir." I took his arm. He would, I thought, in one more minute become sufficiently composed to follow my advice. "I—"

"Dammit, Scacchi," he cried, pointing into the crowd. "There's his lad. As bold as brass. Why, I . . ."

And then he became silent. For Gobbo had wormed his way through the multitude of bodies and now stood before us, grinning like a monkey.

"Signor Marchese," he said with a polite nod of his head. "And my dear friend Lorenzo. Why, I don't know which of you keeps the worse company; that's a fact. A murderer and a magistrate. What pretty conversations you must enjoy."

"I'll have your head on the block before this day is out," Marchese warned darkly. "And your miserable master's too."

"Oh, I think not, sir. For we have only just embarked upon this circuit of the world, and it would be undignified and impolite to make such an early exit from our adventures."

"You scum," Marchese growled.

"Such words do not become a Roman gentleman," Gobbo said, then turned his back upon us and made as if to reenter the throng.

The old man was furious. "Why, I'll . . ."

The mind plays strange tricks. I realised what Gobbo intended in an instant, but witnessing its performance seemed to take an endless age. The old magistrate lunged forward and grabbed the back of his retreating shoulder. At that moment Gobbo spun upon his heels; I saw his left arm jerk back, then forward, thrusting upwards, ever upwards. Marchese gave a soft sigh; his head fell back. There was blood in his mouth. Then that squat body of his tumbled away from Gobbo's blade, back into my arms. His weight was too great for me. He slumped to the cobbles. There was a dark, red stain in his abdomen. It was an assassin's blow: a single stroke upwards, deep into the chest, rising until it struck the heart.

The curious milled around us, murmuring, puzzled, not yet appreciating the horror of what had just taken place. This moment hung in the balance, and still Gobbo stood opposite me, too bold to flee. I was unable to move.

"What's the matter, Scacchi?" he cried across the poor old man's corpse. "Afraid of a little blood?"

Which I was, but that was not why I hesitated. "He was a

good man, Gobbo," I said. "His testimony will see you brought to justice."

He kept his blade hidden, covered as it was in Marchese's blood, by his side. Bodies milled at my back. Faces began to turn. Gobbo sneered at me.

"Justice! Some good that's done your friend, eh? Take that lily-white soul of yours and run, Lorenzo. It's what the likes of us were born to do."

I would not play his game. I shook my head. "I will see some justice done, Gobbo. I will hound you both until it is."

This odd, deformed creature shrugged his shoulders and looked almost fondly at me, as he had done in those days when we first met and I was, to some extent, beneath his wing. "Then more fool you, lad. For I've taught you nothing. Here . . ."

His weapon flashed through the air. Without thinking, I caught it square in my hand. Marchese's blood ran down the hilt and touched my palm.

Gobbo leapt into the crowd, waving his fists as if in fear. "Murder! Murder!" he yelled. "It is the Scacchi villain, citizens. Who, not content with murdering his master, has now felled some poor soul in broad daylight. Murder! Murder! Seize him 'fore he kills you next!"

I dropped the knife, but too late. All faces were upon me, panic and hatred written upon them. I retreated and felt a hand grip my shoulder. Gobbo was gone. I could hear his laughter disappearing with him, like leaves upon the wind.

With a sudden dive, I ducked beneath the arm of my captor and dodged through the crowd to cover the few yards to the water's edge. Then, for the second time in a day, I sought safety in the mire, leaping from the jetty into the lagoon below. The black tide covered my head, and I kicked hard east for the further side of the promenade, beyond La Pietà, where the crowd would still, I hoped, be ignorant of Marchese's fate. Some yards beyond the church, I surfaced, then made my way up the gondoliers' stairs, rolling and bawling like a drunk so none came near me.

As I ran hell for leather into the wasteland on the border of the Arsenale, I heard a familiar sound behind, that of an orchestra starting the first few bars of one of Mr. Vivaldi's favourite tunes. I fancied I could distinguish the tones of Rebecca's Guarneri in the hubbub. Then the music was drowned by the din of boos and catcalls and yells. Not once looking back, I sought shelter in the bramble and elder scrub, where, teeth chattering, I tried to recover my wits.

There the beggar Lorenzo Scacchi wept for his friend Marchese, whose amity had been too short and whose absence made this day seem more dark and forbidding than before.

58

An auspicious première

THE CIRCUS ENDED ON THE STEPS OF LA PIETÀ, AMID the TV cameras and the last-minute hopefuls trying to find a ticket at any price. Inside, the church was filled with the low buzz of excitement. The orchestra, dressed in black, was at the far end of the nave. Fabozzi towered over them from an exaggerated podium. Amy stood alone, between the conductor and the massed rows of the audience.

Daniel walked to the front, accepting the restrained applause with a wan smile, nodded to Fabozzi, Amy, and, finally, the orchestra, then took his place next to Massiter in the first row. He turned and saw Giulia Morelli three seats behind. The policewoman stared at him, unsmiling. A sound behind, Fabozzi's baton tapping the stand, announced the start of the performance. Then Daniel closed his eyes and, for the first time in his life, listened to the work he knew as *Concerto Anonimo* in its entirety, losing himself in the swirling themes and winding alleys of its complexities.

In Ca' Scacchi, transcribing the notes directly from the mysterious score, he had heard the work as a series of voices, violin and viola, bassoon and oboe, each distinct and fighting for its place in the whole. It amazed him now that any human mind could encompass both the individual clarity of each separate instrument and simultaneously meld them into a greater, harmonious creation more magnificent than the sum of each exquisite part. As always, he found himself fascinated by the identity of its true composer. This was not Vivaldi. There was too much of the modern in the piece, and, if the date on the cover was correct, too much verve for it to have been the work of a man in his fifties approaching the end of his life.

Yet this was not any composer he had ever heard; of that he was sure. There lay the overriding mystery. No other work by the same hand still existed. If such a piece were extant, it would surely have been well-known. The concerto had come out of some sudden flash of inspiration which had then disappeared or perhaps been stifled by mishap or design. Something else, too, puzzled him. There was in the work a sense of distance, of alienation, as if the composer had listened to Vivaldi's efforts, absorbed them, and, with a sense of both irony and good humour, transformed them into something akin but separate from what had gone before. This was the act of an admirer, not an acolyte. He doubted any close to Vivaldi's circle would have dared step so closely, and with such impertinent brilliance, on the old man's toes.

Daniel opened his eyes and saw the astonished faces around him. Amy had moved into her first solo, and the voice of her ancient Guarneri soared to the roof of La Pietà with a bold, savage beauty that filled his mind with wonder. He remembered Massiter's admonition to her. Perhaps Amy believed that there was some release in the music, that she could earn her escape from Massiter by playing as she had never done before. Enthralled, he watched the intense concentration on her beautiful face as she tore into the notes, clutching the Guarneri to her neck as if it were part of her body. Once the slow, melodious opening had given way to the rising, relentless surge of the first movement, she had, like all of them, been swept away by its merciless, all-encompassing rapture.

He heard every note of the orchestra resound in the body of the church. Daniel Forster no longer felt shame for his act of deception. Without him this wonder would have lain behind brickwork in a crumbling Venetian mansion, perhaps forever. Without him, it might as well never have existed at all.

Amy cut a searing swathe through one of the most difficult passages, double- and treble-stopping her way along the Guarneri's narrow neck. Close by, someone gasped. It was the only sound that came from the audience throughout the entire concert. There was, as Massiter had predicted, a sense of history in the occasion. For all Daniel knew, this was the first time the work had ever been played in public. Somewhere, he hoped, the shade of its creator could hear a little of its magnificence and feel the awe it inspired in those fortunate enough to share in its debut.

The concerto ran to its own time, trapping them inside the prison of its imagination. It came as a shock when he realised they had reached the closing sections of the third movement, with Amy working desperately hard once more. Daniel racked his head to try to assemble some logical train of events from the opening bars to the fast-approaching conclusion. It was impossible. The work was both a single, simple entity and a collection of complexities, blending seamlessly beneath the surface. Amy stretched for the close. Like those around him, he scarcely dared breathe. Then she was done, in a furious barrage of notes that tore to the roof of La Pietà and continued to resonate, in the church and in their heads, long after she had ceased playing.

When the last tremor of her Guarneri died softly into nothingness, there was a moment of silence. A few seconds later La Pietà erupted with sound. The crowd rose as a mass, not knowing where to applaud. Daniel ducked quickly, squeezed past Massiter without a word, and found a hiding place in the shadow of one of the great pillars. With no composer to cheer, the audience spent its adoration on Amy, who stood before them, shell-shocked, eyes moist and wide, unable to say a word. A small girl in a white dress walked to the front of the nave and handed her a bouquet of red roses. The orchestra put down their instruments and joined the applause, Fabozzi leading them.

Out of view, Daniel watched their faces and wondered. Even Massiter seemed moved, standing to clap furiously and bellow hurrahs. This was a moment to savour. The work was so powerful that none could ever question its value in the future. Amy's performance, too, had surely marked her step into adulthood, more surely than any mere physical act could have done. A dark thought struck him again: that perhaps some pain, some terrible price, was necessary for such greatness. He wondered about his own part in providing her with the key she needed to unlock the genius inside herself.

But then another noise rose. He heard it with dread. A low, insistent chanting running across the audience, echoed by the orchestra. All except Amy, who stood there alone, frightened perhaps, her eyes crossing the bright body of the church and finding his own as he hid in the shadows.

"*Forster, Forster, Forster, Forster . . .*"

The younger Daniel would have fled from the room. He recalled Scacchi and the discussion they had held beneath the Venetian Lucifer. Then he marched out of the darkness, head high, applauding the players as he walked, grinning broadly, hearing the clamour of the crowd's hands rise with each step, feeling like a bogus god walking into paradise.

Amy's astonished eyes followed him as he approached her, took the bouquet from her hands, and threw it to the floor, then, to a roar of applause, held her in his arms, kissed both her damp cheeks.

"Daniel?" she whispered.

"You've earned this, Amy," he said quietly. "This is your moment."

"But..."

She stared at him, suspicious once more. Amy had lived through the piece that night. She knew it better than anyone. She understood, too, Daniel realised, that her first suspicions were correct. He could not be its creator. The puzzlement and the accusation stood in her eyes.

"Tomorrow you must go," he said, then turned to smile once more at the audience. "Don't wait for me. Take the plane to Rome. Then go home."

"I can't," she protested. "We must talk."

The crowd bellowed. He knew he must speak to them.

"Not now," he said, and kissed her again. Then he turned and, with a theatrical gesture, took her right hand and raised it high, above his, milking the audience for applause.

"Friends!" Daniel bellowed over the noise. "*Friends!*"

Slowly they fell into silence, shushing each other in the din.

"Friends," he repeated, and heard his voice echo off the walls. They were seated again, waiting. He looked at Massiter and then Giulia Morelli. They wore the same expression of intense interest.

"What can I say to you?" he asked. "How do I explain myself?"

"Bravo, Maestro," Massiter shouted from the audience, and began to clap, starting a ripple of applause which Daniel swiftly waved down.

"No," he insisted. "Your kindness is overwhelming. I'm not a speaker. When I listen to Amy here and these players of Fabozzi, I wonder whether I'm a musician at all."

"Such modesty!" someone shouted, and he was unsure whether it was a compliment or a taunt.

"No," he answered. "I'm not being modest. I gave these musicians paint and pigment in the hope they might create with them. What you heard came as much from them as from the composer. I owe them my congratulations. I owe you my thanks. But now you must give me some rest. Please. *Ciao!*"

With that, he turned and walked to the back of the church, wandering the narrow corridors until he found a small, empty dressing-room where the clamour outside was reduced to a distant drone. There he sat on a low bench and placed his head in his hands, wishing he had the courage to weep. He felt as if there were poison in his veins.

There were steps outside in the corridor, then a knock on the door. Amy came in. She looked exhausted.

"Dan?" she said. "They want you to go back out there. I don't think they'll go till you do."

He shook his head to clear it and managed to force a smile. "Tell them I'm overwhelmed by their response, Amy. Tell them I'm unwell. Make some excuse for me. Please."

"OK," she said softly, but waited at the door. "Did you mean what you said? That I have to go?"

"Of course," he replied. "It's what you wanted, isn't it?"

She came over to him. "I wanted you, Dan. All along that's what I wanted." She hesitated. "Even if you're a fake, I want you. I don't care."

He looked up at her. "Of course you care, Amy. You must."

"Let me help you," she offered.

"You already have. You'll understand that soon."

She was close to tears again. "Don't talk like that. You scare me."

He stood up, took her face in his hands, kissed her once more, then said, "Go to the reception, Amy. I'll meet you there. Then tomorrow, first thing, catch that plane."

She stared at him, mistrust in her eyes. "You'll come to the party? Just be with me there, Dan. After that I'll go. I promise."

"As you see fit," he said. "Now, be off with you, and talk to those people. This is your night, Amy. Venice belongs to you."

"I know," she replied. "And I wish I felt more grateful."

Then she was gone, and Daniel waited, knowing he would come. After fifteen minutes the noise beyond the door had diminished. He heard the orchestra troop back to their dressing rooms, listened to their low chatter of voices and occasional laughter, feeling painfully distant from their deserved acclaim. A little later Massiter walked in, pulled up the one spare chair, and sat beside him.

"You disturbed me there, Daniel," he declared. "Please don't play tricks. I hate that kind of thing."

"I'm sorry, Hugo. That wasn't my intention."

"Of course not," Massiter observed dryly. "Well. I imagine there's no time like the present. You don't really want to go and sip warm champagne with boring people, do you? Everyone's expecting the pair of us. I think we've both sung sufficiently for our supper recently, to be honest."

Daniel wondered what he was thinking. Massiter seemed resigned to his demands. He had expected more resistance. He wondered, too, about breaking this last promise to Amy. She could never forgive him. Perhaps that was for the best.

Massiter eyed him. He seemed, for the first time in Daniel's experience, almost worried. "You're very privileged. Not many men have seen what I'm about to show you."

"I'm flattered by your offer, Hugo."

"As if I had a choice."

"Of course you had a choice. Several, I believe. You're doing this because you want to, surely?"

Massiter nodded. "True. You're an amusing soul, Daniel. Scacchi coached you well. As, unwittingly, have I, it seems."

Daniel rose to leave.

"But nothing comes for free," Massiter added. "You appreciate that, I hope."

They left by the side door. It was a warm night with the merest sliver of a moon. The lagoon shimmered, its surface reflecting the stars. In the rear of the water taxi, Daniel closed his eyes, fought to stem his thoughts. The music ran around his head still, refusing to leave, circling constantly, a puzzle without an answer.

59

Dissonant notes

Delapole was right in one respect. The Venetians can be an ugly lot when they are crossed. The scribbled messages I had dropped in those lions' jaws had done their trick. I had not sought to accuse Delapole of Leo's murder. Such a ruse would be hard to sustain without evidence; the anonymous writer would be deemed a mischief-maker or worse. Instead, I chose a subject which I knew no self-respecting clerk of the Republic could fail to extend to a wider audience: the authorship of that mysterious concerto.

With a little variation in each, my messages foretold that Delapole would claim the prize and, in so doing, seek to deceive the city. He was, I hinted, a thief, and perhaps worse. This crime was to be perpetrated on an unsuspecting Venice in order that he might fleece the citizens of their money, then disappear into the night. To establish my case, I suggested the readers spread the word and ask those who heard it to demand some proof from the Englishman when he appeared on the podium with Vivaldi's players. If he could lead the players through the opening of the piece—or anything else, for that matter—then let him be acclaimed. If not, then the city should draw its own conclusions and act accordingly.

When I penned those messages, I firmly believed Marchese would be in the city at any moment, walking to arrest the Englishman at the head of a troop of city guards. So much for my prescience. But this was a game of chess, with human players. A precautionary move might turn the balance of a match several steps on from the point at which it is played. The mob was angry. Marchese's murder had spurred their already foul mood. The word was spreading through the crowd that the beloved concerto would not, after all, be played. From his place on the platform, where he paced up and down, looking increasingly nervous, Delapole could see the moment of his triumph turning to catastrophe.

"Music, Maestro!" one wag yelled. "Or has the cat got your English tongue?"

Delapole bowed to his tormentor and walked to the other side of the stage. There was no more sympathy for him there. The rabble was restless. Vivaldi stood immobile, offering not a whit of assistance. The musicians shuffled sheets awkwardly in front of them. Then a drunk came out of the crowd, clambered onto the platform, and snatched the first page of a cellist's part.

"This ain't the concerto," the fellow yelled. "I can read a title page. We've been robbed. They're going to play some of the Red Priest's old stuff, and I've heard that till it's coming out of me ears."

Vivaldi stared at Delapole. The Englishman listened to the baying of the hoi polloi, then walked, with a fixed smile upon his face, to the front of the stage and waved for them to be silent.

"Ladies," he implored. "Gentlemen."

A gang of armourers from the Arsenale, well in their cups,

had gathered at the front to taunt him. "Get on with it, you pomaded bastard!" the largest one shouted. "We came here to listen to them, not watch you parade around like some peacock looking for a mate."

"We will, sir," Delapole replied, glowering at the fellow. "In due course."

"And that new one too!" another yelled. "Not any old rubbish."

"Ah," Delapole said. "If only I could oblige."

With that the crowd fell silent, waiting for his explanation.

"You're the one what wrote it, aren't you?" demanded one of the armourers. "You damn well best oblige us."

The Englishman held his arms open wide. "I had promised to wait to break this news. But yes. I am the one."

He gave them that charming English smile. Not a single pair of hands applauded.

"Prove it, then," the armourer bellowed. "You run your girls through that pretty piece of yours and let's have done with it."

Delapole shook his head. "Nothing would please me more, sir. But we are victims of a criminal. He has stolen our work and left me with too little time to reproduce it for our orchestra here. Next week, I promise. Then I'll have it played for all of you, and free, too, for any who's paid today."

The crowd turned even more sullen at that. Delapole brazened it out.

"We've been robbed, sirs!" he pleaded with them. "By that scoundrel boy Scacchi, who murdered his own master—and his uncle!—only last night. And did so to steal my manuscript from his master's safekeeping, where I believed it would be printed for today. We have no notes, no score, no inspiration for our sweet musicians. What would you have me do but beg my friend Vivaldi play for us and let me work my fingers to the bone into the small hours of the night, re-creating that which I have already once written, as you know well?"

"We don't know nothing," Delapole's nemesis yelled from in front of the platform. "You prove it to us, eh. You make 'em play."

The Englishman's composure broke at that. It was a development he had not forecast. "Why, sir. I do not know this piece as well as my friend. I would not do it justice."

The crowd was enjoying every moment of this. "Oh, come on!" a voice cried. "You're the great composer, ain't you? If you could write that marvel what we heard before, you can surely wave them girls through their paces, eh?"

Delapole glanced nervously at Vivaldi, seeking support. "It would be an impertinence to my friend here."

The Red Priest rose from his seat, walked over to Delapole, and politely placed a baton in his hand, then returned to watch what ensued.

To a man the crowd roared: "*Play! Play! Play!*"

The musicians followed him, waiting for that piece of wood to move and give them direction. There was, he must have realised, no escaping this. He turned his back to the mob, gestured with his hand, and launched into the piece.

I wonder about what happened thereafter. Did he fail through his own efforts or those of the young band of female players who sat before him? Only Rebecca knew his true nature. The rest, I believe, must have guessed it the instant he took his charade one step too far. As he gesticulated hopelessly in front of them, he was revealed. The musicians knew Delapole could no more be the anonymous composer than any of those who baited him from the crowd. He was a fraud, and, to seal his perfidy, he sought to implicate them in his deceit.

So they played as badly as they could while still retaining some dignity. Not a single note was wrong in pitch or duration, but each made its entry into the piece a fraction of a second too soon or a moment too late, so that the movement lurched forwards, then backwards, and finally collapsed into an unrestrained cacophony that stumbled nowhere, like a team of horses that has lost its driver.

The mob began to bay for blood. Gobbo leapt upon the stage and whispered in his master's ear. He had, I suspect, realised that Marchese might have spoken to others before he died. The authorities would take a leisurely interest in Delapole's manifest fraud over the concert. If there was other intelligence to whet their appetites, it might add some urgency to their desire to escort the pair of them into those dark rooms by the Doge's Palace and invite them, under pain of torture, to talk a little of their past.

In my hiding place by the Arsenale, I heard the angry howling of the rabble. That gave me opportunity, for its attention was diverted to the piece of theatre being played out on the platform. Half drenched, I slunk back to the waterfront and cautiously made my way towards the hordes outside the church. Canaletto could have painted this, I thought, and made it look a distant, pretty picture of Venetian pomp and ceremony. From his far-off viewpoint, no one could see the seething hatred that ran through this ugly mass or guess what macabre outcome was now being engineered by Delapole at its heart.

The focus shifted. Someone was moving, but it was impossible to see a thing. A flurry of bodies flocked to a single point by the stage, then flowed forwards. I saw a glimpse of Delapole's silk garments and something else, the black dress of one of Vivaldi's musicians. They had fled down to the waterfront, and there leapt into a waiting boat. Not caring who saw me, I dashed to the edge of the promenade. There, under a rain of eggs, rotten fruit, and less harmless objects, the Englishman was making his exit from Venice. Gobbo sat on his left. To the right, wrapped in her cape, was Rebecca, face as pale as the moon, that fiddle case still beneath her arm.

Delapole waited until his vessel was beyond the reach of the mob's missiles, then rose in the stern and raised his arm in a single salute. He barked at his crew. His gondolier sculled hard for the Grand Canal. The Englishman stood upright in the back of that vessel, not flinching, his lips set in a cold, tight smile. It could only be my imagination which made me fancy that his eyes never left my face.

60

Waiting for the call

GIULIA MORELLI SLIPPED QUIETLY INTO THE POST-concert reception which took place on the ground floor of the Londra Palace, next to where she had sat and listened to Daniel Forster at the press conference that morning. He was absent, as was Massiter. She spoke briefly to the girl violinist, who seemed distraught, overwhelmed by the event, perhaps. There was nothing of moment to discuss with her, even if some rational conversation had been possible over the glasses of Prosecco in which she seemed determined to drown. Amy Hartston had no idea where Daniel or Massiter had gone. The policewoman listened to Amy's half-drunk ramblings about the perfidy of men and her hatred of music, and wondered if this was the same person who had astonished them all this night. Musicians were such a strange breed, she decided, unlike any she had ever met.

When the party began to bore her, the policewoman wandered outside to stand on the waterfront by the *vaporetto* stop. There she smoked a cigarette, happy, content with the evening. It was now eleven. The tourist crowds were beginning to leave the cafés in the square. The raucous noise of the bands, jazz and cheap classical, had now ended. The night began to overtake Venice, and within its folds lay success.

By a quarter to twelve she was growing restless. She pulled the mobile phone from her bag, thinking, for no reason at all, of Rizzo. Rizzo, who was so full of bluster and, in the end, so easy to scare. She was affronted by his death, which had occurred before his usefulness had ended.

She looked at the phone. It was possible Biagio was unable to call. In another city, in another kind of force, she would need none of these tricks. She could confide in her colleagues, put together a team that would do her bidding. But this was Venice, where the lines were always blurred. Until she had what she wanted, hard and fast in her hand, she dared not risk discovery.

Giulia Morelli tossed the cigarette into the shifting waters of the lagoon and listened to its brief dying hiss. Her inner voice began the mantra: *Call me, Biagio. Call me.*

After the campanile bell had tolled midnight, the phone rang. She snatched at the buttons, cursing her own impatience.

"Yes?"

"You wouldn't believe it," said Biagio's distant, scratched voice. "He's almost on our doorstep."

"And Forster?"

"With him. They're both inside now. It's near San Niccolò Mendicoli. Just off the *campo*. I can wait for you outside. It's deserted around here."

She tried to picture the location in her head. She knew the church. It was small, medieval, by a narrow *rio* south of Piazzale Roma. She could take a water taxi and be there in ten minutes.

"What do you want me to do?" Biagio asked.

Such a dainty way of saying it, she thought. They both understood the real question. Two men, both of some repute, had entered a building in a deserted, remote part of the city. She could not think of calling for assistance. There was nothing to report. Or, worse, there was, and the wrong people would hear.

"Wait for me," she ordered. "In fifteen minutes you call them, say there's something suspicious and they should check. That should give us a little time before they come."

"OK," Biagio said uncertainly. He was out of uniform, calling in sick, taking a big risk. She had to protect him if the walls began to fall around their heads. She knew that.

"Biagio," she said. "Don't worry. I'll tell them I ordered everything. OK?"

"You're the boss," he replied.

"Right. And you make that call, whether I've arrived or not. I won't be long."

"And then?"

She heard the hesitation in his distant voice.

"Then we open a couple of coffins," she answered. "And see what flies out with the dust."

61

View from a window

Three times I pleaded with a gondolier to take me across
that short black stretch of water. Three times they refused.
A man without money ceases to exist. I had one item of
value left in the world: the small Star of David that Rebecca
had placed around my neck a lifetime ago. At the *traghetto* I
offered it to the gondolier. He sneered at the precious piece
of silver, then took it and nodded me into the boat. I had
no choice. The alternative was to race through the back
alleys of San Marco and make that long loop over the
Rialto, then down to the Dorsoduro once more. I had not
the time, yet without that small memento of another part
of our lives, I now felt naked.

The September afternoon was waning when I found myself
in the alley by the *rio* which leads to the rear entrance of Ca'
Dario. Swarms of flies ascended from the piles of rubbish
awaiting disposal by the waterside. From the dark chasms
which marked the entrance to the tawdry local inns, eyes
glittered at me as I passed. The city stank. I could feel my
time inside it running out, like sand falling through a glass.
If ever I managed to release Rebecca from this devil's grasp

and take her to safety, I would, I vowed, go down on my knees
to kiss terra firma and swear never to abandon land again.

There was much to be done before that happy state was
reached and little with which to achieve it. I had no means and
no weapon—I had left my only blade on the cobbles outside La
Pietà. No plan, either, save to hope Jacopo would find some
way to smuggle Rebecca to freedom. When I saw that familiar
house, with its forest of curious chimneys, its secure position
by the Grand Canal, and the high surrounding wall, I realised
how fruitless this proposition was too. Delapole had chosen
his abode well. It was, in its own way, a small fortress. There
was but a single entrance to the landward side of Dorsoduro
at the rear, and the same on the canal at the front. To the west
side stood the *rio*, just big enough for a gondola, but with no
access to the building. On the east was an even narrower line
of water between Dario and the adjoining palace, from which
entry was barred by a high wall. It seemed impregnable. There
was nothing to do but wait. Which I did, sitting in the shadow
of the neighbouring garden's alcove entry, and all to no avail.

The maid and the cook left—for good, by the looks of it,
since they murmured darkly about Delapole's meanness as
they passed me. I watched the windows and saw nothing.
I had thought Ca' Dario a small property until now. It was,
by comparison with its neighbours, but not when it came to
guessing where a handful of people might be behind its walls.
The house stood on four storeys, each of a size which might
encompass six or eight normal rooms. I had seen only the
first floor, with its grand parlour opening onto the canal. It
was impossible to imagine where in this miniature castle
Delapole might be making final preparations for his flight.
All I could count upon, I believed, was that he would be in
a hurry. There, again, I was wrong.

Two red-faced men, whom I took to be creditors, came to the door and were sent away by Gobbo with a few coarse words and empty pockets. Nothing else occurred. After almost an hour of inactivity, my patience broke. If the watch were to take note of Marchese's information—which, given his murder, seemed far from certain—they would surely do so soon. Even without this, Delapole must make his exit before long. Either way, we would be damned. I poked my head out into the light and considered the situation. Ca' Dario seemed impregnable, but there was one small possibility for entry. The house possessed a modest walled garden at the rear which, in part, adjoined that of its neighbour where the *rio* either terminated or went underground. I could see foliage, jasmine or oleander, running over the corner of the wall where it met the street. A little way along stood the branches of a small orange tree, bearing tiny fruit, which sat in the neighbour's garden but crossed, a little, into the Dario property.

Gingerly, I turned the handle on the wrought-iron gate behind me. To my good fortune, it was unlocked, so I hastily pushed it open and stepped into the green parterre that lay behind. There was no time for dawdling. The house beyond looked empty. I scrambled up the orange tree until I reached the level of the wall's summit, then rolled over and fell hard onto the puny grass of a small lawn. My blood froze. There were voices, coarse, male ones, close by. I hid in a bush and tried to think. The noise was coming from the front of the mansion, by its private jetty on the canal. If Delapole was about to leave, this in all probability would be his exit route. It was more public than the rear, but less accessible. To fly the city, he needed water transport. It made sense that it would arrive at the most convenient location, then carry him and his cargo away, perhaps to land, perhaps to a passenger ship in the docks.

I considered my options. The ground-floor level of the house was hopeless; the side windows were barred. The first floor, with that grand room where I had betrayed Rebecca to the Englishman, was beyond my reach. If I were to enter the house, it must be at the front, through the same arched entrance they would use to load Delapole's possessions and, last, their passengers.

There was nothing for it. I clung to the damp wall, edged my way along the narrow stone skirt that ran from the garden, by the *rio*, to the canal, and poked my head around the corner. Thank God for the common Venetian. There were three of them, lounging in their boat, with several packing cases around them. Coils of tobacco smoke rose from the prow, where, with their backs to me, the men lay, cursing idly about the whims of rich men who order a boat for five and still decline to board it at six. I felt relieved. Then one of them murmured, "Perhaps he's fancying a bit of rough-and-tumble with that bit of skirt, lads. Can't blame him, eh? She's a pretty one. They were upstairs for a reason, if you ask me."

My heart sank. While they gossiped, I edged along the dank white marble frontage until I reached the narrow jetty, then dashed silently into the gaping arched maw of the entrance. None saw me. I paused against a wall, marshalling my thoughts. There was a small sledgehammer at the foot of the grubby stone stairs that led up to the house proper. I did not want to walk into the presence of either Delapole or Gobbo unarmed. No other weapon was likely to present itself. I lifted the thing, felt its pendulous weight swing beneath my arm, and was then up the stairs, two at a time, into the corridor which ran along the main reception room.

They had said Delapole and Rebecca were above. I had no idea where Gobbo might be. Then I heard something that made me grip that hammer tight in my hands and catch my breath. From above, distant but with that unmistakable, bold tone, came the sound of Rebecca's violin, and behind it Delapole's cold voice.

They were on the floor directly over my head. I could hear the boards creak as he paced the room. A single flight of stairs separated me from Rebecca and our fate. I strained to hear another sound. There was none. Gobbo could not be nearby—perhaps he had slipped out while I was making my furtive entrance at the front. We seemed alone, with only the bored boatmen outside for distant company, and they would not come through the door until summoned.

I tucked the handle of the hammer into the top of my trousers, held the hard iron head firm to my stomach, and ascended the stairs, step by patient step, listening to these twin, related sounds, Rebecca's fiddle and Delapole's commanding tones, becoming louder all the while. At the head of the staircase was an ill-lit landing with a long velvet drape which ran across to the entrance of the room opposite. I briefly saw Delapole's back there as he strode across my vision. Rebecca was out of sight. I slipped behind the curtain and started to skirt along the wall towards the open door. There I moved the fabric a little and saw her at last. She was seated, the instrument in her arms, a single sheet of manuscript on a stand before her knees. Delapole marched around her like some kind of teacher.

"I think not," the Englishman said. "Some part of it runs out of one's head before it is heard, like a well-worn phrase. This is a textbook definition of the cliché, and we must avoid that at all costs."

"Sir," Rebecca replied wearily. "I am tired. I believed we were to depart tonight."

"When Gobbo's met that brother of yours. Not before. Blame him, not me. I'll give them thirty minutes more, and then we're off. In the meantime I shall play with my new toy, if you'll oblige. Music, girl!"

His back was turned. I lifted the drape from my face so that she might see me, but her mind was elsewhere.

"I have had enough," she announced. "I will play no more."

He walked over and knelt beside her chair. "Oh, surely you will oblige me, dear. It is in your own interests. The Devil has the best tunes, always, they say. With your talent and my . . . polishing, who knows where we'll end up?"

"I wish no more of this," she said, and carefully placed the violin back in its case.

"Ah." He looked at her with an expression I would once have interpreted as kindness. No more. "I'll have other sport, then."

With a single arm he dragged her from the chair and threw her abruptly to the floor. Rebecca screamed and clutched at her dress. Not for fear of his intentions, either. She was in pain. The beast took no notice. He was unbuttoning himself, and then, in one swift movement, snatched up her hem and ran his lascivious hands upon her flesh. I felt the hammer tight within my grip and wished I knew whether Gobbo was back in the house with Jacopo. We had a single chance to escape their grasp. I would not allow Delapole to savage her again, but I was determined that if I was forced to strike, I would deliver a blow that granted us all freedom.

Then Rebecca sent every idea fleeing straight out of my head. She dragged herself away from the Englishman and spat full in his face. He paused and wiped the spittle from his cheeks, with a wry smile that said she would surely pay for this impertinence.

"You shall not touch me again," Rebecca said coldly. "I will claw your eyes out if you try. This charade about your talent I'll tolerate if only for the safety of my brother and Lorenzo. The rest you shall not have. I carry Lorenzo's child. I will not have it soiled in my belly by the likes of you."

Marchese's words of warning rang through my head. I felt the strength drain from my limbs and leaned back against the wall, scarcely able to keep the hammer in my grip.

The Englishman stood upright instantly and buttoned his fly. "Lorenzo's child, eh?" he asked without expression. "How sweet. You did not mention this before, my love."

She smoothed down her dress and sat motionless on the carpet, her arms around her knees. I fought to catch my breath and squeeze a single rational thought from my mind.

"I say it now. You mark it well. I'll not have your poison stain what's unborn inside me."

"A child," he repeated, seeming calm and pensive. I tried to catch Rebecca's eye again and failed. If we had to, we must both attempt to tackle him in order to break free.

Delapole strode to the window and stared out at the canal. "You know," he said, "I thought I would not have to face this so soon. You have rushed me, girl. You have lured me into Procrustes' bed before I am ready. Such a waste."

Slowly she stood upright and backed towards the door, still unaware of my presence. "The time is late," she said. "We should be going."

He turned and waved a hand at her. "Oh, no. Now there's new business to conclude. You have demanded it. A child . . ." His face astonished me. He seemed in full possession of himself, yet distant, too, as if another Delapole lived inside his skin and had come to the surface to claim a little time in that long English frame.

"I hear someone come, sir," Rebecca said. "On the stairs."

There was no sound. The house was as silent as the tomb. She could retreat no further without making it clear she intended to leave the room. I waited and prepared to act.

"And I have demanded nothing," she observed. "Nothing but some decency."

"No?" He took a single stride forwards, hands still clasped to his breast. "Oh, come, Rebecca. Admit the truth, for we both know it. There is but one woman in the world. You may call her Eve. You may call her Lilith; it's all the same to me. She takes a man's life from his seed and uses it to breed his death in her belly. Had I known this earlier, I should have ripped that little upstart out of your body before it began to grow. But then we should have been denied the pleasure of each other's company, girl. That would have been such a shame."

"Sir . . ."

He shook a fist at her and came two steps closer. I gripped the handle of the hammer tightly and watched him like a hawk. "*Silence, child!* I'll not let it happen. Oh, no." He reached into his jacket and retrieved something from his person. I stared, aghast. Clenched in his right fist was a long, slim knife like that of a physician's. "You always make it come to this in the end. The same old deception. The same old cure. Now, be still and make it easier for yourself. I'll . . ."

He moved towards her. I leapt out from behind the curtain, swinging that crude weapon in both hands.

"Lorenzo," the villain said softly, staring strangely at me. "Such a rude intrusion does not become you."

The hammer caught him on the right shoulder. His arm shot back. The knife fell to the floor, where I kicked it hard, sending it scuttering into the corner of the room. Delapole tumbled to his knees, his hand clutching the sleeve of his white shirt from which a single point of blood soon began to grow into a broad, round stain.

I took Rebecca's arm. She stared at the Englishman, unable or unwilling to move. "We must go," I told her. "Now."

"Where is Jacopo?" she asked me.

As Delapole squirmed on the floor, he made no complaint, no moan, as if he felt the agony I must have inflicted on him as nothing more than a distant annoyance. "I don't know. He was supposed to be here, helping you escape. The house seems empty."

"Dead, dead, dead, oh, good boy, Gobbo ..." Delapole laughed at us and then, to my amazement, stood straight upright, shook his bloody arm as if to cure it, and gave us both a gracious bow. "One Jew's enough on this payroll, girl. D'you think I really wanted to feed him too? Gobbo went to find him, but not to fetch him back. Now, to return to business ..."

He strode over and, with his one good arm, reached down and retrieved the knife from the corner where it lay. Then he walked back to us, his bloody shoulder hanging from its socket, and struck feints with the blade through the air.

"Lorenzo ..." Rebecca whispered. "It cannot be possible...."

"I saw," I answered. "Now, run."

She went away from Delapole, across to the fireplace, and picked up a long poker which lay there. "Not without you," she answered. "Not without my brother."

Delapole could not decide which of us to lunge for first. He simply stood there, grinning, as if this were some game.

"You will not go?" he asked. "Good. I like that spirit. I like that...."

I almost fell to him. He dashed to one side and swept the air with that long knife, so viciously and with such speed it seemed impossible I had wounded him at all. Seeing that sharp line of metal cut towards me, I pulled the velvet drape to one side, watched it slice through the fabric like a scalpel through soft flesh, then jabbed the hammer into his face. Delapole staggered back, off balance, and Rebecca was there, dashing him in the head with one long arc of her poker. He clutched his skull and mewled like a wounded cat, then fell to his knees. I would have no more of this.

"Come," I cried. "This madman's best left for the city to deal with."

I had her hand. I stared into her lovely face. In that instant we were closer to each other than we had been for days. She moved. Then the creature on the floor roared, "No!" And I saw, flying through the air, that devilish blade. Rebecca screamed and fell to her knees, clutching her thigh. The knife had bitten deep into her leg. Dark blood welled out from the wound and stained her dress. I grasped the hilt, withdrew it, and pulled up the hem. A red slit had opened just above her knee, a good two inches across, and now was bleeding badly.

I tore a strip from her hem. "Tie this," I urged. "It will staunch the blood. And *now* we shall be gone."

Her eyes did not meet mine. Their point of focus lay behind me, and I knew, without turning, what it was.

"Lorenzo," the Englishman whispered, and I was a little cheered to hear a wheeze and some hurt inside his voice.

I twisted round to face him. He was a sorry mess, with a

bloody arm and a bloody head. Yet he stood nonetheless, as erect and forthright as a soldier on parade, and would, I knew, be at me, weapon or no, in a moment.

I covered Rebecca with my body. "You are a stubborn fellow, Englishman," I said. "What must I do? Break your legs so you cannot walk? Beat you until you stand no more?"

He bowed his head again and beamed in that familiar way. "Why, you must kill me, boy. Or wait until I do you a similar honour. This day. Tomorrow. Next week. Next year. It matters nothing to me. I have all the time in the world."

The hammer lay between us on the floor. He shuffled towards it. I could not believe we must fight again.

"You are insane," I said. "Perhaps they will lock you in the asylum, not send you to the block which you deserve."

"Deserts. Deserts. Who gets 'em, eh? Not their rightful owners, I think."

He fell towards the weapon. My foot shot out and pulled it back from his grasp. He squirmed on the floor and looked up at me, still grinning.

"You have a very narrow definition of triumph, Lorenzo," he said. "As do all Italians."

I refused to listen to more and gripped Rebecca about the waist. She seemed close to fainting from the pain.

"Lorenzo!" Delapole barked. "Ask who beds her best. Ask whose tongue is more agile and finds the most delicious morsels. Ask who turns above her sweetly and never allows release until she begs. *Ask whose child she really bears. . . .*"

She moaned and stared at me with open eyes that could not lie. I turned and gazed at the bloody wretch on the floor.

"Oh, fool," he spat at me. "Do you think that fiddle carried no price? I placed it in her lap and followed there soon after. Though her breeding and her other talents remained, I must admit, a secret till you revealed them."

I looked into her eyes, seeking some denial. She said nothing but retreated from my arms.

"Poor Lorenzo," Delapole sneered. "And now . . ."

Whatever else he said escaped me. The redness was rising in my head as never before. If this was what Delapole wished, then so be it.

"Now I put an end to this," I answered, and picked up the hammer.

She watched me begin, then, for reasons I did not at first understand, joined me with the dagger. There, on the second floor of Ca' Dario, we butchered the man we knew as Oliver Delapole, methodically, with the hammer and the knife, as carefully as he must have slaughtered those women who were unfortunate to cross him in the past. We battered and we stabbed, to a constant, beating rhythm that filled the air with blood and the stench of meat, until all the spirit of this fiend was gone from the face of the earth. I knew at that moment that I should never again close my eyes and see an empty blackness. In this place there would forever be this deep, red stain and the plashy sound of metal upon flesh.

He laughed at us between the blows. This was a transformation for us all, and he had wrought it. Towards the last, when the blood was welling in his throat so much he was close to losing the power of speech, he muttered something. It was only after, when we had swiftly changed our gore-stained clothes and planned to stumble out of that charnel house, that I believed I remembered the quotation, though by then my brain was so fevered that I might have imagined it instead. The words were from the English poet Milton, in *Paradise Lost*.

Who overcomes
By force, hath overcome but half his foe.

Only part of Oliver Delapole died in Ca' Dario that evening. The rest now lay inside us, like an infection that had darted into our blood, inseminating it with his devilish seed. By making us his murderers, he became our conqueror. Rebecca joined me in his slaughter that we might share the shame.

This much became apparent in that room by the Grand Canal as the long Venetian day made way for night. Deranged, in despair, I fell towards the great window overlooking the water, as if some kind of redemption lay beyond the glass. There was the strangest sight of all. Not the Venice I knew and now hated, familiar, heartless, and cold as the grave. Another view greeted my eyes, so outlandish I knew myself to be mad. Gone were the gondolas with their lamps, like fireflies on the water. In their place was a multitude of vessels, huge craft that lumbered across the channel, carrying scores of curiously dressed individuals on their backs. Around them were middling boats, bigger than gondolas and twice as fast, all scurrying across the surface with not an oarsman in sight.

The skyline of the city stood out against an aura of queer light, burning yellow yet too bright to be even the fiercest of torches. Outlandish structures, like the skeletons of great beasts, loomed over the western end of San Marco as if about to devour the buildings beneath their giant jaws. This was another world beyond the leaded panes of Ca' Dario, one that was both familiar and untouchable. . . .

I felt the blood turn solid in my veins. Here was some glimpse of paradise, perhaps, or a vision of some coming hell. Paralysed, I stood transfixed by that window, wishing I could reach out through the glass and touch this apparition which lived and breathed somewhere in the universe, quite unaware of my presence. Or so I thought.

Then, beneath me, on the stern of one of those great iron vessels, a face stared back at mine. A young child, a girl in a white dress, looked up, and—like me, cursed with some third eye—peered full into my face across whatever vast chasm of existence separated us. This ghost of the future *saw*. And what she saw sent such screaming terror through her mind . . . at the sight of me.

One lifetime is insufficient. Some of us have more to atone for than a single span can embrace. I watched the child's dread gaze, stared at my bloody hands, and, like a beast, I roared.

62

The treasure trove

MASSITER TOLD THE WATER TAXI TO DROP THEM AT the western end of the Zattere waterfront. Here the ancient city met the fringe of modern blocks that ran from the port north towards Piazzale Roma. There was the smell of marine fuel on the air and, beyond that, car fumes from the vast parking arena which sat at the city's landward limit. But there were old buildings, too, low, stately shapes lurking in the half-lit streets. They walked away from the Giudecca canal, then crossed a small bridge, dodged through a pitch-black alley, and came out in a cobbled *campo* by a featureless church.

Massiter came to a halt in the square, next to a column topped by a small, winged lion just visible in the puny yellow spotlights of the church. He looked around them, sniffing at the air.

"Do you see anyone?" he murmured. Daniel scanned the square and said he could not detect a living soul in the neighbourhood.

"I imagine you're right," Massiter agreed. "This is one of the oldest parts of the city, you know. If they dug a little hereabouts, I can't imagine what they'd find. San Niccolò there is half-Byzantine, and only a little modernised by the vandals."

"It's late," Daniel said. "Let's finish our business, Hugo."

The older man surveyed the empty *campo* once more. "Of course. You won't let me down, will you?"

"Meaning what, precisely?"

"Oh, Daniel. Please. I'm doing you a great favour here. I've had this private storeroom a decade or more, and hardly a soul outside my circle has seen it. Some would love to know its location. Thieves."

"I know no thieves, Hugo."

"Really? The police, then."

"I see no police."

"No."

Massiter set off at a brisk pace to the northern corner of the square. Daniel followed.

"I had a cousin in the movie business," Massiter explained. "He worked on that Roeg film. They made it in that church, mostly. We got together now and then and..."

They crossed a small bridge, moving into darkness. "The point is, a man needs a haven. Somewhere, in those days, where we could take a couple of women. Smoke something. Be private. And later..."

"What happened to your cousin?"

"Dead," Massiter declared without emotion. "An accident. He was a poor businessman. Tragic, really. I felt terribly let down."

They turned a corner into a narrow alley and, after a few paces, stopped in front of a modern metal door, which Massiter swiftly opened. Daniel followed him inside. A series of fluorescent lights came on. He stared at row upon row of packing cases.

"A friend's shipping business," Massiter explained. "Nothing to do with me, you understand. But here..."

He walked along the left-hand wall, then halted in front of a battered green door closed with several heavy padlocks. Massiter took out a set of keys and began to throw the bars back, cursing the stiffness of the mechanisms. Then he reached inside, flicked a light switch, and Daniel saw, leading down into the earth, a narrow brick-lined tunnel with a worn floor of stone steps.

"My fancy," Massiter said, "is that it was a wine store at one time. Perhaps converted from some ancient crypt. Who knows? You did pull the outside door shut, didn't you? Damned if I can be bothered with all these padlocks until we go out again."

"Of course," Daniel replied.

"Good," Massiter said, then reached into his pocket and pulled out a small black handgun. "Here. Take this. If we're interrupted, shoot the bastards."

Daniel stared at the weapon. "Hugo, this isn't my business."

The older man's eyes flared. "But it's very much your business. What's the problem? I can make a single phone call and have the evidence out of here in a flash. It won't be the first time, you know."

"I see."

"Oh, dear!" Massiter said, smiling. "Daniel, you're a fraud, an impostor. You could have been in jail by Monday if you'd gone ahead with this nonsensical notion of baring your breast to the public. Please. Don't play the innocent with me now."

Daniel held out the gun. "I won't use this thing."

"Just hold it for me, then," Massiter answered, and set off down the stairs. Daniel followed slowly, leaving the door open as he had with the outer entrance. There was as yet no sound behind. Giulia Morelli had warned him her timing might be difficult. The gun sat cold in his hand.

After twenty steps, the low ceiling disappeared and a maw of darkness stood in front of them. Massiter threw another light switch on the wall. Daniel suppressed a gasp of astonishment. They stood on the threshold of a vast, curved crypt supported by a forest of columns, each surmounted by a gentle brick arch. The place was spotless, as if it had been recently swept. The worn cobblestones had a dull sheen. Arranged around the capacious floor was a collection of objects hidden under wraps: furniture, the rectangular outlines of paintings, and other shapes he could not recognise. In the far corner, out of place, sat a low, modern bed.

He followed Massiter across the room, towards the crumpled sheets on the low divan. Massiter sniffed. There was the unmistakable outline of bloodstains in the centre of the white cotton.

"Damn," he said. "The trouble with these secret places is one must, from time to time, look after them oneself. I omitted to clear up after my discussion with your friend Rizzo. But then I didn't realise I'd have a visitor."

Daniel's head whirled. "Rizzo?"

"Ah. You never knew his name? The thieving little bastard who sold you my Guarneri. Told me so himself eventually, though I had guessed already, naturally. Never trust a Venetian, Daniel. They always let you down in the end."

Daniel said nothing. Massiter laughed and slapped him on the shoulder.

"No offence taken on my part. I was grateful for it. Finally convinced me I had a pupil on my hands."

"I am not—"

"Of course not! Well, what shall it be?"

Massiter set off around the room, snatching the wraps off each treasure as he passed.

"We have a very full collection here. Some Russian gold, liberated by the Nazis? A Bosnian ikon, perhaps? A reliquary from Byzantium? Or some porcelain by way of Shanghai? No..."

He dashed across the room and removed the cover from a large painting. Daniel was unable to keep his eyes off the work. It was vast and set in a fine gilt frame. The artist's hand was plainly Venetian and familiar. It depicted, with a fluid, savage grace, two naked men grappling to the death, one wielding a flashing silver knife over the other.

"Titian, or Tiziano, if you prefer," Massiter noted. "Cain slaying Abel. Better than the one in Salute, I'm sure you'll agree. That was the trial run for my darling here."

"Where do you get these things, Hugo?"

Massiter glowered at him. "Please, Daniel. One must never ask a collector that." He stared at the painting. "My sympathies tend to lie with Cain, I'm afraid. But I imagine that's what you'd expect."

Daniel stood between Massiter and the tunnel leading to the ground floor. There was, he felt sure, some faint sound above.

"Well!" Massiter urged. "Let's find a gift for you. The Titian is out of the question, of course. It would produce no end of problems for us both in the public domain, and I don't think you're ready—quite—for your own little treasure house. But there are items here that have no difficult antecedents. This is for you, Daniel, isn't it? Not for the auction? I sell myself, from time to time, but I'd be offended if I thought it was mere money that you sought."

There was a distant noise. He hoped that Massiter had not heard it.

"Why do you keep these objects, Hugo?" he asked. "What use are they, hidden away here like this?"

Massiter blinked. "They are *mine*. What other use do they need?"

"And are people yours too?"

"If I desire them. And only if they're willing, of course. I can't tempt the saintly. I go only where I'm invited. You, of all people, must realise that."

Daniel stared at the bed in the corner. Massiter followed the direction of his gaze.

"That's just a bed."

"For what?"

Massiter smiled. "Many uses. Mainly pleasurable. To me, at least."

"Tell me, Hugo. The girl. From ten years ago. Her body was found near here. You took her to that bed?"

"Susanna Gianni? Of course." He shrugged. "At least, I tried. She was beautiful. She owed me much, and would now be even greater in my debt had she lived."

Daniel became more aware of the weapon in his grasp.

"Don't misunderstand me," Massiter insisted. "As I said, I enjoy a little fight. But she was still breathing when I was done. Had she taken my advice to wait awhile and recover her composure, I feel sure she would still be alive now. Whoever threw the poor girl into that canal, it was not me. I didn't wish her dead, Daniel. Why should I, when she had such exquisite uses left? Besides..."

He placed a hand on his chin, searching for the correct words. "I wasn't finished with that child, to be frank. I still feel cheated. There's a mystery there that continues to puzzle me." Massiter walked forward to stand in front of him, eyeing the gun. "You have to choose your gift. That's why we came."

Daniel gazed into his face, seeing no emotion, no humanity there. "I would like the Guarneri back, of course. And I should like the music I found, Hugo. All of it."

"Ah!" Massiter declared. "Scacchi was clever. He saw your potential. Much sooner than I did. Have you thought of that?"

Some foreign flame of anger rose in Daniel Forster's mind. "A fiddle and some music, Hugo. You killed Paul for such small things? And Scacchi too?"

Hugo Massiter bellowed with laughter. "Do me justice, Daniel. I killed them both outright. I had a little fellow I know sneak into that hospital on the Lido and smother Scacchi gently while the stupid nurses were dozing. They were a close pair, in any case. It would have been a sin to leave one alive. I could tell that night I visited. The American was no pushover once I made my intentions clear. He left me little choice."

Daniel's rage left him speechless. Massiter seemed amused by his reaction. "Don't be too cross with me. I would have killed Scacchi myself, out of courtesy, had it been possible. A mite risky, though. It was not done with malice, you understand. I couldn't have him waking up and telling all and sundry about how I called on them, could I?"

"But why did you visit them in the first place, Hugo? They were small men. They were dying. This is all beneath you, surely?"

Massiter seemed disappointed. "I'm amazed you have to ask. Because they had stolen something precious of mine and refused to return it. What greater crime can there be? I was robbed, Daniel, and cheated by that old man. It was all quite uncalled-for."

Daniel lifted the gun and pointed it at Massiter's face. "I could kill you, Hugo. I don't care about the consequences."

"Of course!" Massiter shrugged. "But I can't give you the Guarneri. Or the music. They didn't have them. Said they'd spirited the lot somewhere else. At least they did after Scacchi started his wheezing and I'd stuck that American plenty of times to get him talking. The trouble was, by that time they made such a noise I had no choice but to be out of there. Footsteps on the stairs. I believed they were yours, and I'm not one to hang around when the numbers don't add up. Besides, it was a ruse; I was sure of that. Those two wanted me out of the place. Yet the instrument really wasn't there at all, was it? You see what I mean about the mystery?"

Massiter wore his most pleasant smile. Daniel felt the weight of the weapon in his fingers. The barrel was no more than a few inches from Massiter's face.

"Well? We don't have all evening. What is your price to be? Not the Guarneri, for sure. I don't have it. Me instead?"

Daniel looked into the grey eyes and saw the amusement there. He knew he was being taunted. He lowered the gun and said, "After a fashion."

"Oh?" The sense of pleasure in his expression never diminished.

There was the sound of feet moving on the stairs. Massiter turned theatrically towards the entrance. Giulia Morelli strode into the cellar, followed by a tall dark man in jeans and a white shirt who held, conspicuously, a long police revolver in front of him.

"Captain?" Massiter said pleasantly. "You surely haven't been eavesdropping? Such a rude habit."

Giulia Morelli walked briskly in front of them, then forced Massiter's arms into the air, checking for a weapon. He held his hands above her, amused, holding open his jacket, exposing a fat leather wallet in the inside pocket. "How much? Take what you like."

"What?" she snapped.

"My dear, I can bribe you. Or I can bribe your superior. Or his, come to that. There are so many fleas feeding on one another in this city. Your rank in the pecking order is of no interest to me. What crime is there here to interest you? A little smuggling—"

"Three murders, Signor Massiter," she said. "And Susanna Gianni."

"Ah," he said, remembering. "You still have a bee in your bonnet about that girl. It's all so much history, surely?"

"You're a powerful man. But you won't bribe your way out of this. We may behave with dignity, I think? If we go to the station now, we can avoid much fuss. Much publicity."

"Surely not?" Massiter asked. "I wouldn't want to disappoint you."

She shuffled on her feet nervously. Daniel looked at the stairs. They were on their own. She seemed to expect some support. "I have limited patience," she said. "Please."

"Ah," Massiter said, seeing her companion. "Biagio! You are well?"

She stared at the figure opposite, uncomprehending. The young policeman held the gun loosely at his side.

"*Sì*, Signor Massiter."

Massiter nodded. "I am glad to hear it. And I still owe you, naturally, for that news of our friend Rizzo. And the rest. I remain most grateful."

Giulia Morelli's face fell. "Biagio...?" she asked.

Massiter yawned. "Oh, for God's sake, man. Kill the bitch, will you? She bores me so."

Daniel saw the revolver rise from Biagio's side, and leapt forward, fumbling with his own weapon, struggling as Massiter pounced, then punched him once, hard, on the back of the neck, forcing him to the ground, where two powerful hands wrestled with his.

The cavernous room was filled with an explosion that hurt the ears and echoed around the bare bricks. Daniel looked up from the floor and saw Giulia Morelli staggering slowly backwards, a neat black hole in the fabric of her dark jacket, something liquid pumping from it. Biagio watched greedily, gun ready for a second shot if he needed it. Then she fell against the wall and slumped to the ground. Her mouth opened, her throat formed some unidentifiable word, she breathed blood that ran over her lips and formed a long, dark stain down her chin.

"Damn woman," Massiter cursed angrily, then reached down and dragged Daniel to his feet. The gun was back where it belonged, tight in Massiter's strong fist. "What on earth were you doing, boy? Running with her when you could be running with me? *Me!* The only one who's never lied to you!"

Daniel looked at the fury in his eyes. It was as if this were the greatest betrayal, more cruel than any other.

"I made a choice, Hugo," he replied. "Not the right choice or the wrong one. Merely *my* choice."

The cold gaze never left him. "And I tell you such things, Daniel? That I killed your friends. That I kill who I like. You've a gun in your hand, and still you do nothing."

Massiter eyed the weapon. The gun rose in his fist. He held it to Daniel's face. There was a sound from the opposite wall. Giulia Morelli groaned, still living, but by a thread.

"You're an enigma to me, Daniel," Massiter declared. "At times you show such promise. Then . . ."

A knowing grin broke Massiter's puzzlement. "Of course! I understand! You think I play games with you." The barrel of the gun touched Daniel's temple. "You think I tempt you with empty promises and an empty chamber. Oh, Daniel."

He withdrew a little. Biagio stood next to them, immobile.

"You misunderstand me so."

His hand rose, finger tight on the trigger, then turned. The room rang to the deafening noise again. Daniel saw Biagio's forehead open in front of him, saw the force of the blast, despatched by Massiter's hand from only a few inches, send the policeman flying backwards through the air. He crumpled to the floor and lay still. Massiter stared at his body. "I am a good master," he murmured. "But the police...It's all about money. Nothing else."

The air stank of blood and the sharp scent of powder. Massiter came close to him again. Daniel closed his eyes and felt the metal on his cheek.

"We could clean this mess up," Massiter said. "One phone call. I have people. It would be wise, perhaps, to stay out of Venice for a little while. Keep out of the public eye. But everything blows over here, with a little time, a little money."

Daniel said nothing.

"I'll reward you," Massiter said. "More than anything you can find in this room."

"Go to hell," Daniel whispered, aware that he was trembling now. "I'm not like you."

Massiter gripped his hair and pressed the weapon harder to his cheek. "Everyone's like me. It's only a question of the proportions."

Daniel tried to think of Laura. And of Amy, magnificent in the nave of La Pietà, making such sounds from her instrument. A world lived inside his head, composed, ordered, complete. It could contain him forever and never allow Hugo Massiter entrance.

Shivering, prepared, not frightened, Daniel Forster stood upright in the crypt, waiting to die. Then, abruptly, Massiter's grip relaxed. There was no noise, no sudden pain or blackness. Finally, Daniel opened his eyes.

Hugo Massiter had left the cellar without making a sound. Two handguns now lay on the floor next to the body of Biagio. On the far side of the room, Giulia Morelli was motionless, barely breathing. Daniel could hear her snatched gasps.

He ran to her, picked the phone out of her bag, knowing he

would have to go outside to use it. Then he touched her forehead, felt a little warmth on the skin. She opened her eyes.

"Daniel?" Her voice sounded ghostly.

"Don't say anything. Massiter's gone. You're safe. I'm going outside to call an ambulance. You'll be fine."

She moved a hand to her chest, felt the sticky wetness there, looked at him, and tried to laugh. "Don't talk nonsense. Let me tell you something."

"No. Just wait."

"Daniel?" Her hand clutched his arm. He waited. Something was happening to her eyes. They were fading; the life was falling out of them.

"Daniel..."

Giulia Morelli whispered a single, cryptic sentence, then said no more.

63

Report from the watch

From the journal of Captain Giuseppe Cornaro of the
Dorsoduro night troop, September 17th, 1733.

THE VILLAIN LORENZO SCACCHI IS DEAD. I LUGGED HIS
cursed carcass to the block myself and watched in satisfaction as
the Doge's executioner despatched him to the region where he belongs.
In all my years of guarding the Republic from foul devils, I have never,
I believe, come across a young rogue such as this. His cunning was
matched only by his capacity for cruel violence and, oh!, such damage
has he done. Thanks to this vicious criminal, the city has lost much: a
publisher, his uncle, no less, and owner of a much-reputed name. Then,
in his last hours upon this earth, the life of one who sought nothing more
than to enrich the Republic with his talents and generosity. The good
and meek are snatched into God's bosom by the vile and low. I am no
priest, so I do not pretend to know why such filthy deeds occur. We must,
on the Dorsoduro watch, merely observe their enactment and then
attempt to remedy the consequences as best we might.

The facts of the uncle's murder are well-known. Those surrounding the
death of the English gentleman Oliver Delapole appear to be the subject of
much rumour in the city, a good deal apparently started by Scacchi

himself, since documents in his abode show his handwriting closely resembles that on several of the anonymous notes which have come into our possession. I set down now what we, as the legal authorities, know and in so doing assure those who read this report that there is no more of material value to be gleaned from further investigation. A base criminal is dead. The sad aftermath of his actions lives on. We must waste no more of the state's time and money adding to an executed felon's list of charges.

So that justice be done to the dead Delapole (and the vociferous English consul assuaged) let me state here and now that we find no evidence, save our villain's mischievous lies, of any wrongdoing on his part. There were debts, it is true, but then what gentleman does not from time to time rely a little upon the bank? There was the contested matter of his authorship of this mysterious concerto. I am no artist myself, sirs, merely a hunter of the facts. In this case I would ask a single question: if Delapole did not write this work, as he claimed, then who did? For none other has come forward to place his name by the frontispiece, not even an obvious fraudster. This nonsense about there being a curse upon the piece, I dismiss instantly. If the composer lived—and surely could re-create the work from his own head—why would he remain silent? Even if he never wrote another note in his life, he would be assured fame and fortune for this single effort alone. No, Delapole was the composer, surely, and the gossip spread about by his murderer was merely some ruse by which to ruin him. Thus it seems an even greater tragedy that every last piece of paper relating to this concerto appears to have been destroyed by the scoundrel himself after he bludgeoned its author to death.

The dead Roman I dismiss entirely as a lunatic. I have interviewed those who spoke to him when he first arrived, babbling about Delapole's past and making wild and wholly unsubstantiated accusations. The man was unbalanced. That he knew Scacchi cannot be in doubt. I have evidence that the young rogue stayed with him in Rome and perhaps there unhinged his mind so effectively that the old fellow followed him to Venice and attempted to make mischief. Marchese's arrival threatened to foul

Scacchi's game and the result we know well. I have an army of witnesses who saw him standing over the old man's body with the bloody knife that killed him still dripping in his hand. What more must one require?

Some reason for all this, you shall say, and with justification. The dark depths of Scacchi's deeds are well documented, yet we continue to lack an explanation for them. The answer must lie in a woman, of course. There was one. After we called on Delapole to discuss the matter of Marchese's accusations and found his shattered corpse instead, I went to speak to those who had been in his household. A female, young and beautiful, had been there for several days and was known to Scacchi too. She is gone. Perhaps her corpse lies at the floor of the lagoon, despatched there by this jealous villain. There is no way of knowing, and I venture that it matters little. We understand the nature of the deeds and the identity of their perpetrator. He has met his much-deserved fate. All else is idle chatter, and as guardian of the Republic's citizens, I have no time for that. The beast is dead, and for once I shall not pray for a departed soul. I saw his handiwork. It was hard to believe that the pile of flesh and tattered rags upon the floor in that fine mansion had once walked and talked—and written fine music. Even that it had ever been a man at all.

As to the manner of Scacchi's apprehension, I shall offer a brief description. As I noted, I was sent, with no urgency, to talk to the Englishman on several matters and found, on my arrival, the dreadful tragedy I have described. Close by the house, in an alley near the rio, my guards discovered one who had, it seemed, apprehended the villain as he sought to flee. During the scrap that ensued, young Scacchi—whom the fellow recognised, having seen him in the neighbourhood before—was sorely wounded in the chest and face, the latter so badly that he could speak not a single comprehensible word. Not that it was needed. We could see, with our own eyes, the extent of his criminal deeds and would have held him anyway, without the warrant over his uncle's brutal slaying.

There was, I scarcely need add, no need for the expense of a full trial. That excellent magistrate Cortelazzo hurried from a dinner party to listen to our case while Scacchi slumped, half-dead, on a chair in the dock, with his apprehender beside him. A sterling fellow this chap was too. Had he waited afterwards, I would have commended him for some gift from the city funds. He was, it seems, a physician on his rounds when he encountered Scacchi, panic-stricken and bloody, who demanded money and immediately set about him. For once the villain met his match. The fellow's profession proved fortuitous, for I wonder if the scoundrel would have survived long enough to be dragged to the block without his tending. But like many a Venetian, when it comes to a crisis, he answers the call and asks no reward. After I saw Scacchi despatched by the axe, I turned and he was gone. I have his name, however—Guillaume—and an address in Cannaregio. One day when times are quieter, I will visit him and say a word of thanks. It is from such folk—good Christians all—that Venice is made.

I shall, accordingly, conclude. The world is rid of another villain, though not without the loss of two good and talented men at his bloody hands. That old serpent visited us and found us ready. There is no cause for rejoicing, but I do believe we may allow ourselves a little satisfaction. On a single point I will, however, offer criticism. We would have apprehended Scacchi much more rapidly had we been better informed. The descriptions of him on the city posters—and I know not where they come from—speak of an average lad of average build and comely appearance. Perhaps he wrote them himself, for in real life, bloodied and injured as he was, it was clear to see that Lorenzo Scacchi was the ugliest individual it has ever been my privilege to despatch to Hades. Even without a knife split down it, his face would have been hideous. Furthermore, on his back stood the distinct makings of a hump such as one might find on a cripple or a leper. Had young Guillaume not confirmed his identity for us, I fear he would have escaped, for all our efforts.

Perhaps sweet Jesus smiled on us that moment and, through that good doctor, shone a beam that penetrated this beast's disguise. In future I should prefer a few hard facts to save our Lord the trouble.

64

The edge of the lagoon

DANIEL FORSTER HAD NOT FOUGHT THE CHARGES with much enthusiasm. Two police officers were dead. Large sums of money had been elicited by fraud from several well-known musical institutions around the world. The true perpetrator was Hugo Massiter, as the public and the prosecutors knew. But Massiter was gone, vanished from the face of the earth the night Giulia Morelli and Biagio died. Daniel remained, willing to admit his supporting role in some of Massiter's misdeeds, the only culprit a vengeful criminal system could find. Unable to charge him in relation to the murders, the prosecutors had raised the stakes on the embezzlement case and succeeded in winning a three-year jail term, which Daniel, much to their fury, accepted with a humble shrug of the shoulders.

He found no cause to argue. Some desire for atonement nagged him constantly. He wished for time to think too. In the small, modern cell in Mestre which he shared with an engaging Padua gangster named Toni, Daniel began to construct some explanations for the events which had engulfed him that long, dangerous summer. He was a popular prisoner, teaching his cell mate English, striking up a strong friendship which would, both men knew, survive their release. There were individuals in jail there who were of use to him too. They confirmed what Giulia Morelli had already told him. Scacchi owed money to no one. The house, which was now his, was free of debt. With the balance of Scacchi's estate, he became a man of a little means, even after the fines the court had imposed. Within four months, when it was clear to the prison authorities that he had no intention of trying to run away, he was increasingly allowed out of the jail to spend days in the city to further his education. They were not to know that he would soon abandon his now tenuous links with Oxford for a different sphere of research.

The property had been his first focus of attention. He had sold the near-derelict adjoining warehouse to raise money to pay for the main building's restoration. Within the space of a year, Ca' Scacchi was neighbour to three smart apartments, two of them American-owned, served by a renovated bridge across the *rio*. As he supervised the building work, and the refurbishment of the cellar where he and Laura had found the manuscript, his interest was drawn increasingly to the question of the concerto's authorship. The work was fast becoming a standard item in the orchestral repertoire, performed around the world. The infamous mystery which surrounded its appearance in Venice did the takings no harm at all. All the same, Daniel never once doubted the work deserved its acclaim. It had its lighter flourishes and occasionally stooped to some shameless fireworks in order to dazzle the listener. Yet there were such depths, too, and they continued to astound him even though he now felt he knew every note.

With the help of the supportive prison governor, he had gained an unlimited reader's ticket to the Archivio di Stato, the archives which contained every last surviving document of the Venetian Republic. The building was behind the Frari, a stone's throw from San Rocco. He spent months there, poring over the thousands of pages the city's clerks had scribbled throughout 1733. For weeks it seemed a fruitless task. Then, half a year after he was sentenced, he stumbled over a fragment of a report from the Dorsoduro night watch. Most of the document had been destroyed by damp and mould. A single paragraph remained legible in its entirety, but it was sufficient. There was a clear reference to the "mysterious concerto" and a death connected with the work. There was also a name, that of an Englishman who was, the report confirmed, the undoubted author of the piece, and the revelation that all papers connected with the piece had been destroyed after its composer's death, for unknown reasons. There was no clue why the original should have been hidden behind the brickwork in Ca' Scacchi, though it seemed likely that one of Scacchi's ancestors might have been hired to print the original scores.

Much enjoyable research remained before this single scrap of information could be turned into something resembling fact. Every weekday, he was released from the prison and took the bus to Piazzale Roma, then walked to the archive, trawling its miles of shelves for more evidence. The name Delapole was mentioned elsewhere, though never in connection with music. There were, as the night watch reported, debts. A few fragments of private papers also made comments on the man's character, which was, by all accounts, cultured and charming. Over the weeks, Daniel assembled every last scrap of information he could find about Delapole. When he wanted to think, he would walk round the corner and sit in the upper hall of San Rocco, beneath Lucifer's shadow, and let these facts roam around his imagination, trying to see where they might fit alongside one another.

After ten months he had assembled a story of a kind and come to realise that it could be complete only if he were to tell another tale: that of how the lost concerto came to be found. So, alongside the tragic account of Oliver Delapole, another emerged from his mind: of Hugo Massiter, an act of deception, and a wily friend named Scacchi who came to pay for his cunning with his life. There were lacunae in this account, as several interested publishers were anxious to point out. But Daniel was adamant: this was fact, not fiction. It could have no cosy, rounded closing act. Mysteries would always remain in the story, and he was unsure that even Hugo Massiter, were he ever to reappear, could explain them all.

A deal was concluded. A book made its way into print with a rapidity Daniel found surprising. The anonymous concerto, as it was now becoming known, continued to create a stir around the world. No publisher wanted to miss the bandwagon. By the time he qualified for early release, twenty months into his sentence, Daniel Forster's book was an international success. He was mildly wealthy, with his own mansion in the heart of the city and the promise of a continuing career as a writer. A return to Oxford never entered his head. There remained a more important task.

One Monday in September, Toni called. He had an address and also a suggestion. He had been looking for many weeks and remained unsure. People changed. There were no recent photographs. It made sense to see her first, in public, before risking the embarrassment of visiting her at home.

The following day Daniel sat on the number one *vaporetto* as it crawled across the lagoon towards the Lido. He thought of his first voyage on these flat, uncertain waters, just over two years before in the good ship *Sophia*, captained, for a while at least, by a dog named Xerxes. No one noticed him. He now wore a thin moustache, and his hair was more closely cropped. This change in his appearance helped keep the curious away.

He watched the jetty bob towards him, unsure of his own feelings. Once ashore, he turned south for a mile, towards the residential area where the market was held. This was another side of Venice, more ordinary, more like the outside world. The Lido had cars and buses. The stink of diesel sat alongside the perfume of oleander bushes.

He crossed the canal that led to the Lido casino, then followed a broad, tree-lined avenue which ran to the shoreline. The city hung low in the distance across the lagoon, a tantalising horizon dominated by the campanile in the square. The street was now given over to a busy market. Daniel put on a pair of sunglasses, then strode forward and soon found himself lost in a pushing, grumbling mass of people arguing vigorously among stalls of clothes and vegetables, fish and cheese.

It took only minutes to find her. Laura stood at the counter of a van near the exit, haggling over a vast chunk of Parmesan. She wore the white nylon housecoat. Her hair was tied back as before. She seemed not a day older. He could remember the smell of her, the touch of her skin. Then she was gone, out towards the main road. He followed, but she had already caught one of the orange buses that meandered along the long main drag of the Lido, from the little airport in the north to Alberoni at the opposite tip of the island. Shaking, he pulled out the address Toni had given him, went outside, and caught the next bus south.

It took ten minutes to reach Alberoni. He had never travelled this far in the lagoon. There were low fields of vegetables and marram grass, some small restaurants and hotels, a handful of shops. The houses were rural villas set behind their own fences. They had orange shutters and front gardens with roses in them.

He asked directions of a young woman with a child in a pushchair. The house was down a cul-de-sac leading to the sea side of the narrow spit of land. He walked down the dusty, potholed road and saw the white housecoat again. She was behind a double iron gate freshly painted green. A young man with blond hair was with her. He wore a white cotton T-shirt and jeans and seemed handsome, with a finely chiselled, tanned face. Daniel guessed that he had been gardening, cutting the elegant rosebushes which formed an ornamental shape behind the gate. She had arrived with her shopping. They had been talking. Then the young man bent down, kissed her on both cheeks, and took her groceries.

Daniel's mind was spinning. He stopped in the middle of the road and stared at them. The man turned, bags in hand, and looked at him, puzzled. Then Laura turned too. He was too distant to see her expression. He walked forward until he was no more than six feet away, separated from them by the gate. Her hand went to her mouth. The man said something inaudible, in an accent which sounded American. Another figure appeared, shorter, dressed identically to the one who had kissed Laura, but much older, and with pebble-thick glasses. He stared at Daniel and opened the gate, beckoning. Daniel walked into the grounds, unable to take his eyes off her.

"Guess it's time to be out of here, John," the younger man said carefully, placing an arm around the other. "Laura's got a guest."

"A man?" the older man asked.

"Seems so. You got a name, friend?"

"Daniel," Laura interrupted. "We haven't seen each other in a while. This is John. And Michael."

"First fellow I've seen here," John said, somewhat baffled. "Oh, well. Had to happen. Are we going to that première or what?"

"Sure. Any minute. The film festival," Michael added by way of explanation. "We're kind of in the business."

John waved a set of car keys. "Then let's leave these young

people to themselves. You drive. I'm going to drink." With that he wandered off towards the garage. A white Alfa stood outside, pristine, gleaming.

"Hey, Laura," Michael said wryly. "You can take him inside. It's OK by me. I won't count the candlesticks when we get back."

She cast him a cross glance, which Daniel recognised instantly, then said, "Come!"

He carried the shopping bags. They heard the gruff roar of the Alfa as they entered the door. She led him into a large open room with a sparkling Bechstein grand by the window, then sat down in an armchair, put her feet on the coffee table, and stared at him. He perched on the piano stool opposite.

"You look older," she said.

"You look just the same."

"Flattery. I'm going to seed." She reached behind her head and unfastened her hair, then shook it free. "Aren't I?"

Now that she had let down her hair, he could see it was much longer. "Not that I've noticed."

Beyond the full-length windows was an ornate garden in the English style, with rich herbaceous borders of pink, white, and blue, a sundial, and a colonnaded pergola covered with red roses. Daniel admired it, then asked, "Where do you find them, Laura? It's like Scacchi and Paul all over again."

"Nonsense," she replied firmly. "John and Michael are quite different. Michael is a film producer. And John...helps. They have money. They have taste. They're honest. Most of all, they're absent for most of the year, leaving me here to look after this place on my own."

"And you enjoy that?" he asked, wishing he could erase the note of disapproval from his voice. "Being alone?"

She looked at him, not offended as he had expected. "Daniel. I'm deeply sorry for what happened. I read about you being in jail, and it made me furious. Why didn't you argue? I think we all went a little crazy that summer. I went a lot crazy, but then you know that. You saw me. All the same." She hesitated. Her eyes went to the garden. "I didn't wish to see you again," she added. "I didn't want you to find me. I wish you had not found me now."

"I see," he said softly.

"I'm sorry. I have this new life. I don't wish it disturbed."

"Of course."

Her nose flared, another familiar gesture he recognised. "Well then," she said quietly. "That's that, it seems. You have your career. Your writing. Ca' Scacchi."

"I didn't want Ca' Scacchi, Laura. Half of it's still yours. All of it, if you like."

"Hah! That's why you come! To bribe me!"

He laughed and watched her try to stifle the amusement in her face. "Not at all. I came to make you cross. It struck me that you may not have had the opportunity for this in a while. You seemed to enjoy it so much once."

She pushed back her chair until her face was in the shade. "Please don't play with me, Daniel. I want nothing of Scacchi's. I want nothing of yours. That part of my life is over. Leave me alone."

"I will," he said, "but you must do something first."

"What?"

"Play for me. Play the Guarneri. You must have it. The music too. I had so much time to think in that prison. Play, please."

Her face came out of the shadow. "Are you insane, Daniel? What are you talking about? I play nothing. I'm a maid."

"No," he said firmly. Daniel took the old newspaper cutting out of his pocket and placed it on the table between them. She did not look at the story, with its garish headline and the photograph of the girl. With her longer hair, the resemblance between Laura and the teenage Susanna Gianni was striking but by no means undeniable. Yet he could understand why Scacchi kept Massiter from the house. "You pretend to be a maid, but I know who you are—Susanna Gianni. Whom Hugo Massiter tried to possess and almost killed, twelve years ago. Who has been hiding ever since and now is determined she should be alone because she wrongly believes there's no other way to survive. Perhaps to protect me also. You're like Scacchi—always deceiving in order to protect. That's why you pushed Amy at me, against my wishes. You wished to save her from Massiter too. It's a mistake, Laura. We all need the chance to choose, the opportunity to learn from time to time."

"Daniel!" Laura shook her head and stared at him. "What are you talking about? This girl is dead!"

He remembered the day it came to him. He was in a café near the Frari, wondering about the missing violin and Massiter's hunger for it. "No. It's the only possible answer. Giulia Morelli suspected as much, too, and tried to tell me before she died."

"You're talking nonsense."

He had this in his head, as clear as the tale of Oliver Delapole. "Massiter fooled me into thinking it was the Guarneri he sought. But he'd no interest in musical instruments. He didn't even own one. People were what mattered most to him. He'd always found something odd about Susanna's supposed death. He knew he didn't kill her. He told me so himself."

She did not flinch and simply sat there, arms folded, looking at him as if he were mad.

"That was why he ordered Rizzo to supervise the opening of the grave," he continued. "He could not be there in person, naturally, since it would draw attention to him. Yet he needed to satisfy his curiosity that Susanna was really dead. He'd no idea the Guarneri was in the coffin or, to begin with, that his lackey had stolen it. But as soon as the fiddle came on the market, he saw his opportunity. He knew that if he could acquire it and recognise it for the one he'd bought a decade before, then perhaps you were alive and wished to sell it out of necessity. And from that point on, he would seek you out again and reclaim what he thought of as his."

She raised a sceptical eyebrow. "Your next work will be one of fiction, I presume?"

He ignored the taunt. "Moreover, Scacchi understood the peril of the position immediately. He knew the fiddle was inside the casket, because he had, I suspect, reluctantly placed it there at your insistence. He discovered the coffin had been lifted early, with an authority Massiter had forged. Scacchi's purpose in acquiring the instrument from Rizzo was not for medical treatment or to pay off some gangsters, as he wanted us to believe. It was twofold. To protect you, as he had been doing for a decade. And, at some stage, to restore you to yourself. I believe that last part was imminent when Massiter killed him. You said on the day of the eel contest that Scacchi was about to share his secret with you. What else could it be but the violin? He knew you, Laura, and loved you. He didn't want you to hide behind this disguise forever."

She cast him a withering look. "This is rubbish, Daniel. Did you lose your sanity in that institution?"

"Not at all," he replied. "I found it. Scacchi's ruse would have worked, too, were it not for Rizzo. Massiter discovered his treachery and probably tortured the entire truth out of him before he died. At that point, Hugo knew that Scacchi had the instrument and no intention of selling it. Why would a man like Scacchi do such a thing? There could be only one explanation. He knew Susanna lived and wished to keep her identity hidden. That was why Massiter visited Scacchi and Paul that night, to extract the truth out of them. And that's why they died. To save you."

"You do a disservice to their memory," she said flatly. "These are such sad fantasies. Besides, if I'm that poor dead girl, whose body was in the coffin?"

He smiled. She had struck at his weak point immediately. "I don't know. I asked Piero last week—"

"Piero?" she asked, outraged. "Why pester that simpleton with your daydreams?"

"I asked him what had happened, and whether he had by any chance kept some items of Scacchi's for safekeeping. He blustered and pretended to be angry with me, naturally. As you're doing now."

"Piero's soft in the head!"

"No," Daniel insisted. "That's a game you play. He's a good and loyal friend and has been from the beginning. What I believe happened—you may correct me if you wish—is that he put you in Scacchi's care the same night Massiter attacked you. Perhaps he found you. Perhaps you found him. I don't know. Scacchi listened to your story. He knew Massiter for the man he was, knew that he wouldn't desist from pursuing you. I think also..."

He paused, not wishing to hurt her unnecessarily.

"This tale grows ever more fantastic," she said sourly. "Do go on."

"Your mother died a year after this happened. I don't wish to add to the pain."

She looked at him, wide-eyed, a little frightened now, he thought. "What do you know of my mother?"

"I suspect she believed you should have gone along with Massiter. You were poor. She saw this as some happy accident, perhaps. Your own feelings were secondary. The fact that Massiter appalled you, that he was violent and wished to make you one of his possessions, meant nothing to her. He tried to ensnare Amy through her parents. Much the same trick."

"Theories! Fairy stories! You are trying to deconstruct the past like it's something out of that book of yours. And there's still a dead girl in the coffin."

"Of course," he agreed. "Piero provided the body. He worked in the morgue, after all. I went through the papers from that time. A small boat carrying illegal immigrants from Bosnia capsized off the lagoon the same weekend. Two people died, a girl in her teens and a young boy. Scacchi could manipulate people as much as Massiter when he felt like it. With Piero's assistance, he would have had no difficulty organising the paperwork so that the corpse of a foreigner found its way into the *rio* instead of the crematorium. Then, conveniently, he would identify it as Susanna Gianni. I saw his powers myself."

"Hah! And you think the police would be fooled by that?"

"Not for long. But that is where Massiter's nature worked in your favour. When he feared his attack would be discovered, he exerted all his influence to shift the blame, finally inculpating that poor conductor to bring the investigation to an end. He wouldn't have wanted anyone looking too closely at that corpse. There might have been some physical evidence there which would have led to him."

She was silent. Daniel's mouth felt dry. He had laid out his evidence just as he had carefully planned over the months he had spent assembling it. Yet if Laura continued to deny everything, there was little he could do.

"I don't know if you were his lover before that night," he continued tentatively. "As Amy was. But I'm sure that something happened that evening, more than his beating you. Something so evil that it made you wish to become another person, to divest yourself of your entire identity, even to the point of insisting Scacchi bury your instrument in the coffin."

Her eyes were on the garden, her face turned away from him.

"You must realise that Scacchi had second thoughts on that last matter," Daniel said. "He was not simply keeping you hidden from Massiter by purchasing the Guarneri. At some point he hoped, I believe, that you would resume at least part of your true identity. I think…"

He hesitated again, seeing from her posture that she was retreating further into herself.

"My love," he said firmly. "I've been to that place. I've walked down that tunnel, stood in that room beneath the earth. I've seen the paintings and all his other possessions. I've looked at that low bed in the corner—"

"*Stop!*" Laura's head was in her hands. He rose, walked across the room, knelt in front of her, touched the warm, soft skin of her fingers.

"I'm sorry." He said it quietly. "I don't mean to torture you. Only to say that I, too, have seen inside Hugo Massiter's head. I know what lurks there."

She pulled away her hands and stared at him, an older person now, one who had witnessed something he had been spared. Daniel felt guilt for inflicting such pain upon her. "You know nothing. You haven't the faintest notion what it's like to be devoured by that man and see no escape."

"I've some idea," he replied. "I saw it in Amy's face."

"And she's free," Laura said, half-amazed. Her hand ran through his hair, gently touched his moustache.

"Perhaps," he replied. "As free as one gets. I wonder if any of us escapes him completely. He no longer owned you, yet he marked your life, so much that you became another person and withdrew from the world into Ca' Scacchi."

She gave him a cold look. "Did I? Is that what you want from me, Daniel Forster? A confession?"

He said nothing, feeling foolish.

"If this is all true, Daniel, what business is it of yours?"

"You know why it's my business."

"No," she said. "I won't have it. This is the past, and one shouldn't return to it. You're such a clever one, Daniel. Why could Scacchi not have chosen a fool?"

"We can deny what's happened, Laura. We can't erase it."

"Really?" she replied. "So you think Piero and I should remind each other constantly of a night when he found a naked and half-dead teenage girl and saved her life? And whenever I see a frail old man, I should think of Scacchi when he lay there in his chair, and this crazy stream of words coming from him about the fiddle and Massiter and you, with Paul dead and you asleep in my bed at that moment?"

He tried to speak, but there were no words, though his head felt as if it might burst.

"I hate your hair like this," she said. "It's too short, too spiky. How can a woman run her hands through that? The moustache must come off too. In some ways you have extraordinarily bad taste."

"Thank you," he said, smiling.

"Where did this idea arise, Daniel?"

He recalled that as precisely as the moment he first understood Massiter's true motive for seeking the Guarneri. It was in his prison cell, late one night, when he was unable to push the memory of her from his head. "I thought about the day I went on Hugo's boat. I sat there, with Massiter and Amy. As we left the quayside, I looked back, into that little park. You were wearing jeans and a red T-shirt. And sunglasses, as you usually did outside. You couldn't stop looking at the boat. At the time I thought it was me…"

"Men!" she objected. "Everything revolves around themselves."

"Quite. But it was Massiter, naturally. You wished to see him from afar, to convince yourself his presence remained as malevolent as you remembered."

"I wished to walk onto that boat and tear his eyes out. I didn't like having him near you. But I was afraid. I *am* afraid."

"You were going to see your 'mother,' or so I believed."

"Ah," she said, giving nothing away.

"In prison, when I was bored, I would imagine your life, Laura. I would try to dream what you were doing at any particular time. And what you had done that summer when I wasn't with you. Those visits to Mestre, for example."

"I confess," she said swiftly. "I had a lover. He was a lorry driver with horny hands and bad breath. It was merely a sexual infatuation."

"Rubbish!" he exclaimed. "I imagined it precisely. You wouldn't play in Ca' Scacchi, for fear of troubling the old man. So there was some small musical gathering in Mestre. A string quarter, perhaps. You borrowed a cheap violin. You played beneath your capabilities. But you played, and that was what mattered."

Her green eyes narrowed. "I'm not fond of your talent for imagining, Daniel Forster. It's unnatural."

"I apologise."

"You still apologise too much as well! And there was a lover. Once. I'm not some blushing virgin."

Daniel touched her cheek, then gently, nervously ran his fingers through her hair. "You have a lover now," he said.

"Oh, Daniel." Abruptly she turned away, but not before he saw the sudden change in her demeanour.

"Please play for me, Laura. I've waited a very long time to hear you."

She reached forward, kissed him briefly on the forehead, ruffled her hand through his short, cropped hair as a reproach, and left the room. Ten minutes later, a period of time which seemed to last forever, she reappeared. The white housecoat was gone. She wore a red cotton shirt and cream trousers. A silver necklace glittered at her throat. Her long hair was now on her shoulders, just as it was in the photograph in the newspapers. In her hand was the fat brown Guarneri he had once touched, a lifetime ago, in a warehouse in the Arsenale.

He was lost for words looking at her. It was as if she were some new, changed person. As if Susanna Gianni had slipped out from beneath Laura's skin.

"I don't always wear a uniform," she said in return. "I'm not a nun. Stop doing that fish thing with your mouth, Daniel. It's unattractive."

"I'm—"

"No! Just sit, please, and listen."

Laura stood by the piano, straight-backed, with a determined poise. There was no music. She lifted the fiddle to her neck, tucked it beneath her chin, then brought the bow down on the strings. She chose the most difficult section: the virtuoso finale. Daniel closed his eyes and listened to her play, let the full, bold sound of the Guarneri rise to occupy every last inch of his consciousness.

Amy had performed this magnificently, but she was, next to Laura, a child. Now the piece had an added intensity, a wild, mature beauty it had never before possessed. This was how the work was meant to be played. She had mastered every last cadence and harmony until there was nothing left to change. It was perfection, of an ethereal, almost supernatural kind.

When she finished, Laura raised an amused eyebrow at his silence. "Why do you look so surprised? I can practise here,

Daniel. I don't have to run and hide in Mestre every time I feel like taking out the bow. How do you think I spend these long months of solitude the masters of the house allow me?"

He stood up and, with her permission, took the Guarneri. The instrument was curious: a workmanlike piece of extraordinary size. Yet the sound it made...Daniel gave it back to her. He recalled that day on the Arsenale and some sudden flash of colour in his head. Rizzo feared the fiddle. In a way, he did too.

"Did I perform well?" she asked.

"You were magnificent."

"Thank you! Do you really think that an Englishman wrote such a lovely piece of music? I read your book."

Daniel bristled. "All the evidence points to such a conclusion. Why shouldn't an Englishman have written it?"

Laura laughed. "Don't be so touchy. It just sounds...wrong. I've a fancy it was written by a woman."

"You mean *for* a woman?"

"No. *By.* I feel that when I play. You're the historian. Tell me it's nonsense."

"It would certainly be...unusual, let us say."

She shrugged. "I don't know. Sometimes I dream too much. Do you?"

"Only of you," he replied. "I should like to hear you play in Ca' Scacchi, Laura."

Her face fell. "I can't. Think. You must know why."

"For the life of me I don't. I have a house we both adore, one that feels empty without you. As does my entire existence. From the moment on Piero's boat, I think I knew as much, but I was too stupid to realise it."

Her face fell onto his neck. He felt her arms move around his waist, then the warmth of her tears touched his skin. Laura's voice whispered in his ear.

"Scacchi once told me we were all born hurtling towards Heaven, Daniel. I denied it for both our sakes, but since we met, I have always felt I was born hurtling towards you. I don't know why. It terrifies me that I understand so little about these feelings."

"Then we're the same—"

"No," she insisted. "It cannot be. You don't appreciate that man for what he truly is. A devil. Nothing less. He lives. He waits. He'll come for us one day. He'll devour us because he believes we have given him the right."

"Massiter's gone," he said firmly. "No one knows where."

"He sees us, Daniel. You in particular. With your riches and your book and your fame. Haven't you considered that? You've profited from Massiter more than anyone."

Daniel's train of thought, so carefully organised beforehand, stumbled. "For what reason would he return? Revenge?"

"No! Don't you understand anything? To possess us, Daniel. To own every last part of us. Even our souls."

Beyond the window, above the distant horizon of the Adriatic, the sky was perfect, cloudless.

"You could have killed him." There was a note of accusation in her voice. "I read it. Why did you choose otherwise?"

It was a question he asked himself from time to time, and one it never took long to answer. "Because if I had, I would have become like him. Joined his hell. And I would have lost you forever, and deserved to."

She was unmoved. "That devil will seek us out, Daniel. It's in his nature."

"And what if he does? He has no power unless we give it to him. If we possess each other more fully than Hugo Massiter could begin to comprehend, what's left for him to own? What space will our lives allow him to occupy?"

Laura took her hands away and refused to meet his gaze. "Still, he will come," she said softly. "One day."

"Perhaps," he admitted. "But if I leave here without you, I don't care in any case."

A light fired at the back of her eyes. "And is that the kind of blackmail you hope will win me, Daniel Forster? Walking in here with your scrawny moustache and your spiky hair?"

"I'd rather hoped as much," he said lamely.

"Pah!"

She turned and was gone, out into another room—the kitchen, he imagined. He went to the window and admired the view. A formation of wild ducks crossed the sky in a squawking vee, heading northwards for Sant' Erasmo and, if they were unlucky, the jaws of a certain black dog he knew. There were worse places than Alberoni. It was, at least, the lagoon.

He heard her cough. Laura stood holding two glasses of bloodred liquid. He smiled and held out his hand.

"Wait," she ordered.

In the corner of the room a small ornamental clock struck six. When it had ended, she handed him his glass.

"Spritz!" Laura said, smiling. "Timing is important, Daniel Forster. I like my days divided in an orderly fashion. Not running backwards and forwards as they fancy. You should know this about me."

"Spritz!" he replied, raising his glass. "I had guessed that, to be honest."

"Good. Is there something I should know about you?"

"Only that I'll never cease to love you, whatever may happen. And I'll never leave you, because that would be like leaving myself."

She cocked her head to one side, thinking.

"What is it?" he asked.

"I was remembering the last time you kissed me. You smelled of eel."

Daniel was surprised. It was one memory which had eluded him. "No. That was the *first* time I kissed you. The last was some hours later."

He fell silent. She was staring at the room as if about to take her leave of it. She seemed serene at last. At this moment he could almost convince himself that every last painful act of the recent past was justified by their reunion.

She turned and wrapped her arms around him. She was shivering in the dying heat of the evening. Their bodies locked together, like two pieces from the same puzzle.

"I'm afraid," she said.

"Of what?"

"Of us. Of how I feel when we are together. Of what lies ahead."

He gazed beyond the glass at the low, flat marshland and the empty grey horizon. As he watched, a solitary figure walked slowly across the pebble beach, in the distance beyond the dunes, then passed behind a hummock of marram grass and was gone. There would always be shapes in the shadows. She saw them too.

They held each other tightly.

The doorbell sounded and she trembled in his arms.

Daniel strode to the front of the house. A boy of no more than nine stood there selling apples and pears fresh from the orchard. Daniel gave him some notes and took a few apples. The child disappeared down the drive, half running. When Daniel turned, she was standing in the hall holding a small kitchen knife. He walked up to her, took the blade out of her hands, and said, "Come with me, Laura. Please."

"Of course," she said nervously, and quickly removed the

silver chain, then began to tie up her hair and fumble in her bag for the sunglasses. He waited, wondering if she would seek out the white housecoat too.

"No," he said, taking her hands. Overawed by her beauty, he gently pulled forward her auburn hair until it sat over her shoulders again.

Daniel walked over the threshold of the villa, breathed the late-summer air, and led her outside. Arm in arm, slowly, not speaking, they walked to the small modern promenade, past the restaurants, past the little hotels, then sat by the water's edge.

The lagoon mirrored the gold of the sky. It was a perfect evening. The last of the season's swallows darted above their heads. Families played on the narrow strip of beach. Couples walked hand in hand along the concrete path. In the distance stood the outline of the city, shimmering in the haze on the horizon.

Laura's head fell on his shoulder. He felt the moist warmth of her lips on his skin.

"Who are we?" she asked.

"The blessed," Daniel said, and knew at that moment that nothing, not even Hugo Massiter, would part them again.

65

Chance encounter

From the journal of Jean-Jacques Rousseau, April 1743.

AT LAST THEY DO ME JUSTICE. I TRAVEL NOW FOR A
*post of some rank, as Secretary to the French Ambassador in that
den of sin, Venice. I cannot fault the work; only the location. I have not
written much of the place in my other journals, though I spent a little
time there a decade or so ago. There are sights aplenty and a smattering
of artists too. Yet, though possessed of a memory which scarce lets slip a
face or incident from years back, I must confess I recall nothing of
moment during my interlude in La Serenissima. Nothing, that is,
save the stink of the canals, which even an idiot is unlikely to forget.*

*Sometimes the oddities of fortune have a way of making up for these
omissions. I travel to Venice from Geneva, where I saw my few
remaining relatives. The call of business prevented my taking a direct
route and instead demanded I visit the surly burghers of Zurich for
three tedious days. Then I took the coach to Chur for the mountain pass
to Milan, by Lugano and Como, a crossing so ancient I must be
following in the footsteps of Caesar and his battalions with every mile.*

*This is a long and tiresome journey, and so, of necessity, I must break
it into as many constituent parts as I find convenient, or sit day and*

night on the hard seat of some cold, drab carriage, listening to the coughs and wheezes of my fellow man. Chur is as pleasant a place as any to pause for breath. This is a curious spot, set in a deep valley carved by the Rhine. The natives, part of the canton we call Grisons and they Graubünden, claim descent from the Etruscans and speak a strange tongue known as Romansh. There is a handful of fetching buildings, some fine hotels and restaurants, and an ancient Kathedrale with one of those Gothic altars designed to make you dizzy if you stare at it too long.

With some money in my pocket for once and an urge for a decent meal and a soft bed, I took a room at the Drei Könige, a comfortable establishment not far from the carriage stop. There I dined marvellously on good Swiss boar, potatoes, red cabbage, and ale before retiring to the salon at the rear, attracted by the unexpected sound of a small ensemble. I pulled up a chair, joined the six or so other travellers in the room, and found myself lost in thought. The music was expertly played, though somewhat predictable in content—insipid dance tunes, the kind of fare one must expect from entertainers in an hotel. What caught my attention most, though, was the players: a woman of striking appearance, perhaps in her mid-thirties, with wayward dark hair and a scarlet dress, who worked at a large, sonorous fiddle as if she were born with the thing strapped to her arm; a furtive-looking man a little younger than his wife, playing the harpsichord with rather less skill than his partner; and a dark-haired, if overly serious, child—nine, no more— bowing away on a smaller fiddle alongside his mother, and very well too.

I recognised this couple instantly. Our meeting had been brief—in Venice, of all places—and at least one of them I believed dead, and after some villainous deeds at that. To see this pair, with their offspring, stand in front of me, flesh and blood, was a curious and chilling experience, and one made all the more so by the way in which, after a while, both adults returned my inquisitive gaze. They performed another fifteen minutes more, then, after the merest round of applause, turned their backs on me and began to pack away their instruments. Emboldened by this rudeness, I decided to play them at their own game, and duly strode across to the tiny stage in order to strike up a conversation with these "strangers."

The man regarded my outstretched hand as if it were leprous. "I congratulate your little band, sir," I said with a smile. "I never expected to hear such musicianship in the provinces. Surely you must head for civilisation to reap the acclaim you deserve!"

The fellow gave me a filthy look, one that made my heart skip a beat. The exact circumstances of our acquaintance were still a blur to me at this point. The woman, I recall, was a musician. Yet I knew there were black rumours about his character later, though I had assumed him a gentleman when we first met, if a somewhat pompous one. It would be foolish to discount these tales of his disposition simply because half the intelligence about his fate proved misconstrued.

"Music is music, sir, wherever it is played," he replied in a monotonous country brogue. "One does not need the city's imprimatur to prove its value."

"True, but what worth is a diamond set beneath the ground, dear fellow? Nothing. It is only when the miner brings it to the surface, the jeweller carves it, the lady wears it . . . then it becomes the most precious thing in all the world!"

His eyes, if I am not mistaken, glazed over at this metaphor. A strange symptom of fear, no doubt, for all three of us knew this was a charade.

The lady packed away that gigantic instrument, as ugly to behold as it was delightful to hear, and said with what passed for a smile, "We are mere country folk, sir. Content to earn a living and a bed for the night by our playing and our lessons, nothing more. The city would surely drown us in its tumult and expose our talents as the humble efforts which, in truth, they represent."

She did herself a disservice and knew it. "Not so!" I insisted. "I

*listened most carefully, and you, madame, play like an angel. And
originally, too, for I have not heard those tunes before and there's many
a hotel band I've been forced to listen to on my travels."*

*She beamed at that. Quite rightly, for it was sincerely meant. She
had acquired, I must record, a distinct limp; it spoiled somewhat her
otherwise comely appearance. "Thank you, sir. It is a hobby of mine
to write a little now and then."*

*"Dance tunes," the man interrupted. "Nothing that would fill a hall
outside the inns."*

*"And not all my own," the woman added. "My brother recently
found a position as a physician at the Russian court. We are fortunate
in that he sends us some popular melodies from Moscow occasionally."*

*She smiled, obviously proud of her sibling's achievement, then her
husband broke this pleasant turn in the conversation by observing
sourly, "We know our métier, monsieur. We are travelling players,
and it puts bread upon our table."*

*Such false modesty! "Never underestimate the human spirit, my
friend," I answered. "Handel was the son of a barber, and a trainee
lawyer to boot. If he can overcome those twin burdens, surely you might
fight your way out of the taverns and reach a more appreciative
audience?"*

*They looked at each other, and with my customary acuity, I was able
to detect this was a subject of some tension. It would have been cruel to
prolong this awkward moment, so I reached down, tousled the mop of
dark hair on the young lad, and earned a grudging look for my pains.*

"And you, my boy. What name do you answer to?"

"Antonio," he replied, as surly as a street urchin.

*"Well, Antonio. Let me tell you something. Your parents are fine
people who will educate you well in the ways of the world. But
remember always that each one of us is an individual and must make
his own decisions. If you play so admirably at your age, I'll warrant
you'll be in an orchestra by the time you're twenty."*

He glanced at his father. There was some enforced severity in this little band I could not hope to comprehend. "I only wish to play as well as Mama, sir. And, when I am older, earn the right to own her fiddle."

"And after that?"

"Why..." I swear the child looked at me as if I were a fool. "I'll do the same for my son, and he for his. Until we produce the very finest fiddler there has been in all the world, and one that still plays Mama's instrument too. So even if we all be dust by then, a little of us passes down to the next, and that is as much immortality, my father says, as any man might hope for."

Poor lad, I thought. So stiff and old for his age. He was a comely fellow, having inherited the looks of his mother, not those on the other side, and this might stand a man in good stead. Yet I found it hard to believe these folk did not inhabit some prison of their own making and found themselves bumping into the bars at every turn.

"You'll teach your son yourself, no doubt?" I wondered.

"Aye, sir. As Mama has taught me. Everything."

It was time to throw in a sly one. "Then what shall you teach him of God?"

I found all three of them staring at me then and wondered whether I had overstepped my mark. Unless I was mistaken, the father had blood upon his hands already, and what's one more red stain when your skin is soiled already?

The child looked at his parents for some guidance. The mother nodded at him. "Answer the gentleman. As you see fit."

He drew himself up, took a deep breath, then said, as if reciting a laboured rhyme from the nursery, "We... I think that God is great enough to manage without my adulation, sir. He knows where He may find me in His hour of need."

He said it well too. I patted him on the head, then gave him a coin, which, after glancing at his parents once more, he swiftly pocketed.

"You have all entertained me generously this evening," I said with a smile. "I travel to Venice. May I repay the favour by recommending you to the impresarios?"

The blood drained from the faces of both man and wife in an instant. The child regarded them fearfully. I felt guilty. This was unworthy of me, and I should not have done it without their ungracious reception of my advances. Every story has more than one side. I had no right to read the gutter sheets and assume their rantings represented justice.

"We are content as we are," the man replied icily, then set them packing away their things with more speed. I retired, a little apprehensive, I'll admit. There was a look of utter ruthlessness in the fellow's eyes after my last remark which made me wonder for my life.

That night I failed to sleep for more than a few moments. This strange interview replayed itself in my head and I recalled, too, a little more of the meetings we had in Venice some ten years earlier. As I said, nothing of moment then occurred. Yet looking back now, I detect, I believe, the seeds of some tragedy beginning to germinate beneath the Adriatic sun.

Small wonder a decade on they seek to flee this thicket of deceit. When I rose the following morning, there was commotion in the breakfast room over their sudden disappearance. The landlord and his wife seemed bereft at their flight, nor was it for the usual reason of an unpaid bill. The pair seemed rather fond of this odd and talented family, and looked at me askance when my enquiries set them wondering whether I had something to do with their decision to disappear into the night. Provincials! Am I supposed to feel guilty? Should the hanged man blame the rope?

They were gone. None knows where, or in truth much cares. The world is full of such strangers. One may wish them well, whatever shadows lurk in their histories, but their fate remains entirely in their own hands, for good or ill. Yet these three were not vagabonds at heart. They showed as much in their manner and in their carelessness.

A fugitive must seek a new name each time he renews his existence. And with what paucity of imagination do they seek their disguise!

After a good night's sleep the following evening, I finally remembered the fellow well. He was in the printing trade, an inky-fingered artisan of books. And how would he now be known? Why, only by the stolen name of one of his rivals in the publishers' guild! An ancient house that in its brief day produced some books on Arabic and Hebrew which still grace many an antiquarian's shelves.

Such errors serve the runaway poorly. I wish the family "Paganini" luck. They'll need it.

About the Author

DAVID HEWSON was born in Yorkshire in 1953. He was a journalist from the age of seventeen, working most recently for the *Sunday Times*. As well as his novels, David has also written a number of travel books. *The Blue Demon* is the eighth novel in his Italian crime series featuring Nic Costa. The author lives in Kent.

THE BLUE DEMON

Read on for an exclusive extract from
the new Nic Costa novel, to be published
shortly by Macmillan

Part 1

DIVINATION

Fere libenter homines id quod volunt credunt.

Men willingly believe what they wish.

Julius Caesar, De Bello Gallico,
Book III, Ch. 18

1

The garden of the Quirinale felt like a sun trap as the man in the silver armour strode down the shingle path. He was sweating profusely inside the ceremonial breastplate and woollen uniform.

Tight in his right hand he held the long, bloodied sword that had just taken the life of a man. In a few moments he would kill the president of Italy. And then? Be murdered himself. It was the lot of assassins throughout the ages, from Pausanius of Orestis, who had slaughtered Philip, the father of Alexander the Great, to Marat's murderess Charlotte Corday and Kennedy's nemesis, Lee Harvey Oswald.

The stabbing dagger, the sniper's rifle . . . all these were mirrored weapons, reflecting on the man or woman who bore them, joining perpetrator and victim as twin sacrifices to destiny. It had always been this way, since men sought to rule over others, circumscribing their desires, hemming in the spans of their lives with the dull, rote strictures of convention. Petrakis had read much over the years, thinking, preparing, comparing himself to his peers. The travelling actor John Wilkes Booth's final performance before he put a bullet through the skull of Abraham Lincoln had been in Julius

Caesar, although through some strange irony he had taken the part of Caesar's friend and apologist, Mark Antony, not Brutus as history demanded.

As he approached the figure in the bower, seeing the old man's grey, lined form bent deep over a book, Petrakis found himself murmuring a line Wilkes Booth must have uttered a century and a half before.

'"O mighty Caesar . . . dost thou lie so low? Are all thy conquests, glories, triumphs, spoils, shrunk to this little measure?"'

A pale, long face, with sad, tired eyes, looked up from the page. Petrakis, realizing he had spoken out loud, wondered why this death, among so many, would be the most difficult.

'I didn't quite catch that,' Dario Sordi said in a calm, unwavering voice, his eyes, nevertheless, on the long, bloodied blade.

The uniformed officer came close, stopped, repeated the line, and held the sword over the elderly figure seated in the shadow of a statue of Hermes.

The president looked up, glanced around him and asked, 'What conquests in particular, Andrea? What glories? What spoils? Temporary residence in a garden fit for a pope? I'm a pensioner in a very luxurious retirement home. Do you really not understand that?'

The long silver weapon trembled in Petrakis's hand. His palm felt greasy. He had no words at all.

Voices rose behind him. A shout. A clamour.

There was a cigarette in Dario Sordi's hands. It didn't even shake.

'You should be afraid, old man.'

More dry laughter.

'I've been hunted by Nazis.' The grey, drawn face glowered at him. Sordi drew on the cigarette and exhaled a cloud of smoke.

'Played hide and seek with tobacco and the grape for more than half a century. Offended people – important people – who feel I am owed a lesson, which is probably true.' A long, pale finger jabbed through the evening air. 'And now you wish me to cower before someone else's puppet? A fool?'

That, at least, made it easier.

Petrakis found his mind ranging across so many things: memories, lost decades, languid days dodging NATO patrols beneath the Afghan sun, distant, half-recalled moments in the damp darkness of an Etruscan tomb, talking to his father about life and the world, and how a man had to make his own way, not let another create a future for him.

Everything came from that place in the Maremma, from the whispered discovery of a paradise of the will sacrificed to the commonplace and mundane, the exigencies of politics. Andrea Petrakis knew this course was set for him at an early age, by birth, by his inheritance.

The memory of the tomb, with its ghostly painted figures on the wall, and the terrible, eternal spectre of the Blue Demon, consuming them one by one, filled his head. This, more than anything else, he had learned over the decades: freedom, of the kind enjoyed by the long-dead men and women still dancing beneath the grey Tarquinia earth more than two millennia on, was a mayfly, gloriously fleeting, made real by its impermanence. Life and death were bedfellows, two sides of the same coin. To taste every breath, feel each beat of the heart, one had to know that both might be snatched away in an instant. His father had taught him that, long before the Afghans and the Arabs tried to reveal the same truth.

Andrea Petrakis remembered the lesson more keenly now, as the sand trickled through some unseen hourglass, for Dario Sordi and his allotted assassin.

Out of the soft evening came a bright, sharp sound, like the ping of some taut yet invisible wire, snapping under pressure.

A piece of the statue of Hermes, its stone right foot, disintegrated in front of his eyes, shattering into pieces, as if exploding in anger.

Dario Sordi ducked back into the shadows, trying, at last, to hide.

2

Three days earlier . . .

'Behold,' said the man, in a cold, tired voice, the accent from the countryside perhaps. 'I will make a covenant. For it is something dreadful I will do to you.'

Strong, firm hands ripped off the hood. Giovanni Batisti saw he was tethered to a plain office chair. At the periphery of his vision he could make out that he was in a small, simple room with bare bleached floorboards and dust ghosts on the walls left by long-removed chests of drawers or ancient filing cabinets. The place smelled musty, damp and abandoned. He could hear the distant lowing of traffic, muffled in some curious way, but still energized by the familiar rhythm of the city. Cars and trucks, buses and people, thousands of them, some from the police and the security services no doubt, searching as best they could, oblivious to his presence. There was no human sound close by, from an adjoining room or an apartment. Not a radio or a TV set. Or any voice save that of his captor.

'I would like to use the bathroom, please,' Batisti said quietly, keeping his eyes fixed on the stripped, cracked timber boards at his feet. 'I will do as you say. You have my word.'

The silence, hours of it, was the worst part. He'd expected a reprimand, an order, might even have welcomed a beating, since all these things would have acknowledged his existence. Instead . . . he was left in limbo, in blindness, almost as if he were dead already. Nor was there any exchange he could hear between those involved. A brief meeting to discuss tactics. News. Perhaps a phone call in which he would be asked to confirm that he was still alive.

Even – and this was a forlorn hope, he knew – some small note of concern about his driver, the immigrant Polish woman Elena Majewska, everyone's favourite, shot in the chest as the two vehicles blocked his government vehicle in the narrow street of Via delle Quattro Fontane, at the junction with the road to the Quirinale. It was such a familiar Roman crossroads, next to Borromini's fluid baroque masterpiece of San Carlino, a church he loved deeply and would visit often, along with Bernini's nearby Sant'Andrea, if he had time during his lunch break from the Interior Ministry building around the corner.

They could have snatched him that day from beneath Borromini's dome, with its magnificent dove of peace, descending to earth from Heaven. He'd needed a desperate fifteen-minute respite from sessions with the Americans, the Russians, the British, the Germans . . . Eight nations, eight voices, each different, each seeking its own outcome. The phrase that was always used about the G8 – the 'industrialized nations' – had come to strike him as somewhat ironic as he listened to the endless bickering about diplomatic rights and protocols, who should stand where and with whom. Had some interloper approached him during his brief recess that day, Batisti would have glanced at Borromini's extraordinary interior one last time, then walked into his captor's arms immediately, trying to finish his panino, without much in the way of a second thought. Anything but another session devoted to the rites and procedures of diplomatic life.

Then he remembered again, with a sudden, painful seizure of guilt, the driver. Did Elena – a pretty, young single mother who'd moved to Rome to find security and a new, better life – survive? If so, what could she tell the police? What was there to say about a swift and unexpected explosion of violence in the black sultry velvet of a Roman summer night? The attack had happened so quickly and with such brutish force that Batisti was still unsure how many men had been involved. Perhaps no more than three or four from the pair of vehicles blocking the way. The area was empty. He was without a bodyguard. An opposition politician drafted in to the organization team out of custom and practice was deemed not to need one, even in the heightened security that preceded the coming summit. Not a single sentence was spoken as they dragged him from the rear seat, wrapped a blindfold tightly round his head, fired – three, four times? – into the front, then bundled him into the boot of some large vehicle and drove a short distance to their destination.

Were they now issuing ransom demands? Did his wife, who was with her family in Milan, discussing a forthcoming family wedding, know what was happening?

There were no answers, only questions. Giovanni Batisti was forty-eight years old and felt as if he'd stepped back into a past that Italy hoped was behind it. The dismal seventies and eighties, the 'Years of Lead'. A time when academics and lawyers and politicians might be routinely kidnapped by the shadowy criminals of the Red Brigades and their partners in terrorism, held to ransom, tortured, then left bloodied and broken as some futile lesson to those in authority. Or dead. Like Aldo Moro, the former prime minister, seized in 1978, held captive for fifty-six days before being shot ten times in the chest and dumped in the trunk of a car in the Via Caetani.

'Look at me,' a voice from ahead of him ordered.

Batisti closed his eyes, kept them tightly shut.

'I do not wish to compromise you, sir. I have a wife. Two sons. One is eight. One is ten. I love them. I wish you no harm. I wish no one any harm. These matters can and will be resolved through dialogue, one way or another. I believe that of everything. In this world I have to.' He found his mouth was dry, his lips felt painful as he licked them. 'If you know me, you know I am a man of the left. The causes you espouse are often the causes I have argued for. The methods . . .'

'What do you know of our causes?'

'I . . . I have some money,' he stuttered. 'Not of my own, you understand. My father. Perhaps if I might make a phone call?'

'This is not about money,' the voice said, and it sounded colder than ever. 'Look at me or I will shoot you this instant.'

Batisti opened his eyes and stared straight ahead, across the bare, dreary room. The man seated opposite him was perhaps forty. Or a little older, his own age even. Professional-looking. Maybe an academic himself. Not a factory worker or some individual who had risen from the street, pulled up by his own boot laces. There was a cultured timbre to his voice, one that spoke of education and a middle-class upbringing. A keen, incisive intelligence burned in his dark eyes. His face was leathery and tanned as if it had spent too long under a bright, burning sun. He would once have been handsome, but his craggy features were marred by a network of frown lines, on the forehead, at the edge of his broad, full-lipped mouth, which looked as if a smile had never crossed it in years. His long, unkempt hair seemed unnaturally grey and was wavy, shiny with some kind of grease.

A mark of vanity. Like the black clothes, which were not inexpensive. Revolutionaries usually knew how to dress. The man had the scarred visage of a movie actor who had fallen on hard times. Something about him seemed distantly familiar, which seemed a terrible thought.

'Behold, I will make a covenant . . .'

'I heard you the first time,' Batisti sighed.

'What does it mean?'

The politician briefly closed his eyes.

'The Bible?' he guessed, tiring of this game. 'One of the Old Testament horrors, I imagine. Like Leviticus. I have no time for such devils, I'm afraid. Who needs them?'

The man reached down to retrieve something, then placed the object on the table. It was Batisti's own laptop computer, which had sat next to him in the back of the official car.

'Cave Eleven at Qumran. The Temple Scroll. Not quite the Old Testament, but in much the same vein.'

'It's a long time since I was a professor,' Batisti confessed. 'A very junior one at that. The Dead Sea was never my field. Nor rituals. About sacrifice or anything else.'

'I'm aware of your field of expertise.'

'I was no expert. I was a child, looking for knowledge. It could have been anything.'

'And then you left the university for politics. For power.'

He shook his head. This was unfair, ridiculous.

'What power? I spend my day trying to turn the tide a little in the way of justice, as I see it. I earn no more now than I did then. Had I written the books I wanted to . . .'

Great, swirling stories, popular novels of the ancients, of heroism and dark deeds. He would never get round to them. He understood that.

'It's a long time since I spoke to an academic. You were a professor of ancient history. Greek and Roman?'

Batisti nodded.

'A middling one. An over-optimistic decoder of impossible mysteries. Nothing more. You kidnap me, you shoot my driver, in order to discuss history?'

The figure in black reached into his jacket and withdrew a short, bulky weapon.

'A man with a gun may ask anything.'

Giovanni Batisti was astonished to discover that his fear was rapidly being consumed by a growing sense of outrage.

'I am a servant of the people. I have never sought to do anyone ill. I have voted and spoken against every policy, national and international, with which I disagree. My conscience is clear. Is yours?'

The man in black scowled.

'You read too much Latin and too little English. "Thus conscience does make cowards of us all."'

'I don't imagine you brought me here to quote Shakespeare. What do you want?' Batisti demanded.

'In the first instance? I require the unlock code for this computer. After that I wish to hear everything you know about the arrangements that will be made to guard the great gentlemen who are now in Rome to safeguard this glorious society of ours.' The man scratched his lank, grey hair. 'Or is that theirs? Excuse my ignorance. I've been out of things for a little while.'

'And after that you will kill me?'

He seemed puzzled by the question.

'No, no, no. After that he will kill you.'

The man nodded at a place at the back of the room, then gestured for someone to come forward.

Giovanni Batisti watched and felt his blood freeze.

The newcomer must have sat silent throughout. Perhaps he was in the other car when they seized him at the crossroads near the Viminale. Though not like this.

He looked like a golden boy, a powerfully built youth, naked apart from a crude loincloth. His skin was the colour of a cinematic Mediterranean god. His hair was burnished yellow, long and curled like a cherub from Raphael. Bright-blue paint was smeared roughly on his face and chest.

'We require a sign,' the man in black added, reaching into his pocket and taking out an egg. 'My friend here is no ordinary man. He can foretell the future through the examination of the entrails and internal organs. This makes him a . . .'

He stared at the ceiling, as if searching for the word.

'A haruspex,' Batisti murmured.

'Exactly. Should our act of divination be fruitful...'

The painted youth was staring at him, like a muscular halfwit. Batisti could see what appeared to be a butcher's knife in his right hand.

On the table, a pale-brown hen's egg sat in a saucer with a scallop-shell edge.

The man with the gun said, in a clear, firm voice, '*Ta Sacni!*' Then he leaned forward and, in a mock whisper behind his hand, added, 'This is more your field than mine. I think that means, "This is the sanctuary". Do tell me if we get anything wrong.'

The golden boy came and stood behind him. In his left hand was a small bottle of San Pellegrino mineral water. His eyes were very blue and open, as if he were drugged or somehow insensate. He bent down, gazed at the egg and then listened, rapt, captivated, as the man in black began to chant in a dry, disengaged voice, 'Aplu. Phoebos. Apollo. Delian. Pythian. Lord of Delphi.

Guardian of the Sibyls. Or by whatever other name you wish to be called. I pray and beseech you that you may by your majesty be propitious and well disposed to me, for which I offer this egg. If I have worshipped you and still do worship you, you who taught mankind the art of prophecy, you who have inspired my divination, then come now and show your signs that I might know the will of the gods! I seek to understand the secret ways into the Palace of the Pope. *Thui Srenar Tev.*'

Show me the signs now, Batistic translated in his head. The youth spilled the water onto the table. The knife came down and split the egg in two.

The older one leaned over, sniffed and said, 'Looks like yolk and albumen to me. But what do I know? He's the haruspex.'

'I cannot tell you these things,' Batisti murmured. 'You must appreciate that.'

'That is both very brave and very unfortunate. Though not entirely unexpected.'

The naked youth was running his fingers through the egg in the saucer. The man pushed his hand away. The creature obeyed, immediately, a sudden fearful and subservient look in his eye.

'I want the code for your computer,' the older one ordered. 'You will give it to me. One way or another.'

Batisti said nothing, merely closed his eyes for a moment and wished he retained sufficient faith to pray.

'I'm more valuable to you alive than dead. Tell the authorities what you want. They will negotiate.'

'They didn't for Aldo Moro. You think some junior political hack is worth more than a prime minister?'

He seemed impatient, as if this were all a tedious game.

'You've been out of the real world too long, Batisti. These people smile at you and pat your little head, caring nothing. These,' he dashed the saucer and the broken egg from the table, 'toys are beneath us. Remember your Bible. "When I was a child, I used to speak like a child, think like a child, reason like a child; when I became a man, I did away with childish things. For now we see in a mirror dimly . . ." '

Batisti recalled little of his Catholic upbringing. It seemed distant, as if it had happened to someone else. This much of the verses he remembered, though.

'But faith, hope, love, abide these three,' he said quietly. 'And the greatest of these is love.'

'Not so much of that about these days,' the silver-haired man replied mournfully. 'Is there?'

Then he nodded at the golden boy by his side, waiting, tense and anxious for something to begin.

Visit **www.panmacmillan.com** to read more about all our books and to buy them. You will also find features, author interviews and news of any author events, and you can sign up for e-newsletters so that you're always first to hear about our new releases.